THE TRAITOR

The Katori Chronicles
Book 4

A. D. Lombardo

BOOKS BY A. D. LOMBARDO

The Katori Chronicles:
The Half-Light
Mariana's Secret
Rayna's Sacrifice
The Traitor

The Traitor

The Katori Chronicles Book 4
A. D. Lombardo

Published by Nichols INK

ISBN (Paperback): 978-1-7333376-6-3
ISBN (Ebook): 978-1-7333376-7-0

Cover design by A. D. Lombardo
First Edition 2021

www.ADLombardo.com

I dedicate this book to my son Connor,
who no matter the hour
finds time to listen to my story ideas.

ACKNOWLEDGMENTS

What can I say about the creation of book four? It was never meant to be its own book, yet here it is. Scrapes from Rayna's Sacrifice left in shreds on the editing floor brought to life during a pandemic.

When I published book three days after the world shut down, we all sat and watched everything around us change. Many struggled to find a new sense of normal and cope with being cut off from friends and family. I for one found it challenging, but I am blessed to have people who never gave up on me.

For all those writers who suffer writers block and never give up, bless you. It took a writing class, my editor, and fellow writers to wake my muse and help stir the passion to complete this book in what felt like an upside-down world.

As always, I must thank my son, Connor, without him I would have never found this passion. A big thank you to my devoted husband; he supports me in so many ways without question. 2020 hit us all hard and we each came out stronger.

Special thanks to my family and friends for your continued support. And as always, Buddy, thank you for walking into the office every night reminding me to keep writing.

A. D. Lombardo

CONTENTS

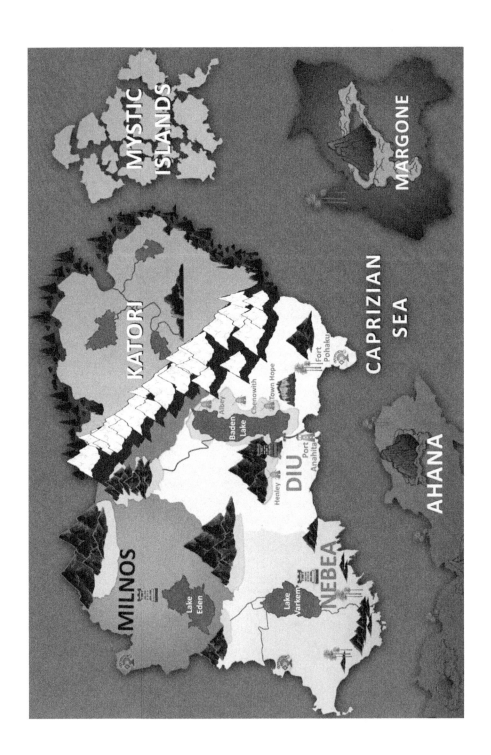

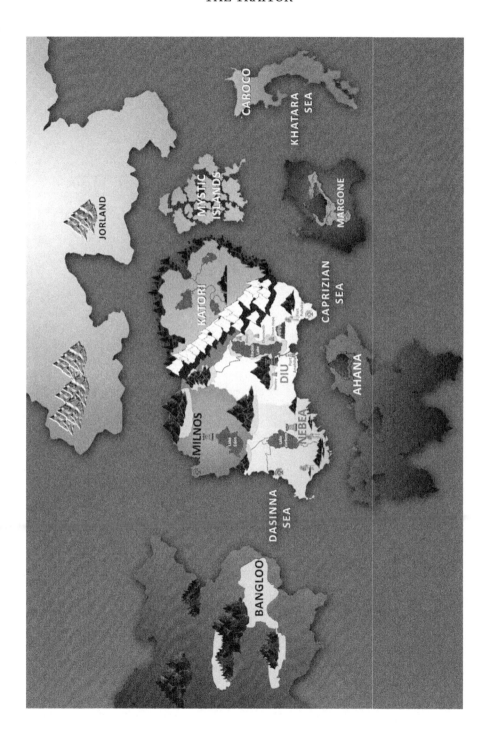

PROLOGUE

Queen Nola strolled outside from the King's council chamber, her gold embellished boots leaving prints in the fresh snow. The winter sun felt warm on her face but made her green eyes blink against the change in brightness. She leaned against the stone railing, wrapped in her blue velvet coat with white fur trim for warmth. Her towering view over the palace gardens and the sprawling Diu city beyond gave her pause. She did not care about these people, but she enjoyed her status above them.

The cold wind bit her nose and swept her golden locks to the side. Regent Lucas Maxwell stepped away from the other council members and joined her outside. "Diu is a beautiful city," he said, interrupting her thoughts. "Small compared to Milnos, but it has its charm."

Queen Nola scanned the dwindling crowd before returning to the power-hungry ruler of Milnos. A man old enough to be her father, who beheld her with lustful eyes and contempt all at the same time. She hated him, but he was a useful pawn.

Regent Maxwell reclined against the stone railing. The wind tugged at his long wavy hair and gray beard. Nola watched his beady eyes study the three stone archways behind her. She knew he was waiting for the other councilmen to leave and give them privacy. Reading men, understanding their desires, manipulating them to do her bidding—it was almost too easy.

When the chamber behind them fell silent, Maxwell crossed the divide between them, tilting his head to kiss her. His beard tickled her nose, and she pushed him away before he could grab onto her.

"I suppose Diu does have some charm," she muttered, avoiding him. She continued to play hard to get, stepping around a large evergreen potted plant.

The corner of his mouth curled with sly intent, and Nola watched his gaze comb the length of her. "I guess it's a shame we plan to burn it all to the ground."

There was no denying the thought of destroying Diu—and the man Nola had grown to hate—thrilled her to the bone. Her glee bubbled to the surface. "With Iver dying and Prince Kai gone, I will put Aaron on the Diu throne. These people will bend under his rule, and with my guidance, we can annex this country into Milnos without lifting a finger."

She could tell her plan had struck a nerve. Maxwell crossed his arms and leaned away from her. "Why the change of heart?" he scoffed. "I thought we agreed Diu must burn once we put your brother Landon on the Milnos throne."

It was true; all Nola ever wanted was to destroy the Galloway family line and the city of Diu. Glaring back at Maxwell, she held her nose high. "Illegitimate or not, I am King Bannon Penier's daughter, his firstborn. Yet, as a woman, I have no claim to the Milnos throne. Bannon hid my birth and sent me away to Ahana." The memory and loss of her father set her blood to boil. Although she wanted to consider Milnos her homeland, she had no power there. Her own people did not know her.

"Growing up on Ahana, I lived in a tropical paradise," Nola continued. "My father, King Penier, ensured my mother and I wanted for nothing, but I wanted recognition, as did my mother before she passed. My father may have killed Iver's father and uncle, but that was because they interfered in Milnosian affairs. Iver Galloway had no right to execute my father in return. I will have my revenge."

Maxwell chuckled. "Come, my dear, you are no stranger to wealth and power." He stepped closer to her again. "Your reputation on Ahana is what brought you here. The bustling port below your estate filled with travelers: kings and dignitaries—men seeking their fortune or secrets." He brushed her chin with his fingers.

Nola smiled at the truth behind his words. She had learned the old craft from her mother—potions, hypnotism, magic—and lies and secrets had become her stock-in-trade. "Yes, my lavish lifestyle and spy network attracted them all—King Iver was no exception." The thought of those early years twisted her nose as if she smelled something foul. "Mariana kept a keen eye on him, never letting him out of her sight. The woman looked down on me. I know it. She thought she was better than me."

Thoughts of the previous queen curdled Nola's insides. She hated Mariana with the darkest parts of her soul, and it suited her fine if her son paid the price in her stead. Yes, she would make Kai Galloway suffer if it was the last thing she ever did. Any who wronged her must pay.

Maxwell's laughter echoed off the stone palace, breaking her contemplation. "And still," Maxwell applauded her, "you made it your business to get close to the widowed king."

Her own chuckle tickled her spine, remembering the ease with which she had seduced Iver and became his queen. "A broken man is a weak-minded man." She gleamed. "Iver was too trusting."

"I implore you, Nola—leave this city, destroy it or let it falter without leadership, but come home with me to Milnos. I need you. Your brother, Landon, will take care of you. We belong in our homeland; this backwater does not deserve a flower as sweet as you. They do not treat their royals with enough reverence here. You should stand above the people, not shoulder to shoulder."

She kept her face soft, hiding her distrust. "My father shared your disdain for these people," she said, then shook her head. "Landon promised you a place by his side, so you do his bidding. You have no more claim to the Milnos throne than I. There we have no power, not *real* power, but here we control trade routes. Money and power blossom in Diu, we need only take it. You have debts, Maxwell—Bangloo will come to claim them, and Milnos will no longer cover your wasteful ways. Let Diu fund your bad habits."

Nola knew one thing for certain—she had power as the Queen of Diu, but only while Iver lived. Once Iver died, a man needed to sit on the throne. If Kai did not return, she would see to it that Aaron would be the next king, or she would convince others that Kai, Iver's eldest, was unfit to rule. "No," she refused, "as a half-sister to Landon Penier, I would sit in the background. In Milnos, there is no guarantee he will publicly recognize me at court as his sister. He and I have spoken only a handful of times, and there are no guarantees." No, she had grown fond of the influence—Diu city was under her control. All she needed was Iver and Kai out of the way.

"Diu is no place for you, Nola."

"We have discussed this." She held back the sarcastic tone she felt collect in her throat. "Kai has abandoned Diu city for his mother's beloved Katori people. Painting him as unworthy of the crown will be easy; he has no loyalty to the Diu people. And if he does return, I have a plan to turn the world against him. Mark my words, Iver will be dead and six feet under—one way or another. And I shall place the crown on Aaron's head while the city mourns, long before anyone can protest."

"Not good enough," Maxwell seethed. "I hate this country—their very existence disgusts me. They must be crushed for their audacity against Milnos in the war. I have noticed a change in the skies—the disappearance of dragons. Every year there are fewer and fewer in the sky near the Katori Mountains. In the past month, my men report there were no sightings over Baden Lake. I believe the beasts are dying off."

Nola nodded in agreement. "Even Iver's dragon, the one he used to keep traders in line, went missing and is presumed dead. No dragons mean the Katori people will no longer be a threat, and with Diu's army and Fort Pohaku's naval fleet under our control, we could conquer Katori next." The facts were there; Katori was ripe for conquering. She liked the sound of this news.

His greedy eyes swelled with joy. "In time, Katori and Nebea will fall under our boots. We will control it all. Our power may even rival Bangloo."

She knew Maxwell's hatred for Diu ran deep, but the Regent's shortsightedness exasperated her. Clearly, it was a waste of time try convincing Maxwell with logic. He would never allow her to keep even a scrape of control or power. She would need to continue to bend him to her will, or at least convince him it was his idea Diu should be hers.

Nola moved to a stone bench sheltered from the winter breeze, then motioned Maxwell to her side, offering him the seat next to her.

He accepted but eyed her with a sideways glance. "There are no words to change my mind, Nola. You know full well that I will have my revenge for the years of bowing to this boy, King Iver, and the Cazier family from Nebea. They killed my king and kept me from the throne. My men will kill every last one of them, and I will cleanse Milnos of any Diu vermin."

She nodded, reassuring him of her allegiance. "Is everything in place for Landon to assume the Milnos throne during your winter festival?" she asked, batting her eyes at him. "Tolan and Amelia will not be a problem, I hope."

Maxwell leaned in closer and took her hand in his. She smiled at his foolishness. "My dear Nola, Tolan was tossed into prison weeks before I left. Amelia loved these Diu people—she even married one. I tried to convince her the morning of her wedding to reject the offer, but she refused. After imprisoning Tolan, I could not take her constant blubbering. I locked her in a tower where she can rot for all I care. The girl is of no use. She was to deliver Kai to Milnos and failed."

The heat from Maxwell's hand warmed Nola's cold fingers. She knew all too well his disdain for women and his belief they were playthings— tools or trash that deserved no real power. Someday she would need to manipulate her bother Landon into killing the Regent when he was no longer of use.

Caressing the back of his hand, her green eyes locked on his. One thought bloomed in her mind and curled the corner of her mouth. In a soothing tone, Nola spoke. "My dear Maxwell, continue your plans for Landon." She tapped his hand with the rhythmic cadence she preferred and let her hypnotic stare renew the connection she had forged over the years.

From around her neck, she clasped a black crystal dangling at the end of a chain. It had been handed down generation to generation, and now she alone wielded its power. Ensuring her influence over the Regent was secure in this matter, she focused on her desires. "Remember, the Milnos people will rally together under their one true king. You will be my brother's advisor. Landon will need your guidance. With years of experience ruling Milnos, you will play an important part in our country's future. Only then can we be together."

Maxwell's lost look told her he was under her spell once more. She whispered into his ears, seeding his mind with her desires. Before she could secure her place, Kai must be removed—permanently. "Maxwell, send a unit of Milnos men into the Zabranen Forest to disrupt the Katori tribes north of Albey. We must flush Kai out from his hiding place in those mountains. I have plans for the young prince, and for his father. Trust me, Maxwell, and I will give you all you desire. You do trust me, don't you—my love?"

There was no response. The layers of manipulation made the man putty in her hands. Nola wanted to instruct him to jump to his death down the five-story drop, but she still needed the man, as did her brother, Landon. Instead, she changed the rhythm of her tapping to a slow rub. "Maxwell, listen to me. You are tired. Sit here in the sun and rest your eyes. You will wake in a few moments and feel refreshed, confident in your strategy to control Diu through my son Aaron."

Nola rose and stepped inside the council chamber, leaving the Regent where he sat.

CHAPTER 1

Snow Wolf

The golden sunrise raced down the Katori Mountains and sparkled through the ice-covered trees. Kai's breath floated on the frozen air in white puffs. There was something safe about solitude. Or so he told himself, as he did every morning as he ventured out alone. A yawn took over his face, reminding him how little sleep his nightmares afforded him, trapped in constant contemplation over his ability to change the future—and save his father.

One lifelong burden still haunted him: could he save his mother, Mariana Galloway? He knew the risks he was taking today, his mother was a powerful Beastmaster who had lost her mind after spending a decade trapped in her dragon form. If he hoped to understand her condition, he needed to comprehend the dynamics behind the multiple creatures twisted within her comatose mind. His teacher, Basil, cautioned restraint and set limitations—but Kai knew that if he hoped to revive her, he needed to take risks.

Standing in the snow-covered forest below his grandfather Benmar's cave on the Katori mountainside, Kai sniffed the bitter cold, and a sense of mystery urged him to let his magic flow outward. The energy within his aura rolled down his spine and washed over the forest in a tidal wave. The magic within each animal living in the forest pushed back, instilling the desire to run.

Soundless footfalls pressed into the snow as Kai weaved through the forest at a heart-pounding pace; his Nebean black wolf, Smoke, joined him. Crystal-like branches glistened above him. Each step pressed into the undisturbed snow, leaving a trail of silent destruction. Down the mountain they went; the faster he ran, the happier he felt. Then he noticed them—a pack of wolves hot on their heels. Snow leopards and mountain lions joined the growing collective.

Remembering the lessons his friend Ryker, another Beastmaster, had taught him, Kai no longer relied on his ability to glean—the ability to see the energy that flowed through all life set aglow with his mind. Instead, he traced the vibrations through his aura to create a deeper magical connection to his surroundings. His skin became even more sensitive to his surroundings—opening his mind and enhancing his ability to connect to nature.

Ryker is right. I can do more than see the world—I feel connected to all life around me.

Enthralled by the connection, Kai focused on the power spikes that each creature emanated back through his aura. The hair on his arms and neck raised, and his very essence compelled the beasts to run after him. Somehow, he knew, they felt him as much as he did them. Their energy brought a sense of peace and harmony. On a deep level, he realized that he connected each animal to the rest of the growing pack, like the hub in the center of a great wheel of life.

Beasts that should be at odds came together. Slowing to an easy jog, Kai let the other creatures close in around him. Smoke took the lead down the mountain. Kai gleaned the area. Trees and animals alike were set aglow. He noticed the flow of energy around them brighten. Together they were creating power, and it washed over him like an ocean.

A spark danced from his fingertips as he touched a few of the pack members. In his mind, he saw their design, the golden thread that created their form. The power rushed up Kai's arms into his spine, instilling knowledge he had not recognized before. The power of creation set his crystal aglow, his stone blessed by Alenga during his Conhaspriga that enhanced his magic, showing him the possibilities to use the golden thread to become any beast he chose. He studied the subtle differences between each creature and variations within their structures. The beauty and peace within nature coursed through his heart—he had never known such harmony or balance.

Bright sunlight trickled through the thinning forest. Smoke cornered sharply, taking them to a large clearing; Kai joined Smoke in the center. The mismatched pack entered, circling until they found a spot and sat facing Kai. A kinship formed between him and the other animals. They spoke to him in a way he could not put into words, but there was understanding. A trust brought them together, and he knew they would come if he called. The moment lingered, and he nodded to them in acceptance.

As the pack dispersed, Smoke leaped onto a stone perch and glanced back. Kai felt more than heard his companion's call, and he followed. Smoke hopped from the overlook and darted ahead, leading Kai through the dense pine tree forest. Far down the mountain, the trees began to thin. When they reached a clearing, Smoke stopped. The cold, crisp air whipped through the open meadow, but that did not bother Kai's exposed hands and face.

Kai's mouth curved upward at the recognition of their surroundings. Before he saw the wolf, he felt her presence. Her wild nature floated on the wind. Hidden in the snow- and ice-covered trees, she waited. Her pure white fur blended with the snowy surroundings, and her golden eyes focused on Kai. The snow wolf was nearly as tall as Smoke; her thick coat fluttered in the wind. The intensity of her stare struck Kai—then, he heard her mind speak to him.

Beastmaster, we would walk with you.

Kai nodded in acceptance. She darted into the clearing and rubbed her white fur against Smoke. The pair coiled around each other in a display of affection. Smoke turned and licked the side of her face. Kai nodded to her. *Anjo*, he spoke to her with his mind and offered his outstretched hand to Smoke's mate.

Although she was a wild creature, Kai felt naming her gave her a special place in his heart. Anjo allowed Kai to run his hand down her back as she circled him. Out of the trees came three white and two black wolf pups. Two of them: one white, the other black, shared Smoke's ice-blue eyes, while the rest favored Anjo's golden irises. Kai knelt in the snow to greet the pups; they licked at his hands and face.

"My, how you've all grown!" Kai searched the forest west of their position and saw their den, a dark cave protected by pine trees and brush. "This is the first time I have seen your pups this far from the den." He glanced and Anjo and Smoke; he saw a sense of pride in their puffed-up posture, which made him smile more.

An impulse tugged at Kai's soul. The energy from his interaction with the pack still coursed through his veins. The bubble of power still begged for purpose. Although each Beastmaster understood they could only take one animal form, like his mother, Kai had a stronger connection to beasts—and also like his mother, he had discovered the ability to balance multiple strands within his core.

Holding his crystal, he felt the stone's power amplify his magic. The excess of raw energy added to the magic he pulled from nature, and it made his skin feel hot. Heat radiated off his body, melting the snow beneath him. The power was almost more than he could handle, so he released the white crystal; the dangling stone burned bright. Hands outstretched, he touched Smoke and Anjo.

Loyalty and trust reverberated through his connection. In his mind, he called upon all creation. A spark illuminated his soul, and the sequence coalesced into two unique golden chains. He understood the structure of each wolf—he felt their strength. The spiraled-looking ladders showed him the similarity and variation between the two wolves.

Embracing the knowledge of creation within both chains, he blended them into one unique strand before connecting it with his own. As the change took over, he felt the snap of his form latch onto the new thread. He relaxed and accepted the change, assuring an easy transformation. The shockwave put him on all fours, and chills rushed down his spine and out his limbs. Fur erupted over his skin. He felt his face change and fangs grow. His hands curled into large white paws.

Of all the transformations he had performed, this one by far felt the most challenging. Even with the pack's extra power, there was pain in the shift, forcing him to pull from nature to ease his burden. The completed transformation left him disoriented. He shook his mane. Prancing in place, he tested the movements of his new body.

The call of the wild compelled him to howl into the wind. Smoke and Anjo echoed his call, as did their pups. Their reply filled him with excitement. Kai stepped up to Smoke; his companion's head was lower than his own. Kai realized that his wolf-form was taller than the average man.

The face of his teacher, Basil, came to mind. His teacher had cautioned him against creating a new creature, even discouraged him from anything besides his dragon. Kai imagined that only the most reckless, rebellious Beastmasters who dared to make a new beast would understand the intensity he experienced. Kai embraced his creation, reveled in the euphoria. The overwhelming desire to run coursed through his wild heart, but the words of Ryker echoed in his mind. *Hold fast to your real life. Find the balance between your two worlds.* He knew how important it was to remain focused on controlling his mind.

Rayna, the love of his life, remained his touchstone to his real life, and thoughts of their years together calmed his excitement. Her laughter echoed in his ears, her smile anchored him, and thoughts of their future warmed his soul.

Anjo barked playfully, drawing his attention. Her pups hopped in the snow and darted off through the woods. Kai followed. As a pack, they ran through the snow-covered forest. Icy snow crunched beneath his massive paws. Smoke darted around an immense boulder and his speed increased. Kai kept pace. A scent caught in Kai's throat. The more he sniffed, the stronger the sensation rippled into his core, forcing instinct to take over. The smell of something wild piqued his interest. Cold air whipped through the trees, and he lost the scent. Smoke did not.

The black wolf darted through the forest. Kai spotted a rabbit hopping on the snow; their arrival caused it to run. The smell filled Kai's mind and spurred him to chase the creature. The little thing was fast; he was faster. He closed the distance with little effort. A white wolf joined him in the pursuit. Thick underbrush and dense forest made it difficult to get close. Around trees and between rocks, it zipped. The smell of it stirred beastly desires.

The more he tried to catch it, the more it consumed his mind. He snapped his jaws into the thicket, trying to get a taste. The white creature slipped through the vines with its fur intact. The black wolf advanced around the clump of vines, forcing the rabbit back into hiding. They had it surrounded. Kai dug at the snow and pushed into the brambles; he wanted the tiny beast so bad he could nearly taste it.

Razor-sharp thorns caught in his thick fur. One barb pricked the edge of his nose. The pain startled him, and blood trickled down his muzzle into his mouth. A whisper on the wind called to him, and a woman's voice called to him. It was Alenga, their goddess of all creation.

Kai, remember who you are. Run home.

Smoke and Anju barked; the wolf pups dug at the snow, searching for a way inside the thicket. The rabbit tremored in fear, trapped within the brambly vines.

That name—*Kai*. It sparked a memory. The face of a girl, the warmth of her hand, and the smell of her hair. He could not recall her name, but he knew her—cared for her. His mind raced, but he could not think clearly. The smell of fear oozed off the rabbit in front of him. Yet he stepped back.

Tufts of white and black fur clung to the brambles. His fur. While the other wolves barked, one stopped and ran to his side; even within his confusion, he recognized a connection between them. Thoughts of a man echoed from the great black wolf:

Kai, find Ryker.

Again, the name shook him. *Kai*. The memory of the black wolf resounded with a name—*Smoke*. Their bond eased his confusion. A sense of urgency forced Kai into action. Before his wild desires clouded his mind, Kai ran down the mountain. One thought was on his mind—find Ryker. Wild urges tugged at his nature. Through the trees, he smelled other animals.

Holding firm, he focused on the hillside of Matoku unfolding in the distance—a bustling city built amongst the snowy trees. How he knew the name or where to go, he was not sure. By leaps and bounds, he made short work of the vast distance.

Entering the city, he noticed the black wolf as it ran by his side. Again, Kai struggled to remember the wolf.

Smoke . . . is that you?

His mind fought to cling to memories. Kai and Smoke slowed to weave through the crowd. People and beasts in the city stopped and stared up at him. Their wide eyes shocked him as they parted to yield the path. Smoke led Kai through Matoku, up the hillside; their pace became swift once they had more freedom to move. A row of bulky trees connected by arching vines came into view, and an instant familiar feeling washed over Kai. A massive black wolf sprang from its resting spot. While she was tall, like Smoke, Kai still looked down at her.

Her name eluded him; he felt a connection, and after a sniff, she let him get close. Smoke disappeared into an arched, vine-covered entrance among the trees, and then returned with a man in black. Kai's mind offered him the name—Ryker.

Keen brown eyes gleamed with recognition, and Ryker approached Kai.

"Beautiful beast, I've not seen the like." Ryker looked up at him, offering his open palm. "Come to me, Kai, I know it is you. Are you trapped, lost in your new creation? Risky to attempt alone. Where is your teacher?"

Those words rang true; Kai felt lost. Memories danced around the borders of his mind, hidden in shadow. Faces, just out of focus, tugged at his heart. Conflicted by the desire to run wild and drawn to remain.

He stepped closer and lowered his head to Ryker, allowing the man to touch his fur. Kai felt a strong desire to collapse.

"I am here with you, Kai," Ryker said in a soothing voice. "Feel the sun on your face. Let its power fill your soul. Remember, Mariana, your mother, and how you saved her. She needs you now, more than ever. Think of Rayna, the love of your life. Search your heart for the devotion you feel for her."

Each name resonated within him, restoring his humanity, especially the repeated use of his own. Faces, voices, and moments raced from the recesses of his mind. He watched Ryker's movements. His cupped hand floated out to his side, folded over, ending in a push against Kai's furry chest. Soon both hands joined in the exercise. Ryker began to move his feet, stepping with the movement. Kai knew these moves from a time he could not quite remember.

"Find the balance between your two worlds." Ryker continued to move, and Kai felt his chest start to warm. "Separate your spirit from the golden thread you created. Embrace the light of your crystal—your touchstone."

Beastmaster magic coursed through Kai's veins. The memories of his life stepped to the forefront of his mind and freed his heart. Light blossomed in the shadows of his mind, and he released the golden thread and clung to the white light—the touchstone which infused his magic. Thankful there was no pain as his body sloughed off the beast. He felt the edges of his crystal warm his hand when he returned to his proper form.

Depleted by the shift, Kai slumped to one side.

The strong arm of Ryker held him upright. They sat in silence while Kai collected his bearings. Slowly the surroundings became more and more familiar. Smoke sat in the grass next to Shiva, Ryker's wolf. Her piercing blue eyes were half-closed. Everything was as it should be.

Kai finally spoke, sitting up straight on his own. "Thank you, Ryker." He then told his old friend everything, sharing the morning's events on the mountain and his encounter with the wild pack. Even in the retelling, he felt the magic raise the hair on his arms. This new magic was now somehow a part of him. Kai leaned back on his elbows and crossed his legs at the ankles. His strength continued to return, and he asked Ryker, "Who did I look like, Smoke or Anjo?"

"Anjo the snow wolf, yes, this explains your coloring," Ryker responded. "She was your other inspiration. I should have known. Your fur was mostly pure white, like Anjo's, with a fine edging of black around the eyes and muzzle. Part of your mane, up around your shoulders, had black streaks, as did your tail. The ears were pitch black and came to a point, but what stood out were your eyes."

"Were they blue like Smoke or golden yellow like Anjo?"

"One of each," Ryker responded. "Impressive. Again, I must ask, where was Basil during your little adventure this morning? I am guessing since you came to me, your teacher was not with you. If you plan to take risks, your teacher, Basil, should guide you. What is wrong with you? This is not the first time you went off alone. If you need someone to talk with, find your uncle Haygan. It feels like you are pushing people away."

The shame of his choices forced Kai to look away. He knew the truth—they both did. Ryker sighed, and Kai felt his friend's frustration. "These skills should not be practiced alone." Ryker paused, and Kai turned back to see the seriousness in the man's dark eyes. "We each have teachers for a reason. They do more than teach you the ancient movements of moving magic or show you how to manipulate it. They teach you how to build trust."

Kai knew that he was tempting fate if he did not stop this reckless behavior. "I promise to be more careful." He wanted to believe the lie, that he'd actually be more careful—but he had already become a shuk, a black panther, and a horse, all on his own. There was no reason to think he needed Basil to teach him anything. His teacher only held him back.

"Well," Ryker said, patting Kai's shoulder, "either way, it was good you ran to someone you knew to help bring you back. Instead of creating new creatures, your time would be better spent practicing the shift into your dragon form, like the Guardians recommended. The mastery of one beast will serve you far better than a collection of beasts. Can you yet shift multiple times mid-flight, or bring out only your wings and fly as a man?"

The truth was, he had not practiced these skills because none of them would help him understand his mother. An odd silence floated between them. Kai did his best to hide his intentions, but he found it difficult to look Ryker in the eye. After their travels to save his mother, Ryker was like a second father to him, and the man's Beastmaster nature gave him insights into Kai's spirit he could not truly hide. Guilt hung on Kai like a wet shirt, and he sat staring a nothing; his mouth would not form the lie neither of them would believe.

"Fine. If you will not heed my warning, you should at least know that your next transition into your new snow wolf should take less energy. I can only imagine that the moment with your pack provided the extra magic you needed. But you must remain mindful of the balance between beast and man. Consider having Rayna with you; she is undoubtedly your strongest connection in this life. If any memory can hold you in this life, it is your love for her."

"Thank you," Kai muttered. "The moment simply swept me away." Again, he lied, this time more to himself to ease his guilt for not taking Rayna with him to practice his magic.

The huff from Ryker made Kai sit up straight. "Heed Basil's lessons, or you will find yourself permanently trapped. I know you have heard the story, but it is necessary to understand the risks. Even with Basil nearby, you could be lost. The Katori Beastmasters, who created the first two dragons, had no beast to emulate—only their imagination to guide them. Their designs took immense power. Every drop of magic went into the formation, leaving nothing behind to reach the light. The wild nature of the beasts took over, and they reveled in their new form. Those with them could not coax them back, and they flew away."

If there was any guilt or fear, Kai ignored it. Everyone assured him there was no rush to learn or expand his magic, but he believed the real reason was because nobody trusted him with that much power. If there were even a chance he would be like Keegan—his biological father who had corrupted his gifts in a belligerent quest for power—then he was sure the Elders would banish him, just as they had done with Keegan. Kai knew that the Elders wanted to control him, to protect him from that fate—but Kai needed no protection. He could handle his powers all on his own.

A hush fell between them until Ryker stood and offered Kai a hand up. "Your mother, Mariana, she would be proud of you. While she was one of a rare few capable of changing into multiple animals, it has been centuries since any Beastmaster did what you accomplished today. None since the dragon and the shuk have we Katori created an original creature not already found in nature."

The thought of Mariana being proud of him touched his heart. He visited her each day as she lay comatose, but he still wondered if bringing her back was the right choice. "Are you coming to visit my mother today?" He knew the answer but asked anyway.

"I am not one for an audience." Ryker turned away. "Kendra's mother, Yana, and your grandfather, Lucca, never leave me alone with her. As if I, of all people, would do her harm." He tossed his hand back in a mock wave and started to leave.

"You know," Kai called after him, "tomorrow the Elders intend to announce where Davi and his people will live. Both Yana and Lucca will be here in Matoku. Could be the perfect time to visit my mother in Hiowind."

Ryker glanced back, his one eyebrow raised, then he disappeared into the forest with Shiva trotting after.

CHAPTER 2

Destructive Lies

The warm weather was a surprising change from the snow-covered countryside only two days prior. Smoke sat next to Kai, and they watched the Kodama manipulate the landscape, sprouting new evergreen holly bushes and winter flowers. It pleased him to see Rayna flourish in her new home with new friends. He only wished he could settle the argument raging inside his mind—stay or go.

Lucca cleared his throat and interrupted his contemplation. "Kai, when do you intend to speak with Davi and the other Katori outcasts? It is high time you honored your commitment to bring them home. Davi and his people will not listen to the Elders, but they will listen to you."

There was something to be said for his grandfather's ability to sound calm yet instill intensity. There was no use delaying the inevitable. Alenga herself had asked him to bring her children home—Davi and his family, and any Katori outcast who wished to return to Katori. Kai thought about his responsibility. "I will speak with Liam," Kai responded. "I know Alenga granted Liam the power to restore the tunnels of her crystal mountain, but how will we hide the entrance? Will people be able to pour through the mountain, or will you place Guardians at the temple?"

"When you can control light, you control what others see. Lumens can create light from nothing, but we can also reflect light to create an illusion. Besides the magic you see while gleaning, we can distort light to create barriers, much like Benmar, your grandfather, a Beastmaster with the ability to bend light to become invisible. One of his ancestors must be a Lumen. My own daughter, your mother, could deflect light, and I would not be surprised if the ability lies within you to manipulate light as well. But back to the point at hand, speak with Davi and get Liam to focus on the tunnels."

Although unsuccessfully, Kai did not want anyone to know he had been practicing the ability to bend light. Keegan had tried and it drove him mad; he did not imagine anyone would be in favor of him trying. "Very well, I will speak with Liam about his willingness to change projects in favor of the tunnels and Alenga's temple. But there is something else I need to do before visiting Davi." He eyed his grandfather, hoping he would catch where he was going.

"Diu?" The word escaped Lucca's mouth, dripping with disappointment.

The topic was a sore spot they never managed to avoid, and today would be the same. "It is time for the Winter Festival, and I need to see my father, Iver." Kai noticed the disapproval in his grandfather's eyes. There was no argument he could win when it came to Diu. It was Kai's home, and Lucca refused to understand the importance it held. Nobody understood why he could not let go.

"The Winter Festival is a celebration. We, too, welcome the new year with Alenga's blessing. You need not travel to Diu, and there are traditions here you should experience. There is nothing there for you now."

Lucca offered as if it were a suggestion, but Kai heard the finality in his grandfather's tone.

"Diu is my home," Kai insisted. "I am their prince, and they bid me to return. Iver is my father, despite what you want . . . or the fact Keegan's blood runs through my veins."

Lucca's eyes narrowed. "Home is where you choose. You committed yourself to Katori and gave up the outside world on the day of your blessing. Are you choosing Diu over Katori after all this time? I know you fly to Albey more often than you should. You visit Shane, swap letters. The Guardians watch him; I hear he is an honorable young man, a Half-Light as I understand, but he is not Katori."

The fact his grandfather had the Guardians spying on him raked his backside. "Do you question my loyalty?"

"I do," Lucca admitted. "And I am not the only one. These men who wait for you in Albey—Dresnor and Drew—you should have sent them home, back to Diu. Told them you were not coming back."

There was a small part of Kai that agreed with his grandfather. He had several opportunities to tell his Kempery-man Dresnor that he would not be coming back to Diu, but Cazier's most recent letter carried sad news of his father's illness. "Am I a prisoner?" Kai demanded. "I keep your precious secrets; is that not enough to demonstrate my loyalty?"

Lucca crossed his arms and glared at Kai. "An interesting choice of words. Are the Katori secrets not your secrets, too?"

Are my loyalties really so divided? Kai looked to Smoke, but he offered no response, only turning his head away. "Why must I cut Diu off like an unwanted appendage?" Kai said, turning his attention back to Lucca. "Iver is dying, and he needs me." Kai knew there was more to his desires, things his grandfather would never understand.

"Do you think me naïve?" Lucca stepped closer to Kai. "Diu is a dangerous place, and it carries great risk to you should you return. Iver is not long for this world. I am sorry, but nothing can save him. This Queen Nola brings outsiders to Diu. Milnos must not turn its gaze on us, or they will be on our doorstep. We must protect our own."

"Of course, you have spies everywhere. You know everything. So, tell me, any news or sightings of Keegan?" he asked, watching Lucca's expression harden. "I know you hate him, but we need to be ready for his inevitable return. It has been two months; he knows my mother is alive, and he will come for her."

"I will not speak about—him." Lucca's eyes grew angrier. "Nor should you. He is gone, period. Not even that man could heal from those devastating wounds. I hate that they came by my hand, but the man is gone. Enough talk of this."

The truth, Kai knew the man lived; he was not sure how, but he felt it in his soul. "We cannot turn a blind eye to Keegan. We must search for him, or at least his crew, and confirm he will not rise from the ashes."

"I said enough!" Lucca shouted a little too loud, and a few bystanders turned a wary eye. "I will not discuss this." He tossed his hand up, halting Kai's rebuttal.

The pain welling in his grandfather's eyes filled Kai's stomach with guilt. If Keegan was indeed dead, his grandfather carried the burden. He knew all too well that taking a life carved deep scars into a man's soul. "I am sorry, grandfather. As you wish, I will let this go."

◆ ◆ ◆

Hand-in-hand, Rayna and Kai walked around Matoku, the ancient section of the city buried long ago. Their pace was quick. Even Smoke sensed the urgency and kept to the path, not wandering off. Kai needed to persuade Liam to abandon the ancient city restoration in exchange for repairing Alenga's Crystal Mountain temple and the tunnels for the return en masse of Davi and his people.

The deeper into the ancient city Kai traveled, the louder the ground rumbled beneath his feet. He watched Liam and the other Stonekings direct a massive flow of soil and rocks down into a hollow across the ridge. Kai hung back alongside a line of bystanders. The Stonekings' movements were swift, and Kai could see the forcefulness. Each surfed the outskirts on the wave of unwanted dirt, revealing stone pathways, broken statues, gazebos, and several petrified trees in its wake.

When Liam returned, Kai cocked his head, directing his friend away from the others. When they were alone, Kai spoke. "Liam, my grandfather asked me to speak with you about restoring Alenga's temple.

I have been tasked with bringing home the lost Katori children, as they call them."

"Why? Because the word 'outcast' leaves a bad taste?" Liam rolled his eyes. "You know, even the Elders see them as foreigners. I do not care what the Elders say, these people only wanted to explore the possibilities outside of Katori and were punished for it. Now they want to force them back home because of a vision?" Liam shook his head.

There was truth in his friend's words, and Kai hoped that his friend might understand his desire to return to Diu. "I agree with you. People should have a choice to live where they want, but this is not up to us."

"Why the rush?" Liam crossed his arms. "I am not finished here. We have discussed this already; the city restoration project is important to me, and I want to see it through."

His friend's agitation was understandable. "I know what this means to you." Kai took a moment to watch Rayna laugh with her sister. "Before I can return home to Diu, I must convince Davi and his people to come here. I fear for my father's safety. Something bad is happening in Diu, and I must get to the bottom of it before my city . . ." He let his voice drop off, noticing Liam's raised brow.

Liam glared at him. "Funny, I thought Katori was your home now." He sighed heavily before continuing. "You have responsibilities here now, but I am sure Lucca gave you this lecture already. I am only two years older than you, but even I know as the grandson to an Elder, you need to set an example. You made a vow to give up the outside world. Hiowind is your city now, or Matoku if you so choose."

The truth was Kai was still not sure where he belonged. He came to gain power and find his mother, but Diu was his childhood home, and part of him knew he would always feel connected to the people and the memories of his past. Why did he have to choose? He looked to Rayna, still talking with her sister; she had uprooted her entire life in Diu to explore Katori. *How did she embrace the move so easily?*

Heat swelled in his veins. "I will not turn my back on Diu." His tone carried weight, and he stepped into Liam's space. "You do not understand. Nobody does. I will not hesitate to do what is needed."

Liam matched Kai's glare, and his bronze complexion accented his anger. "It is no longer your place to interfere with the affairs of Diu. Or are you still their prince and would-be king? Your loyalty is either to Katori and our secrets, or to Diu and their petty disputes over power."

Kai took a step forward again, and with it, a knot formed in his stomach. "Why does my loyalty mean choosing?"

"You cannot keep one foot in Diu while you try to make a home in Katori." Liam narrowed his gaze. "Someday, you will have to choose. I will do whatever the Elders ask, and if they insist, I will start clearing the tunnels for the return of the outcasts, but don't ask me to agree with your real motives in going to Diu."

He could not believe what he was hearing. Why did Liam continue to question his loyalty? "Don't make me choose." Kai felt his heart thunder in his chest. "I will not be a prisoner of old Katori beliefs that were never my own. I will live where I choose and help whom I choose."

"You sound like Keegan more and more."

The mention of Kai's birth father was a stab in the back. "How can you possibly compare me to *him*?" Kai spat. "That monster tried to kill Rayna. We are not the same."

Refusing to speak any further, Liam stormed off and rejoined the restoration group.

◆ ◆ ◆

Sleeplessness was no stranger to Kai. Alone, he traveled toward Alenga's ancient city between Hiowind and Matoku. A brisk breeze tousled his blond hair as moonlight danced down the warm white stone pathway beneath his bare feet. Past decisions and new questions rattled away in his mind. Once again, the burden of everyone else pressed on Kai's heart.

He never asked to be Katori—all he ever wanted was his mother back. Although he had fulfilled Alenga's prophecy of rescuing her, she still slept. Had he made a mistake? There could be no room for doubt—Alenga's visions were real. They *had* to be. Or were they merely dreams of what he wanted to happen? Did his imagination create the perfect outcome to satisfy the fantasies that arose out of his childhood abandonment?

But if his dreams about saving his mother were real, then he would have to face the fate of his father and the role his vision implied. How could he be destined to kill Iver, the man who raised him? Blood father or not, Kai loved him and refused to accept his destiny. There must be a way to change fate—after all, another vision helped him save Drew from dying.

Still, he walked alone because his restless soul gave him no peace.

Smoke, ever his loyal companion, appeared at the tree line and joined Kai on his journey. Their shared bond gave him the comfort he was not entirely alone to face the future. They walked in silence through the newly changed landscape of the unearthed structures from the past. The old city, Alenga's city—once lost to Katori, now rediscovered.

Kai marveled at the massive city, which seemed to spring up overnight. Liam and his Stoneking masters continued to remove the mountain of dirt and stone that once hid Alenga's ancient city. The Kodama planted new Bodhima trees covered in cosmos vines, which towered overhead. Crystal clear water danced in fountains and gushed along narrow illuminated channels, breathing life into the hardscapes. Stone obelisks, statues, and gazebos decorated the newly planted gardens, each a little different than anything seen around the other cities of Katori.

Surrounded by a garden in full bloom stood the enormous ancient Agora. One corner remained dark and partially covered in rocky black soil. The rest looked new; pink coral stone accented in white ivy embellishments and illuminated with golden yellow crystals, which Kai presumed were empowered by Lumens.

The waterfall that once concealed the entrance now flowed freely around the structure in a narrow channel randomly lit with tiny blue crystals. Kai crossed a small bridge and entered through what was once the round stone door. Three grand archways now stood open. Inside, moonlight poured into the large pool located at the heart of the Agora.

Unsure what possessed him, he once again returned to this sacred place to pray Alenga would speak to him like the night he slept here before discovered by the others. But since they had unearthed the Agora, the intensity felt faded like a washed-out old painting. And yet, he knew there was great power here.

Before Kai could take another step, he felt a presence, the sense of someone staring at him. Eyes closed, his breathing slowed; he reached out with his sight and gleaned the room. One slow glance around the ancient Agora and his mind came to an archway half-obscured by a mountain of dirt. Her elegant form and brilliant glow lifted the corner of his mouth.

"Rayna, you should be asleep in Hiowind. You need your rest to continue working on restoring the city. Why are you here?"

"Why are *you* here?" She strolled across the vast stone floor toward the center. "I go where you go, remember."

A lump formed in his throat, a knot filled with shame; he swallowed his guilt and tried to smile. "I come here to ask Alenga to deliver me from my fate. Lift the burdens from my soul." His truth washed over him as he spoke. "I will not kill my father. I must fight my destiny."

He watched Rayna's decerning eyes trace the moonlight across the floor. "What is your question, Kai?" Her tone toyed with his raw emotions.

"Why me?" he asked as she passed around behind him.

"These are extraordinary times, and your faith demonstrates your worth. The very fact you search for a peaceful resolution proves you can navigate the responsibilities of leadership. I cannot presume to know the path you walk, or Alenga's will, but you must continue to have faith. Maybe your vision is significant; maybe it's a warning to stay away because Nola is corrupt and means to use you against Iver. Or maybe it is a metaphor telling you to let go of him before Nola destroys your memories of him."

Kai turned to face her. "Tell me what to do. If it is my fate to kill my father, and I have no choice, I guess I am a puppet on a string. Do I play out a doomed life, or are there choices I can still make? I refuse to accept my vision, I must save my father, not let him go." Kai waved his hand at her.

Rayna's chuckle struck a nerve, but he held his tongue, waiting for her response. "You are no puppet." She stopped to face him, and her eyes held fast to his. "Every step you've taken has been yours and yours alone. Own your choices, Kai."

"So, my visions, are they real?" Kai grabbed at the various moments of his past. "My dreams predict the future. I saw Drew die, and yet I saved him. The dragon's breath plant would have killed me, yet you saved me because I told you to research the plant. I have changed many things. Why is this any different?"

The wisdom in Rayna's eyes surprised him, and he looked at her anew. She took his hand. "Your dreams are a glimpse into the future. Telling me to research that plant fulfilled your vision and my destiny to save you. The men who attacked Port Anahita and tried to kill Drew never changed, but your decision to charge in rather than being frozen in fear saved your friend. What you chose now is still up to you." She drifted away from him again. "Real or not, the choice is still yours to make. Stay here in Katori or go home to Diu. I support you either way."

Kai took her hand and said softly, "We should go home."

There was more to his misery he wanted to share, but he kept it to himself as they made their way back through Alenga's city. Diu waited for news of their prince's return, yet he offered only ink on paper as to his well-being. His pending return he left unanswered. A disheartening thought shook his soul; he did not want to return. Yet if he were honest, he did not belong here either? The Katori life demanded secrecy, and like his mother, he must be willing to die for those secrets.

The freedom to live in the open and use his magic without fear required that he live here, in Katori—but no matter how he fought the urge, Diu needed him. His family and friends needed him. He wanted nothing more than to go home and see his father, the man who raised him, called him son, and loved him as his own.

Rayna's pace slowed, and she pulled Kai into an illuminated arbor made from a dwarf Bodhima tree covered in cosmos vines. She cocked her head to capture Kai's eyes. "Mind telling me what distracts you still?"

Her beauty left him breathless. The pale pink glow of the cosmos vines kissed her cheeks. Overwhelmed by the desire, Kai pressed his lips to hers. She kissed him back. Then he returned them to the path. "I apologize—not for kissing you, of course." He glanced down and saw that the blush on her cheeks remained even though the pink hue of the cosmos flowers were behind them. "I'm only sorry for wasting the time we have together. For not being present."

She slipped her hand into the crook of his elbow. "Do you want to talk about anything? Or do you want me to guess?" She paused. "Is this about what Cazier's letter said? I am guessing you want to go home to Diu."

The letter he'd received two days earlier was still etched in his mind. Master General Cazier reported ill omens and bad tidings—Iver's health continued to decline, Riome remained lost at sea along with any answers about who was helping Nola, and Diu was tearing itself apart. And if that were not enough, his cousin concealed one last message:

Diu is now a dangerous place for the next would-be king. Stay away until I send for you.

"Saying everything out loud makes it real." He looked at her knowing he was not ready to face fate. "I cannot accept that my father will die, or that I can do nothing to save him. Then there is Nola; Riome was meant to discover her secrets and bring back proof of her duplicity, but Riome is missing. I know Nola and Landon are related, but I have no proof. I know she is drugging my father, but I have no proof. Riome was meant to find proof. I know Nola needs to be removed from power, but queens are difficult to dethrone, and she has a power I do not understand."

Her eyes pleaded with him to trust her. "There must be a way I can help you. Do you want to go back to Diu together?"

Fear rotted his mind and broke his spirit. "I don't know what I want," he lied more to himself than to Rayna. "I must solve this on my own." He hated being short with her, but he was tired of everyone questioning him.

"You want to search for Riome," Rayna stated, and Kai knew she was right. "I imagine you rack your mind on how to save your father, all while trying to avoid being crowned the next king of Diu. You fear your friends, Dresnor and Drew, have lost faith in you. Not to mention that you worry Dresnor will march into the Zabranen Forest to find you. How am I doing?" she asked but did not wait for Kai's response. "The burdens of being a prince pull you back to Diu, but your life in Katori demands unyielding loyalty." Rayna stopped them on the path. "You train nightly with the Guardians, hoping they will grant us freedoms to come and go on the other side of the Katori Mountains."

"I *must* train with them," Kai interrupted. "They have such control, and I need to understand more than Basil will show me right now. They shift in and out of their beastly forms on a whim while they push and pull magic between them. And yes, as a Guardian, I would have freedoms."

Rayna went on as if he had said nothing. "After everyone is asleep, you travel to Matoku to sleep on the floor of the ancient Agora in hopes of receiving a new vision about Iver. You want to return to Diu, but what if your mother wakes? Before dawn, you travel up the mountain to practice your transformations without Basil."

He felt bewildered by her knowledge of his coming and goings. He was always so careful to go quietly and return before anyone noticed. "How do you know all of this?"

Again, she ignored his interruption. "Then there are everyone's doubts about your loyalty. I heard your argument with Liam and another with Lucca. Have I missed anything?"

Every word was accurate. Rayna knew him as well as he knew himself. He sighed deeply. "I don't know what else to do."

"Do you doubt your calling?" Rayna's tone was less a question than a statement of fact. "Is Alenga's messages unclear? She wants you to bring home Davi's people. Start there—and stay here in Katori." She took a breath and waited.

The silence was deafening. Rayna's truth struck him hard. "You know I do not doubt Alenga's intentions," he said. "I only wish to be released from my fate." Then he felt his back stiffen. "But who controls my fate? Do I even have a say? My visions are gaining in clarity." It felt like a hand had been thrust into his chest, wrenching his heart and straining his breathing. "I don't want to kill my father, but my dream is clear. Why am I there; why is Nola there? Maybe I could stop her if I knew what Riome learned. If only I knew how . . ."

The pleading words fell from his lips like dew on a water-laden leaf. Rayna remained steadfast, and her eyes were without pity. He knew she was trying to help, and he felt shame for burdening her with his troubles.

"We should speak with Benmar. He will know what you should do," Rayna insisted, and Kai agreed.

CHAPTER 3

Battle Pains

The morning was ice cold. New snow danced in the air, refusing to fall. Kai stood at the entrance of his grandfather Benmar's cave with Smoke by his side. The sounds of a steaming teapot pulled him into the warmer living space of the cave. "I wish Benmar were here, but nobody has seen him in days," Kai said as he took a seat close to the fire.

Rayna nodded. "I had hoped grandfather Benmar could help you balance your desire to save Diu and the probability you should let them go."

He had a feeling she hoped Benmar could talk him out of going to Diu, but avoiding fate was not the answer. "Riome is the key to everything. There must be a way to search for her. Wherever she is." Thoughts of Riome drew Kai into contemplation. Had she taken one too many risks? Would he ever see her again?

"Do you mean how you searched the world for your mother?" Rayna pulled the teapot off the fire and poured water into two cups with tea leaves. "Riome is not Katori. Are you sure this is possible?"

The smell of vanilla bean pulled Kai's nose into the air. "I am not sure if it is possible," he began, then paused to consider if her bloodline mattered. "Riome is a Half-Light. The only times I used my magic to call out was with you and Kendra, and we were close together. When I searched for my mother and Keegan, and they were oceans away, and it took more power." He saw Rayna shutter at the mention of his father.

Her physical wounds had healed, but her emotional scars were still raw. Not wanting to linger on the topic, Kai continued. "Being full-blooded Katori might make a difference, but I had help the first time—Kendra talked me through it. My second solo attempt at reaching out with my sight across long distances left me drained and incapacitated for hours."

Hot steam swirled around the spoon in Rayna's hand. "Is there something I could do to help you?" she asked, pouring honey into her tea.

The answer seemed simple enough. Rayna was Katori, and she could help collect the extra energy Kai needed, but would it be enough to allow him to search for a Half-Light? Kendra had once said that he could search for anyone—now he was older, more powerful. *And* he had his crystal. He took a sip of tea and looked around at the stone dwelling.

There was magic in everything, but sunlight and growing plants would provide a stronger connection to the world. "I think you can help. I know in theory what to do, but I need more power. Plus, your Kodama healing abilities could keep me from passing out as my mind travels the world on the light."

He took another sip of tea and continued to tell Rayna the process. She agreed they needed to be outside, and she knew just the place. She told him that she would take them to the eternal summer garden the Kodama created to explore their powers. Empowered by other Kodama magic and nature itself, Rayna would be stronger—and so too would Kai.

Kai's silver dragon cast a dark shadow over the Kodama sanctuary, a plot of land encircled by Stoneking magic. Even in his Beastmaster form, he could sense their power vibrating within the structure, a constant hum. One thing he had never noticed before was a ring of yellow crystals, set aglow, presumably by Lumens, embedded into the tall rock formations. As he neared the ground, his scaly dragon body felt the warm air move in a delicate but steady breeze. Had even the Weathervanes contributed to the creation of this special place?

His wings fluttered the trees surrounding the glade as he landed. Smoke and Rayna hopped to the ground and he transformed back into his natural form. The change in weather wrapped him in warmth and he removed his coat and placed it on a nearby rock with Rayna's cloak. The magic-infused air surrounded them, and he saw it pour into Rayna. The Kodama sanctuary cradled her in her arms bonding with her as the animals of the forest did to him.

"Not sure why, but I never noticed how this sanctuary connects with you."

"It was not always so. My openness to the land, and the growth of my magic creates a stronger connection. Each plant I nurture makes me stronger, connects me to the world. But this place," she waved her hand around the clearing, "is special to the Kodama. Many of the older trees are living people, the Kodama who loved nature and chose to be a tree. If I listen, I can hear them whisper. But we did not come here for me; we came to help you find Riome. What do I need to do?"

"You are right, please sit with me." He motioned to a sunny spot and sat on a grassy knoll, Kai closed his eyes. With a deep breath, he recalled Kendra's instructions. Sunlight melted into his head and shoulders. He infused the energy with memories of Riome. Images of her flooded his mind. Years of hand-to-hand combat training and the various accents and disguises she used on missions flashed before him. Kendra's words echoed in his ears: *Memories possess a power all their own.* He focused on the energy her memories created and pulled it inward.

Speaking to Rayna, he instructed, "Collect the energy from the air and the earth and blend it with your own. Push your energy to me. See the power I pull from the sunlight in the meadow. Allow our surroundings to strengthen you. Share what you can with me, and I will mix it with my own."

Connected to his sight, Kai gleaned Rayna's movements. Like Kendra, her cupped hands swirled through the air as she folded magic and pushed it at Kai. Around them, he noticed the flow of power. His gleaning revealed particles of light swirling through the air. The green crystal around Rayna's neck glowed, as did his white stone.

At first, the magic flowed slowly and easily into him. Waves of Rayna's magic merged with his; he grasped at the raw energy and began to shake. His soul felt momentarily overwhelmed, but he knew what he needed to do. Rayna's magic and the power within their surroundings needed to be shaped by his desire to find Riome.

Drawn inward, he summoned his magic. To his surprise, the depth of his power seemed limitless. Rayna's magic compounded on itself. Sweat dripped down his brow. His body shook with more intensity.

"Hold on as long as you can!" he heard Rayna call. She sounded very far away even though she sat close.

Mentally, he grabbed onto the raw power he'd created and thought of Riome. In an explosion of magic, he felt his mind punch through the air and a focused white light darted over the Katori Mountains. A blur of white, green, and brown landscapes rushed below Kai. His eyes watered as if stung by the wind pressing against his face, yet he physically remained seated in the green meadow.

Before him, a city of black metal rippled across the landscape, and Kai's mind flew toward the sprawling city of Milnos. Its massive size dwarfed anything he had ever seen. He knew Diu was around five miles wide, but Milnos was fifteen miles, with three rings of massive walls. His mind raced past the black iron gates toward the towering ironclad fortress. Then his mind neared the coast and darted out over the ocean. Clouds blew past him, and he felt a special connection tug him downward.

Thud.

A decisive blow to the ribs knocked the air from Kai's lungs, and he felt pressure squeeze his midsection. The wooden decking struck his side, adding to the intense pain he felt. Disoriented and in agony, he wiped the sweat from his eyes and rose to his feet. The salty ocean air filled the billowing sails above his head. He was on a ship in the middle of the ocean.

Someone in the crowd shoved him forward. A sharp pain raced up Kai's leg, but there was no time to look down. Instinctively, he raised his hands to protect his face. He danced on his toes around the behemoth of a man in front of him. Sweat and blood dripped from his opponent. "Nobody calls me a cheat and lives to tell the tale. Least of all, someone like you," the man snarled.

Encircled by shouting bystanders, they continued to exchange blows. With lightning-quick reflexes, he dodged to avoid several strikes before landing a few of his own. With every bone-crushing hit from the man's boulder-like fist, Kai experienced shockwaves of pain. After the last blow stuck Kai's brow, he felt warm blood trickle down his face. He wiped the blood from his temple and caught a glimpse of his hand—not his hand. Too small. Feminine.

A man shouted, "Gut her, Harker. Worthless woman. She probably cheated you."

The man handed Harker a blade. A glint of steel flickered in the sunlight, and Harker snickered. "Your time is up, little girl. It seems your mouth got the better of you. I told you there was no way you could best me. I promise to cast your dead body into the sea," he boasted.

The crowd laughed and cheered him on. Kai heard a feminine laugh below their chatter; a chuckle he recognized spilled from his lips. "Now we're getting somewhere," he mocked in Riome's Port Anahita accent. "I told you I don't cheat at cards, but at fighting, well, you've met your match. I am smarter and faster, and I promise to be quick."

The man's nostrils flared at her mockery; all sweat and fury he charged, blade at the ready. Riome shortened the gap with her swift feet, dodged the outstretched weapon, and slid beneath Harken. Her first kick knocked out his knee, dropping him to the deck, and her second sweeping motion sent the man's outstretched hand around into his own skull—blade first.

The crowd hushed as Harken took his last breath.

"Anyone else?" Riome asked calmly. "No? Drinks all around."

The crowd cheered as the whiskey and rum flowed freely. Riome entered the captain's quarters and collapsed into a chair. "Where were we, boys? My turn to deal?" She scooped up the cards and started to shuffle.

Everything went black, and Kai felt two hands shake his shoulders. He opened his eyes, and the sun bloomed behind Rayna's head as she leaned over to him and caught him in an embrace. "Blessed be Alenga!"

His heart pounded in his chest. Everything around him felt electric, causing him to breathe heavily. Calming his nerves with a few deep breaths, he tried to sit up.

Rayna released him and sat back on her heels. "What happened," she asked, stunned. "I felt you pull the magic through me. Then you began to shake harder. At one point, I heard you mumble, but it was unclear what you were saying. Then you coughed up blood and doubled over in pain. I didn't know what to do. I tried healing you; then, your head started bleeding. What happened?"

There was no explanation. "The first time I did this, I was young, and I did not have my crystal. I had not come into my full power. Maybe the intensity of my crystal-infused magic blended with yours and . . . *drew* me into Riome. It's the only way to explain it—I experienced everything she did. She was fighting with someone else. I didn't have any control, but I felt all her pain. Every blow felt real." Kai rubbed his ribs; the sharpness gave him a real concern for Riome's survival.

The warmth of Rayna's hand pressed into his temple, and he felt her heal the cut. She then healed his ribs, but the taste of blood lingered in his mouth.

"Wherever Riome is," he said, "she is alive, but I fear for her. Smugglers and thieves are bad company, and her current shipmates would just as soon kill her than look at her. They just might, if she can't keep out of trouble."

◆ ◆ ◆

Back in Hiowind, Kai sat in Lucca's chair watching the moon cross the sky. Afraid sleep would bring visions of his father's demise, he thought instead of Riome. Never in his life did he think his magic could pull his spirit into another person. Or that this person's experiences could affect him physically. If only he could talk to his mother, she would know how to help. She was said to be one of the most powerful Katori in history. But still, Mariana had not stirred in her slumber.

Night after night Kai avoided sleep, but time was catching up to him. The land of dreams demanded he slumber. The sour feeling in his gut as his head touched the pillow warned him the dream would not be good. Visions pack a mighty punch, and reality and fantasy can confuse perceptions. He was not ready to process a message from Alenga. His heavy eyelids drooped more and more until he lost his battle. Sleep took him, and the world of dreams and nightmares folded its arms around him.

Storm clouds thundered overhead, startling Kai. The crack of lightning broke through the darkness, and the glint of armor flashed through the trees. Kai crouched. Voices on the road called out.

"I am telling you, I saw someone!" the man shouted in the rain. "Queen Nola pays us good money to guard the road. I will not have some vagrant sneak by on my watch."

"Come on, enough searching," another man shouted. "There's nobody out here. I am going back to the tent. The men patrolling closer to Diu will find your ghost." He stomped off.

The ground beneath Kai smelled of pine needles and mud. Every part of him ached as the rain trickled down his cheeks and into his eyes. The labored breathing offered little strength to his tired limbs. Poised to move, he waited for the soldier to leave. The downpour continued; the lightning flashed, and the path seemed clear. Once he was confident it was safe, Kai attempted to stand but fell hard on his knees.

His leg hurt, and he rubbed his hand over a bandaged gash. The pain in his ribs concerned him—both sides hurt, but the left side felt like two ribs had broken. There was no denying it; he was in trouble, but he also felt an urge to keep moving. On his hands and knees, he crawled through the muck into the woods, away from the road. Each movement agonizing, each breath precious.

Thunder cracked against the sky and a flash of light flittered through the trees. In the distance, there was the dark outline of a broken shack. Cleaved in half by a massive fallen pine and covered in vines, it was barely visible. But he needed refuge from the storm—and somewhere to hide.

With every ounce of energy, Kai pulled himself to his feet and stumbled toward the dilapidated hovel he hoped might give him respite. It had only looked like thirty feet, but each step was small, making the distance feel insurmountable. The next two consecutive lightning strikes lit up the destroyed cabin. Splinters of tree and cottage mingled in a mass of destruction. Moss and ivy consumed the decaying wood and worked to reclaim the forgotten home.

The crooked door hung on one hinge, which creaked when Kai pulled at the handle. The effort sent a sudden pain into his side, and he stumbled inside. The place was small even before the tree chopped it in half. Inside, the remains of a simple home sat waiting for company; a tiny table and two chairs, a smashed hutch filled with shattered dishes, and a small wooden chest that held unknown treasure under the window.

There would be no food in this long-lost home, but desperate to rest, Kai opened the chest, hoping for a blanket or used coat. Inside he found an old navy-blue dress, a brown cloak, and a pair of brown shoes. The pain pulled him to his knees; he could hardly breathe, and a sadness deeper than he had ever known panged his heart. "Don't give up," Kai heard a soft voice whisper as he pulled something from the pouch secured to his chest.

The next strike of lightning and the glint from a metal blade captured a reflection—Riome!

Kai woke from his dream with a shutter. Not only was she alive, but she was coming back to Diu. Somewhere in the woods surrounding the city, she lay severely wounded, maybe dying. He shot from his bed. There would be no time to explain; he needed to go. Riome needed him, and he might be her only chance for survival. It was still hours before dawn, and he knew he had to be quiet if he hoped to sneak out with no one the wiser.

Dressed in black, Kai pulled on his boots and ran down the spiral staircase of his grandfather's Bodhima tree, the Cosmos vines illuminating in a pale blue glow as he woke them from their slumber. Smoke bounded after him. At the bottom, Kai stopped. "Sorry, Smoke, where I'm going, I cannot take you with me."

From the darkness, a voice whispered. "I see no reason why Smoke can't go. He has flown with us before," Rayna called, stepping into the dim blue light.

There was no point in asking why she was awake or how she knew he was leaving. He spotted the pack strapped to her back, the black pants, thick cloak, and hiking boots. She was ready for travel, the same as him; except that she had managed to bring supplies.

They were three black figures darting through the night, traveling high into the hills away from Hiowind. It felt wrong to leave without letting anyone know, but he needed to get to find Riome, even if it meant going to Diu without permission. This might be his only chance to stop Nola. There was no time to waste arguing his cause or his method of travel. He would need to transform into a dragon and keep high enough—and circle wide enough—to avoid being spotted.

Although he was fast, it still took them hours to fly over the Katori Mountains, Albey, and Baden Lake to Thade Mountain. Dawn threatened to peek over the horizon as Kai landed on the massive overhanging rock known as Eagle Peak. The same place he'd met Sabastian, Ryker, and Simone with his uncle Haygan long ago.

Rayna and Smoke hopped from his back, and he transformed back into his natural form. No sooner did he arch to stretch his back than he felt a gust of wind and saw the hint of blue light. Sabastian dropped a few feet behind Kai.

"I saw you coming from miles away." Sabastian patted Kai on the back and angled around him to greet Rayna. "Dear Rayna, it is a pleasure to see you again. Why are you two here?" He shot a displeased look at Kai.

Tension swelled in the pit of Kai's stomach. Even though Sabastian was Kendra's husband, he did not give his trust freely to Kai at first. And although he helped Kai battle the Guardians last spring, it did not mean he would agree with Kai returning to Diu. He could only hope that because Sabastian was a friend to Yulia, that her daughter Riome would be just as important to him. He hoped his friend would understand him landing near Sabastian's treetop home. There was no time to mince words.

"Riome is in trouble," Kai said bluntly, "and I am here to search for her. My vision puts her in the woods outside of Diu. She is avoiding the Diu patrols, hiding in a small cabin cleaved in half by a tree, and she is severely wounded."

"What I asked was, why are *you* here?"

Sabastian's tone felt harsh, and Kai stepped back.

Had he done something wrong? Surely Riome's friends would want to know. Yulia, her mother, needed to know. "I came for Riome," Kai insisted.

"Did you?" The intense expression coming off Sabastian came in waves, and Kai felt stunned. "As a Beastmaster and the grandson of an Elder you know better than to show your dragon form."

He did know better, but he was careful. "Why can dragons no longer fly over Diu and Baden Lake?" Kai asked. "My grandfather Benmar did it for years. My first flight was over the lake. As a boy, I saw dragons many nights. Now they are disappearing from our skies. Why?"

Sabastian chuckled. "I see the Elders still provide no explanations. First, you and I both know nobody tells Benmar what to do, but even your grandfather now heeds their warnings. When your mother was presumably killed by a dragon, they were all ordered to remain on the Katori side of the mountains to avoid war. The black dragons are less of a concern; Simone is practically invisible at night, but you, my boy, look like a roaming star in the sky. Granted, my eagle eyes give me an advantage, but it is prudent to listen. The Elders want the world to believe the dragons are disappearing."

Kai opened his mouth, but Sabastian held up his hand, halting the question forming on his lips. "The Elders have their reasons. Keeping the dragon numbers a secret is better for Katori and better for the dragons. It is not our place to question the Elders."

"Since when do you follow the rules?" Kai chided. "Riome needs me, so here I am."

"You did not need to come yourself," Sabastian scolded, turning his back on Rayna to square off with Kai. "And I follow the important rules. But this is not about me; it is about *you*. Your own cousin, Cazier, warned you to stay away from Diu. Yet here you are. Do not give me an excuse about some vision—you could have sent word and we would've found Riome ourselves. So, tell me the truth. You *wanted* to come to Diu. You know Simone could have come; she would do anything for Yulia. No, you took a foolish risk, driven by your desire to come back here."

Every excuse Kai could think of fell flat in his mouth. Sabastian's words hurt, but it did not make them less accurate. He had been looking for a legitimate excuse to come to Diu, to save his father and face Nola. He set his path wide knowing the risks of flying over Baden Lake at night, but in those final hours, he cut close to Diu in order to reach Thade Mountain.

"Do I need to justify wanting to help find Riome?" he thundered as boldness formed in his bones. "So, what, you are sending me home?"

There was no denying the heat building inside Kai. If he were a dragon right now, he would spray fire. A blue glow emanated from Sabastian's crystal, and Kai felt the flow of magic pour into the seasoned warrior. "My Guardian days may be behind me"—Sabastian opened his arms wide—"but my loyalty to Katori remains steadfast. This is something you need to learn."

"I won't go!" Kai barked. "I came to help Riome, and you cannot stop me."

Smack! Sabastian's hands slammed together.

A burst of golden light poured from Sabastian's fingertips directly into Kai's eyes. The heat was intense, and the light pierced deep. In great pain, Kai dropped to his knees, covering his eyes. He screamed in agony. Hot tears streamed down his face, and he tried to blink his vision clear.

Everything was dark. Kai could not see. "What have you done?" he cried.

Rayna darted to Kai and touched his face. "I am here, Kai," she soothed. "You burned his skin and his eyes!" she gasped in fury at Sebastian. "His eyes are blood red. Why would you do this?"

Sabastian knelt and touched Kai's head. "Go home, Kai, back to Katori. Tell Lucca, Haygan, and Simone you are going to visit your father in Diu. No need to ask for permission, but they deserve to know where you went. Second, travel with your men. Kempery-man Dresnor and Captain Drew have discovered Davi's community. They often visit, inquiring about you. Only then can you return to Diu the proper way. Not like some thief in the night."

Kai blinked his eyes; still, he saw nothing. "How?" he begged, "I am blind. How did you do it? How can a Beastmaster create light?"

"Consider this a lesson." Kai heard Sabastian's tone harden. "Think before you act. Never go against an opponent you don't fully understand. One of my ancestors was a Lumen; my mother called me her 'golden boy' because I could make light with my fingers. Many thought I would be a Lumen, and over the years, I learned how to control the light, use it. You have seen me fight only once, but it doesn't mean I used every trick I know. You must remember that the best warriors keep a few secrets for that once-in-a-lifetime moment. You should have paid attention to the flow of magic. I purposefully pulled in excess—I wanted you to notice. Not that you would know how I would use it, but you should have known something was coming. In a full-on battle, the best of us can sense the shift, find the source, and be prepared. You never want to get blindsided again. I knew Rayna could heal you, but we learn the best lessons the hard way."

"Let me help you," Rayna massaged Kai's temples. Her hands warmed steadily, and he saw the light bloom in his field of vision. As his sight returned, he saw Sabastian and Rayna kneeling on either side. Rayna's eyes were soft and sincere, while Sabastian remained severe and persistent.

"Kendra has told me about the tension building in Diu. I see her less and less these days, but I slip into the city from time to time. Many here in Diu are fearful over the health of their King and they question the rumors surrounding their missing Prince. Kai. You will have to choose." Sabastian rose and offered Kai a hand up. "Time to go home."

Humbled by the moment, Kai accepted the gesture. "What about being seen?"

"Dawn will provide your escape. Shortly after the sun breaks along the horizon, there is a bright streak in the sky. The pale colors of dawn – white and yellow are perfect for you. It will last long enough for you to get well over Baden Lake. Go due east into the sun, north of Chenowith until you reach the mountains, then cut north behind Albey toward Benmar's cavern. Fly as high as Rayna and Smoke can tolerate—the rising sun will continue to ensure you go unnoticed. You know the path, do not deviate. And one last thing. Respect your elders, Kai. Maybe, just maybe, we know a little more than you think."

Kai wanted so desperately to stay, but he nodded with understanding. Lucca and the other Elders would notice they were gone. They might go searching, something he should have considered before leaving. Like it or not, he did owe them the respect of telling them about his decision to visit Diu. "Sabastian, thank you for searching for Riome. There are five days until the Winter Festival." Kai took Rayna's hand. "We will return to the palace in three. Let Kendra know whatever you find."

Smoke slipped around Sabastian as Kai transformed and jumped up with Rayna. The trip back with little rest would be difficult, and Kai did not enjoy returning with his tail between his legs.

CHAPTER 4

A Just Cause

Sabastian's warning to not deviate echoed in Kai's mind. He wanted to listen, but before flying back to Katori, he slipped north, dropping into the dense forest a few miles from Davi's community. He had promised to go straight home, but he needed to speak with his men. He owed them a face-to-face meeting after months of silence.

Sprinting through the forest, Kai and Rayna reached the Katori outcast village, and true to Sabastian's report, Dresnor and Drew were there making inquiries.

Kai whispered to Rayna, "It might be better if I go in alone to speak with my men. If you are with me, I have little leverage to travel back to Katori. I will need a reason to leave. If Dresnor can send for a ship, we may return to Diu before the festival. Wait for me near the first waterfall; I will catch up with you and Smoke there."

Green ivy and moss sprouted around Rayna, covering her in a delicate camouflage. She nodded and disappeared into the foliage behind Smoke.

Alone, Kai sauntered into the Katori community, stopping to talk with one man and laughing loudly. He wanted Dresnor to spot him first. He did not want his old friend to know he had come here, hoping to find him. Perfected over his years of pretending during his spy training, Kai did his best to act surprised when Dresnor called.

"Prince Kai!"

"Dresnor, what brings you here?" Kai said, offering a hand in feigned surprise and delight.

Dresnor's cold expression left Kai hanging in midair.

Kai let his hand fall, pursed his lips, and offered a nod. "I am glad you are here. I was coming your way after I spoke with Davi. Rayna and I would like to return to Diu before the Winter Festival. The last word I received about my father was Cazier's letter. I need to go home."

Dresnor huffed. "Home, is it? Still home, I mean. It seems you prefer living among the Katori over your own people. The last news from you was nearly two months back. I come here every three days inquiring about you. To what do we owe the honor now?"

Drew held his tongue, but his posture gave Kai the impression he felt the same as Dresnor. "My love for my father, for Diu, remains unchanged," Kai tried to assure them. "But I would be lying if I said I do not love my mother's country. The Katori are good people, and I am thankful for their hospitality. They saved my life, and I have worked hard to earn their trust." Then Kai shot back, "Something I thought I already earned with you."

The tension did not improve. Cold stares lingered, and clamped jaws left little room for pleasantries. Davi intervened. "Welcome, Kai. I am sorry to see Rayna is not with you. I trust she is preparing for your departure."

"Thank you, Davi." Kai broke his focus on Dresnor to offer a hand to Davi. "Rayna and I are ready to travel, but my grandfather would appreciate one last dinner before we go to Diu. As I am sure you can imagine, he is particularly unhappy we plan to leave, but family is very important. I will not abandon my father, nor will I forget the relationship I have with my grandfather." He gave Dresnor a stern look.

"One last thing, Kai." Dresnor stepped in close. "I hear Nola has Diu soldiers looking for you and Rayna. The longer they go without news, the more manpower they will throw into the search—or at least that is what Nola wants the citizens of Diu to believe. Each passing day proves her point: either you have abandoned them, or you are dead at the hands of the Katori. Your letters no longer carry weight. They could use a little hope, the city you once called home. There is much unrest—the fall harvest was lacking, and the winter has been cruel."

Guilt seeped into the cracks of Kai's heart. Diu was his childhood home, a place he would forever love but belong to no more. A fact he was coming to realize the nearer he got. "Can you make the arrangements?" Kai pressed Dresnor. "Send for the *Dragaron*. I wish to be home swiftly to see my father before the festivities."

Dresnor bowed, "Your Highness, Prince Kai, I will be honored to see to your preparations. I will send a letter on the afternoon ship. Enjoy dinner with your grandfather; I expect the Grand Duke's ship could be here tomorrow early evening, or the following morning at the latest. Either way, we should be in Diu with days to spare before the festival."

The brevity in Dresnor's tone left Kai sour, but he kept his face neutral while saying his goodbyes.

◆ ◆ ◆

Running at a quick clip, Kai darted through the forest. The smell of earthy pine and melting snow was a welcome aroma to his Beastmaster nature. Thankful for the moment alone, he thought about telling his grandfather Lucca that he needed to say goodbye to his father before he died. If this was Iver's time to die, he owed him for a lifetime of love. Nobody could begrudge Kai one last moment.

The use of magic pricked Kai's senses, giving him an uneasy feeling as an unnatural fog rolled through the Zabranen Forest. Suddenly worried about Rayna and Smoke, Kai ran faster. Each footfall pounded into the soft wet soil, and red mud splashed his black boots. Greeted by the sounds of rushing water, Kai weaved through the trees to follow the narrow trail along the river.

When Rayna's familiar form emerged through the mist, Kai quickly noticed she was not alone. Two Katori Guardians he recognized from training waited with her. The Weathervane, Gail, stood silently weaving her hands in a pattern he recognized; she was creating the mist. Dressed in deep purple and black with a longbow slung across her back, she stopped and looked to her fellow Guardian. The menacing brawny Stoneking, Mekael, carried two battle axes, several daggers strapped to his chest, and one shoved into his boot. His stoic profile made him difficult to read, but Kai knew both were deadly serious.

Before Mekael could tell Kai why they were here, beasts of all sorts rushed through the trees. Concerned by the multitude, and their distress, Kai reached out to an oncoming black panther. Their minds joined, and he felt the creature's fear. The animal stopped in front of Kai as he knelt on one knee.

Why do you run? What have you to fear? he asked with his mind.

The panther responded, Men in black attack anything that moves, animal and mankind alike. They wear a raven on their chest.

Shocked by the news, Kai connected to his sight and gleaned the forest. The vast distance was no challenge for any seasoned Katori, and Kai's range was more than adequate. Animal upon animal darted in fear. His mind drifted deeper northwest until he found Davi's village. True to the panther's story, men with swords were attacking the Katori villagers, who were struggling to fight back. Volley after volley of flaming arrows rained from the sky. Flames licked at the trees and danced from structure to structure.

"Beastmaster," Mekael interrupted Kai's gleaning, "you should return to Katori. It would appear that Diu and Milnos soldiers march on the Katori outsider camp. I glean at least five hundred warriors."

Stunned by Mekael's order, Kai stepped toward Rayna and took her hand. "I will not abandon Davi and his people. If you are going to help them, let us come with you!"

"You are no Guardian, boy," Mekael thundered. "It is our place; other Guardians are already on their way. We will defend our people, but we do not need an unseasoned Beastmaster boy in the way. The girl would be of more help; as a Kodama she could heal the wounded, but she should stay here until it is over."

Two thoughts tabulated in Kai's mind as he slowly collected energy from the sunshine and the rolling waterfall. First, he knew there was no arguing with the Guardians, even though he wanted to help. Second, he knew Rayna would agree with him to stay and fight.

"Very well, Mekael, but I should not risk my dragon form with so many outsiders in the woods. We will run up the mountain to the winter caves until the battle ends.

Gail nodded. "Wise choice, Kai. Make haste; we will report after the battle."

"You are—with me, Rayna." He let his tone fall between a question and a statement.

"Always," she winked at him with understanding.

Mekael and Gail darted off toward the action without another word while Kai, Rayna, and Smoke ran in the opposite direction. Deeper into the woods, Kai stopped. "You know I mean to help, right?"

"I meant what I said," Rayna replied. "I am always with you, I may not be able to use magic to fight, but my skills with a sword have improved. I only wish I had my bow since it is my weapon of choice. You mean to travel as your snow wolf, do you not?"

Kai nodded in agreement. "They do not know I can become anything but a dragon. I can only hope my slow collection of power went unnoticed. If we can slip through the wintery forest to the battle before anyone detects us, the Guardians will have no choice but to let us fight."

Pleased with their plan, Kai took hold of his white crystal and transformed.

◆ ◆ ◆

Hidden on the edge of chaos, Kai shifted back to his natural form. Flames and smoke licked at the sky as Katori men and women battled against an enemy set on their destruction. The scene unfolded, and he suddenly realized there was a new decision to make. The enemy was a mix of Diu and Milnos men fighting together—coordinated, seasoned soldiers. Half of them were his own people.

The battle made him sick. How could Diu attack innocent women and children? He watched a Milnos warrior scoop up a young child as her mother pounded his back, and the man ran her through with his sword. How could his men, Diu men, allow such atrocities?

Kai momentarily froze, torn by his loyalty to both sides. Rayna said something, but the devastation stole his focus, and her words faded into the background. Along the ground, something brushed his ankles. Deep green vines scurried up the trees concealing their location. He turned to look at her.

"It is hard to watch, but we cannot hide. I cannot fight against Diu, but I cannot stand by while my Katori family gets slaughtered. I know what I need to do." He motioned to the green curtain of ivy.

Rayna moved the vines to create an opening. Before they got far, Kempery-man Dresnor and Captain Drew came into view. Their swords lashed at their assailants with fury and determination. His men were fighting with the Katori villagers. "Look, Dresnor and Drew fight for Katori. Why?" Kai asked, more to himself than Rayna. "See if you can find a bow to fight with, but be careful."

Kai darted into the fray and scooped up the first sword he could find. The fallen Milnos weapon was well-balanced but heavy, and the steal was brightly polished with nary a nick to its edge. Angry embers danced, spreading the flames to three mounds of hay. Women ran for cover with small children wrapped in their arms, while other women battled alongside the men. Arrows flew overhead dropping two Milnosian soldiers and Kai looked back to see Rayna nod as she notched another arrow.

A Milnos man twice his size charged at Kai with sword drawn. Flames reflected off the warrior's silver-and-black raven armor. Sweat and blood dripped from the man's bristly face. With speed and experience, Kai pivoted clear of the sword swipe. A smile curled the corner of the

Milnos man's lip. "You have skill, little Katori trash. No matter, I will beat you into submission. Join the others in chains, or I will kill you here and now." The man spat in the mud. "And I do you hope you chose the latter."

Unmoved, Kai let the man take the lead. The first strike came swiftly, but Kai deflected, studying the man's stance and recovery. Each powerful blow came heavy and fierce; anger grew in the man's eyes as Kai bested him. The Milnos warrior's frustration began to show, and he pressed harder, a move Kai knew would be the man's undoing. Within moments, the larger man overstepped, giving Kai his opening to dispatch him with his dagger.

More Milnos soldiers charged from the left, and Kai ran in their direction, avoiding the Diu men on the right. Moving from man to man, Kai outsmarted men twice his age with ease. His Katori speed and years of training left these men helpless to defend themselves.

As the rain started, Kai felt magic lift the hair on the back of his neck. It was an unnatural rain, but he was thankful it slowed the progress of the fire. Across the battlefield, he spotted five Katori Guardians, Mekael and Gail among them. Their skill unequaled, they left a trail of bodies in their wake; soldiers from Diu and Milnos alike were cut down. While they outwardly used no obvious magic, Kai sensed the occasional burst of energy from them.

With a clear opening, Kai joined his men. "Fancy meeting you here," Kai shouted, taking on two Milnos soldiers trying to flank Dresnor. "What is happening?"

Dresnor swapped blows with his opponent. "I told you, Nola has men searching for you. When I tried to explain, they called me a liar and a traitor." Another man charged Dresnor and pulled him into the heat of battle.

Drew continued. "Regent Maxwell ordered this forest cleared on behalf of Queen Nola. These men claimed you were dead since no one had seen you for months!"

Kai continued to fight but shuttered at the fact this was his fault. It was clear the battle was under Milnos leadership, but the Diu men fought with fury. And, why not? They thought their Prince was dead; they would most certainly fight without hesitation. Somehow, Kai needed to get their attention. It was the only way to stop the carnage.

After a quick scan of the periphery, Kai spotted the men in charge: Five riders set away from the battle, their uniforms spotless and decorated with metals. With them stood two flag bearers, one Diu and one Milnos—the man with a horn. "I am going to put a stop to this," Kai shouted to Dresnor. At least until he heard Davi scream, "Naia, look out!"

Kai turned to see a brut of a man charging Naia, Davi's wife. Her small stature was no match for this rugged soldier. She deflected the first two blows with her sword, but the man's force knocked her to the ground. Kai did not hesitate; he sucked at the air and held it tight. The perception of time slowed to a crawl and the air thickened. Barely affected by the alteration, Kai raced across the village center, pushing against time.

The Milnosian's sword swung slow and steady; the man was ready to strike Naia's defenseless form. It did not matter to Kai who or what anyone saw; he used every ounce of speed he had to traverse the field and reach Naia. Her face was frozen in fear, hands raised to deflect the oncoming blow. Placing himself between Naia and the advancing sword, Kai blocked the strike and punched the unsuspecting man.

As time resumed, the man flew backward twenty feet, landing with a thud on the ground. The man did not get up. He laid cupping his jaw, wailing in pain.

Naia thanked Kai with a nod and darted to Davi. Dresnor and Drew stood in shock and awe at how Kai moved. More men charged, and the fight continued.

Kai darted past them to reach the commanders. The Milnos general, a well-decorated man, held his nose to the air.

Kai shouted. "Stop this battle at once!"

The man turned his head. "Who is this boy? Take him away, chain him with the others," the general shouted.

Frustrated, Kai turned to address the Diu captain, a man he recognized, although the man's name eluded him. "I order you to stand down! Call the men back!"

"Or what, runt?" the Milnos general shouted, kicking Kai with his boot.

The blow knocked Kai into the Diu Captain's horse, but he did not fall. Determined to make the general listen, Kai yanked the man's leg, pulling him from his saddle. "Or I will consider this an act of war against Diu! My father, King Iver, will put you in chains. Diu is my country, and you have no authority over these people."

"Petulant child, how dare you touch me." The general rose to his feet and dusted his uniform. "Do you know who I am?"

"Do you know who *I* am?" Kai shouted back. "I am one you seek, Prince Kai Galloway. I am not dead. Call your men off, or I will toss you and your pretty uniform into the middle of the battle."

The Diu captain hopped from his horse. "Sound the retreat!" he called to the bugler. "Your Highness, Prince Kai Galloway . . . Blessed be Alenga, is it you? My name is Beekman," he bowed in respect. "I serve King Iver."

Kai finally matched the name with the face. He gave a weary smile. "It is truly me."

The sound of retreat sounded across the field, and the soldiers pulled back into formation, sorting into Milnos and Diu units. Dresnor and Drew joined Kai, their swords drawn in defense. The general grumbled and complained, but Kai ignored the man.

Kai looked from the Diu soldier to the angry general, "Captain Beekman, escort the general back to Diu. He will answer for his crimes against my people. These people may be Katori-born, but this is Diu soil, and I will not stand to have my people attacked. He had no right to kill innocent men, women, and children."

"You have no authority over me, boy." The general pulled his arm free from the captain. "Your own queen sent us here to fetch you and deal with the riffraff on Diu land."

A second trumpet call sounded, and the Diu soldiers folded around Kai. Beekman drew his sword. "Take this man into custody," the captain ordered, pointing at the general. "Your Highness, may we escort you home? There is a ship near the tip of Baden Lake, the *Jadear*. We can be back in Diu within a day."

Kai shook his head. "Thank you for the offer, Captain Beekman, but I must decline. My Kempery-man Dresnor will see me home on a ship departing from Albey."

Dresnor's eyes gleamed. "Actually, I must insist, your Highness." His Kempery-man motioned to Captain Beekman. "your safety is my primary concern. We should travel with these Diu men; I can send for Rayna in the coming days."

Rayna darted through the crowd, Smoke at her side. "I am here, Kempery-man Dresnor, and ready to travel." She took Kai's hand and squeezed it.

"Ahh, yes," Dresnor leaned in close. "I should have guessed she would not be far from your side," he whispered, barely loud enough for Kai to hear.

Before Kai could protest, Beekman called for horses and returned to his mount.

Unable to protest, Kai climbed up onto the offered horse. Drew assisted Rayna before climbing onto his mount. The heavy rain matched Kai's weary heart. Watching him depart, Davi stood with Gail and Mekael in the center of a smoldering village. Their somber expression twisted Kai's stomach in knots. Getting forced to go back home was not what he had planned, but he knew that fighting to save Davi and his people was a just cause. He glanced up toward Thade Mountain and remembered Sabastian's words—do not deviate.

CHAPTER 5

Winter Festival

The *Jadear* was not the *Dragaron*. The Grand Duke Dante's cutter sailed swiftly, but this ship moved like a fat whale on sand. Captain Beekman was distant, as were his men. Not rude, but they did not extend Kai the respect a prince deserved, even by Diu standards. These men were in no hurry to return to Diu. In fact, Kai noticed they were using the wrong sails, and they were set at an incorrect angle to use the breeze efficiently.

Rayna leaned against the railing, her long hair blowing in the wasted wind. "We are not moving at a swift pace, even for this vessel," she whispered. "First, the ship's captain removed the general's shackles, insisting it would be enough having the General confined to quarters. Looks to me like the crew fear the Milnos General, and now we are barely floating in a breeze that I am fairly certain could blow me across the lake without this ridiculous ship."

Kai laughed. "Want me to toss you overboard in a basket?" he jested.

"You laugh, but you know I am right." Rayna pulled her hair together and secured it with a leather tie.

He knew she was right. The crew had too much familiarity with the Milnos men. "There is little we can do but make the best of this and get to Diu."

"I noticed Dresnor and Drew are keeping their distance. Who is ignoring who?" She nudged Kai toward them.

The gap between him and his men narrowed, and Kai felt a lump form in his throat. There were no words to explain where Rayna and Kai had been all this time. Dresnor either had to be angry or accept the lie that he'd worked to pay off his debt for the cure of their sickness, but he could not tell his friend the truth. Still, they could not remain at odds. "Dresnor, I meant to tell you earlier," Kai addressed his Kempery-man, "thank you for helping my friends. It means a lot to me that you defended them."

Stone cold eyes stared back at Kai. The silence between them lingered, but neither man spoke. Captain Drew broke their standoff. "Well, nobody calls Dresnor a liar or a traitor." He chuckled halfhearted.

Dresnor remained stoic. "I could not stand by and let anyone attack innocent people, Diu-born citizens or not. They did not deserve to be killed, burned in their homes, or dragged away in chains."

"Well, thank you again." Kai nodded with respect and turned to walk away.

"Your Highness, are you returning to Diu for good?" Dresnor asked as if he already knew the answer but wanted to hear it from Kai himself.

This was not a conversation Kai wanted to have. Fresh after any battle, emotions ran high. Nightmares plagued the noblest of men, and he knew Dresnor bared the weight of every choice he made in a fight. Those lives were on his hands, good or bad. Just looking at Dresnor, Kai could tell his Kempery-man had slept very little in recent weeks. Kai blamed himself for putting his man through such tribulations.

"Let me be as honest as I can, Dresnor." Kai stepped in close to his friend. "I love my father and Diu, but there is a new part of my life now that calls me to know my mother's people. Do I really need to choose? Can I not visit my grandfather in peace? Can I not explore the world without abandoning my people?"

"Unfortunately, you are a prince," Dresnor responded with an emotional distance Kai had not felt in years. "Diu is a small kingdom, which allows many freedoms other countries do not have. Our traditions are lenient compared to Nebea and Milnos, but it is time you took on the responsibility of the eldest heir to the throne."

"Are we no longer friends, Dresnor? There was a time you trusted me with your life. Do you mean to say my loyalty is in question?"

"Loyalty?" Dresnor glared. "You wish to discuss loyalty? I have spent months waiting with no visit from you, only letters delivered by Shane. Do you have so little regard to my service you could not come yourself?"

There was no denying Kai had put his own desires above Diu and his men, but he did not back down. "I ordered you home," he reminded Dresnor.

Rage boiled in Dresnor's eyes, and the warrior latched onto Kai's shirt. "You have no idea what your order meant for us. Redmon and Albey finally went home to Diu; they've spent these past months in prison for abandoning their post."

Drew's hand clasped around Dresnor's, and their three faces came together. "Let go, Dresnor. You are drawing attention to us. Your Highness, our apologies, we are here to serve, but you left us little choice. It was clear to me that you graced us with a visit earlier today, but you had no intentions of coming home. I sense even now that you will return to Katori the first chance you get."

Dresnor released Kai's shirt, and the three men took a step back. Kai brushed his shirt smooth. "I will not justify this insult." He felt the heat well in his veins. "Remember your place, Dresnor. You will not address your Prince in this manner again."

♦ ♦ ♦

Months of adventure made Kai's return to Diu feel bittersweet. Captain Beekman led the march through the city. Kai rode between Dresnor and Drew, Rayna rode behind, and Smoke kept pace, running beside her horse. The citizens were a mix of sweet and sour. Some cheered while others booed his return. Their behavior made Kai wonder if returning was a mistake. How he wished he had consulted the Elders, or at least his grandfather Lucca, for advice.

Diu had been his home for seventeen years, but Diu no longer felt like home after his time in Katori. The city was loud, and the people were brash. Kai saw the separation between the classes as he never had before. In Rimtown, the poorest of the poor offered him no welcome. Midtown greeted him with halfhearted cheers and scowls. One person shouted, "Go back to Katori! You are no prince of Diu."

The words hurt. Entering Hightown did not improve things. More people cheered, but a few held their noses high and appeared displeased by his return. On nearly every street corner along their path, Milnos guards glared and whispered. The farther into the city they went, the more he noticed the Milnosian men outnumbering the Diu soldiers.

The stroll through the palace felt awkward. Many of the faces he expected to see had changed. The usual guards were replaced with strangers; even the Mryken guard dogs were different. Nobody was the same, not even the servants. Many glared at him and offered no sign of respect, making Kai feel like a stranger in a strange land. Eager to find some sense of normalcy, he used his Beastmaster magic to connect with the Mryken guard dogs. They held their posture but greeted him with the respect of a Beastmaster.

The guards escorted him to his room, but they remained outside his closed door. Kai leaned against the door and wished Smoke were with him, but then he figured Rayna would sleep better if the great black wolf stayed with her.

His once-stately room felt excessive and wasteful for one person. Walking around his desk to the shelves, he let his fingers traced the spine of an old book. Everything was just as he had left it. The only thing missing was the personal items he'd asked Kendra to burn.

"I did not think you were ever coming back." Seth's voice startled Kai, and he spun around to see his half-brother's silhouette in the doorway, his arm in a sling.

Kai offered a kind smile. "You've grown, little brother."

"I *have* grown." Seth puffed up his chest. "Not enough, though. I'm still not as tall as you."

Seth ran to Kai, and they embraced. The guard at the door interrupted. "Your Highness Seth, perhaps you should wait for your mother to speak with this traitor."

Taken back by the words. Kai let his half-brother go. "I mean my brother no harm." He wanted to chastise the guard for his insult, for addressing a prince in this manner, but he did not know this man, and something about him gave Kai the impression he did not see him as *his* prince.

Seth closed the door. "Pay him no mind, he is the Regent's man. You are home and everything will be better now."

Doubt stabbed at Kai's heart. He did not belong here, and those men knew it. The word traitor shook his core. Did they really see him as a traitor? Had he been gone that long?

"You were noticing my growth," Seth reminded Kai, salvaging the conversation.

"Give it time, little brother, you are only twelve." Kai tussled Seth's hair and gleaned his brother's arm. A white hairline crack streaked across the bone beneath the skin. "What happened to your arm?"

"I fell off my horse. Sigry says in a few more weeks I should be able to get rid of the and sling. Since you left, life is not the same." Seth stepped in close and whispered. "One thing remains—mother keeps things from me. She must think I am blind. I know she has plans for Aaron. While she includes me in some discussions, it did not take long to realize my suggestions were of no value. So now I keep my nose in a book or ride my horse, and mother ignores me."

"But you listen, right?" Kai studied his brother's posture. "You know something."

"I do," Seth whispered. "She harbors ill will toward you. Ever since mother and father returned from sea to find you gone, she started spreading rumors about you abandoning the Diu people. People believe you've been living in the woods among the Katori and that you do not wish to return."

Seth paused to look around the room. His hand covered his mouth.

Kai gleaned the room and the secret passageway to ensure they were alone. "Seth, what is it?"

"Mother told Dante you are not the true heir to the throne. That Iver is not your real father. She is the one who utters the word *traitor*. The guards listen and believe her words as fact. Do not let the uniforms fool you, most of the new men are not even from Diu. They are Regent Maxwell's soldiers from Milnos." Seth nodded to the door, suggesting that the man outside was such.

A lump formed in Kai's throat; Seth had no idea how right Nola was about his parentage. "Do you trust me?" Kai asked him.

"More than I trust my own mother. I have the feeling she is doing something to father. Every time they are apart for any length of time, he improves. Then, when they are together, he backslides and can barely say three words together. She caught me in their room one day. You would have thought I'd committed treason by her reaction." Seth shook his head. "I was touching some bottles on the night table, trying to talk with father. She has not let me see him since—four months ago this happened."

Kai grabbed the back of Seth's neck and pulled him close. "Do you trust me?"

"Why do you keep asking that? Yes, of course I trust you. Mother claims the Katori mountainfolk have brainwashed you against Diu these many months, and now you are one of them. I don't believe her—but *what* really happened to you, Kai? Even I can tell there is something different about you."

There was no time to test Seth's loyalty. And Kai could not share what he knew or burden his young brother with his destiny. "I only hope that you never lose faith in me. Remember these words—I love our father. And you."

"I believe in you, Kai. I know your loyalty is true. Tell me you are here to stay." Seth's eyes begged to hear it was so.

Confined to his room, Kai had no idea what came next. He had been separated from Rayna at the palace entrance, and his only solace was gleaning her arrival to her parent's home within the palace grounds. Wishing they could go back to Katori did not make it so. "Dear brother, I wish I knew what to do next. I need to speak with Cazier. He must know I am here, and maybe he can help me see our father."

"Do you plan to stay?" Seth pressed.

He did not imagine Nola would let him get anywhere near Iver. Given his vision about his father's impending death, and his role in Iver's demise, he clung to the hope he could somehow change his destiny. "I am here for the Winter Festival. Maybe longer," he responded.

"I believed you would be the next king." Seth fidgeted with his cuff link. "Dante and Cazier agree."

Kai wanted to calm his brother's concerns, but frankly, he did not have the words.

"I heard the Regent," Seth persisted. "Though mother . . ." He swallowed hard before continuing. "Mother has plans for Aaron. Not me, of course. He is her favorite. She says I look more and more like father every day. My brown eyes and darkening hair, I guess."

"Seth, Nola loves all her children." Kai tried to reassure him, but Seth wasn't wrong. She did tend to fawn over Aaron; the green-eyed boy version of herself.

Knock, knock, knock.

The door opened. "Prince Kai." Kendra strolled in carrying a tray of food and wine. The guard closed the door behind her. She placed the tray on the table and embraced him tightly. "You made it." She pressed her hand against his chest and touched the crystal hidden under his shirt. "Safe and sound I see. And feeling stronger, no doubt." She gave him a wink.

He understood her double meaning. "It was a challenging trip," he said, playing along, "but thankfully Rayna and I both made it." He gave her a telling nod. "I am sorry we arrived so abruptly. I had hoped to be here under different circumstances. I deviated from the path, I'm afraid." He hoped she would get news to Sabastian, but he could not say more in front of Seth.

A guard pushed open the door, and Queen Nola entered. "Seth. There you are. Come, my son, it is rather late. Off to bed with you." She shooed Seth from the room.

Seth nodded to his mother, but he gave Kai a desperate look. "I am so happy you are home, Kai. Goodnight." His shoulders slumped as he glanced at the guards.

"Goodnight, little brother," Kai offered, avoiding Nola's glare. "I am happy to be here, as well. I will see you in the morning."

The room went deathly silent. Nola hovered in the doorway for many moments before finally stepping inside. Kai watched her every move as she fingered the flowers on the tray and then poured a glass of wine.

"You've had us quite worried gallivanting through the mountains," she said, masking the barbs in her voice with what seemed like affection. "We cannot trust these mountain people who squat on our land and refuse to pay our taxes. Given your father's precarious condition, I suggested we send troops to search for you and bring you home. At first, Cazier convinced the council there was no need. But in the end, everyone saw reason. It is good my men found you, saved you. And now here you stand, safe and sound."

The squeals of a little girl echoed down the hallway; Kai smiled at the thought of seeing his little sister, Cordelia. Kai nodded to Nola. "My father. I would like to see him, if I may."

"Not now, Kai. It is much too late." Nola rushed to the door. "Maybe in the morning if he is up for visitors. We should talk, you and I, after the festival. About your future. About the future of Diu, and your true place in it."

She started to leave, but at the door, the cutest little girl appeared, dressed in a pink gown and a smile that could melt the coldest of hearts.

Kai waved at his half-sister—he marveled at how much she had changed. He knelt to greet her. "Little Cordelia!"

His sister giggled, but Nola caught her arm and spun her around. "It is late, my princess, time for bed." Mother and daughter departed.

Kendra closed the door and rushed to his side. "I have so much to ask and even more to tell! Haygan tells me your crystal remained white. Is it true?"

He nodded in acknowledgment and pulled the stone free from his shirt. "Haygan is a father now. Simone had a daughter."

She marveled at the white crystal. "Did Haygan make it home in time?"

Kai shook his head in remembrance. "Only just. A moment later, and Haygan would have missed the entire birth. Her name is Nevaeh."

"What a beautiful name." Kendra leaned against the bedpost, looking tired and worry-worn. "You need to be careful of her. Queen Nola has become a powerful woman in your absence. The king is barely a figurehead. Iver is bedridden, and Nola makes changes and not all good ones. Men, those most loyal to your father, have been dismissed, replaced by these new guards, men loyal to the Regent. The Queen's decision to bring Milnos into a position of power over Diu makes no sense to me. Iver still lives, and her relationship with the Regent feels wrong, but any who question, or gossip go missing. Between Nola and these men, they foster gossip about your disloyalty." Then she changed tacks. "You've heard of Landon's escape?"

"I have. Was Landon's escape Nola's doing?" he asked.

"I cannot be sure. A few weeks prior, Regent Maxwell came for a visit. Landon coincidently escaped the same day Maxwell departed."

"Nola is the illegitimate daughter of the late King Bannon Penier of Milnos," Kai admitted. "Landon is a Penier—they are brother and sister. I am sure Nola enlightened him before she helped him escape our dungeons."

"Really?" Kendra covered her mouth. "Daughter to King Bannon." Her expression turned to real concern.

Kai looked out his balcony doors. "Has anyone heard from Riome?"

"Riome? No. I cannot say I have heard anything." Kendra's brow knit together. "Why?"

"She was missing—lost at sea. I do not have all the specifics, but she was posing as a cabin boy on my father's ship. Riome hoped to discover the hold Nola has on my father. Undo the spell. And discover who else might be involved in her conspiracy. I had a vision she was trying to return to Diu, but her wounds and soldiers on the road forced her to hide out in a cabin. I do not know where. Sabastian searches for her." He looked at Kendra, puzzled she had not heard this news. "I informed Sabastian almost two days ago. How do you not know?"

Kendra's eyes fell. "I have not seen my husband in weeks. I am forbidden to leave the palace. The queen watches me, and her new maids watch me—I am Katori, and there are whispers around the palace that suggest I should not be trusted. People talk of you in the same way. I had hoped to be replaced like the other Katori maid, but Cordelia begged the Queen to keep me." She touched his shoulder. "But if I hear anything, I will let you know."

Kai nodded, understanding the risks. "It is late. You must return to Cordelia before Nola suspects something."

♦ ♦ ♦

The following evening, the Winter Festival arrived in a display of grandeur and indulgence. Lace runners trimmed in gold and silver replaced the traditional blue-and-white table decor. Garland made of cedar boughs, holly, pinecones, and red roses swooped around the chandeliers and stone walls, filling the room with the smell of nature. Gold-trimmed plates and crystal goblets decorated each place setting.

Lords and ladies from around the land came to celebrate the Winter Festival. Many guests brought gifts; however, the queen did not receive each offering. Instead, they were displayed on an elegant table for all to see. Most were gifts fit for a queen: jewels, rare books, paintings, golden statues, and glass figurines.

Nola's royal chair sat on the dais; the King's chair was nowhere to be found. Kai was sad that his father would miss the event—but he was thankful Nola did not take the seat for herself. Aaron and Seth sat on either side—there was no place for Kai. Given his limited freedom, it surprised him Nola would let him near any of the city's elite. Guards kept him on a short leash, never more than a few feet away, and they often blocked his path if he wandered too close to the Queen.

The great hall felt empty to Kai without his father, and the celebration felt hollow and fake. To the best of his recollection, this was the first Winter Festival that Iver had ever missed. He divided his attention from the grand hall, gleaning the King's chamber to monitor his father's labored breathing while pretending to have a pleasant time. Sigry sat with Iver, and four armed guards stood vigilantly in the hallway.

Still, gifts, wine, and food flowed freely. Nola's opulent outfit was beyond lavish for a Diu queen, bedecked in jewels and gold, cut lower than it should and off the shoulders. The new crown upon her head looked grander than anything Kai had ever seen. He watched the spectacle from the periphery. Regent Maxwell hung on every word Nola uttered, offering her his arm as they mingled with guests. Unfamiliar people strolled around the room as if they owned the palace—their style of dress and accents were foreign. The best he could discern, they were from Milnos. Most of them hovered close to Regent Maxwell and the Queen. He also noted those not in attendance—either not invited or who chose not to attend. Lord and Lady Henley and the entire Chenowith family were nowhere to be seen. When Kai asked after Amelia, the Regent said that she had been unfit for travel.

Convenient, Kai thought. The man was hiding something; he was sure of it.

The more he looked at the mix of faces, the fewer he recognized. Several Kempery-men, his father's men, were not in attendance.

Watching Nola flit across the dance floor, laughing and fawning over Maxwell, made him wonder if she had ever cared for his father.

"Prince Kai." Dresnor nudged his shoulder and handed him a wine glass. "This is not the Diu we left nine months ago. Men I knew and trusted are either gone or standoffish with me. I warned you that we should have returned sooner."

Kai sighed. "Neither of us could imagine Milnos moving in on Diu, especially like this. The Diu lords and ladies must believe the Queen is forging alliances. What am I to do?"

"I hear words like *brainwashed*, *cult*, and *traitor* wrapped around your name. Our once-beloved prince is now considered an outsider. Milnos men walk our halls and guard our queen. Foreigners have replaced most of our captains, and nearly half of our soldiers were discharged."

"Too much has changed." Kai kept studying the room. "Diu is becoming an unsafe place. Philip, I want you to consider reassignment away from me, away from Diu. I asked for the release of Kempery-man Redmon and Albey from the dungeons. Dante assures me he set them free upon my return."

Dresnor gulped down his wine. "No, I belong by your side. I spoke with Redmon after his release; he and Albey were reassigned to Admiral Roark, they left this morning for Port Anahita. I tried to get them to speak with you, but they refused."

The idea that his men wish to avoid seeming him left an uncomfortable feeling in his gut. Even those most loyal were distancing themselves. "Let's not talk here." He nodded, weaving them through the thick crowd. Dresnor followed. To lose the guards, Kai darted across the dance floor and exited through a servant's corridor. They walked down to the gardens behind the palace, through the gate, and into the garden maze.

In the darkness, Kai spoke. "I don't want to blindside you, Philip, but in the coming days, your faith in me will be tested. Do not ask me to explain. I tell you this so you may protect yourself and those we care about most. I know you doubt my loyalty, but I swear to you that I do love Diu. Katori has not changed me so much, I would *never* renounce my home or my father. In fact, I am here to protect my father at all costs."

Kempery-man Dresnor's stern eyes locked on Kai. "I do question your loyalty to Diu, but do not question mine. You have changed, and there are secrets you refuse to share. I see a distance between us I hope to repair. We have an unspoken bond, a bond of brothers. I will not abandon you. But you must tell me: What do you know? You are keeping something from me."

Kai looked at his friend; there was nothing he could say, so he ignored the question. "Help me by going to Fort Pohaku. Admiral Roark owes me a favor. I sent word asking for your safe passage. Cazier assures me the admiral will accept you at your current rank, and you leave tomorrow morning on his ship out of Port Anahita. Drew should go home to Henley; I hear his mother is unwell."

Dresnor huffed. "Are we having two different conversations? I beg for honesty and you offer reassignment. How dare you decide without even asking me? I do not want to go to Fort Pohaku. I am no seaman, and I have no desire to leave Diu. You had no right to make this decision—my life is here."

The anger in his friend's tone was mild compared to the seething expression he forced on Kai. "I am giving you an order, Dresnor. I need to know you will be safe, but more importantly, when I call, I need to know you will be able to help me. Alive, you can help; dead or in prison, you cannot."

"Clearly you suspect something is about to happen," Dresnor said slowly, "and yet you are keeping it a secret like everything else. I thought I knew you. Your time in Katori has changed you. I am sorry, but I do not trust this new person I see. The Kai I knew would never keep such secrets from me."

He could not argue; his friend was right, but he was committed to keeping the Katori secrets, just as his mother had all those years. "Philip Dresnor, I trust you with my life, but there are secrets I cannot tell you because they risk the lives of others. You have seen too much already. Yulia protected our ship in the storm, Rayna healed me from a poisonous plant—and might I remind you, you called her a witch—and now you witnessed me saving Naia."

Kai saw the regret in his friend's expression.

Dresnor looked away. "I apologized to Rayna, and I never pushed you to explain. Not really."

Through the trees, Kai sensed Yulia approaching. "I don't have time to explain. I just ask for you to have faith in me, now and in the coming days. Remember me as the man you know. Someday, I will explain. Pray I am successful in my quest, and your faith will not be tested."

Yulia opened the gate. "Prince Kai. May I speak with you?" She entered the maze and stepped from the shadows; the moonlight danced on her cheeks.

"Dresnor, please do this one last thing for me," Kai commanded.

Dresnor left with a nod.

Yulia's fierce expression said volumes. She wanted results. "I want to know what you are doing to find my daughter. Have you any news? Has Riome returned somehow in secret?"

Kai cringed at the memory of Riome suffering after her fight on the ship. His vision was brutally realistic. "Yulia, I know you are worried. I spoke with Cazier earlier this evening, and there is no news."

Sadness washed over Yulia's face. "Sabastian and I searched for Riome without success. Even with the gift of sight, it took us days before we found the little cabin this morning, cut in half by a tree. It was not near Diu at all. It was a few miles outside of Port Anahita. Signs of my daughter were few; we found dried blood inside, and the empty wooden chest. It appeared she spent some time there, but . . ." A look of disappointment burdened her eyes.

"This is good news," Kai insisted, his heart lifting. "You and Sabastian are both excellent trackers. Were you able to pick up her trail? Anything outside the cabin? She must be coming to Diu, but she would know to be cautious. Trust no one is her motto."

"Marks in the woods indicated she was still traveling toward Diu, but we lost her tail once she neared the road. A caravan of horses, people, and wagons concealed her path."

Kai felt the disappointment in Yulia's tone. "Riome is a fighter. If anyone could survive, it would be her. I will search for her myself—I promise. By now, she could be somewhere within the city walls." He touched Yulia's shoulder, offering comfort.

The deep contemplation in Yulia's eyes implied she had a plan. "I will search the southern half of the city if you could take the northern part? Dead or alive, I must find my daughter."

"I know of a few places I could search first," Kai acknowledged, "and then there are the tunnels and towers. My access from the palace will make it easier for me to search. Focus on the south end of the city near the warehouse district, then move west to cover the inns and taverns and circle back northeast toward the Central City Gardens. There are some high-end gambling establishments that stay open late. Riome knows the owners; the private rooms upstairs would be an excellent place to recover and allow her to send for help."

"Thank you, Kai." Yulia offered a shallow smile and walked away.

CHAPTER 6

Wicked Intentions

A bustling fire heated the King's chambers, and three oil lamps gave the room a warm glow. Queen Nola wiped the sweat from her husband's brow, eyeing the maid collecting the bed linens. The round woman spoke no words and made no eye contact. Nola hated the pleasantries with those who were unnecessary—and to her, everyone was unnecessary. Pretending to care was not her favorite activity, but she knew it served a purpose, and she was rather skilled at pretending.

Knock. Knock. Knock.

"I am done with the city's problems. Send whoever it is away." Nola ordered the maid, turning her nose away from the soiled linens and a waste pan in the woman's arms.

The door swung open. Golden light poured around Regent Maxwell as he stood in the frame. "Your Majesty, Queen Nola. May I have a word?" He bowed in the asking, cutting his eyes to the guards at the door while moving to hasten the maid's exit.

Nola motioned him inside and grabbed a glass of wine that lay in wait on a nearby table. "Enter, Regent Maxwell, but leave the door open."

She did not care what the maid or guards thought of her, allowing this man into her chambers, but she needed to control the rumors and lies whispered about the palace. All necessary gossip needed to circle focus on Kai, not her exploits.

"Why do you bother me, Maxwell?" She strolled to the balcony and pushed the doors wide. A cool breeze blew fresh air into the stale room. "Could this not wait till tomorrow?" she said with disregard, loud enough for the guards leaning into the doorway.

"Your Majesty, I humbly beg your forgiveness for the intrusion," Maxwell responded, staying near the door, "but you wanted to be informed when the *Dragaron* returned from collecting taxes. They are unloading now; my men are escorting the payment to the vault as we speak."

Nola turned away, using her back to conceal her actions, and poured a few drops of liquid from a vial she kept hidden in her gown pocket. She watched the orange substance blend with the wine as she gently swirled the cup.

I must keep him pliable, she reminded herself.

Every step she took was necessary, and the Regent was a pawn to ensure her future. To keep him under her influence, she needed to refresh her hypnotism over the man. Wine and sinder root made everyone pliable. Even those with a strong will, of which Maxwell was not.

Taking in a deep breath, she steeled herself for the Regent's grubby fingers and aggressive behavior. With a turn and a nod, she motioned Maxwell to join her on the balcony. She hated this man as much as every other man she had ever met. To her, men only cared for or respected wealth and power. For now, Diu concealed Maxwell's debts and bad habits, which gave her the upper hand. There was no benefit to her in relinquishing her position.

She watched Maxwell eye the sleeping king. Hatred narrowed the man's gaze, and his hand unconsciously clenched his sword. The click of his boots as he left the carpeted chamber and crossed the stone balcony brought a sly smile to her face. "What brings you to my door, Maxwell?" She pretended to sip the wine. "The ship arrived hours ago; we watched the guards from my council chambers. Don't tell me you could not spend another moment apart." She batted her eyelashes and tossed him a look.

Maxwell eased in close. The man's breath smelled of ale and his beard of tobacco. His eyes shifted to parts of her where they did not belong. She knew what he wanted, and she hated him for it. There was no love between them, but his desires allowed her to get close. Up close, her skills could manipulate any man, given the right incentive—and a potion if necessary.

"My dear," Maxwell whispered, getting closer, "you are divine in that gown. Why do you deny me the privacy to take advantage of you?"

No, there was no love left in her heart. The only man she ever loved was her father, and Iver killed him. Maxwell was only a pawn in a grander scheme to restore her family to the throne of Milnos and exact revenge on the Galloway family line. "Oh, Maxwell." She fiddled with his decorative medals. "You know you cannot come to the King's chambers. What would the lords and ladies of the land say?"

"You know I don't care about your reputation, my dear." Maxwell grabbed her neck with his thick fingers. He spoke quietly so no one would hear. "I grow weary, waiting for that man to die. I am a patient man, but why don't you kill him already?"

His touch made her skin crawl, but she kept her eyes delightfully locked on his. Hidden in her bosom, she felt the dark crystal against her skin. Her mother's stone ebbed with power; she had used it too much today. Still, she pulled at the magic, begging it to control this man. His eyes fell blank, and she offered him her cup. "Drink, Maxwell."

Maxwell downed the entire cup. Nola chuckled at the weak-minded man in front of her. The remnants of her influence mixed with new suggestions that forced him to comply. Thankful that the stone did her bidding, she whispered to the man under her spell. The sinder root allowed her to squelch the passionate nature bubbling inside the man for a time, leaving him feeling satisfied and remembering whatever she told him to believe. But the root was only a momentary solution, for she knew a buildup of the herb would cause an immunity to its influence, forcing her to resort to mixing potent herbs, which always lead to sickness, as it had with Iver.

Over Maxwell's shoulders, Nola heard men talking near the chamber door. Their loud noises drew her inside, and she pulled the Regent along, ordering him to retire for the night.

"Your Majesty, Queen Nola," one guard stepped to the side to let the Regent exit. "As you requested, we wish to inform you that Prince Kai is returning from his stroll in the palace gardens. The maid informed me his evening meal would be delivered to his room per your instructions."

Nola felt drained, but exhaustion was not an option. The time was now. Tonight, she needed to activate her plan. She was tired of waiting. "Thank you," she nodded and closed her door.

When Nola reemerged, she wore a different gown, shapely yet conservative. A dress she knew accentuated her youthful beauty and represented Diu style, perfect for the occasion with the unsuspecting Kai. In the pocket of her dress, the refreshed vial pressed against her hip. The long walk to the opposite end of the palace took longer than she wanted. She needed this done, one last move to finish the game.

Ahead of her, she watched the guard change outside Kai's room. Then Kendra entered, carrying a large tray of food and wine. Taking advantage of the open door, Nola strolled in behind the maid.

"Thank you, Kendra." Nola waved her hand in dismissal. "Leave us."

Kendra set the tray on the table and departed. Nola watched Kai eye the tray and the open wine bottle. She knew he did not trust her, but she needed him to play his part. His attitude around her verged on the side of arrogance, and that made her angry. But she kept her composure, took a seat, and offered a pleasant smile.

Kai crossed the room to join her at the table. "You said you wanted to talk, but I have a few questions first. Must I remain confined to my chamber? Why am I a prisoner in my own home?"

Nola poured two glasses of wine. She offered Kai a cup and took a sip from her own. She noticed Kai did not drink. She added food to a plate and offered it to him. He accepted but did not eat. Filling her plate, she continued to ignore his question. "The council believes you are not to be trusted; there are those who speculate about your return. Captain Beekman informs me he had to force you to return."

A grumble emanated from Kai's stomach, revealing his hunger, but he refused to eat anything. "It did not happen that way," he insisted.

The fireplace cast angry shadows across the room, matching Nola's mood. As she watched the flames dance and the embers disappear up the chimney, she continued to manipulate the truth. She had Kai trapped in more ways than one. Beekman had painted a picture, and Nola simply altered it to suit her needs. There was little he could do, and they both knew it.

"The way I heard it, your Kempery-man, Dresnor, I believe, had to insist you travel with Captain Beekman." She wiped her mouth and dropped her napkin back into her lap. "Speaking of your men, I have it on good authority that all have requested reassignment. Well, all but one—Captain Drew Henley, resigned his position. Everyone seems to be distancing themselves from you. There are even rumors that the baker's daughter was in tears upon her reunion with her parents. I hear she feared she would never see them again. Has she also abandoned you? She has not come to the palace asking to see you even once."

The queen delivered each comment like a punch to the gut, hoping to incite Kai, but he held his tongue. Nola leaned back in her seat and continued to let her words swirl around the room. "My dear, we all make mistakes in our youth, but you are a prince; you cannot afford mistakes. The kingdom no longer trusts you. You fought against Diu men to protect Katori outsiders."

"They are not outsiders!" Kai snapped back. "And I did not fight any Diu soldiers, only Milnosian men."

She could see the anger build in his eyes; this made her happy. "Dear Kai," Nola leaned forward, "they are the same. The Milnos men traveled under my authority to save a Diu Prince, and in turn, you attacked them, killed some of them. It was all I could do to calm Regent Maxwell after the treatment General Zhao received at your hand."

Kai pounded his fist. Her plan to flush him out had worked better than she could have hoped.

"The man ordered the slaughter of men, women, and children if they refused to be taken prisoner!" Kai shouted. "I could not stand by while this happened in my kingdom."

Guards stormed the room; swords drawn, they approached Kai.

"Your Majesty, we heard yelling and banging," one man insisted.

Nola patted the air. "I am fine. The prince is passionate, that is all. Leave us." She motioned to the door, and the men complied. Even without applying any effort, Kai was playing the part she hoped—aggressive and unpredictable. This outburst would add to her plan.

Her mischievous grin bounced between them, and Kai let out a shallow sigh. "My apologies, Queen Nola." She could tell he said the words but did not mean them.

She relaxed back into her seat. "Accepted."

A long pause lingered until Kai spoke. "You are correct; I am passionate about my people, all the citizens within Diu borders. The Katori people have lived there in the foothills for generations."

"With Iver unwell, the Diu citizens look to me to protect them." Nola refilled her glass. "If Iver—well, *when* Iver dies—they need to know the country will be in good hands. I cannot in good faith suggest you become our next king. The heir apparent or not, without the council or the city behind you, I am afraid you have no power."

She let the words circle his head, and she watched the doubt bubble in his expression. When he pushed back from his uneaten plate, she feared he would open the door and order her out. Instead, he offered a polite bow and gestured to the balcony. "Forgive me, Nola, I need some air."

Alone in the room, Nola emptied the entire contents of the sinder root vial into her cup; she needed to be sure Kai's mind would bend to her will. With her cup replenished, she stepped outside into the winter air. He stood hunched over with his hands grasping the stone railing. Her first thought was to push him over the rail and let him plummet to his death. But she had to remember that patience was a virtue, and killing two birds with one stone took control.

Joining him in silence, they looked over the sprawling city. Nola could almost hear his aggravation thunder in his chest, and it tempted her to touch his back. To her surprise, heat emanated through his shirt and vest. He turned, and she could see the challenge of her unwanted affections bubble on his lips, but he swallowed his words.

It had been nearly a year since Nola had hypnotized him; she doubted there would be any lingering effects. Still, she gazed at him with her green eyes and searched for their bond in the fading sunlight. "We do not need to be enemies, Kai." She stared with profound kindness, focusing on the crystal tucked within her bosom. The stone had very little energy left to give; she was too tired to offer it power, and it pulsed in refusal.

"The thought of my father dying . . ." Kai let his words fall away, and he leaned against the stone railing with his hip.

The sheer depth of his sadness should have melted Nola's heart, but then she wasn't sure she had one. She ran her hand over his crossed arms. His skin was warm; her touch was soothing. "You will be alright, Kai." She whispered, leaning close to his face. "Trust me—I am here for you."

"How did it all come to this?" Kai begged with a lost expression.

She almost felt bad for him. Almost. But she could see Mariana in his eyes, and it restored her hatred. Keeping her true feelings hidden, she tilted her head. "I understand, Kai." She tapped his arm and pulled once more on the magic within the dark stone. Then she felt a snap as she was drawn deeper into his eyes. The crystal complied.

"You fear Iver is all you have left." Her rhythmic touch electrified her fingertips as power flowed through her. She felt his will bend, but not enough.

His breathing slowed, but she felt his mind push against hers. The crystal gave her keen insights on the power of the mind, and Kai was strong—stronger than any man she had manipulated before. The smell of wine from her cup gave her an idea. If he did not drink on his own, she would introduce the substance another way. Over the years, she had drunk enough of the sinder root potion so it no longer affected her, and she knew how to use its mind-numbing properties.

Yes, this was the only way, Nola thought. Holding a gulp of wine in her mouth, she kissed Kai square on the mouth. The taste of dark cherry, earthy oak, and the bitter potion danced on her tongue. She let some of the liquid slip into Kai's mouth, then pulled back and watched him swallow. Nola stared into his eyes and pulled on the magic within her crystal. It gave just a little, but with the wine, it was enough.

Kai went slack, and his eyes looked a thousand miles away. "You see me, Kai, as I see you. Hear me as you once did. We cement our bond tonight—you will be mine." She continued to tap his arm. "Look into my eyes and hear only my voice. I am your queen. Drink, drink the wine, I insist." She handed him her cup.

Lost in her eyes and mesmerized by her words, Kai drank. He drank every drop. She had him; she could taste it, just as she could taste the wine on her lips. "Say it," she commanded him. "I am your queen."

"You are my queen," he responded, hypnotized by her words and the sinder root.

One question burned in her mind. "Why did you come back here, Kai?" Nola held his gaze and tapped on his hand.

He spoke without hesitation. "I came to save my father. Save him from you."

Well, honesty. Nola did not expect Kai to be so forthright. "We both know you are no prince of Diu," she prodded, hoping to confirm the rumors that he was not Iver's biological son. "But you will serve me. You love me, say it is so." She kissed him again to test her influence. Kai pulled her close, and she let the space between them collapse.

Even the strongest of men cannot resist the stone; I will rule the world someday.

Keeping her wits, Nola took a breath and stared into his eyes. She watched Kai lick his lips and felt his hands pull at her waist. "I do love you, my queen. I am yours to command."

"I need you, Kai," she teased. "You will free us from Iver's evil grasp, by killing the king. The moment is upon us, and you will need to be ready. Remember the commitment you made to me. Keep it buried deep until I pluck it out. Come." She took him by the hand and led him inside.

Drawn to her like a moth to a flame, she watched Kai follow without question. Poor, innocent boy—Galloway or not, he would be her puppet. Now all she need was to lead him to his doom.

Ready to take her final walk to the King's chambers, she reached for the door but heard shouting. It was Kendra.

"Where is the queen? Queen Nola?"

Nola pushed Kai into a chair and grabbed his chin with her hand. "Remember, my dear prince. You will serve me when I call. Now hide this moment deeply; hide this truth for now. Rest, and I will call on you soon." She watched his head roll against the back of the sofa, and he stared helplessly at nothing.

CHAPTER 7

Escape

A familiar voice called to him. "Kai, wake up." Kendra shook him. He felt her presence but lacked the ability to respond. She slapped his face and called his name. Still, he stared. Again, and again she shook him. Cold water drenched his face, and he snapped awake.

"What? Why am I all wet?"

He looked to see Kendra's face.

"Nola did something to you," she whispered. "Last night, I gleaned your room. You were on the balcony, and you were talking, and then she kissed you—twice. I could not believe my eyes. I did not know what to do." Kendra's eyes were wide with panic.

Kai recoiled at the thought. "That cannot be true," he insisted. "I love Rayna, and Nola is, well, married to my father. I would remember . . ." His stomach tossed at the possibilities.

"She has you under a spell. Like Iver, she has done something to you." Kendra ran her fingers over her lips and then pointed at his. "Your lips, they are stained red, same as last time you missed the better part of a day."

Kai licked his lips and tasted the wine. Small crystals around his mount tingled on his tongue. "There must have been something in the wine." He tried to recall the previous night, but his mind hit a wall. "I

87

do not remember anything. I remember you bringing a tray, and I remember her sitting at the table we talked, but that is all. What else did you see?" He feared her answer but braced himself for the worst.

Shame crept over Kendra's face, and tears welled in her eyes. "There was an accident," her voice shook, and she wrapped her arms around her body. "I spilled hot tea on Cordelia." Tears ran down Kendra's face. "I wasn't paying attention to how much I was pouring. I was gleaning your room, and . . ." she sobbed again.

Kai did his best to comfort her. "You didn't mean to do it."

She wiped her face and continued. "I love Cordelia as if she were my own. I have spent every day with her since she was born. I ran to the hallway and shouted for help screaming for Nola, and the guards opened your door. Nola came running out of your room. I thought she would murder me on the spot when she saw the girl's hand and leg. Cordelia said she spilled her cup, but I know better. I believe Nola did, too."

He could see Kendra's love for his little sister. "So, I have been sitting here all night and half of today?" he asked, but knew it to be accurate by the stiffness he felt in his body. His head hurt, making him wonder just how much wine he consumed and what Nola had laced in the cup. And more importantly, what might have happened if Kendra had not interrupted.

"This is the first time I could leave your sister. Nola is with the council, and I came through the secret passageway from the library."

Kai thought about the possible lingering effects of the wine and whatever Nola used to cloud his mind and the potential outcome linked to his vision. He could not allow her to control him. This had to be how she planned to force Kai into killing his father. "If Nola did use an elixir to induce a trance, I need to get it out of me and avoid her until the effects wear off. Have you ever seen an herb called lobelia?" Kai asked, developing a plan of his own.

Kendra nodded with recognition. "I know it. I believe Sigry keeps some, but why would you want a poisonous flower known to induce vomiting?" She glared at him with concern. "Sigry will never give it to me, and he rarely leaves his medical room these days unless to tend to Iver. He studies journals and rare books, searching for a cure for your father."

A smile crept over his face. "You are going to do me a favor. I need to search for Riome tonight; I promised Yulia I would help find her daughter. I need to know what Riome discovered about Nola's plot to kill my father. But how can I if Nola intends to return to my room every night? Besides, I cannot wander around the city slums and tunnels with Diu guards following my every move. I need to be irrefutably sick for the next several days." He thought of Rayna and her study of herbs. She would be pleased he remembered the name and its use. Now he had to hope he remembered how much to take safely.

"When you bring my evening meal, place the lobelia in the flower bouquet; I will do the rest." He patted her hand and pointed to the secret passage hidden behind Gianfranca's portrait.

Once Kendra left, Kai set to play his part. With a splash of water around the hairline and collar, he appeared sweaty and exhausted as he opened his door. "I am unwell and unable to take my daily stroll through the gardens," he complained to the guards. "Please extend my apologies to Seth, we were to go riding this afternoon."

Confident he had them convinced, Kai waited for Kendra's return. Like Iver, Kai took to pacing to sort out his mind. His stately room suddenly became too small for the problem he faced. How could he tell Rayna that he had kissed Nola? The more he walked, the smaller his room became—and the bigger his problem.

Gleaning the small baker's home within the palace grounds gave him no peace. Rayna sat with her family; his wolf, Smoke, sat at her feet. She looked sad, like she had been crying. Since the day they rode into the city, he had not spoken with her. Although Kendra said she was free to move without guards, to his knowledge, she had yet to step more than a few feet outside her parents' cottage. Doubt caught in his chest. Had he truly forced her from her parent's home all those months ago? Did she regret their move to Katori?

When a knock echoed through his door, Kai hopped onto his bed just as the door swung open. He expected to see Kendra, but Nola stood in the frame. "I hear you are unwell." She approached his bedside. "The council kept me very busy today, or I would have come sooner. Maybe we can have dinner together." She stood at the foot of his bed.

"Your Highness," Kendra called, entering with a small silver tray. She placed it on the table and approached Kai, holding a wet cloth in her hand. "Please excuse me, your Majesty, Queen Nola." Kendra put a cold compress on Kai's head and slipped a vial into his hand. "Prince Kai complained of a headache and stomach cramps. Sigry has sent me with a compress, bread, and water. He will prescribe a tonic if the prince continues to feel unwell."

Kendra feigned concern as she glanced from Kai's eyes to the tiny vial.

Kai wrapped his hand around the dark green vial, trusting Kendra knew what she was doing. Ready to play his part, he sat up and coughed profusely. "May I have some water, Kendra," he begged.

Nola held up her hand and turned back to the table. "I can pour water, Kendra. You are no longer needed. Go."

With the Queen's back turned, Kai drank the contents of the vial. The contents burned down his throat. While he had never had lobelia, he was sure he never wanted to drink it again. He hated the taste, and he could only hope Kendra supplied the right amount as he did not know how she managed a liquid form in only a few hours.

Before Kendra reached the door, Kai became sick. He vomited all over his bed coverings. Red wine from the previous evening stained his white bedding. Queen Nola shouted, "Kendra, come back!" Nola backed away, disgusted, covering her nose and mouth. He noticed a brief look of concern as she turned away. "You should send for Sigry," she motioned and left.

The door slammed shut, and Kendra gave him another vial. "Drink this down," she insisted.

He did as she instructed, and he felt the cool liquid squelch the fire in his throat and belly. Next, she handed him water, and he downed the entire glass. "What was that?" he held up the two glass vials, one green, one blue.

"I tried to get the lobelia," Kendra confessed, "but Sigry no longer has any. Riome's room on the other hand contains many poisons and cures. In Riome's absence, I have been studying her notes, hoping to find a cure for Iver myself. She wrote about these two potions in a recent journal entry; I could only hope I understood the mixture and grabbed the correct amounts."

She handed him some bread, and he nibbled it slowly. "So, you poisoned me?" He felt nauseous and covered his mouth, but nothing new came up.

"I did what was necessary; Sigry is not the right person to trust with this. He might have suspected something if I had asked for lobelia." Kendra removed the soiled linens and headed to the door. "I will be back with fresh bedding. Riome's diary recommends plain bread and water for the next hour. The effects may linger if I gave you too much. Should you feel sick while I am gone, use the waste bin by the bed."

The door closed with a thud, and he looked at the bin. The very thought of being sick again made him retch, and he was thankful the container was close.

The next knock at the door was a maid Kai did not recognize. She was a brute of a woman who refused to make eye contact. Her beefy hands yanked the remaining linens from Kai's bed, and she replaced everything with new gold and blue coverings.

"May I get more water?" Kai rasped, tugging the fresh quilt over his chest after he climbed into the freshly made bed.

Her only response was a curt nod. By the time the maid returned with more water, he felt surprisingly better, but he hid his progress by keeping his eyes closed as she came and went.

CHAPTER 8

Little Sister

Once Kai was sure his room would remain undisturbed, the secret passageways and underground tunnels made escaping the palace easy. The memory of the first night he discovered the corridors made him chuckle. He missed the old days of ditching guards and running spy missions with Riome. Tonight would be anything but fun. This time, he searched for his teacher and friend in a city he hardly recognized, hoping to save her life.

Much had changed about Diu in the time Kai was away. Rimtown never looked this dirty. Trash and mud littered the streets. While parts of town had always been rough, he did not remember hungry beggars. Homeless people sat on corners and lay in alleyways. Pickpockets bumped into unsuspecting travelers, stealing what they could. Only a few random guards patrolled, and they steered clear of dark alleyways and hot spots. Kai could not believe what he saw.

Riome once taught him that the old and poor go unnoticed. She was right. The outskirts of the city were falling apart, and nobody seemed to care. Kai could feel the tension within the crowded streets; men mumbled under their breaths, disgusted with life. The scowls on their faces seethed with anger—and a hint of pending treachery. Most wore threadbare clothing, pulled tight around their hunched shoulders.

Disguised in a dirty shirt and rugged pants, Kai blended in; even his thin overcoat had patches and several holes for good measure. He kept his eyes down and his hands in his pockets. He padded through the streets, muttering under his breath. If Riome was indeed back, there had to be news of her return. There were three inns she frequented when she worked this part of the city, and he had already checked one location with no luck.

One street short of the Tabour Inn, Kai ducked into the alley that ran behind the large establishment. Checking the alleyway was the best place to start—no signs of her. He shuffled by two vagrants smoking at the corner as he doubled back to the front. Satisfied nobody was following him, he gleaned the establishment for Riome. After speaking with the barkeep, he decided she was not here, either.

While his disguise was right, he was no match with Riome's skill in masquerade, so he had to be careful about asking too many questions or making direct contact lest someone recognize him as their prince. He no longer trusted anyone in the city. Even the few city guards appeared disgruntled and quick-tempered, and keeping clear of them seemed the prudent choice.

After crisscrossing town, he reached another inn. After he checked the streets to make sure they were clear, he ducked inside. It was time to speak with a few locals. Still, in his mind, he searched the patrons and the upper rooms. From room to room he gleaned, setting the inn aglow in his mind. He had to be sure Riome was not hiding in plain sight behind a disguise.

After Kai scanned the bar, he sat on an empty seat and ordered an ale. The barkeep turned his nose at Kai's grubby appearance but served him when Kai produced the proper coin. From his stool, he listened to the other patrons. Many complained of higher taxes and food shortages, while others speculated about their next king. Most believed Aaron would rule, but a few wished Seth, the quieter of the two twins, would take the throne. Not one person mentioned Kai as their future ruler. Instead, his name provoked anger and distrust.

Each time the door opened, he hoped it would be her.

Tired of listening to the conversations around him, he inquired with the owner, spinning a tale about getting separated from his family—a grandmother and his younger brother. There was no way to know what disguise Riome might be using. She could be an older woman or a young boy; anything was possible. Kai convinced the man to check his logbook in the hopes that one of them had inquired after him and secured a room.

After having no luck, Kai quickly flipped through the pages before the man snatched back the book. Every name on the pages were couples or families, all in town for the Winter Festival. The owner had no lodgers that matched the description. Appreciative, Kai offered the man an extra coin and drank his ale.

After an hour of listening to people complain, Kai left to check one last establishment. It was the least respectable, the Red Rain Tavern. If you want to go unnoticed, you stay in the worst place in town. Still, after inspecting the inn, asking the owner, and listening to the patrons, Kai accepted tonight was a waste of time. He was no closer to finding Riome than when he started.

There had to be a way to find her. Playing his part, he stumbled out of the Red Rain Tavern and tripped over the foot of an older man hunched outside. The smell of urine and vomit turned Kai's stomach. Cautious, Kai stepped back as the man held up his leathery hand. "Spare a coin, mister?"

The smell was unbearable. While Kai felt terrible saying no, he was confident the man would only spend the money on ale. "Sorry, none left. I have some bread in my pocket if you want that?"

The man's pale blue eyes swelled with pain. "Pffftt. No, mister, I need ale. My head is pounding."

The man's foul breath nearly made Kai retch. Evidently, the various liquids he had consumed and thrown up were still working their way through his system. He stepped back and vanished down the next alleyway. If Riome were in trouble, she would need to become invisible; searching public places was wrong, he decided.

How do you do hide in a city this busy? he wondered.

Kai took to the rooftop to think. The crisp night air was welcoming.

Even at this late hour, people were everywhere. Kai watched them from his perch, studying who they were and their purpose in the night. Gamblers and vagrants. People with nothing but time on their hands, many itching for a fight. The slightest shoulder bump sent fists flying, which did not always draw the guard. There was not one kind word among them.

They are homeless, Kai realized. *They have nowhere to be, no place to call home.* Most sat outside begging for food as people stumbled out of pubs. *So, where do homeless people go?*

He hated the idea, but he needed to get dirtier. Blend in with the lowest of the low. If people were to confide in him, he needed to look and smell the part, maybe even follow a few to find where they slept.

In the next alley, he found trash piled in the street. Food and dirt would have to be good enough. He tore the knee of his pants into a gaping hole. He hoped the addition of more dirt on his face and food stains on his shirt would do the trick. In a back alley, he stumbled around until he found an old woman sitting alone.

He sat down a few feet away. It didn't take long for the woman to give him grief. "Push off—this is my spot. Go on, get. Find a new place."

A burly barkeep opened the door to the street. The woman stood with her hands out. "Can I have some food, sir?"

He dumped his trash into the bin outside. "Take what you want." He slammed the door behind himself. Kai heard the steel bolt slide into place seconds later.

Cautiously, Kai moved closer, watching her edge around the trash heap. He could smell remnants of the pub's dinner. Leftover bits from unfinished meals coated the trash, but it did not deter the woman as she scavenged with her fingers, eating bits of bread and stew. "Get out of here—this is mine." She croaked as sauce dripped down her dirty chin.

Hands up, Kai humbly leaned away. "Don't need food tonight. I need a place to sleep. Where could I find a safe place?" he asked in a humble voice.

She eyed him suspiciously, then sniffed him like a dog. "Near the sewers," she croaked. "Guards won't bother you there, smells too foul— too many rats. But if you prefer, the water drainage pipes don't smell bad, but there are still rats. Take your pick."

He nodded with gratitude and backed away.

If Riome was nearby but unable to come into the tower for fear other vagrants might see the secret entrances, then he figured that she had to be hiding in one of these two places. Since he was already on the outskirts of town, he searched the sewers first. Near the entrance, a few people lined the walls. He had never smelled anything so foul, and the odor intensified the deeper he went. Still, he searched several tunnels with no luck.

How could this be happening here in Diu? He shook his head; this was not his city, not the one he remembered. How could a thriving city crumble in nine months?

Hours of walking underground did him no favors, and before long his stomach started to feel sick. Rats scurried everywhere. People threw stones and stabbed at them with sticks. Kai shook his head in disappointment. There was no way to find her down here. It would take days to search the tunnels properly. If he were a Stoneking, it might be easier, but for him, the thick stone made searching with his mind nearly impossible. He had to hope Riome was not here and that she would pick a cleaner, healthier hiding place.

Partway through Midtown, Kai started getting strange looks. His attire was no longer suitable for the slightly cleaner parts of town. He would love to change, but he did not have any options. Stealing clothes on a cold winter's night would not be easy. Down the next street, he climbed up three balconies to the rooftops. From above, he could travel unnoticed.

Building by building, he made his way across Midtown. There were two places to access the water pipes. These tunnels were smaller, but he was happy to know they should not smell. The hinges on the tunnel's iron gate creaked from lack of care, and he sniffed the air—musty but not filthy. Angry faces greeted him as he hunched inside. It was at least a little warmer, and it certainly smelled better.

He pulled the gate closed and stepped over sleeping bodies. With his sight, he gleaned the tunnel as far as he could see, about fifteen feet. He searched for Riome's brightness, hoping she would stand out among these people.

He called for her. "Little sister, are you here?"

"Shhhh," was his only answer. An angry homeless man scowled at his rudeness.

Frustrated, Kai continued. More tunnels, more turns. He walked hunched over. Pipes dripped on his head, and the musty smell of filthy people added to the intolerable conditions. Two rats scurried over his boot. The farther he walked, the fewer people he found, until there were none.

He could see why they chose this tunnel. The heat from the pipes warmed the space against the winter conditions outside. But there was no sign of Riome, and he made his way back to the exit, discouraged. While he had not searched every inch, he was confident she was not here.

The wind whipped through his hair. Snowflakes flitted by his face. It was a few hours from dawn, and he smelled and looked disgusting. There was no way he could walk the streets back to the palace. The guards patrolling Hightown proper would turn him away, and they most likely would force him back to the slums in Rimtown. None would believe him to be the Prince of Diu, and he most certainly did not want to give them cause to question his activities.

Once again, he took to the rooftops. Alone in the night, he strolled casually across each building with no one the wiser. People slept in their soft, warm beds while he walked above them. Only when necessary did he shimmy down to access another row of buildings on the next street.

The last set he needed to cross was a line of warehouses, stores, and shops. Their flat roofs would leave him exposed and easy to spot by the guards on the palace walls above, but he could not risk taking the streets. He kept low and moved quickly. Along the north wall, there were three access points. One would access the palace dungeons, one the old armory, and the last would come out near the barracks. The one he wanted would take him to the armory where he had spent countless hours training with Riome and Dresnor, the same tunnel he used to exit, which would provide him clean clothes and a way to reenter the palace. Riome had shown him the access points years ago, allowing them to come and go undetected.

The first entrance he came to led to the barracks. Laying on top of the warehouse, Kai watched the guards patrol on the wall above and the street below as he gleaned the depths of the tunnel. He found it to be empty. He waited for the opportunity to hop the small gap between two buildings. The next access point was for the dungeons. This time he hid behind a chimney and waited for the guards to pass on the walls above. As he paused, his eye caught a glint of light.

There was something metallic inside the tunnel grate, but from this distance, it was too dark to tell what. Kai took a hopeful breath, closed his eyes, and with one last prayer, he gleaned the tunnel. The spark of a Half-Light burst in his mind. Focused on the form, he saw her face— Riome. He had found her. In an instant, he scaled the side of the building by sliding down the steal drainpipe.

Frantic to get to her, he dropped to the ground with a thud. Hidden in the shadows, he detected her shallow breathing and weak pulse. Once the guards passed his hiding spot, Kai dashed across the darkness. The iron grate was cold against his hands. "Little sister!" he called to her quietly. "Are you awake?"

A moan came from the tunnel. Kai pulled open the gate, hopped inside, and closed it behind himself. Riome lay in a heap. Her clothing was ratty and damp, and she smelled of farm animals. Her hand was clammy, her face feverish.

"Can you move?" he whispered, seeing her injuries.

Riome did not answer. He ran his hands around her boy-short hair. There was a partially healed gash on her head and a deep cut across her eyebrow. There were bruises everywhere, all in various shades from black to yellow. The jagged gash on her leg concerned him; an infected wound by the look of it.

Gently, Kai pressed on her abdomen. She twitched as he pushed her ribs. "Riome, we can't stay here. You are in the tunnel leading to the dungeons. We need to get to the next one to access the armory tower. Can you move?"

He shook her lightly. Riome opened her eyes and closed them again. Moving her with broken ribs worried him. If she could not walk, he would have to carry her. The last thing they needed was to attract unwanted attention or hurting her more. "Riome, can you walk?"

He wrapped one hand around her waist, and she put her arm over his shoulder. She groaned as he brought her to her feet. Her legs stiffened. "I can." She grabbed his arm. "Wait. Where is it?" She pointed, "Is it there? Find the blade."

Kai searched the entrance, where he found a silver blade, which he figured was the glint of steel he saw three stories up. He stuffed the knife into his coat pocket and waited for the guard to pass. Kai opened the grate and helped Riome down the narrow street. Back into the shadows, he weaved them through the darkness. Closer and closer to the next access point.

Closed shops gave them the empty streets they needed to move undetected. Three blocks later, they hid in the shadows as two guards walked down the street on patrol. Their opportunity to cross was coming. Two new guards met, spoke briefly, and parted. Patiently Kai waited, but he could feel the weight of Riome sag next to him. She was finding it harder to stand. "Hang on. We are almost there." He hoisted her against his hip.

One step into the street, Riome stumbled. On the second step, she fell; Riome was unconscious. Kai scooped her into his arms and ran to the third access point leading to the tower. The gate hinge creaked; he could only hope nobody heard them as he climbed inside and pulled it closed. The gate rang out in proclamation as he closed it behind them.

His boots sloshed in the water as he crept farther into the shadows. Voices converged on their location, and Kai backed deeper into the dark tunnel. They had been too loud. There would be no explaining to the guards what they were doing in the tunnel; the men would arrest them. Riome hung limp in his arms, then her labored breathing stopped. Kai shook her, and she gasped.

While he understood the concept of invisibility, the gift had eluded him with every attempt. He prayed to Alenga. "Hide us, please," he begged, recalling his grandfather Benmar's instructions—to become invisible, you absorb light.

Seeking the wisdom carved into his lineage, Kai thought about his two grandfathers' abilities—invisibility and the power of a Lumen to bend light and distort the truth. Both manipulated light. Desperate to hide them, Kai pulled at the light around them. The patrolling guard stopped. Kai held his breath. The man shook the metal grate; it popped open. A rat scurried over Kai's foot, but he did not move.

Another guard peeked into the darkness. After a few mumbles, they glared again into the tunnel. One man entered. His form blocked the outside light. "Hand me a torch," the man demanded. "I can't see anything in here."

Kai focused—gleaning his own light, he drew it into his core and he felt the heat building. He pulled on the energy he saw around Riome's collapsed body in his arms and again he noticed an increase of heat. His gift of gleaning revealed the flow of energy that he absorbed into his core. Light from the guard's torch washed down the tunnel. Kai felt the warmth of it pass through his body.

Holding on to the light, his muscles began to shake, *just a moment more, please,* he begged.

"Empty." The guard shouted as a rat scurried over his boot. "Rats. Filthy vermin. Let's go; there's nothing here." The man backed out and closed the gate.

Letting go of the light, Kai collapsed to his knees. Heat poured out of Kai's skin, and his heart and lungs felt cold without it. Heart pounding, he held Riome tight against his chest, protecting her head from the stone as he slumped against the wall. There was nothing in the tunnel to replenish his magic. The flow of water within the pipes had little to give, and the hard stone gave even less.

Knowing he was Riome's only hope he collected his strength and rose to his feet and continued down the tunnel. The old armory was cold and dark. Their old training room smelled stale, and months of dust covered everything. *Good*, he thought. *We should not be disturbed.* From the rack, he pulled a few of the old quilted tunics. He placed them under her head and hid her behind the shield rack. "Riome, I have to leave you here. I need to get help."

She moaned. Her eyes fluttered.

Kai used the inside of his thin overcoat to scrub the dirt from his face. He removed his disguise and grabbed the clean shirt and pants he'd left on the rack. While the change was a visual improvement, he still smelled foul.

On his way up the eastern spire, he contemplated whom he could trust. Riome needed Sigry's knowledge and medicines, but could the old man be trusted? His cousin was the only person who could help— Riome's father, Adrian Cazier. Utilizing the secret tunnels, Kai worked his way to the master general's tower and the second-floor bedchamber.

Adrian was asleep atop his covers; a book lay on his chest. Kai jostled his cousin. "Wake up."

Adrian woke, grabbing for the blade he kept at his side. Moonlight trickled into the room and revealed Kai's face. "Looking for this?" Kai handed Cazier his weapon.

Cazier turned his nose away. "You stink. What have you been doing?"

"Cousin, I found Riome," Kai whispered, unsure anywhere was safe. "Do you always sleep fully dressed?" He asked helping ease Cazier upright.

Adrian's eyes bulged. He swung his feet to the floor. "I did not mean to do more than rest my eyes for a moment. Where is she?" He pulled on his boots. "Take me to her."

"She is safe for now, but she is sick. She has two broken ribs, gashes on her head and thigh, and many bruises. The cut on her leg looks infected. I found her in the tunnel for the dungeons' access point. So much has changed in Diu, I did not know where to take her. I left her in the eastern spire in the old armory."

"We need to move her before dawn. Get her to my tower. I can have Sigry tend to her here in my room. I trust him. He is loyal to your father. Loyal to me. Retrieve my daughter, and I will get Sigry. But do not be here when we return—I cannot have you mixed up in this. Your reputation is tarnished enough; I cannot have the lost Prince of Diu caught in a spy scandal."

Kai nodded. "I can use the secret tunnels, but I need to move fast before the maids start their day. Send me a note through Kendra when I can visit. I will send her to help bathe Riome."

◆ ◆ ◆

When Riome was safe in Adrian's room, not wanting to track filth through the palace, Kai stopped by the laundry to drop off his mud-caked boots. Before he could get through the kitchen, Lizzie spotted him. Her expression demonstrated fear and caution. "Kai, is it really you, my dear boy?" Lizzie touched his arm as if unsure he was not a ghost. "My, my, you are a sight for sore eyes. I feared I would never see you again, but do not dally here. The Queen must not find you here; things have changed in the palace. The kitchen is no place for a prince." She bowed ever so slightly and grabbed him around the waist for a quick hug.

"Dear Lizzie, how I have missed you. I hope to ease the worries around Diu, but right now, could you do me a favor? Please send food to the master general's room. Could you also send food to my room? I would appreciate the help." He hated to beg and run, but she was right—the kitchen was no place for the supposedly ill prince.

"Certainly, Prince Kai." She waved his smell from her nose. Her eyes pinned him with a look of concern, but she mustered a smile. "Now, go take a bath."

◆ ◆ ◆

An hour later, Kai found himself eating from a bountiful tray of food in his room provided by Kendra. "I need to tell you something," she started.

He swallowed his food and wiped the corner of his mouth. "Later Kendra, I need your help first. I found Riome. She is in the master general's quarters. I need you to help bathe her and provide fresh clothes; Cazier is expecting you. Sigry will tend her wounds, but if you know any Kodama healers in the city who could help her, I would appreciate it."

"I am happy to help." Kendra turned to go. "And I will try to inform Riome's mother, Yulia. She will want to know her daughter has returned. But I must tell what I heard about Rayna."

Half chocking on his water he read the concern in Kendra's eyes. "What? Tell me, is she alright?"

"I overheard the lavender girls in the laundry gossiping about how Rayna tried to see you, twice. The first time the guards turned her away and during her second attempt with different men, they manhandled her, one instructed she should understand her place while another soldier threatened a night in prison by order of the Queen. I do not want you to leave, but this is not a safe place for either of you."

Her concerns sank in, Kai was playing a dangerous game with Nola and if he did not do something, Rayna would pay the consequences. "I will get her out of the city, thank you for telling me."

CHAPTER 9

Free Your Mind

When Kai slipped into the tower through the secret passageway to check Riome's condition, the hour was late. He was pleased to see Sigry had wrapped her ribs, tended her wounds, and given her medicine to help with the infection. Although her complexion had improved, she only woke in short spurts and her feverish ramblings continued. All Kai and Cazier could do was wait for her to recover—or hope a Katori healer was found.

"I thought I told you to stay away from Diu," Cazier said through gritted teeth. "Did you not read my hidden warning?"

Kai nodded. "I saw the message, but I had to see my father. He is much worse than your letter implied."

"His condition was better when I sent the letter. Iver gets worse by the day. I hate to say, but I am not sure how much longer your father has left, which means that my primary goal is now to keep you safe. If he does not recover . . ." Cazier looked away. "You are the future king."

"Cousin, my father is strong," Kai insisted, not wanting to believe anything else. "We need to find a cure for the poison Nola is using on him."

"You don't think we've tried?" Cazier huffed. "Sigry has tried to cure him, but the old man swears it is not poison, at least none he understands. And, of course, Nola holds a vigil of her own every night.

She is rarely far from his side for more than a few hours. Even if Riome were well, she would be unable to get close to Iver to study him. I have no idea what ails him. The only time Nola leaves him is to hear the council instruct young Aaron. She aims to put him on the throne, you understand. Dante does whatever she commands."

"So, Dante is her lap dog?" Kai curled his lip. "Explains why Dante allows her to keep me hostage in the palace."

"He obeys his queen." Cazier craned his neck to look outside. "The Grand Duke is no traitor—he is loyal to the crown and the Galloway name. But unlike you, Nola is here acting the part. Dante has no idea about our suspicions, and Nola paints you in a displeasing light. We still need real proof of her duplicity, something we both hoped Riome could discover."

Riome sat up, clutching her head. "Must you two chatter all night?"

"You're awake!" Kai hurried to her side. "You have been in and out these two days."

She scoffed. "It will take more than a few broken ribs, being stabbed in the leg, and nearly drowning to kill me."

She looked at them both sternly. "My father is right, Kai. It would be best if you were not here. When your father dies, Nola will not let you become king. It's not safe here. She spreads lies about your time in Katori. Even in the middle of the ocean, people talk of you and your disloyalty. You are no longer the beloved prince."

Kai leaned away. "I have been gone too long, but I will stop Nola, one way or another."

"Don't be foolish," Riome barked. "This conspiracy against you and Iver is big—Regent Maxwell and Milnos big. I would not be surprised if your friend Tolan and his bride Amelia are executed or imprisoned in the coming days. You remember your friend Tolan, right? The one meant to rule Milnos in your stead. My network has no news of their fate; I am currently cut out of events in Milnos."

Kai waved her off. "Lucas Maxwell is a power-hungry tyrant, but he would never imprison or murder his own daughter. Tolan, maybe, but Diu would never stand for that. His death would start a war."

"You think?" Riome clenched her fist. "Maxwell will not allow Tolan to be king of Milnos. Nola wants revenge for the death of her father, King Penier. Maxwell will help Nola if he gets what he wants, which is wealth and power. She wants Iver dead and Aaron on the Diu throne. The only person I could not find was Landon—the would-be heir to Milnos is still missing. He is a Penier, and I imagine he has a desire to reclaim his birthright. Given the military expenditures, Maxwell has overextended his city and they grow weary of his other spending habits."

"Well, if Nola rules Diu through Aaron, and unites Diu with Milnos, there would be no war," Cazier mused, interrupting their argument. "What proof do you have the city of Milnos is behind this?"

"Milnos steel," she answered, pointing to the blade on the table.

Inspecting the blade, Cazier thumbed the pommel and traced the curve of the blade before passing it to her. "So, the knife came from Milnos?" he questioned. "And you suspect that Maxwell is behind this?"

She nodded. "The stamp on the blade and pommel is the iron skull, a blacksmith's symbol in Milnos. Plus, the curve of the blade is most definitely Milnos. I took the weapon off an assassin spy. His tattoo—the Milnos raven and an iron skull. Foolish tradition. Gang tattoos. The Iron Skulls run a shipping trade between Milnos and Bangloo. Thieves and murderers, mostly."

"What was this man doing on my father's ship?" Kai interrupted.

"My guess, he was hired to kill Iver—on the ship or after they arrived in Bangloo. We were less than a mile out from Bangloo when I discovered the assassin onboard. We fought below deck. The man was good; I was better. I killed him, and as I tossed him overboard, a crewman called out. My only choice was to fall into the sea and swim for shore. I could not risk discovery with blood on my hands, plus I was not the cabin boy I pretended to be." A fit of coughing overtook her, and she pointed to the water pitcher.

Kai offered her a glass but did not interrupt.

Riome took a sip and continued. "The ship I boarded to return with my proof was less-than-friendly—a slave ship from Bangloo to Milnos. The next two ships were not much nicer, smugglers and thieves. I spent most of the trip fighting for my position on the ship or defending my winning streak. I tried to find out who hired the man willing to kill a king, but let's just say I pressed the wrong people without proper support. But at least I know where to look now."

She rubbed her neck, her eyes lost in a memory. The fading yellow bruises formed a large handprint around her throat. Kai contemplated her suffering. He knew firsthand at least one fight she had fought to defend herself, and he could not imagine everything she went through to get home with this blade and her story.

It started to sink in that he needed time to think. First, Rayna was not safe in Diu. He needed to take her home before he dealt with what was coming. His vision was coming—the death of his father at Kai's own hands—but he still did not know how to change how his destiny intersected with his father's.

Kai stood up. "I must leave. I will take Rayna back to Katori. She will be safe there, and Riome can get a message to me through her mother's network. Yulia and Kendra are searching for a healer to help you recover. I would bring Rayna to you, but I am not sure I can risk her getting caught inside the tower. Nola's spies are everywhere."

"Agreed." Cazier leaned forward. "I will consult my other spies to discover what I can about this hired assassin and see if my network can get inside Milnos. You need to leave at first light. I want you safe away from any other would-be killers, until I can trace this conspiracy to Nola or Maxwell. Do you need a ship?"

"I do not." He paused to think. Now was no time to sleep. "I will leave now." Kai stood and went to the door. "I will be back. Before my father dies."

"Is that wise? To come back, I mean." Cazier glanced at Riome for confirmation.

Kai turned to face his friends. His family. "Do you trust me?"

"What kind of question is that?" Riome scoffed. "Of course we trust you."

"Remember that. Remember the man you believe me to be right here and now. Please do not doubt my loyalty. Many people doubt me, but I could not bear to lose either of you. I may need my friends more than ever in the coming days."

Cazier rose from his chair. "Kai. You're speaking nonsense."

Riome's expression, however, remained calm. "I do not understand, but we will be ever faithful to you. Despite what we hear."

Confused, Cazier looked back and forth. He threw his hands up. "Clearly, you know something I do not and refuse to share. I will do what I can." He took Kai's arm. "Take care of yourself."

"You too, cousin. Take care of Riome. She needs you now."

"I am right here, and I am no cripple. I could still beat you both," she mocked.

"Take care, little sister." Kai knelt next to her and kissed her on the forehead.

Before he could escape, Riome pulled him close. Her eyes locked on his, and she placed her hand to his ear. A ticking sound filled his mind. The metal pocket watch felt cool against his skin. Riome's stare locked him in place.

"Listen to the sound of my voice, my dear." The lilt in her voice had changed.

Kai tried to pull away, but she held him in place. "Remember what I told you that night. I asked you to listen and bend your will to mine." Nola's voice echoed in his head.

Visions of Nola flickered through his mind. Their foreheads were nearly close enough to touch. The tick, tick, tick of the watch set a rhythmic spell where only her voice mattered. Thoughts of Nola washed over him as her voice twisted his memory. Brown eyes, green eyes. Riome's face, Nola's face. The two faces blurred behind the voice and the constant ticking trapped his mind with a hypnotic rhythm.

"See the light dance in my eyes; I lead you by the hand.
Unravel the string to break the ties; there is power in a grain of sand.
Time does not wait for thee; remember, I am not your kind.
Before the hands of time stop, unlock the key to free your mind."

Locked on her eyes, Kai listened. His eyes played tricks on him as Riome's face became Nola's and back again. The words in the rhyme and the tempo of the tick-tock transfixed his mind as she repeated it once more. The constant tick-tock of her watch lulled him into a deep haze of nothingness.

"Close your eyes, Kai." Nola's voice echoed in Kai's head. "Hear only my voice. Nothing else matters; I am your queen. Discover the seed I planted. Open the lock within your mind. Remember my truth."

Each breath was slow and easy. Riome's words dug deep into his mind. He recalled his time with Nola. The taste of wine on his lips, the taste of her. Her words locked him in a promise. "I am yours to command, my queen. I promise to serve you with my dying breath."

"Do you remember the task I bid you perform?" Riome asked with Nola's voice.

Nola's request rang in his head. He fought to form the words. "You want me to free us; you want me to kill the king."

"Excellent, my dear. Who is Iver to you? Is he your father?" she asked lightly.

"Iver is my father," Kai responded.

"Yes, my dear. Remember my commands. You must obey your queen. When next we meet, I will free you from my commands, but you must heed my words. Tell me your name."

"I am Kai Galloway."

"Search your soul, and you can choose," Riome added.

Riome continued to plant new seeds. "Hold on this truth—truth has power. I need you to save Iver. I am your queen, and I order you to obey. Focus on the idea within your mind. Remember your own heart. Let go of my words and their control over you. Free yourself—SAVE IVER!"

She lowered the watch and washed her hand over Kai's face. His eyes closed, and he sat back on his heels. The fading tick-tock left him in silence. In the darkness, he searched for his inner truth. The love of his father, Iver, bloomed brightly. Nola's conflicting statements now muddied his mind, and he shook his head as he opened his eyes.

"What did you do to me?" he asked.

"I pulled a weed and planted a seed." She looked at Cazier. "Like Iver, Kai was hypnotized to follow Nola's commands. You heard it here from his very lips. She means for Kai to kill Iver. Two kings with one blade. She will place Aaron on the throne and take Diu down from the inside."

"Am I cured—free?" Kai asked, hopeful destiny no longer held him within its grasp.

She hummed. "I doubt you will ever be free of her. It is not my specialty—the mind. During my early studies, I discovered the rhyme in a teacher's journal. He wrote how combined with the use of the tick-tock of a watch it could be used to hypnotize someone. What I gave you was a choice. Two commands battle within you—mine and hers. Do not let fear control you. If she means to use you, be ready. Fate places you at a crossroads; given this foresight, be prepared and be swift before her words cloud any clarity you now have. But know this, Kai—you should not face her. If you are not here, she cannot use you."

"How did you know Kai was compromised?" Cazier questioned.

"Kendra told me she feared Nola did something to him the day she found him dazed in his room. She told me that she found Kai, his lips stained with wine, staring at nothing." Riome leaned back. "You had lost time. Unable to remember parts of your day. Haunted by a feeling, Kendra trusted me to help you. That was enough for me to realize what Nola had done."

Hope—real hope, for the first time—washed away the impending doom. Fate no longer had him by the throat. "Thank you, Riome. Cazier, I must leave and take Rayna far from Diu. I will not risk her safety if something goes wrong. I beg you, do not do anything with this information. Nola is not yet within our grasp. I plan to return because I can stop her now."

"Wait, what?" Cazier took hold of Kai's arm. "This is not right. I cannot sit back while Nola plans to murder my King—your father and use you in the process. I changed my mind, you will stay here under my protection within the tower until my spies can uncover the truth." Cazier's expression swelled with worry.

There was no time to argue, Kai knew it, and he could see Riome knew it too. "Father," Riome used their family bond to distract Cazier, extending a hand to draw him closer.

Cazier sat beside his daughter, and Kai backed up to the door. With his cousin preoccupied, he slipped away without so much as a goodbye.

CHAPTER 10

Shattered Dreams

Dark hazy clouds cast a heavy gloom over the palace grounds. Wanting to go unseen, Kai knocked on the back door to the Kendrick cottage. He waited. Levi answered. "Mister Kendrick, may we talk?" Kai stepped back and motioned to the dark shadows behind the baker's home.

Levi's discerning eyes left Kai's and peered back into the house. Kai followed the man's focus to see Rayna with her mother, holding hands. "You have a question to ask, son. Before you ask, I need to know you have my daughter's safety in hand," Levi said as he followed Kai outside.

"You know Rayna means everything to me, and I would do anything to protect her. I apologize for my distance, but I did not feel it safe for her to be in the palace, especially since I spent the better part of my stay under armed guard."

"That may be so, but Rayna tried to see you, twice. She will not tell me what happened, but she was quite upset."

"Mister Kendrick, I only learned about this tonight. So much has changed since we left. I do not recognize any of the guards and most of the staff has changed. All the more reason we need to leave, and I need to ask you something." Studying the baker's face, Kai hoped the man still trusted him with his daughter. "Before I ask, you should know I love your daughter; more than my own life, which is why I come to your house at such an hour. I believe we must leave. For her safety more than mine. I hope to return, as there is important business I must see to its end. Through it all, remember that I love your daughter."

"Ask your question, Prince Kai." Levi gave him a reassuring smile. "I have heard the rumors around your disappearance, but I know why you left—for the cure. My daughter would not explain why you were gone so long or if you planned to stay, but I trust my daughter. You are most likely my future king, but you are much more to my family. I have never felt less than equal around you, and for that, I am grateful. Your kindness to my daughter, a girl below your status, tells me the kind of king you will become."

Kai took a deep breath. "Mister Kendrick, please trust me when I say that I will keep your daughter safe, but I cannot promise when she will come back."

"Ask your question," Levi repeated.

"Sir, I would like to ask for your blessing in marrying Rayna."

"Son, I know my daughter's heart, and I believe I have seen enough to know yours. Never in all my days have I seen two people more right for one another. You have my blessing. Whatever trouble you are in, I know you love her, and she loves you. I just hope that is enough to hold you together."

"Thank you, sir." Kai shook Levi's hand. "I am afraid we need to leave right away."

Levi nodded and rejoined his wife and daughter inside. Rayna said her goodbyes. Dot kissed her daughter on the cheek. "I love you, my dear, remember what I told you, whatever troubles you face, they are best handled together. Please take care of my daughter, Prince Kai." The baker's wife touched his shoulder.

Kai offered the best smile he could muster. "I promise."

"I love you too, mama." Rayna wiped a tear from her cheek and hefted a leather bag over her shoulder. Smoke darted into the night. Rayna looped her fingers between Kai's and followed him across the yard.

Considering they had not spoken in days, he was thankful that she came without question, but he was surprised when she pulled her hand free of his. He tried to catch her eyes, but she kept them on the ground as they stuck to the shadows. "What is wrong? he asked.

Rayna did not respond until they were father from her parent's home. "Do you still love me?"

"Of course, I love you! Why would you . . ." The kiss with Nola smacked him in the face. Rayna knew. She must have seen them together.

Before he could explain, they spotted Yulia. "Why the rush?" Yulia questioned when they reached the bare trees of the apple orchard.

"There is no time to explain, Riome discovered a plot to kill the King and I fear things may get worse before they get better." Kai marched toward the center of the orchard. "I must get Rayna somewhere safe. If everything goes in my favor, I will save Iver, either way, I will not let Rayna suffer the Queen's wrath. I have only tonight learned the queen's new guards regard Rayna as a threat. They spoke of questioning Rayna. Yulia, can you give us a cover? Fog. Maybe even snow."

Yulia rolled her hands over and over. Washing one over the other, she pushed outward, and Kai saw fog flow into the orchard from beneath her feet. Stepping around the apple orchard, she intensified her movements while pushing and pulling at the sky. The temperature dropped with the developing moisture. The thick clouds overhead began to weep with fat snowflakes.

Kai looked to Yulia. "I can only assume you wish to remain here to watch over Riome. Have you found a Katori healer who can help her?"

"I know a woman I can trust who lives in Henley, and she plans to come tonight. Where are you two going?"

The concern in Yulia's voice resonated with his fears. He had no idea where he was going. Where would Rayna be safe? Returning to Katori was risky since Kai did not properly inform the Elders about his trip to Diu. Would they let him leave again to save his father? Not to mention he left Davi's village in embers after the battle even though his one mission from Alenga instructed him to help bring the lost children home to Katori. He could only hope Davi and the others were safe. "Chenowith, maybe? Or Albey? Maybe we could find Shane?" Everything came out as a question.

Yulia pulled Kai and Rayna in close. "Go to Benmar. Your grandfather will help you. He is probably the only man you can trust. No offense to Lucca, but as an Elder, he cannot act as a grandfather because he must remain neutral for the Katori nation."

Still keeping her gaze from Kai, Rayna nodded in agreement. "Yulia is right. Benmar will help you."

"You know the big island near the center of Baden Lake?" Yulia turned to the side. "Draw a straight line in your mind from here to home. See it in your mind, Kai." She demonstrated the action with her arm. "You will cross over this island first. Let it be your guide that you are on target for Benmar's cave. I will give you as much cloud cover as I can."

Yulia stepped back, pulling Rayna with her. Kai wanted to understand Rayna's coldness toward him, but there was no time, so he stepped into the shadows along the edge of the orchard. The newly formed clouds shrouded the area in gray gloom.

The falling snow melted into Kai's scalp. He took one last look at the towering palace and the balcony of his father's chamber before closing his eyes. Hidden within his soul, he found the golden thread of his dragon. One hand clung to his crystal while his mind embraced the braid to spark his transformation. White light beamed within his fist. His shoulders curled inward, and he felt his bones twist and expand. His skin stretched and thickened.

He embraced the change and fell into the magic swirling around him. The evolution felt natural and empowering. His spine rippled with new vertebrae, and his clothes dissolved into his change as he flexed outward. Wings unfurled from his back and his fingers grew into sharp talons. A long-spiked tail sprouted and slithered through the grass. His eyes expanded into amber orbs. His face changed to accommodate massive teeth. Kai became the silver dragon.

He restrained the urge to screech and spray fire. With amber eyes, he saw the snow float around him. Anxious to depart while the snow and fog lasted, Kai lowered his massive wing to the ground. Rayna and Smoke climbed onto his back, their weight barely noticeable. Kai cut his amber eyes back to Rayna. A look of sadness swelled in her eyes. Her behavior made him question everything—how could he possibly explain what he feared she now knew. *Would she ever forgive him?*

With one swift motion, he pushed off the ground and burst into the sky. His silver wings blended with the white and gray mist. With three beats of his wings, they were above the clouds. Midnight blue and purple expanded across the starlit sky, and Yulia's cotton clouds stretched on as far as he could see.

Behind them, he sensed the snow falling over Diu. Clear of the city, he dipped below the clouds, and Smoke barked with excitement. Rayna's legs clamped against his back. Focused on her face, he held onto his dragon form and the life he loved.

Below them, Baden Lake unfolded, dark and vast. Rain pelted his dragon face. He felt Rayna shiver. He pumped and pumped his wings up above the clouds out of the freezing winter weather.

The fresh air filled Kai's nostrils as he increased his speed, taking them higher. He felt the heat well in his throat, but he resisted the urge to belch fire. The heat of it washed back down his throat. He felt Rayna squeeze his warm neck. Her gratitude resonated with the stroke of her hands across his scales. They flew like this until he spotted land through the winter clouds.

They were flying over the big island. It was a relief to know they were on target. The rain clouds parted, and he flew lower over the lake. He watched his dragon reflection on the water. His amber eyes blinked at the sight of his massive wingspan. He flexed his back. Dropping near the surface, he let his talon skim the waves. Water splashed his belly. Far in the distance, his dragon eyes spotted the shoreline blooming along the horizon.

The approaching shore reminded Kai they must go unseen. Forcing his wings to beat harder, he climbed into the dark sky while he scanned the town of Albey and the woods to the north. A trail of lights trickled through the hills, leading deep into the forest.

Ascending the Katori Mountains, he caught sight of a bright light illuminating a vast cave entrance. A man stood in silhouette—his grandfather, Benmar. Kai flew toward the cave and landed with a thud. Rayna and Smoke crawled down his back, and he returned to his proper form.

Exhausted from the flight, Kai sat on the ground, collecting his bearings. Benmar touched Kai's shoulder. "You mind telling me what is going on? The Katori Elders are in an uproar. Milnos and Diu soldiers attacked Davi's community, and as I understand, you were there. Lucca is furious you left, by the way."

"Let him rest," Rayna insisted, using her hands to collected energy and push it to Kai, recharging him.

"Thank you, Rayna." Kai's raspy voice wavered. "Grandfather, did Davi's people come home to Katori?" He searched his grandfather's eyes, then he looked to Rayna to assess her mood.

"They are slowly moving through the mountain," Benmar acknowledged. "You should be here to witness Alenga's blessings. The gift of sight returned to all so far, and some have powers as you would expect from a Katori born going through Conahspriga. Nobody knew Alenga would grant gifts to an adult after the time of Conahspriga passed. As I understand, many are settling into the new city between Matoku and Hiowind. A few left, to where I do not know."

Kai listened to the news about his friends. It was good to hear they would be safe on the Katori side of the mountains. "I appreciate you welcoming us here, and I hope you will take care of Rayna and Smoke, but I must return to Diu."

"Wait, return to Diu?" Rayna grabbed Kai's hand. "Don't you dare leave without me. Why did you bring me back? Is this about Nola?" She studied his face.

The confusion in her eyes broke Kai's heart. He knew he planned to leave her behind, breaking a promise to face whatever came their way together. But crossing destiny was his risk to take alone, and there was no time to explain what happened that night with Nola. Not now.

Moonlight and tiny stars gleamed, bathing Kai with their power. His strength grew. Benmar stood and helped him to his feet. "Whatever your plan is, Kai, know that I will always be there. You are not alone in this. Let me help you."

Believing those words might have swayed Kai to alter his course, but deep down, he could not accept anyone else cared for Iver the way he did. Nobody understood that changing his father's fate was up to him. "I will not put anyone else at risk."

A dark shadow drifted overhead, blocking out the stars. Kai sensed the approaching black dragon—Simone. Lucca slid from her back after she touched down, and Simone transformed at his side. Saying nothing, Simone escorted Rayna and Benmar toward the cave entrance, leaving Kai alone with his other grandfather.

Lucca stared through the lingering silence. Kai could almost see his grandfather moderating his breathing to slow his racing heart before he spoke. Kai broke the silence. "Grandfather?"

"I would ask where you have been, but I already know. Diu is no place for you, grandson."

Kai looked to the others standing in the distance; their backlit silhouettes offered no emotional support. "Lucca, I do not have time for idle conversation, nor do I wish you to chastise me. What do you want?"

"I want to know what you're planning. I wanted to believe you embraced the Katori way of life. I hoped you would give up the world on the other side, yet now I find you left without telling me. You nearly started a war with Milnos and Diu against Katori in order to save Davi, and then you returned to Diu for the Winter Festival, and now I see that you have been flying over Baden Lake against the Elder's orders. I am aware King Iver is unwell and that he may soon die. Are you home for good, or do you mean to revisit him?"

The question lingered for barely a moment.

Kai clenched his jaw. "Seems to me you're hiding behind your great mountains, protected by your cliffs and avoiding the world. You should know, there is nothing I will not do. Nothing, if it will save Iver. He is my father, and I will save him. Destiny is wrong and I know I can do this now."

"I do not want to fight. Not when we have come so far, you and I." Lucca stepped toward Kai. "You speak of things you do not understand. You sound like a child. I have a nation to protect. All the Elders want is to protect our way of life. Our secrets are necessary."

"Stop trying to control everything and everyone!" Kai shouted. Irritation crawled over his skin. "Have you not learned your lesson? You tried to control my mother. Ryker. Keegan."

"I do what was best for my people," Lucca hammered back. "I had no idea Keegan would turn out the way he did. He was a good boy when I introduced him to my daughter."

Months of pent-up resentment bubbled to the surface. Every bitter thought Kai ever had toward Lucca vomited from his mouth. "You did what was best for you. Years ago, after Keegan kidnapped my mother and she reappeared in Diu—married to Iver—you could have come to her and welcomed her back into your life. No, you shunned her and the outsiders that she chose. Not once did you ask what she wanted or why she hid."

Any peace between them was now shattered. There was so much at stake, and Lucca was still trying to control the outcome. Tired of holding back, he lashed out. "When I was old enough, you could have reached out to me. Iver would have understood; you were Mariana's father. Instead, you kept secrets. You even tried to keep me from my birthright. You set the Guardians against me. Would you have cared if they'd killed Rayna— killed me?" Anger reverberated from his core. Kai clenched his fists and continued. "Why can't you let me do this one little thing for myself? I know what I am doing—I can stop his death."

Lucca was unmoved. "I am sorry you feel this way. However, you cannot change what is meant to be. Iver's fate is not in your hands."

"Don't be so sure. I know now what destiny planned, but I am in control now, not Nola. I *will* change fate. I will save Iver." Then Kai transformed into his silver dragon and disappeared into the night sky.

CHAPTER 11

Even Kings Die

Kai circled the city, floating above the clouds. Yulia's magic-induced storm still lingered, with thick clouds blocking the moonlit sky and covering Diu in snow. His dragon-wings floated on the wind. Round and round he went. His amber eyes focused on the king's chamber. His father's room—Iver was alone. Dawn was coming, and he needed to land while the snow still fell.

Kai dove through the night. He pushed his wings tight against his body, wind streaming around his aerodynamic form. At the last moment, he swept his wings wide, halting his descent. Seconds before his claws touched the balcony outside his father's chamber, he transformed back into his proper form.

His heart pounded with emotion. Kai thought of his father's withered, frail body. Nola had denied him access to Iver's chambers before, but tonight he was determined to see his father. Even if this would be the last time, he wanted to say goodbye.

Kai gathered his strength and gave one last prayer to Alenga to help him. "Please hear me, Alenga, change my fate. Let me save my father."

The pounding of his heart slowed, and he pulled the balcony doors open without a sound. The dank room smelled foul. Death lingered in every corner. Sickness dripped from the bedsheets. Studying his father's gaunt and pale face, Kai approached and touched his father's hand. Clammy.

Iver opened his eyes. Hazy eyes peered up at Kai. "Son, is that you?" His raspy voice begged for an answer.

Kai's heart broke at the sight of this once great man. His muscular form was now skin and bone, near death. "Yes, father. I am back. Come to make you well."

Visions are a terrible thing: gift or curse, Kai was unsure. Knowledge is power, something he learned at an early age, but knowing did not necessarily tell him how to change things. Still, he was not prepared for this horrible moment etched across his spirit. Anxiety swelled, and his heart pounded violently. His hands trembled.

No amount of preparation could squelch the sick feeling. Kai had to believe Alenga showed him the next moment, not to scare him, not to trap him, but to empower him. It was a risk to let the vision unfold. While he did not know who would wield his blade, he felt it necessary to let it play out. He thought of Riome's seed planted as a key to free his mind.

A key in the lock clicked and the door opened. Light from the hallway cut through the room, blinding him momentarily. The silhouette stepped forward, and Kai saw Nola's familiar form. Kai turned his face towards his father. It was time. He leaned on the bed to listen to Iver's labored breathing.

"How did you get in here?" she snarled, but then she closed the door, and Kai heard her lock it.

The room swelled and Kai felt a thickness press on his mind. "You came, my dear," Nola spoke with a new tenderness. "We have longed for this moment. Remember the commitment you made, and the promise hidden deep within your mind. I am your queen, and you promised to be true." She approached and leaned into his side.

His mind felt like it was drowning in the lilt of her voice. The memory of a command given. All the seeds within his mind bloomed at once. Obey—Kill the king—Choice—Save the king. Her warm hand pressed into his shoulder and slid down his arm; together, they withdrew the dagger from the scabbard on Kai's hip. He felt the energy flow from her touch.

Kai thought about the blade in his hand, and he felt her guiding him. "I remember, my queen, all the words you told me."

She squeezed his hand with her own. Fear and faith battled within Kai's soul. Then he heard these words again. Riome's face, Nola's face, Nola's voice:

See the light dance in my eyes; I lead you by the hand.

Unravel the string to break the ties, there is power in a grain of sand.

Time does not wait for thee; remember, I am not your kind.

Before the hands of time stop; unlock the key to free your mind.

Candlelight flashed across his blade. The palm of his hand began to sweat as Nola's grip tightened. The memory of her words continued to guide his will. The tightness in his soul loosened. A tiny speck of light awoke his mind. Broken were the ties of her commands.

I love my father.

He angled the point downward and tried to resist Nola by pulling the blade away from his father, but her white-knuckle grip forced the dagger forward. Kai pulled it back again; his mind became cloudy and lacked focus. Nola leaned into him, and he felt a strange power press against his mind. The dagger eased toward Iver again. Kai felt her breath on his ear. "Make this easy, Kai."

Riome's warning echoed in his mind.

You may never be free of her.

Before he could stop her, she plunged the knife into Iver's rib cage to the hilt. He felt the warm blood oozing from the wound. His mind suddenly free, he gleaned the injury; she had missed the heart.

I am sorry, father.

Nola yanked the blade free. Her vile green eyes glared at Kai. Her lip curled into a sly grin. "You've made this too easy, Kai. Thank you." Nola ran and opened the door; the blood-covered blade glinted in the light from the hallway.

"HELP! HELP! The king is dead. Murderer! TRAITOR!" she yelled for all to hear. "Kai has murdered the king!" She held the knife in the air.

Behind him on the wind, Kai heard a voice.

Run, boy. Fly away.

Was he hearing voices now? The open balcony beckoned, but there was no one there. He could not very well transform into a dragon and fly away with Nola watching. From the hall, dogs barked and men shouted. Without a moment to lose, Kai shoved Nola through the doorway. She fell to the floor. Kai bolted down the hallway with the guards and Nola in pursuit. Tears ran down his face as he punched the first set of guards and kicked them away, darting down the stairwell. More men charged him on the next landing, and others descended with Nola hot on their heels.

"Take him!" she ordered. "Kai killed the king!"

Two men blocked his path, swords drawn, bringing Kai to a halt. Before he could disarm one of them, a Mryken guard dog pounced against his backside, knocking him into the wall. The beast latched onto Kai's arm, and Kai yelled in pain as the animal's teeth dug into his skin. He reached out with his mind to call the dog off. The Mryken let go and stood next to Kai, but it did not matter—more men charged him.

From behind, someone punched Kai in the head, pitching him forward. His vision filled with stars as another man landed a strike to his ribcage. He fought back but there were too many. Guard after guard surrounded him, swords at the ready. The Mryken growled in Kai's defense and Kai ordered the beast to stand down.

"Arrest him!" Nola handed the guard the blood-soaked blade, Kai's initials on the hilt.

Heartbroken, Kai's eyes fell into a trance as he looked down at his blood-stained hands. He had done it—killed his father. The voices of the guards swarming around him echoed distantly in his head. One guard shackled his wrists, then two men yanked him by the arms and hauled him down the hallway. He remembered little of the winding stairwell to the dungeon. Even as they removed his chains and his sad form crashed onto the cold stone floor, he was still in shock.

Above him, he heard the chiming of bells—death bells for his father. The thought made him retch until he dry-heaved and collapsed in the corner. He pressed his hand to his broken heart and felt his crystal beneath his shirt. His little piece of Katori, missed by the careless guards. He removed the chain and tucked it into a hidden leather pocked hidden within this boot.

Guards outside his cell speculated, but he did not have the will to listen to their rumors. "Did you really kill the king?" one of them asked with a laugh.

Recognizing their Milnosian accent, Kai stared frozen at a dark spot on the floor. These men were not from Diu, and they most likely were here because of Regent Maxwell. Confiding in any of these men would not serve him well.

They did not leave him for long. A beast of a man entered his cell, all muscle and mass. Kai noticed a tattoo on his arm—the Milnos raven and an iron skull, *this man belongs to the Iron Skulls.* Kai gulped in fear backing away from the man, but it did not matter. The guard beat him more than questioned him, and the few words he did say were thick with Milnosian brogue. Kai took his beating in stride; he cared little for his own life now. There was nothing worth living for now that Iver was dead and the Katori would no longer trust him. He was even sure Rayna would hate him for abandoning her—again.

The next man to enter Kai's cell took a different approach, asking him how he could murder his own father. The man wore a Diu captain's uniform, but he had no sword on his hip. His seasoned gray hair and chiseled jawline held a controlled demeanor and reserved tone. Still, Kai kept his eyes on his hands. He could not face this man.

"Speak, boy. Why did you kill the king? I was hoping you could speak to me, or they will send in another to beat the answers out of you. Who helped you enter the king's chambers? Where have you hidden Iver's body?"

Kai's silence infuriated the captain, but still Kai said nothing. The man's questions danced around his head but made little sense. No tears fell; he was empty. Nothing felt right. How could he have failed? He had been so certain he could change his destiny, that he could change Iver's fate and save them both. Was this punishment for challenging fate? How could this vision be any different than saving Drew or anyone else?

Nevertheless, every hour they sent in a man to beat or question him. Over time their words seemed jumbled and unreal. He felt numb and broken, inside and out. By the time a familiar face came into Kai's cell, he could hardly see. His eyes were swollen, his ribs broken, his entire body ached, but he did not care. He wanted to lay down and die. He deserved to die.

"Sorry I did not come sooner," he heard Cazier's voice echo across the stone cell. "The queen is distraught over the loss of Iver, but I know it is all show. She called the council together, demanding the guards walk us through what happened. Meanwhile, the Regent had the freedom to oversee your questioning, and this is the first time they let me through." He paused, then asked, "What happened, Kai? All you had to do was stay in Katori or hide in my tower until we had our proof from Milnos."

A warm tear rolled down his bruised cheek. "You wouldn't understand," Kai started, "I thought I could . . ." He coughed, and a sharp pain stabbed him in the side.

"Riome warned you not to return. Unless you give me something, I doubt I can help you, "Cazier pleaded, lowering his head to Kai. "Who helped you get back into the palace? Did you use the secret passageways, but more importantly, who was with you? Confide in me, and I may yet help you."

Tears streaked through the dried blood around Kai's puffy eyes, and he tasted it on his lips. He coughed blood, trying to speak. The look on Cazier's face was utter disbelief. As Kai tried to lift his head from the stone floor, he felt dizziness take hold, and he blacked out.

Kai lingered in and out of consciousness, waking occasionally to find himself alone and wallowing in a pool of his own blood. When he finally found the strength to sit up, he looked around his cell. Five-by-ten, dank, dark, moldy. Likely his final resting place. There were no windows, and the only light came from the hallway outside the iron bars. The small drain in the floor stunk of vomit and piss.

There he sat for two days with no food, only a bucket of filthy water. In the silence, his demons plagued his mind. Over and over, he saw the blade slide into his father's chest, the blood spilling from the wound, Kai helpless to stop the flow. Tormented by what he had done, Kai begged for death, wondering why they had not strung him up the first day.

When Grand Duke Dante Carmelo appeared at his cell, Kai wept all over again. The reduced swelling on Kai's face gave him a clear view of his old friend, but Dante's eyes held no kindness.

"The evidence is irrefutable—you are a traitor. What in Alenga's name did the Katori people do to you?" Dante asked, but he did not wait for an answer. "Clean him up. The council will have words with him before sentencing."

The Grand Duke left with no other words.

The next man entered. Kai winced as the guard came close. "I would take my turn beating you, traitor, but they want you able to answer for your crime. Undress," the guard ordered. "I will be back."

Kai did as he instructed, stripping down to his undershorts. The man returned, hefting a large barrel of water. "Bathe."

Thankful the beatings had stopped, Kai approached the open barrel. His father's blood still stained his hands, embedded into the creases. There was no time to weep—he dipped them into the cold water and scrubbed his face and hands the best he could before washing his chest and emptying the remaining contents over his head. He tried to rinse away as much of the stench as he could.

The waiting guard handed him fresh clothes: a white shirt with black trousers. Everything stuck to his wet body. His broken spirit begged for more rest, but the guard shackled him and escorted him from his cell, forcing him up the steep, towering stairs. Each step was a struggle, every breath painful.

Joined by additional guards, they escorted Kai to the grand ballroom. He entered the center archway and was shocked by the number of people there. The guard at his back shoved him hard. The blow rippled through his ribs, causing him to stumble. Righting himself, he took in those in attendance.

On the dais, Queen Nola sat with Aaron to her right and Seth to her left. Seth's red eyes and distraught expression hurt Kai the most. Dante and Cazier stood to the side, unwilling to look him in the eye. Sigry stood arms crossed near the windows, his face stern and unforgiving. He did not see Riome—not at first, not until he gleaned the secret passage. Her expression was solemn, but at least she was there. Nearly a dozen lords of the land stood glowering at his arrival, their attire more suited for war rather than a social gathering at court. The remainder of the grand room was a mix of Diu and Milnos soldiers standing at attention in their armor.

Grand Duke Dante Carmelo spoke first. "Kai Galloway, you have been found guilty of murdering your father, King Iver Galloway." The man's tone was a mix of grief and anger. "Before we pronounce your sentence, we want to know who helped you. We know you were not alone. It is our belief that another person helped you infiltrate the palace. Your room was empty several hours before the murder, and you were nowhere within the palace. Before the murder, nobody saw you enter the king's chambers. Queen Nola claims she locked the door, and the guards attest to her unlocking the chamber doors while they were on rounds when she found you. Did Kendra give you her key?"

There was nothing Kai could tell them. He had come alone and entered from the balcony, a feat he knew Dante would find impossible given the five-story elevation. With nothing to say, Kai stared at the bottom step of the dais.

"Tell us what happened, Kai?" Master General Cazier pleaded. "Who took Iver? Cousin, please, tell us where you have hidden Iver's body."

The pain in his cousin's voice shattered Kai, but he held his emotions in check. He had no answers for them. Nothing they would believe, anyway. He wanted to beg Cazier's forgiveness, but there was no use — he had done it. Brainwashed or not, he was guilty.

The crowd roared in anger, calling for war on Katori; men banged their swords to their shields. Kai looked at his hands; specks of blood outlined the edges of his fingernails. Whatever sentence they announced, he deserved. Ready to hear his fate, Kai raised his eyes to meet Nola's. She was stern and unforgiving, but Kai saw the glint in her eyes. They both knew the truth; he had not been alone in his father's room. Nola was as much to blame as he.

Seth bolted upright; his white-knuckled fists balled in anger. Tears spilled down his cheeks. Unable to control the anguish boiling within, he stormed down the steps and pounded Kai's chest. "I hate you. I hate you. I HATE YOU!"

Unable to respond, Kai stood there and took every painful blow. Sweat formed on his head as Seth struck his broken ribs. He bent in pain, but he still refused to beg for his brother's forgiveness. Cazier pulled Seth away and escorted him out. Sounds of his brother's torment echoed from the hall.

Dante cleared his throat. "Kai Galloway, if you would name your accomplice, you would be sentenced to life in prison rather than be sentenced to death. Please, boy, who was with you? Who stole our king's body? Do you not deny these accusations?" the Grand Duke begged one last time.

Lost in a daze, nothing made any sense to him.

"If you will not give us what we ask, you are hereby sentenced to death by hanging. You have two days to get right with your maker. May Alenga forgive you, because I cannot. Guards, take him away," Dante ordered before storming out of the grand ballroom, unwilling to look at Kai a moment longer.

Hearing his sentence did not scare Kai as much as he thought it would. Instead, it was a relief. His eyes caught a glimpse of pride flicker across Nola's face. She had won, and he had helped her. Everything she had ever said to him rang in his ears. Her instructions to kill Iver, her profession of love, even her kissing him—all of it came flooding back. He had been a fool to think he could stop her.

The memories made him sick, but he held back his urge to vomit. There was no way he could prove she was involved. Iver was dead by his blade. The proof stained his hands, not hers. By the time he returned to his cell, he again felt sick to his stomach. Alone in the dark, he sat, saddened by what had happened and confused as to how he was so foolish to fight fate—because, for the first time, he lost.

CHAPTER 12

Lost at Sea

Lack of sleep corrupted Kai's senses, and the appearance of a dark silhouette startled him. The flicker of flames danced on the walls, the iron gate, and the guard. The man unlocked the door and stepped inside. Although Kai was unaware of the time, it felt too early to be morning. He braced himself for another beating.

The guard leaned against the wall opposite Kai, and his metal armor scrapped the stone. Kai sat up to get a better look at the man. He had seen him before, days ago—one of the first to beat him until he passed out, a Milnos captain covered in battle scars with little desire to listen to any protesting Kai tried on the first day. The man who broke him in more ways than one.

The guard's lack of conversation did not surprise him, but his hands-off approach left Kai uneasy. He did not know why the man only stared until he broke their long silence. "Well done, my boy, well done. I knew you had my darkness. Killing a king, impressive, and your father to boot. Well, stepfather. I hope you know you started a war. Milnos warriors are pouring into Diu every day with plans of attacking Katori."

Kai looked at the man in confusion—until the stranger's face and body started to twist and change. Before his eyes, the guard standing in front of him morphed into Keegan. Pale pink scars covered parts of his face, still fresh from the burns inflicted months ago by his grandfather Lucca. But clearly, Keegan was healing.

"Why are you here, Keegan?" Kai snarled. "Have you come to gloat?"

"My, no! I have come to offer you aid." Keegan knelt and grabbed Kai's arm. The sensation of power coursed into Kai as he felt the healing power of a Kodama ripple through his body. His ribs healed, his vision restored, his broken hand mended. Every cut and broken bone made whole again.

His strength returned, Kai stood and backed away. "Why would you heal me after everything that happened two months ago?"

Keegan stood up and gleamed with delight. "We should not dwell on the past right now. Not while everything I have ever wanted is with our grasp. You did more in a single night than I managed to do in decades. Diu blames Katori for brainwashing you, and Milnos is all too willing to crush, well, anyone."

Visions of war and chaos filled Kai's mind, weighing heavily on his shoulders. "It will never come to war. The Master General and the Grand Duke will stop this madness. The Katori Elders will force Diu to see reason, that I was only visiting my mother's country for the first time in my life."

"Son, you are trying to convince the wrong man. And honestly, anything you say now will only prove the point—you care more for protecting the Katori than your Diu countryman. Men prepare to march toward the Katori Mountains to seek out any Katori they can find. Your dear Kendra is a fellow cellmate, only five cells down from you this very moment, now wanted for treason. The Diu council believes she helped you. Word is spreading through the kingdom; Kai Galloway is a traitor. Fort Pohaku has orders to lead ships in mass around to Katori."

Knowing Kendra shared his fate weighed heavy on his heart. Kai was so focused on trying to change his fate that he did not consider the ripple effect to those around him. "And this pleases you, why?"

Keegan chuckled. "This means war on Katori. They will have no choice but to defend themselves, and I can tell you they will win—but at a cost. The world will discover magic, and the common man will be on the wrong side of its power. No longer a myth or mystery. Even among my Caroco countrymen, they have no real idea the depths of our power. The fear I instill keeps them on a short leash, and our secrets do not extend beyond their shores. Now all will feel the full force of our might. The fear of the Caroco people will be compounded a hundred-fold around the world. None know the might of the Katori nation, but they will, everyone will. They will shutter in fear."

Kai refused to believe it. "Katori will never reveal its true power. The Katori Elders would not allow magic to dominate this world. I believe they will fight back, but not with obvious magic."

"If I had known killing a king would result in war, I'd have killed Iver years ago. Join me, Kai, and together we can rule. We can put the Katori people where they belong, in a position of power. No more hiding on our side of the world."

Kai shook his head in refusal. "I will not join you, Keegan." He thought of his crystal hidden within his boot, unsure how he could use it to send the man away.

"I was afraid you might say no." Keegan's finger touched Kai's forehead. "In due time, my boy, in due . . ."

Everything went black as Kai collapsed.

◆ ◆ ◆

Sunlight poured through a bank of windows. Kai blinked. He felt rested as he sat up. The space was a wooden masterpiece; the craftsmanship was like nothing he had ever seen. He assumed he was in the captain's quarters of a ship. The toss of the vessel was rougher than he expected from a boat crossing Baden Lake. He rose to look out the wavy glass. Dark blue waves churned behind the ship with no land in sight. He opened the window, and the salty ocean air assaulted his nose.

He was not on Baden Lake, but on the open sea. Wondering how far out they were, he gleaned the distance. Not so much as a sliver of land developed along the horizon; the shore was beyond his natural ability. All he could do was base his location on the sun's angle and Keegan's mention of Caroco. If they boarded in Port Anahita, he could only hope they had yet to pass Fort Pohaku. *There must be a way off this ship,* he thought.

An abundance of anger brimmed in Kai's chest, making it difficult to breathe. A deep, hollow desire pulled his soul down to a level of hate he never felt before. His mind bubbled with thoughts and feelings he could not understand. A tingling sensation sent goose flesh down his arm, and claws surged from his fingertips and then retracted as if a figment of his imagination. Kai winced in pain but held in the cry. Something was wrong, but he did not know what.

Instinctively he reached for the crystal he wore around his neck—it was gone. He thought back, he checked his boot—missing. Keegan must have taken it to prevent Kai from using his magic to escape. As the tightness subsided, he gleaned every inch of the ship, gathering intel on his captors. The vessel held heavy armaments, thirty-two cannons, and over one hundred men. The cargo was laden with weapons, gold, and jewels.

On deck, Caroco men crewed the ship while Katori Weathervanes created a substantial breeze to propel them across the ocean. On the ship's bow, Keegan stood focused on his outstretched hand while he held Kai's crystal in the other.

Kai let go of his sight and slumped against the desk. An overwhelming level of frustration made his head hurt. Rubbing his temples, he turned toward the window. As the pain subsided, he felt a lightness return to his soul. Each breath came easier, and the anxiety passed.

"Good, you are awake." Keegan strolled into the cabin, startling Kai. "How do you find your accommodations? Or rather, my quarters?" He approached the bank of windows but left a respectable amount of space between them.

"You stole my crystal. Return it," Kai insisted.

Keegan ignored his plea. "We sail to Caroco to collect reinforcements and continue to stoke the battle that is about to consume this world. But more importantly, once there, I will show you how the rest of the world should bow to our greatness. You will come to understand how life as a Katori should be. Let war tear this part of the world to pieces, and then we can collect the broken bits and rebuild it as we see fit."

This could not be happening. Kai searched his mind for an answer. There had to be a way of escape.

"I have no interest in being a god, Keegan," he finally spat. "Return my crystal and let me go. If there is going to be a war, I must try and stop it. Or at least be there to fight."

Keegan laughed. "And on what side will you stand? Diu is a large country but weak. They have never stood alone in any battle—not without the mighty Katori dragons or the powerful Nebea supporting them. Or will you stand with your Katori brethren, who indubitably will crush their neighbors even if Milnos comes to their aid?"

Kai choked on the picture of Diu at war because of his foolish attempt to fight destiny. Had he stayed in Katori, his father's death would not be his fault. His father might have died, but not by his hand, and his mother's people would not be blamed. He let his eyes fall on the waves behind the ship once more.

Kai did not hear Keegan leave. The shifting sun and hunger led him to search his room. The door was locked, but he found wine and rum in a wooden rack, a mound of fruit on a silver tray, and a loaf of bread wrapped in cloth. No water. Desperate for sustenance, he ate a hunk of bread and two apples, tossing the cores into the sea.

A third apple rested in his hand; he wanted to eat it, but visions of Rayna caught in his throat. He had abandoned her. She was safe, but the last moment they shared was abandonment. He promised they would never be apart, yet he left her behind. Had he been so desperate to confront his fate that he let his ego blind his ability to trust the one person who trusted him the most?

Thoughts of her and their brief but tremendous happiness pang his heart. Years of wishing they could be together had been within his grasp, and he wasted it. So many times he had chased after danger or put her in harm's way; she deserved better. Maybe being with Keegan was what he deserved—a captive in a strange land.

Before he could wallow too deep, the cabin door opened and a woman entered. Kai knew her instantly. The curve of her face, the shape of her eyes, and the bounce in her dark brown hair. Rayna's mother brought in a tray of cooked food. The hatred in her eyes swelled with tears. "I would kill you myself if I could," she professed. "but Keegan would have my head. I blame you for the death of my daughter."

"Blame Keegan, he ordered her execution," Kai thundered back. "Not that you did anything to stop him or the Weathervane ordered to strike her tree with lightning." He did not know her name, and his wonderment must have shown.

"My name is Fenia," she offered. "Rayna's father is Demir. We were not good parents, but she was still our blood." Her honey-colored eyes stared through him.

Kai felt Fenia's anger, and he could see her broken spirit. Rayna's loss weighed heavy on this woman. She may not have raised her daughter, but there was something akin to love there. Compelled to spare her continued pain, he sat on the edge of the desk. "Rayna lives," he spoke softly. "After you all fled, we dug her from the earth where she hid under her burnt tree. She was barely breathing, but alive all the same."

Fenia darted to his side, and she grabbed his shoulders. "Don't lie to me for sympathy. I will not harbor my daughter's killer. I will kill you or see it done when I get the chance."

"I speak the truth." He pushed her away and slipped around the desk. "Do you think I could stand here knowing her murderer stood on deck? I would fight Keegan with my dying breath because I could not live without her."

His words sank deep into the Fenia. The shift in her expression bounced between joy and sorrow. "I still will not help you. This life is not for the weak. The one rule in the real world is a kill or be killed. Denmir and I made a mistake following Keegan, but we owned it. When Rayna was born, we had two choices—feed her to the sea or pay a trader to escort her to Katori. We could not let her grow up with Keegan, so we paid very well to see her safe return. My golden bracelet embedded with five jewels delivered her to her Aunt Mina."

The very thought that Fenia trusted anyone in her line of business made Kai roll his eyes. "Rayna was not delivered to Katori," he announced. "She was dumped in Port Anahita with little more than a blanket, her name stitched on the corner. Luckily good people raised her before the worst happened, and when the time came, I took her to Katori."

Doubt narrowed her gaze. "Don't judge me, boy. You know nothing. Nothing about me, my life, or the man we follow. Your father is a monster, but much of what he preaches, we still believe. He charmed us at the start. We only wanted to be free. Free to live and travel and not hide our true selves. Keegan wanted power, and we did not care about the cost of our choices. Our rebellion felt satisfying at first, but over time that changed."

Kai could see the history of fear in the woman but questioned her anyway. "Why didn't you leave? Go back to Katori?"

A single tear spilled down Fenia's cheeks. "You can only watch so many fellow Katori die at his hand before you surrender to your fate. Live and fight at his side or die at his touch. This life has not been all bad. I don't mind most of it; besides, I wanted to live. Still do," she insisted.

The hope that Fenia might help him gave him courage. "You must help me escape," Kai pleaded. "I need my crystal. Keegan took it from me."

She frowned. "You have no idea what you ask. And in any case, we are too far out to sea—you would not make it. A young Beastmaster, dragon or not, has no hope of flying to shore. You have flown how far—a few hours, at most?" She questioned with her tone and eyes.

"I have crossed Baden Lake, twice in one night," he declared, confident that it mattered.

Fenia cocked her head. "Should I be impressed?" She turned to face the windows. "Let me guess, you changed back and rested before your return flight? Boy, we travel with Weathervanes at the helm. They drove us south half the day into the open sea well before we turned east. Even I cannot glean the shore at our distance, and I am one of the best. We must avoid the trade routes running between Port Anahita and Fort Pohaku. It has hardly been a day, but our distance traveled is equal to nearly two days with average winds."

Hearing they had not sailed beyond Fort Pohaku was good news. Knowing his geography well, he knew he needed to get off this ship before the final point of land below Fort Pohaku. It was true, in his dragon form, he had no idea if he could traverse an ocean, but the ability to become a manta ray meant he had choices. "How long?" Kai searched Fenia's eyes. "How long until we pass the Point of Diu?"

She shook her head. "I don't know, another day, day-and-a-half. But you are not getting off his ship. Resign your fate, as we all have. Without your crystal, you cannot transform. You belong to Keegan. He will not give it back until he knows he can trust you."

"Fenia, please. I must warn Katori. Diu means to send ships around the coast. For your daughter's sake, help me."

"Do not use my daughter against me. It will not change my mind." Fenia stormed out.

Frustrated that he had pushed Fenia too hard, Kai leaned against the wooden cabinet filled with wine. There had to be another way off this ship. If she did not help him, he would make his own way. But how? He could not swim to a shore he could not see—not in his human form, anyway. And without his crystal, there was no transforming into any creature.

The setting sun dipped into the sea, scattering orange and red across the sky. Thoughts of his mother and the time she spent hiding in her dragon form without her crystal stirred an idea in Kai's mind. All those years ago in the garden, she had transformed on her own. No crystal aided her. Maybe he did not need his crystal, either. His next thought was the memory of her screams—he thought they were because she fought the change, but now he wondered if the transformation was painful without the stone. Either way, he had to try.

Imbued with new courage, Kai resolved himself to escape; with or without his crystal, he could not waste any more time waiting for Keegan to whisk him around the world. No, he needed to act now if he hoped to stop a war.

Kai jostled the cabin door's handle. It was still locked. No matter, he searched the desk for anything to pick the lock. A knife or letter opener would be ideal, but he would settle for a pin—no such luck. He tapped his fingers on the desk. There had to be something he could use.

Maps cluttered the surface. Kai slid the individual sheets into a stack, sorting the disorganization. Before him, a black feathered quill stood proudly. The find brought a curl to the corner of Kia's mouth. He snatched the pen from its holder and inspected the tip. The metal shaft and flat tip were ideal for his needs.

Of all the tricks Riome had taught him, this was the first time he felt thankful for this intrusive skill. He knelt on one knee and examined the lock. The flat point of quill fit perfectly, and with a jiggle and twist, he heard the lock click open. Free from his latest prison, Kai opened the door and peered into the passageway. It was dark but empty.

Venturing into an alcove, he saw his freedom through a bank of windows. Moonlight kissed the deck a few feet away. He took one step, then another. A glimmer of hope lifted his spirits as he stood at the forward hatch. Men worked the rigging and moved about the ship, but none noticed him. Not wanting to reveal his location, Kai twisted the handle and opened the door. Salty air assaulted his senses, and the sounds of the ocean gave him pause. He had not thought beyond his cage. Without his crystal, he was unsure about transforming, but his mother proved it was possible.

Careful not to pull too much magic from any one source too quickly, fearing it would alert the other Katori, he felt the evening breeze on his face. He extended his hand and let the moonlight absorb into his skin. Even the sea and her bounty within offered him power.

Deep within the recesses of his mind, he called upon the golden thread of creation. Multiple coils spun in his mind; all the creatures he knew floated within reach. Without his crystal, they all felt overwhelming, each pulsing with power, begging to be set free. The dragon, his first beast form, roared with life, demanding his attention. Kai embraced the cord and merged with the design of his dragon. His insides ripped and tore apart, and pain shot down his spine as the shift reconstructed his body. His head's expansion caused severe throbbing, yet the fear of discovery kept the desire to scream locked tight.

As his throat morphed and extended, the transformation felt like swallowing gravel. Each shift was like a million pinpricks rippled repeatedly over his body. The cracking of bone and growth of new mass sucked every ounce of power he had. The intense change hurt beyond belief and twisted his mind. He never imagined how much the crystal amplified his magic and softened his shift. The pain his mother suffered all those years ago finally became real.

The transformation complete, his emotions roared with anger and desire to fly free. The dragon's mind was strong, maybe stronger than his own, and it wanted control. Focused on the memory of Rayna, he held thoughts of his life close. The first beat of his wings lifted him from the ship. Men shouted. He pressed his wings down for another lift, but something—or rather, someone—landed on his back.

"Not so fast, boy." Keegan touched his scaly neck. "Easy now, Kai, let's not do anything rash, like fly away."

Kai heard a voice inside his head. It sounded like his own voice, ordering him to land on the deck. Bewildered by the instructions, he tried to flap his wings, but the voice pressed harder, and he landed on the deck with a thud. He had no control over his own body or mind.

Keegan's voice spoke to him, and he stroked Kai's dragon neck. "I must say, no Beastmaster has ever transformed without their crystal. It looked painful, but I am impressed. If I had not taken to the crow's nest, I would have been forced to shoot you from the sky."

Familiar magic whispered to Kai; his crystal was being pressed against his scales. He wondered why Keegan would offer him any kindness. "Transform back, my boy. I can't lose you yet, and there is no room on my ship for you in dragon form."

The magic within the white crystal sang to Kai. He felt the call and serenity of its power hidden within his stone. Combined with the magic from Keegan, he transformed back into his proper form. His father jumped to the deck behind him. Pride beamed on the man's face, and Kai seized the opportunity to snatch his crystal from his father's hands.

"By all means," Keegan relented, "take it. The crystal does not work for me; believe me, I tried, but you do not need it. Again, impressive. I know of no Beastmaster in our history who could transform without their stone. Sure, Weathervanes can still manipulate the climate and Stonekings can move stone, and some Kodama can heal minor cuts and wounds, but we are each limited without our crystals. You should not be able to shift."

The warm crystal dangled once more around Kai's neck. A peace emanated from the stone. "I will not stop," Kai seethed. "Every chance I get to flee, I will take it."

Keegan motioned to a massive crossbow mounted on the front of the ship. Kai remembered the weapon and how it felt getting shot with the large bolt through his wing.

"I believe you," Keegan motioned to a Caroco man who turned the weapon toward Kai and yanked it into firing position. His father continued, "Which is why, for now, you must be chained below decks. You will remain under constant supervision until we arrive in Caroco. And then, when the time is right, we will collect your mother. Maybe she can talk some sense into you. I know she is alive—well, mostly. The report I heard said that Mariana is an endless sleep."

Kai rushed at Keegan. "Leave my mother alone!"

An iron-like grip latched onto Kai's neck, and his body fell limp. "Careful, boy. Your willful nature is going to get you killed, and I have plans for you." Keegan tossed him to the ground. "I am tired of this battle between us. You will learn your place, or I will find other methods to teach you respect."

His father motioned to a nearby man who forced Kai below deck and shackled him inside a steel cage.

CHAPTER 13

Keegan's Darkness

Dawn poured through the porthole within Kai's cage. His black steel box was barely large enough to stand in and not wide enough for him to lay flat. Using all his strength, he pushed and pulled at the bars. They did not bend, not even a little. The bolts held fast and showed no signs of breaking.

Disappointed by his failure, he tugged at his shackles. His chains were heavy, even for a Katori. He studied the texture and gleaned the metal. Like his cage, the restraints were made of steel. It was beyond anything he knew. Still, he yanked on his bonds. Surely the wood would give way, he thought, but it did not budge.

"You will not break your chains," a man called from the shadows. "The powder mixed within the metal makes it harder and heavier than anything a Katori can break, even a Beastmaster like you. If you do manage to pull the bolts from the hull, you will sink the ship and drop to the ocean floor. Terrible way to die, if you ask me."

A moment later, Denmir stepped into the light.

The man's sunken eyes surprised Kai. "I know you. You are Rayna's father."

"I do not deserve that title. Twice my Fenia granted me the gift of fatherhood, and I tossed my girls away. My girls hate me, and my wife blames me for our lot in life. Sure, it was adventurous being rebels—but it did not stop at adventure, as you will soon see for yourself. Keegan has darkness I never thought possible from a Katori. Once you cross that line, you become like him, and we are all doomed."

Part of Kai wanted to care, but this Denmir made his choice—twice, for that matter. "Do not look to me for pity. You made your choice. Blame this on youth if you wish, but we both know you had a choice. Even now, you continue to follow him. But I saw you both that day on the beach. You did not kill Rayna when you had the chance. In fact, you held back when you fought me, I know it. You are not heartless like Keegan, though I think part of you does enjoy the fight."

It was clear that his words struck deep; Denmir did not hide his shame. "Fenia tells me our Rayna lives. Is this true?" He pressed his face into the bars to stare at Kai. "I must hear it for myself. I must see the truth in your eyes."

Denmir's pain ran deep, his eyes welled with tears, but none fell.

"Rayna lives," Kai acknowledged. "She was lucky. Keegan nearly killed her—or do you, like Fenia, want to blame me?" He stared back, searching the man's soul.

"I do not blame you. I blame myself. As you said, I made a choice, and it cost me dearly. It still costs me. Fenia is angry, but she knows Keegan is to blame. He ordered the lightning that struck Rayna's tree and we did nothing to stop him."

The weight of the world seemed to fall on Denmir's shoulders, and he slumped in disgrace. Silence lingered, and Kai watched the man battle his internal demons before clearing his throat and continuing. "Fenia, my dear wife, is not ready to face the truth. She still blames everyone but us. Our choices put our daughter at risk, not Rayna's love for you."

"Set me free," Kai interrupted. "If you care as much as you imply, let me go. I must warn Katori before Diu and Milnos retaliate. I have to stop this war before it starts. I must protect Rayna."

Denmir shook his head and sat quietly in the corner. "I am not here to free you; this is my shift. I am to keep an eye on you. Keegan rules us—get used to it."

Kai shook the bars, desperate to get free. "Please Denmir, I can stop what is coming if I can get free. With each passing hour, we near the point of Diu—Fort Pohaku is my last chance to escape."

Denmir returned to shadows unwilling to respond. And Kai continued to rattle around in his cage.

When the next guard thundered down the stairs, Denmir left. A man with rust-colored skin and emerald eyes towered over Kai, a head taller than the steel cage. The blue crystal dangling around his neck marked him a Beastmaster. He unlocked the cage and pushed Kai toward the stairs. "Come, Keegan has something to show you," the man insisted.

On deck, Kai was nearly blinded by the bright afternoon sunlight. Before him, the Katori Weathervanes, Kodama, and Beastmasters stood at attention. Their eyes were fixed behind him, and Kai turned to see Keegan standing by the railing.

"Time to embrace your new life, son." Keegan eyed him with pleasure. "I believe it is time for you see the effects of our power and the decisiveness of our methods. For now, you watch, but soon you will join us in battle." Keegan motioned to the Weathervanes, and he took possession of the helm.

Under their magical influence and Keegan's direction, the ship came about and surged through the water. Waves broke against the ship's prow. Worry swelled in Kai's chest. A sense of dread consumed his heart. Something terrible was coming; he could almost taste it.

Around him, he saw the others flex their muscles in preparation. Kai studied the sun and their new direction. If his assumptions were correct, they were sailing toward land. Would they make landfall? He could not help but wonder what Keegan had planned. On land, Kai had a greater chance to escape; the possibilities rolled around his head. This could not be what his father hoped to show him. No, they were not going ashore—and he did not have to wait long to learn their purpose.

At breakneck speed, Keegan's ship cut through the ocean waves. Along the horizon, a ship came into view. "Trade routes, my boy. You must learn them. Know when and where to strike. While we could take on an entire fleet, there is no use declaring war on ourselves. Instead, we need to create chaos and implicate the Katori if we hope to further incite war." Keegan explained. "Our purpose today is to send a message and drive a wedge between their two nations."

Listening to Keegan tell stories of conquest and death made Kai wonder if he would ever escape. This was not the life he wanted, but he saw no means of escape even with his crystal. For now, he would need to gain this man's trust and possibly find the opportunity to run.

The Diu pennant, a silver wolf on a field of blue, flapped in the wind above the trade ship's white billowing sails. The other vessel slowed, allowing Keegan's superior craft alongside. Kai wondered why they would yield until he noticed their flag bore the Katori colors—three golden stars on a field of white. The other captain would feel no fear coming about, allowing the would-be friendly ship to get close.

The gangplank lowered, connecting the two ships. Keegan shoved Kai in line behind four Katori Beastmasters, and they crossed to the other ship.

Joined by eight Caroco men, Keegan addressed the captain. "Fair weather we are having."

A white-bearded man with leathered skin stepped forward. "Name is Captain McCrory. We sail from Port Anahita to Fort Pohaku with supplies. May we be of service?" The captain's eyes drifted up the Katori flag whipping in the breeze and back to the strange men on his deck. Kai could almost see the realization sweep through the man's mind. Too late.

Keegan crossed the divide and latched onto the man's throat. "Captain McCrory. What cargo do you carry, truly? Food, weapons . . . gold?"

The captain's eyes revealed his precious bounty.

"Gold! How lucky are we." Keegan glared back at his men. "See to her bounty, boys. We must relieve her of her burdens before she sinks beneath the sea."

The Caroco men scattered about the ship, disappearing below deck. More men from Keegan's ship poured over the gangplank to assist in removing anything of value.

Meanwhile, Keegan continued to grasp the helpless captain by the throat. Kai could see the fear in the older man, and he knew he would not see another sunset. Keegan's grip around the captain's neck did not tighten, yet the man gasped and contorted his face, the only part he could still control, while the rest of his body drooped as if no longer attached. Lines deepened on the man's aged face as his bone structure became more pronounced and his muscles withered. Watching the lifeforce drain from this man horrified Kai.

There was no bond between Keegan and Kai, not like the one he shared with Rayna, yet he felt his father's pleasure as he sucked the lifeforce from the captain. He could only imagine the shared blood between father and son provided the bridge. The thoughts and feelings emanating from his father made Kai sick to his stomach, but he swallowed the bile down.

Covering his mouth, Kai noticed the faintest glimpse of light emanating from his father's black crystal. A stone once white, much like his own, but now the tainted crystal matched the hate and death which consumed his father's soul.

Keegan tossed the spent corpse to the deck and moved to the next victim.

When they first boarded, Kai was unsure what to expect, but his father's demonstration reinforced his need to get off this ship to warn the others, Keegan was destroying Katori goodwill. With great speed, one by one, Keegan and his men began to dispatch the crew. His father took some with little more than a touch, others with the flick and twist of his blade—all but one. When he finished, Keegan took a stance beside Kai and surveyed his handiwork, with the sole survivor kneeling before them. The man was dressed too well to be a crewman; Kai assumed he was a merchant with money by looking at his clothes and shoes.

"Padar," Keegan motioned to a nearby Weathervane. "Drop the skiff and set our survivor on his way. See that he has a strong wind to ensure his little lifeboat makes landfall today. I would hate for him to be unable to tell the tale. The Katori are the real villains—a nation of sorcerers and witches of old, come to destroy them all."

Keegan pulled the shaking man to his feet. "Tell them, tell them all. Katori comes for Diu in the coming days. We are tired of hiding from the world. Soon, you will know our superiority."

A child's scream broke the moment as Keegan shoved the man toward Padar and turned toward the entrance to the cabins on deck. A little girl had been discovered hiding inside a barrel by one of Keegan's men.

"Shall I eat her?" The bloodthirsty Beastmaster transformed into a black panther and chased the girl. Kai watched in horror as a well-dressed girl in pink—who could be no more than ten—ran toward the merchant, but the Beastmaster pinned her to the deck inches from the open arms of safety.

"Father!" she cried, squirming with fear.

Keegan knocked the panther off his prize and helped the girl to her feet. "No!" he barked. "Not the child."

Why is she so special? Kai wondered, noticing the softer expression on his father's face as he smoothed the girl's dark black curls around her face.

The little girl backed away from Keegan, and her father scooped her into his protective arms and wiped her tears. "There, there Violet, papa is here." The man soothed his daughter but kept his fearful eyes on Keegan.

"Remember, Papa," Keegan mocked, "tell Diu the Katori nation is coming for them. We will arrive in days." Keegan motioned to the dinghy, and the father did not hesitate.

Sadness and anger pounded in Kai's chest. This misfortunate ship and her crew. Was this his fault, too? He could not help but wonder. Had he not pressed fate and provoked this war, would this ship have gone unnoticed? Another burden he felt was his to carry.

As the weathervanes brought the ship about, they angled them south and provided a gust of wind to fill their sails.

There must be a way off this ship, Kai thought, praying for the souls lost today. He faced Keegan. "You are proud of this? Killing those people and provoking a war?"

"This is all I have ever wanted. For the world to feel our might, to live free and rule over the weak." Keegan laughed, and his crew joined in his celebration. Their jubilation and cheers burned Kai's soul.

He could not believe they all wanted this life; his father had to have some good left in him. After all, he did spare the child. "How can you . . .?" Kai wanted to argue but he saw little point. How could he convince any of them there was another way to live free without creating war and chaos?

"Son, we enjoyed these years, but I want more than piracy now. Always have." Keegan stepped closer. "I would not change this life. Do not think I will waste my time sitting on a throne with a ring of gold around my head. I want to rule the world, yes, but not from a chair or hiding on my side of the world. I am tired of keeping my distance; the time to strike is now, thanks to you. Seeds of mistrust corrupt even the most loyal friendships, and I say we can finally be free to live without hiding. The world looks to Katori now with new eyes. Revered by all, our nation once demonstrated peace and goodwill. I say it is time we demonstrate our might and power like we did during the Great War and the time of dragons."

Every concept felt like a slap in the face. Kai spat, "Is peace so foreign to you that you only find joy in chaos?"

The delight in Keegan's eyes turned dark and angry without warning. Kai felt his father's rage and instinctively reared back and used his fists to protect his core. "You know nothing of risk." Keegan charged Kai with intent but did not touch him. "I live with the Katori secrets, keeping to my side of the world. Those who see my greatest power live in fear. A fear so strong they would sooner end their own life than cross me. Up until recently, any who witnessed my magic firsthand were usually dead and unable to tell the tale. But now I must show the world and ensure the stories are told. I will accelerate this war to create a better world for all Katori, and all who fall in line."

Keegan gestured to his men.

"I have lost men. Your mutt Ryker killed a few of my Katori a few months back. We risk our lives every time we go out. I am mortal, my boy—I can die. Well, many have tried to kill me." Keegan laughed and pushed Kai hard in the chest. "Enough talk, take him below."

The Weathervane wind whipped around Kai. "Admiral Roark will get you one day," he muttered under his breath as the guard pulled his arm.

"What was that?" Keegan looked around, "Admiral Roark?"

A Caroco man shouted, "navy man who serves King Iver, . . ."

"I know who he is. Do you think this man could best me?" Keegan swung back around, ego danced in his eyes. "You have more faith in this man than me, after everything you know about the Katori, about me?"

Kai did his best to conceal the depth of his relationship with Roark, but the spark in Keegan's eyes told him his father saw through him. "Your pulse quickened. Most would never notice something so subtle, but I see it—I hear it. Roark means something to you. When will you ever learn? Have no ties in the world, and nothing can hurt you."

Guilt formed in the pit of Kai's stomach, devouring him from the inside out. "Leave him be!" he shouted.

"How can I prove to you I am the superior warrior if you have more faith in this Red Warrior? I will pluck this man from his bed, and hang him from the gatehouse of Diu with the Katori pennant pinned to his chest. If he is their best man, I will show them how little he can protect his people."

Renewed focus narrowed Keegan's eyes. "This man runs Fort Pohaku, let us pay him a visit. Test his mettle. Man-to-man, blade against blade. What do you say, men? Another deviation before we go home to gather reinforcements for war?"

The men cheered, and Keegan bowed to Kai, "to Fort Pohaku, post haste. We shall ferret out this man and put him on the end of my sword before we deliver his corpse to Diu and it's pretending Queen."

Bile welled in Kai's throat. What had he done? The rusty man of color grabbed Kai's arm and returned him to his prison. Once again shackled below deck in his steel cage, Kai thought about the differences between this man and the one he called father. Iver and Keegan were nothing alike, and now because of him, the good man—Iver, was dead while the other roamed free. The lack of emotion in Keegan's words raked Kai's heart. No matter how he tried, there was no finding goodness in this man. Maybe there was no white light left. Keegan's soul truly matched his black crystal. Thoughts of Roark dying because of his yammering took him to a dark place. Never before had he deliberately wanted to kill another person, but Keegan was testing his limits.

From his steel cage, there nothing he could do. Who else would suffer because of this man? Rayna, his mother? Kai had to find a way free, or Roark would become the next victim.

CHAPTER 14

Freedom

Moonlight bounced off the ocean waves and into Kai's tiny prison. Salt mist splashed through the porthole and landed in his hair. Clutching his knees to his chest, he sat pondering his next move while Keegan's ship sailed to Fort Pohaku. Heavy laden with precious bounty, they eased through the waves.

Sounds of a new guard thundered down the steps along with another figure. Fenia approached his cage. "I brought you food and water." She handed the cup and plain bread through the bars.

"You must help me, Fenia," Kai whispered. "I must warn Roark."

Fenia pressed her finger to her mouth. "Shhh, before you get us both killed. You have no more choices. You made a mistake, as we all did; now you live to serve Keegan. He is too powerful to deny, you did not ask to join his cause, but like it or not you are a part of this now, for life or death."

Her words shocked him. "I will not live my life pretending I have no other choice. Keegan might as well kill me now because I will spend every waking moment trying to escape."

Her eyes filled with worry. "You do not know what you ask. Keegan will kill me—painfully, but only after he kills Denmir before my very eyes. He already uses my husband to heal his wounds. Keegan has taken years from him to restore the damage done to his precious face. I try to

157

help heal Denmir each night, but without time on land, I no longer seem to regain my Kodama power."

The memory of his grandfather, Lucca, burning Keegan to a crisp to save them all brought a terrible sorrow. "I am sorry for Denmir."

He wanted to mention Rayna in the hopes that he could convince Fenia to let him escape, but that would be using her daughter against her, and he would not do that again.

Instead, he gulped the contents of his cup and handed it back to her. Fenia left him alone in the darkness. Alone with his questions, his choices, and his guilt.

Helpless to escape, Kai thought about Rayna. He missed her more than words. He wondered if she would ever forgive him, and he thought of what he might say if she gave him half a chance to explain. To feel close to her, he craned his neck to look out at the night sky. The full moon was a golden yellow hue. Kai whispered, "I am sorry, Rayna. I should have listened to you. I will love you for the rest of my days."

"Shut up over there," his guard called from the corner.

Kai sulked in silence, watching the moon. With each roll of the ship, he thought of their destination. He would not live like a rat in a cage. Nor would he stand by while Keegan killed Roark and started a war. As a lifelong prisoner, the thought of everyone he loved dying made him bold. He would rather die than follow in his blood father's footsteps and join him in this war.

Kai resolved that there was only one way to stop Keegan from killing Roark. He gleaned through the darkness to sense the guard; the man was asleep. Kai decided this was his chance.

His chains were anchored to a square plate that was secured to the hull by four black bolts the size of a child's fist. Placing his feet on either side, he yanked on the chains. They did not budge. Again, he tugged. Denmir's words rang in his head. *You will not break your chains.* Kai did not want to drown at the bottom of the ocean, but he would not stand by while his father murdered Roark or killed anyone else.

Kai wrapped the chains around his palms to get a better grip; for leverage, he bent his knees, pulled with his upper body, and pushed with his legs. His hands, arms, and shoulders ached from the effort. His legs began to shake, but nothing changed.

Again, he took a deep breath and pulled with all his might. Magic seeped into his crystal; power sent more than requested. Kai accepted the energy and his stone glowed brightly. The bolts held fast, but the wood groaned and creaked.

Kai's knuckles were turning white as the chains began to crush his hands. He did not stop. His legs pushed on either side of the steel plate, and he yanked with his arms. Sweat rolled down his face. Something snapped around the bolts securing the metal plate. There was no going back, he would stop Keegan, one way or another.

A crack formed. Tiny at first, then water began to trickle, and the pressure built behind the break. Kai gleaned the expanding crack; the ocean begged to come inside. The damage spread along the seam just below the waterline. One more pull and the plate would come free.

"STOP!" Fenia shouted, hopping down the stairs two at a time.

The guard rubbed the sleep from his eyes as he looked at the gush of seawater pouring in around his ankles. "Are you mad!" he shouted, scrambling up the steps in terror. "You'll kill us all!"

The ship creaked louder and groaned as the seam burst and more water began to fill the compartment. Kai grabbed the bars of his cage. "Let me go, Fenia!" His eyes begged her for mercy. "I must stop this war before it tears the world apart!"

Fenia hesitated as the ship listed to one side. Denmir bounded down the stairs into the knee-deep water. He looked to his wife; she held the keys to free Kai. Crates sloshed about in the rising water. Denmir snatched the keys and unlocked Kai's cage, then removed the shackles.

"Go," he pleaded. "Tell my daughters I am sorry."

"I am not a bad mother," Fenia said as the water reached her waist. She looked lost, as if all the life and fight had gone out of her. "We wanted to love them."

Kai looked at their sorrowful eyes. They were asking him for forgiveness, but there was nothing he could say to absolve them of their choices.

Voices shouted above, and three men came barreling down the steps. Kai ducked into the shadows and waited for them to pass. Focused on the condition of the ship, they did not see him. They grabbed tools and wood to repair the hole in the hull.

Not wanting to waste this opportunity, Kai dashed for the steps—but not before he gleaned his father's location. Keegan stood at the helm, barking orders. Weathervanes manipulated the waves to tilt the ship and lift the damaged section out of the water. Kai gripped the railing as soon as he emerged on deck. The crew was frantically scrambling to tie themselves to the masts or railings. Many of them clung to ropes, trying to reach the damaged wood with tools and metal bracings.

Without hesitation, Kai let go of the railing and dove into the water. The cold ocean water cradled him in her bosom. The memory of his mother's manta ray called to him. He needed to stay hidden, so he searched for the thread of creation. As if it had been only yesterday, he remembered the design of the majestic rays. Taking hold of the gold braid that would transform him, he lit the spark within his soul. The sequence merged with his own and shifted the pieces to fit the manta ray form.

Arms outstretched; he pointed his feet. Light burst from his crystal and enveloped him with a blue radiance. His body morphed. His skin turned dark, and wing-like fins formed from his shoulders to his feet. A tail grew.

His broad outstretched wings flapped up and down, propelling him through the ocean. Water slipped around his sleek body and washed over his gills. The possibility of reaching shore before Keegan and the exhilaration of his transformation hastened his speed. He left behind the chaos of the ship and swam for shore, ever hopeful he would find someone willing to listen to his warnings given he was not a murder.

Along the farthest reaches of his gleaning ability, he searched for the shore. He wanted to shift to his dragon, but he could not risk coming to the surface, not yet. He needed to put as much distance between him and Keegan's ship, but terrible pain began to overtake him. The cold water wracked his leathery skin. His new form was acclimated to the warm waters around the Mystic Islands, but this far south, and in the middle of winter, he could feel his manta-body going into shock. Feeling the desire to sleep, Kai forced himself to swim.

He needed his dragon. Unsure if it was possible, he searched for the golden thread of this dragon. Faint in the back of his mind, he saw the dancing coil of light.

Reach for the white light, he heard an echo in his mind.

Faith pushed on his heart. He continued to swim for the surface, faster and faster. Embracing the white light, Kai felt his soul release the manta ray, and his dragon's spark gleamed. Understanding the order of things, Kai let his mind wrap around the dragon. As his body morphed from manta ray to dragon, he burst from the ocean and soared into the sky.

Clear skies welcomed Kai's silver dragon. The deep purple glittered with millions of tiny stars. He was happy to be one of them. Just another star in the sky, according to Sabastian.

Kai's amber eyes scanned the horizon. There was no shore in sight, but he could not afford to stop. First, he spotted a ship, so he flew higher to avoid detection. Then he noticed another in the distance to his left. Scanning to the right, he saw another.

Miles apart, each ship sailed along the shipping lane between Port Anahita and Fort Pohaku . Thoughts of the trader ship sunk near this very spot pushed him faster; he could not let everyone believe that Katori had been behind the slaughter. People needed to know Keegan's desire for war. He had to warn Roark.

As darkness fell across the sky, he realized how tired he felt from hours of flying. Letting his wings rest, he floated on the wind as long as he could. Each time he pushed himself higher he could glide for miles before he sank back down to the ocean's waves.

Drifting lower in the sky, he spotted lights on the horizon—Fort Pohaku. The three points of the fort beamed against the darkness.

His wings weary, and his body heavy, he pushed harder. Each beat was exhausting, each breath brutal; he did not give up. The pounding in his head pressed into his massive skull. To keep his mind sharp, he focused on Rayna. The curve of her face, the smell of her hair. He thought of the day they met at the bakery in Port Anahita, her arrival in Diu, and their countless walks through the apple orchard.

Flying lower and lower, Kai did his best to keep the above the splashing waves. Kai glided above the water, keeping to the west of the fort. Remembering Sabastian's warning about how visible his shiny silver scales were in the night sky, he decided twenty feet from shore to let go of his dragon braid and grabbed the natural white light of his soul. His body transformed back to his human form in a flash, and he dropped into the sea.

Wave after wave rushed him toward the shore. The closer he came, the larger the swell. He was utterly exhausted as he tried to swim to the beach, and the crashing surf pushed him under. Angry ocean waves pulled and pushed and sucked him under before the ocean spat him out to the shore.

In a haze, Kai rolled along the edge of the wet beach before passing out.

♦ ♦ ♦

When he awoke, he saw the side of a man—a man he knew all too well.

"Dresnor, how did you find me?"

Kai sat up to look up and down the beach. They were alone.

His friend did not turn to look at him; instead, he asked, "Answer my question first. Are you running because you are innocent, or because you cannot face the punishment for your crime?"

Everything Kai knew twisted in his confused mind, but he had to have faith in his heart. "I swear on the name of Alenga, I am innocent. I did not kill my father."

The world needed to know the truth about what Nola and everything that happened. But first, he needed to band his friends together.

"Now you answer my question," Kai insisted. "How did you find me?"

"We are about to go to war, and you are worried about how I found you?" Dresnor curled his lip, looking disgusted at Kai. "We received word you had escaped Diu prison. The Queen insists the Katori brainwashed you. Roark was about to board a ship to sail for Katori when one of our vessels rescued a tiny skiff with a merchant and his daughter spouting talk of Katori witchery and a planned attack on Diu City.

"Now, come dawn, Admiral Roark plans to sail toward Port Anahita, rally the troops, and defend Diu. Although, I am sure he also hopes to join in the hunt for you, too. I came out here to pray to Alenga. I asked her to guide me because I am lost and do not know what I should do. That is how I found you."

Kai nodded and realized the only way his men would follow him again was through trust. Trust he needed to earn. "Dresnor, you are my closest friend. I am sorry that I have kept secrets from you. I swore to these keep secrets because I was protecting others, but now I understand we are on the verge of war. A *war I* started—and one I hope to end before blood is shed on either side."

Dresnor cocked his head. "Why should I follow you?"

There was no point in hiding his truth any longer. The only way forward was together. Kai stood and took hold of the crystal around his neck. He let the moonlight and the power from the crashing waves poured into him, which fed his magic—causing his crystal to glow. The golden thread of creation spun in his mind begging him to meld and embraced his inner dragon.

Dresnor hopped to his feet and drew his sword. "By Alenga's name," he shouted. "What manner of sorcerer are you?"

Visions of his mother's sacrifice and her years of suffering weighed on his heart. Did he have the right to expose Katori's secrets? Caught between the choice, he feared that revealing his dragon-form would only reinforce the tale of sorcery delivered by the merchant and his daughter—he would tell anyone who listened that the Katori are killers, and Kai would be one of them. He let the magic seep back to whence it came. The light in his crystal faded, and he sank into sadness. "I am no sorcerer. I thought . . ." He let his words fall on the sand. "It was only a parlor trick."

Dresnor lowered his sword, but only slightly. "But how did you make the stone glow?" he asked, pointing his sword once more at Kai's chest, now only inches from the dangling crystal.

What an interesting question, but it was the wrong question. He tucked the stone beneath his shirt and pushed the tip of Dresnor sword away. "I am me, the boy you helped shape into a man. The man you fought beside at Port Anahita. What you do not know is that I am Katori-born. Iver was not my father, but he loved my mother, and he helped her hide me from the man we all know as Keegan—my birth father. The very same man who attacked the Diu palace with Landon; the leader of the Caroco army who sent men to kidnap or possibly kill Aunt Helena in Port Anahita if Tolan had not stopped them."

Disbelief and shock overtook Dresnor's face, and Kai could only imagine the questions that were forming on the man's tongue. "I do not believe you. But why would you lie? Is this part of the brainwashing from Katori? How did they convince you of this nonsense?" He shook his head, refusing to accept Kai's story.

"Trust me, Dresnor, this is not a lie. I still consider Iver to be my father, and Iver told Cazier the same night he told me. The Master

General can attest to the truth of this, but we there is no time for all these questions."

Dresnor relaxed but kept his sword unsheathed. "But, I have so many questions, yet they seem small in comparison to the chaos surrounding you. So, if you did not kill Iver, who did?"

"Nola," Kai answered flatly. "She is the sister of Landon Panier, the illegitimate daughter of King Bannon Panier. Her desire is to avenge her father by manipulating, well, everyone. She plans to put Aaron on the Diu throne, but she needed Iver dead and me out of the way—either dead or in prison."

"What proof do you have?" Dresnor demanded. "If I understand what I have heard, you were found in Iver's room, your hands covered in blood, and Nola witnessed you stabbing him."

He knew his word was not enough after all the secrets and the lies; proving his innocence would be impossible against a queen's word. "Nola manipulated me with some potion and a spell, but I have no tangible proof, only my word. I did not do this. Nola wielded the knife, put it in my hand, but I did not thrust the blade. She alone shoved the dagger into my father. She brainwashed me. Cazier and Riome know this to be true."

"So, if you did not kill him, and you were all alone, except for Nola, who took Iver's body?."

The look on his friend's face did not make sense. Those words, that phrase rang in the back of his head. He vaguely remembered the council asking the same question. Kai's jaw dropped, bewildered. "What do you mean, who took Iver's body?" The last he remembered his father's body lay in a pool of blood, dying. "I ran. My father was still in his bed when I pushed Nola into the hall and took out the first set of guards. At the bottom of the stairwell, more guards cornered me—too many. Nola ordered my imprisonment."

"You had to be working with someone, or someone followed you or . . ." He shook his head, visibly sorting the different possibilities. "This does not make sense. Well, I find this all impossible. You may not know who took Iver, but you were not alone. Someone else was there, helping you." Dresnor's brow furrowed. "There had to be."

It was difficult to recall every second of that moment, but the sound of a voice whispering—run boy, fly away, came to mind. "Keegan," Kai suggested with a bit of uncertainty. "He stands the most to gain. He wants this war. He broke me out of my cell, put me on a ship. He is on his way here as we speak; he plans to assassinate Roark and make it look like it was the work of Katori. He is intent on starting another great world war."

The confused look on Dresnor's face coincided with Kai's feelings. Keegan was a crazy man, and it was up to Kai to put an end to this war before it started. "Look, Dresnor, before I turn myself in, I want to see Rayna one last time."

"Turn yourself in?" Dresnor cocked his head. "I thought you were innocent?"

"I am," Kai reassured him, "but somehow between now and everyone reaching Diu, I must find proof. Maybe I can find my father's body and the person who took him. I must stop this war before it starts, before minds are too clouded with hate and power nobody remembers or cares about the truth." Kai thought about his time on the vessel. He had searched every part of the warship. If Iver had been there, Keegan's ego would have been keen to gloat. "His body was not on Keegan's ship, not that I saw, which means Iver could still be here on the mainland."

"You obviously have a plan . . . So, let's hear it."

The look between them darkened, giving Kai an eerie feeling. Did his Kempery-man dare share his thoughts? Not that he had much of a plan, only the makings of one. "I must go to Henley. I need Drew by my side. He needs to know the truth, and maybe he can help me search. Find Iver's body and proving Nola's guilt is the only way to stop Diu and Katori from tearing each other apart." He knew this could be the biggest mistake of my life, but he had little to lose. "Then I hope to go to Chenowith before reuniting with Rayna. She is with my grandfather."

"So," Dresnor chuckled, "this grandfather character, he does exist? I was sure he was another lie?"

"Of course, he is real. What did you think I made him up to trick you?" Kai realized what he said, and Dresnor's eye roll confirmed it. He had lied a lot. "I am sorry, Dresnor, my stories were for a good reason. I wanted to travel to Katori and get to know my mother's people, and they would never let an outsider enter. I had no choice but to leave you behind."

The wheels spun behind Dresnor's curious eyes. "What would you have me do? There is no way you can go to all those places before Roark or Nola catch you. It's well over two hundred miles from here to Diu city. Four days in the saddle, and you have no horse. Two-and-a-half days by ship, and you have no vessel."

There had been little time to develop a strategy—Kai wished Tolan were here. He was the strategist, the man who could see events unfold without visions from Alenga. This felt like a chess game, and he was out of practice. The crashing waves beat the beach, and the making of a plan came together.

"I need you to convince Admiral Roark to meet me outside of Diu city on the bridge over Stone River, below the dam. Tell him I mean to surrender, but only with everyone present. Say in four days. If he is already planning to hunt me down, he need not look anywhere but on that bridge. It is good he is already planning to bring his army; we will need an army if we mean to take back Diu. Milnos men have overrun the city, and I plan to stop them. But neither Milnos nor Katori is the real threat; Keegan and his Caroco men are."

Dresnor's eyes narrowed, pondering the request. "How am I to convince Admiral Roark not to kill you on sight? If I am honest, I nearly killed you myself when I found you. Our history is the only reason you are not dead or in chains. I needed to know why you killed your father. I hoped you would confide in me and tell me where you hid Iver. Now you tell me this foolishness, that you are not Iver's son. Your new truth makes me trust you even less."

The realization that everyone wanted to see him dead made it clear how unlikely anyone would trust him again. "I did not kill my father, I told you, Nola made me hold the knife . . . she was the one who drove the blade into Iver." The words twisted in his mouth. "Please, Dresnor, you must trust me. Tell Admiral Roark that Landon Panier means to become the next king of Milnos. Remind him that Tolan, his son, was meant to wear the crown in my stead. I pray his son is well. Also, if there are a legion of Milnos men in Diu, doing her bidding, maybe he should question Nola before he seizes me."

"No, I don't owe you anything." Dresnor moved away from Kai. "You lied to me more than once. How do I know you are not lying now?" his distrustful expression only intensified as he raised his sword and aimed at Kai's chest.

"Please, old friend. I need time to prove I did not do this."

Dresnor's eyes were distraught. "I am not sure what I believe, but I think you should leave before I change my mind. I cannot help you, not after all your lies. Iver is dead, and no matter the role Nola played, you even admit that the knife was in your hand. I read the report after you were imprisoned—you did not deny killing your father. Nola is distraught over her husband's loss; the nation mourns, and you are playing games. No, Kai, I must stick to the facts. Our friendship must not interfere with justice. You best start running. Roark will come by ship to hasten the end of this foolishness, as you say, and defend Diu from a Katori attack. Two days, not a moment more."

There was nothing left to say. Dresnor had all but drawn a literal line in the sand, and they were on opposite sides. Kai backed away, taking with him all the power the moon, ocean, and wind could offer. His boots splashed in the fading waves. With all his might, he ran down the beach. His chest ached, not from the exertion but the loss of a friend. The one person he thought would help him was now threatening to arrest him.

Kai ran like the wind. Only when he was sure he would go unseen did he shift his form to become his silver dragon. The night sky welcomed him into her realm, unfolding the world for him to fly free. Thin gray clouds streaked across the sky, providing modest cover for his escape.

Having never flown over the southern Diu countryside, Kai was unsure of the markers he should use to ensure his path. Now was not the time to get lost in the dark, his best guess was to follow the coast toward Port Anahita than fly inland toward Henley, all while trying to go unnoticed.

CHAPTER 15

The Hunted

I am innocent, Kai reminded himself, watching the coastline morph into the countryside. He tried to convince himself they would all come to know the truth. If only he could figure out how to convince the world. But even if he found Iver's body, he was unsure it was possible.

Circling over Henley, Kai searched for an army, men who might lay in wait should he consider seeking sanctuary with an old friend. He saw nothing out of the ordinary; no camps or marching men sent to hunt him down. Still, he wondered if this were another mistake. Dresnor had no faith in him. Why would Drew or Robert, Drew's father, be any different?

Kai yawned. Heavy eyelids weighed on him. He wanted to rest— needed to rest. He shook off the drowsiness and searched for a place to land. Lights from Henley twinkled below. Two main gatehouses, both well-lit stone arches on opposite ends of town, looked heavily guarded. Deep in the northern woods, Kai dropped from the sky with ease. His dragon form disappeared when he released the golden thread. Through the trees, a light flickered as he released the magic back into his stone.

Less than a mile from the town, he used his Beastmaster skills to sense the animals around him. They were at peace; no signs of alarm. The city walls lay between him and safety. The various access points and guard stations were child's play compared to Diu security, and Kai slipped in undetected without breaking a sweat.

Kai snuck to the manor and gleaned Robert in his study, rifling through a stack of papers on his desk. There had to be a way to reach Robert without entering the estate. Kai considered the risks: getting captured or putting his friend in jeopardy.

Maybe I can call Robert to me? He thought as a yawn stretched his face and brought water to his eyes.

He had never used his mind to call to anyone besides Rayna and Kendra. Would it even work on Robert? After days with little to no sleep and hours of flying, Kai's strength was waning. Every step took its toll. Lethargic and weak, he stumbled closer to the estate, needing a safe place to rest with someone he could trust.

As Kai had done so many times before, he held onto the light within his soul and pressed it inward. Weakness shook his body; the power did not build as it should. Kai pushed his thoughts toward his friend, and Robert looked up; his head cocked to the side. Confused but not drawn, he went back to reading.

Stars pricked the edges of Kai's mind, causing him to yawn uncontrollably. His fist clenched his crystal, calling for more power as he pulled at his surroundings. The wild, forced energy struck Kai, putting him on his knees. There was no giving up; he needed help. He knew he was in trouble. From the woodlands around the estate, he drew strength. His head began to pound.

Kai focused on memories of Robert, their friendship. A knowing welled in his soul. Unable to control the magic, he focused on Robert and pushed the pulse with one thought attached—*help me, Robert.*

A spear of light bolted from Kai's mind, across the yard, and into Robert. Kai saw papers flutter from Robert's hands as the man slammed back into his chair. Robert rushed to the window, and their eyes met briefly before, dizzy and weak, Kai collapsed in the darkness.

♦ ♦ ♦

Dawn's pale-yellow light peeked through the windows and woke Kai. Across the room, the sofa had the form of a slumbering man. Propped up on his elbows, Kai realized that he was inside the estate. Robert rolled over and caught Kai's bleary eyes, "Good, you're awake. You had me worried."

Dread bubbled in the pit of Kai's stomach; he sprang to his feet. Lightheaded, he dropped back on the bed. "How do I get inside?"

"Rest, Kai," Robert said, tossing aside his blanket and moving to Kai's side. "you've only slept a few hours. I cannot imagine what you've been through these past few days."

Fear gripped Kai's gut. "I am sorry, Robert, I should not have come here; this was a mistake. Who else knows I am here?"

"You are safe here, Your Highness." Robert rose to help Kai stand. "I carried you in myself to the guest room. No one knows you are here—I promise. Stay here, and I will get you food. You must be starving." Robert left in a rush, allowing no time for Kai to respond.

In his solitude, Kai thought about the past several days. Every choice he had made weighed on his heart. How wished he had listened to Lucca and stayed in Katori; let nature take its course. At the time, he did not want to accept the truth of Iver's fate. Now he was left with the memory of his hand wielding the blade.

After an hour, Kai began to worry Robert might turn him in or send for Diu soldiers. He put his hand on the doorknob and listened—silence. His history with the Henley family made his heart ache as he pondered the possibilities that this man would report him to the authorities without really hearing his story.

The handle twisted in his palm, and Kai backed away. Robert entered with a brown leather satchel. "Sorry Kai, I could not very well disappear with a tray of food at this hour without questions. As the lord of Henley, I have a duty to my citizens. I needed to see to several matters of state. I packed a bag in case you wanted to take provisions with you when you leave."

There it was. Robert had not asked him to leave, but he did not intend on harboring him. "Why are you helping me?" He looked to Robert for answers. "You were my father's best friend, years ago, when he had friends. You should hate me, like so many others. Do you believe I murdered my father?"

Robert gulped, confirming that coming here was a mistake. He should not have involved the Henleys in his tragedy. Robert would be the last person to help him. He needed to leave. Before Kai could go, Robert touched his shoulder. "Why did you come here? What did you expect? I have only the news from Diu to believe, in addition to months of you lying to my son. Drew told me he was there when they sentenced you. You did not deny the charges. He said you were a broken man. Do you have anything to say?"

Images of his father and the blade flashed in Kai's mind. Guilt twisted his insides. There were chances to avoid this fate, yet at every turn, Kai all but ran to his father's bedside, blade in hand. Lucca, Sabastian, even Riome had warned him—but on some level, he thought he knew better. He thought that Alenga's vision meant he could stop what was coming. A lump clogged Kai's throat. "I am innocent," he insisted. "I am not sure how to prove it, but I must try. If only I could find Iver's body."

Robert's face contorted. "How will returning Iver support your case?"

"Whoever has Iver must know something. As they said, I was not alone in the King's chamber. I only saw Nola and my father, but I did hear another person tell me to run. I believe Keegan was there, too. He broke me out of prison. The only explanation I have is he was there and knows the truth. Or one of his people know. Either way, I need to find Iver's body and the person who was in that room."

"Keegan? The man who attacked Diu and possibly Port Anahita?" Robert looked confused. "Why would he care about rescuing you from prison?"

The truth was a closely guarded secret, but he had to be honest. "Only a few know the truth," Kai explained. "Keegan is my real father. My father—Iver, admitted it to me and the Master General years ago. When

Iver married my mother, he knew she was pregnant. Iver promised to raise me as his own to hide me from Keegan."

The room fell silent, and both contemplated the implications. Robert's softened expression gave Kai hope he had made a dent. Maybe he stood a chance of convincing the others. There was more to Iver's death than anyone knew.

Then something occurred to him. He thought back to his trial and tried to recall the faces in the crowd. "You mentioned Drew was in Diu during my sentencing. I do not remember seeing him."

"Well, you were severely beaten, according to Drew. Your eyes were swollen shut, little more than a slit. Not sure you saw much of anything." Robert studied Kai's face and body. "Come to think of it, considering this was two days ago, you look unscathed for a man beaten half to death."

There was no real explanation, at least not one Robert would believe. "Keegan has healers," Kai was all he said. The lie tasted bitter in his mouth; one he could not bring himself to finish. He began to feel like a caged animal. "Can we get some air?"

Robert searched the hallway while Kai waited alone. Thoughts of betrayal made him hold his breath. When the door swung open, Robert motioned for him to follow. They moved down the corridor to the spiral wooden staircase. Robert paused only a moment before descending, ensuring they continued without detection. Kai took the coat Robert offered. Out a small door, Robert led him into a simple garden.

The crisp air kissed Kai's face. His footprints were the first to leave their mark in the undisturbed snow. "Thank you, Robert." His breath floated away on the breeze. "Where is Drew, if I may ask? I was hoping to speak with him."

The request seemed harmless, but Robert's expression held more concern than Kai thought possible. Drew was his oldest friend; they were nearly brothers. Robert whipped his head to the stables. Kai followed the uneasiness and watched for movement.

"My son went to Diu to deliver the city taxes. I am expecting him and his men home later this evening."

The worried expression on his friend sent a sense of dread down Kai's spine. "Forgive me for saying, but every time I mention Drew, you react like there is something I should fear. What should I know?"

A flurry of snow blew between them. Robert remained silent. Kai did not want to be the cause of tension. "I should leave. I came here to tell Drew that I did not murder Iver. I wanted his help proving my case, but I will not set you at odds with your son."

"You must understand that my son loved being in service to Diu. He dedicated his entire life to the Galloway family, to you, and now that is over. I do not know what I believe. I know what I hope, but the truth has yet to come to light. If there is a way to prove your story, you must find it. Please do not ask my son to follow you on this path."

"Who are you speaking to, father?" Drew stepped into the garden and caught sight of Kai standing in the shadow of a large tree. Anger flared Drew's nostrils and narrowed his focus.

The depths of his friend's rage pulled Kai back a step. "Before you overreact . . ."

Drew's reaction was swift and unyielding as his unsheathed sword flew into action without warning. Kai ducked away from the strike and slid behind the tree. He had no weapon to defend himself, only his speed. "Please, Drew! Let me explain." He could see the layers of anger and disbelief resting on his friend's shoulders; he would not yield.

"I am a Diu Captain, or at least I was before you took that from me!" Drew swung his sword again this time nearly catching Kai in the chin.

Darting around the snow-covered garden to avoid his friend's sword, Kai begged. "Listen to me, please. I need your help."

"How dare you come here after what you did," Drew spat. "Why would I help you? You lied to me, to everyone. You are a traitor and a murderer. Do you deny it?"

Drew stepped through the snow closer to Kai.

Robert followed and grabbed his son's arm. "Please, Drew, before you make a mistake, hear Prince Kai out. Then we can call the guards."

"Do not call him a prince!" Anger boiled behind Drew's eyes. "He does not deserve the title. How could you kill Iver? That man loved you. I loved you like a brother."

The anguish on his friend's face bore a hole through Kai's heart. As painful as it was, he explained everything that happen, sparing no detail, starting with the night Riome hypnotized him and learned Nola had brainwashed him into killing Iver. He explained how he slipped into his father's room through a secret passage accessible from the music room on the floor below. Explained how Nola slid the blade into his hand and guided it into Iver's chest. He told everything he could remember.

Drew stopped Kai before he could continue. "Lies. I do not believe you."

Kai wanted to explain further but Drew pulled away from Robert. "I was there two days ago." Drew narrowed his gaze. "You were barely recognizable. There was a deep gash in your cheek. I saw when Seth hit your ribs, and you doubled in pain, I am guessing from a broken rib maybe two. None of those wounds would heal in two days."

"Healers," Kai confessed. "Keegan has special herbs..."

Anger swept over Drew's face. "Are you making fun of me? Do you think I am foolish? Father, call the guards. I will watch Kai, make sure he does not escape." Drew pointed to the door as he unsheathed his sword once more.

Kai stepped closer, frantic to convince his friend. "Were you willing to believe any of what I said?"

"I do not believe the Queen tried to kill the King," Drew said bluntly. "I cannot believe she cast a spell on you; there is no such thing. Her dedication to him over the time while you were away showed real strength and loyalty. She weeps for her lost husband. Father, go, do not stop until you reach the stables. My men should be finishing up. Bring them here."

Robert left as his son instructed. Drew stared at Kai. Clumps of snowflakes began to fall, and Kai drew on the magic around him. There was little time to concern himself with any Katori who might notice a power shift. He needed strength now more than ever. Although Drew deserved the truth, Kai held up his hands. "I am not making you out to be a fool, Drew. I only need time to prove my innocence."

Given the small space they shared in the garden, there was little room to avoid Drew's blade. They circled as if sizing each other up for battle, only Kai had no weapon, and Drew's massive shoulders left little doubt who was the bigger man.

Drew cocked his head as if ready to strike. "Why did you do it? Why should I believe anything you say? You are no prince; you said so yourself."

The truth was a lot to process, and Kai could tell his friend was stalling. If Robert was coming with the guards, he needed to flee. "Do what? Kill Iver? I told you, I did not do this. You must believe me, please. I am still the man you knew. We were friends once. Queen Nola is behind all of this."

"Enough lies!" Drew shouted. "I cannot let our past cloud my loyalty. You once saved my life, but I will not help you break the law. Friends or not, I must do the right thing. You must accept Diu's judgment. You have lied too many times, Kai."

More snow fell, soaking Kai's head and collecting on his shoulders. "Even if I am innocent?" he implored his friend. "If I go back with you, they will hang me without searching for Iver's body, or the person who was in the room that night with me and Nola. Please, I need time! Give me at least two days," he pleaded, hearing voices clamoring around the front of the house.

They both knew it was now or never. Kai wanted to believe his friend would help him, give him the benefit of the doubt, but the trust was no longer there. Even as the words escaped his friend's mouth, Kai knew he had wasted too much time.

"Do not run, Kai—you must not run," Drew begged, looking back for the oncoming guards and then back at Kai. "Running proves you are guilty."

Robert and Drew were his last hope in Diu. Sadness sank into Kai's chest as he stepped backward, pressing his back into the tall cypress hedge. "I am not running. I am searching for the truth, and right now, I am the only one who cares about the truth." Power seeped into Kai's core, and renewed strength permeated his body. "Have faith in me, Drew. I did not kill Iver, and I will of my own free will return to Diu. Two days from now, meet me on the bridge over Stone River, the long bridge below the rock dam around Baden Lake's south rim. I promised Dresnor I would turn myself in. Roark is sailing with his soldiers to Diu. Bring your men, and I will be there, with or without Iver. Remember, in two days."

Then he threw himself backward and crashed through the hedge into another part of the garden. Drew gave chase. But as they both knew, Kai was quicker. Kai slipped through the estate gate and dashed into an open field. The change in the weather covered the countryside in fresh snow. Lost in the blizzard, he would be impossible to track without help.

With exceptional speed, Kai put distance between himself and the town of Henley. When he reached the forest, he gleaned the manor. Drew had returned to the estate. Hunters were gathering—men in Robert's employ, men who once saw him as their Prince, trackers capable of finding him in any weather.

The air filled with the sounds of dogs barking. The estate's hounds surely already had Kai's scent. Drew would be relentless. If Kai hoped to confuse the hunters, he would need to make for rockier ground. When the time was right, he could become his dragon and take to the skies beyond Drew's reach.

CHAPTER 16

Redemption

Kai's dragon's shadow soared over a blanket of white storm clouds. Up above the world, he was free. A small part of him wanted to fly away and never stop flying. Yet he was tethered to this world and the people he loved; he could not abandon them.

The tree-covered apex of Thade Mountain came into view. He circled toward Eagle's Peak and sank beneath the clouds. His feet landed with barely a sound as he transformed moments before his claws scrapped the stony ground. Here the snow fluttered like tiny specs unwilling to land.

Sabastian's abandoned tree stood as a testament that he was all alone. There was no one left to help him; no one left to believe in him. He did not heed Sabastian's warning, and now he would pay the price. Would Rayna even stand with him now? He wallowed in his solitude, feeling hopeless.

The sounds of eagles lifted Kai's eyes to the clouds. Two larger-than-average birds soared out of the storm. Even without the golden tips, Kai knew who they were. His heart skipped a beat. Were they friends or foes? Would Sabastian be any different than Dresnor or Drew? While Sabastian held no love for Diu, he was an honest man.

Sabastian landed first. Next came a white-bellied eagle with dark wings—Kendra transformed in midflight and dropped a few feet in front of Kai. Her eyes welled with tears as she pulled Kai into her arms. Kai felt her pounding heart against his and he melted into the mother's love he always felt from her. No words passed between them, but the truth of her faith in him poured through her arms, giving him the hope he desperately needed.

When he finally stepped back, he saw her wet cheeks. "You're alive!" she cried, wrapping her arms around him and hugging him tightly once more.

He held her and nodded. Tears of his own rolled down his face. She did not accuse or question him, only offered support. "Thank you."

"How did you escape the dungeons?"

Kai noticed Kendra could not help the stray tear that slipped through her regained composure. "Keegan," Kai admitted.

"I knew Seth did not help you, no more than he helped me. Nola put Seth in prison for the thought he betrayed her."

Her words struck Kai; another person was paying for his choices. "Poor Seth," he mumbled under his breath. "Please do not lecture me." Kai felt the weight of the world on his shoulders. "I know I made mistakes, but I only did what I thought was best. Right now, I need to find Rayna, explain what happened, why I left her with Benmar. Then I will find Iver's body and return to answer for my crimes. Kendra, I am innocent. I did not kill Iver, but without his body or the person who took him, I cannot prove anything."

"I know everyone else has abandoned you, Kai." Kendra glanced at Sabastian, then back to him. "But I am not sure how we can help. You do not have time to find Iver's body and save Rayna. She is no longer with your grandfather."

Sabastian interrupted. "She is as stubborn as you. In her attempt to follow you, she traveled to Chenowith; however, by the time she arrived, news of Iver's murder had already reached them, followed by the news of your escape."

Kai's confused expression must have been evident because Sabastian explained further. "After your skirmish at Davi's camp, I went to Katori to tell the Elders you were now traveling to Diu with your men. The Elders thought it best to begin bringing home the Katori outsiders."

The phrase "your men" struck Kai. Could his friend really believe he supported Diu over Katori? Had he made a choice yet? No, he did not know to which life he belonged. "So that is how Lucca learned I was in Diu. He asked me to stay, but I was too angry to listen. I was sure my mission was to save Iver and change fate. So, how do you know Lord Chenowith has Rayna?"

"After you ran off to Diu, I begged Lucca to help you," Sabastian continued. "I had hoped we would venture to Diu and bring you home before something went wrong. He said no, you were free to make your own decisions. So, I traveled to Chenowith to ponder my options."

"Drink is more like it," Kendra chided.

Sabastian folded his arms over his chest. "While I was there, I learned about what you had done and that Kendra was also in prison. By the time I was able to travel, another day had passed."

Kendra put her hand on Kai's shoulder. "Dante ordered every cell emptied, hoping to find you. Prisoners were herded into the prison courtyard as they searched. In the chaos, I escaped through the tunnels; I know the palace better than anyone. I wanted to find you myself, so I combed the streets, and that's when I overheard a guard." Her hand touched her heart, and Kai saw real fear in her eyes. "Lord Chenowith sent word to Diu that he had Rayna. I am guessing Rayna is to serve as bait to lure you out."

Sabastian acknowledged the story. "We saw the *Dragaron* set sail this afternoon. They will be swift to Chenowith and back. You can be sure that by dawn tomorrow, Rayna will be thrown into the palace prison. Alenga helps us . . ."

The words crushed Kai's spirit; another mistake that would be his fault. He broke his promise by leaving her behind. Guilt was a powerful force, and it began to eat away at him.

You are too late. You will lose everyone you love . . .

With less than two full days left before he promised to return to Diu, Kai stood on Eagle's Peak. So much had transpired in this spot. His life changed forever when he saw his first two Beastmaster transformations and learned that Haygan was his uncle. Now tonight, he would make another life-altering decision—save Rayna instead of himself.

He would make amends with Rayna, even if it meant he would not have time to search for his father's body. He could not go to his death knowing in his last moment that he had broken Rayna's heart. He needed her forgiveness. But first, he needed to save her from his mistakes.

"I will save Rayna," he declared, "but I need to find her first." Kai knew memories, like nature itself, held great power. Baden Lake was nearly three hundred miles wide, and he would need immense range if he hoped to pinpoint her location. The love he felt for his mother helped him find her an ocean away, but his love for Rayna was even more powerful. The view of Baden Lake below with the city of Diu in the distance reminded him of all the memories he had with Rayna.

He looked to his friends. "Please lend me your strength to ease the burden of gleaning. I cannot risk being drained right before saving Rayna."

They gave him a nod.

The moon kissed his head and blessed him. The stars giggled with delight and blessed him. Even the wind did its part and rushed up to bless him. Kendra and Sabastian each set a hand on his shoulder. Given freely, he felt their magic swirl into his core. Collecting all the power within his soul, he gave it purpose, wrapped in memories of Rayna; his gleaning ability would focus on her energy and draw him to her like a moth to a flame.

Releasing the molded magic through his gleaning sight, a dart of cosmic power and light shot from Kai. His mind traveled on stardust over the treetops and across the wind-swept waves of Baden Lake. Miles of rippling water raced beneath him as his mind's eye flew toward Rayna's spirit. Near the distant shore, he saw the *Dragaron* underway, still within view of the Chenowith docks. Rayna's gleaming outline sparkled with

Katori magic. She stood alone facing the bitter winds. No chains held her; her eyes had no tears, but her gleaming form held a brilliance, a beacon to his soul. He sent her a whisper on the wind—*I am coming, Rayna.*

Her mouth curled ever so lightly, and she thought back—*I know.*

As his mind dropped the connection, he started to smile, but it quickly faded. From the position of the *Dragaron,* he knew that Sabastian was correct; Rayna would be in Diu shortly after dawn. The seven or so hours while they sailed would be his best chance of rescue before she reached the city—or the Diu dungeons.

Various possibilities sprang to mind. He could fly down to her, but the shimmering scales of his silver dragon would reveal his arrival and break the promise to hide the truth of dragons. Sending Kendra and Sabastian might be an option, but this was his mistake. No, this was something he needed to do himself—but for once, he would ask for help. There was no weakness in admitting that he could not do this alone, no shame in admitting he was wrong.

He turned to face Kendra and Sabastian. "I need your help. If I am to save Rayna, I need to reach the ship before dawn. The storm is subsiding, and the clouds are fading. Will you carry me over Baden Lake and drop me in the water near the ship?" His voice sounded distant to his ears, and he felt outside himself.

Kendra nodded. "I am out of practice carrying people; there is no way I am strong enough. I think Sabastian is your best choice. While you save Rayna, and I will begin to search for Iver. I will start with Thade Mountain and the surrounding farms until Sabastian returns."

"Thank you both for believing in me and helping me correct this mistake." He looked between Kendra and Sabastian, and then he confessed, "I have no idea how to ride an eagle."

"You have the easy part," Sabastian said. "Lay against my back and maintain your balance. But I am more concerned about the distance you need to go. I cannot carry you the entire way. Eagles typically fly a little over one hundred miles in one go—a Katori eagle, double that. Alone, at top speed, I can make it across in about four hours, but with your added weight, I must rest before returning." Sabastian shook his head. "I am no dragon; I can only carry you so far and still make it back to shore."

Baden Lake was massive, he knew that firsthand, but he had not considered the limitations of an eagle against his dragon. Flying across the lake to rescue Rayna and escape would not be possible for an eagle Beastmaster. "Understood," Kai responded. "If you can get me close, I will do the rest. Take me as far as you can before you need to turn back."

Sabastian raised an eyebrow. "Should I be concerned? You cannot use your dragon. Do you plan to swim the rest of the way?"

Kai shook his head. "I can become other animals. The eagle design and other birds of flight elude me, but water and land creatures feel very natural." Given they had little time to argue, he was thankful they did not push because he had no idea what he would do once he fell into the water.

A brilliant white light seeped through Sabastian's fingers as he drew on the magic within his stone. Kai watched with amazement as feathers erupted over his friend's changing form. The speed of the transformation was quick, but Kai's Katori Beastmaster eyes noticed the ripple of change, and for the first time, his senses felt the subtle draw of power raise the hair on his neck.

"Time to go." Kendra wrapped an arm around his shoulder and squeezed. "We will see you in two days; I promise we will find a way out of this. Do not give up hope."

He nodded and stepped up behind Sabastian. Excited and nervous, he took hold of the wings close to the eagle's head. As Sabastian fell forward over the edge, treetops rushed by. Soring down the mountainside under other circumstances would be exhilarating—this was not. Kai did his best to stay centered as he clung to Sabastian's eagle. He knew the risks his size posed. Sabastian's eagle was only a foot taller than Kai and not much wider. There was little room for error if Kai shifted in flight.

Focused on remaining calm, he thought of a creature, a construct which only existed in his mind, a beast born of fiction. He needed something nobody would see coming. It needed to be dark, it needed to be swift, and it needed to be strong. With no such animal to emulate, he risked being lost in a new creation.

Ryker once reminded him about the first dragons, and how dangerous it was to create a novel beast from nothing but one's imagination. His snow wolf was not original, not really—it was more a blend of Smoke and Anjo. The experience remained fresh in his mind, along with the memory of nearly getting lost in the attempt.

Of all the creatures Kai knew, the dragon was the strongest, the snake was the fastest, and black was the color of night. To go unseen, he would need to blend them into something new. As they flew over the lake, Kai started to sense the flow of magic. He would need power if he hoped to transform, but he did not want to take anything friend required. The wind flowed into Sabastian, restoring him and prolonging his ability to carry a passenger. Collecting moonlight, he pushed his strength into the eagle's wings and felt them lift higher.

Kai, you will need all the magic you can collect for yourself, he heard Sabastian speak to his mind.

His friend did not know how right he was. As they continued, he took magic from the moon and the clouds and the star-filled sky; from the depths of the lake, he drew power. His skin began to tingle with anticipation, and his mind detailed the creature he needed. Power flowed freely, and Kai felt it build faster than he ever remembered before.

Wind-driven waves reached for him in the night; the tiny mist of water told him they were flying lower. Sabastian was getting tired from the hours of flight. They had flown a great distance, and with each beat of his wings, they flew a little lower. His friend had reached his limit. With no land or ships in sight, Kai said goodbye.

Thank you, Sabastian, Kai thought with his mind. You can let me go alone from here.

Good luck, Kai, he heard back just before Sabastian rolled over midflight.

Baden Lake swallowed Kai whole. Her bitterly cold waves greeted him with open arms and concealed his entry. His crystal already was aglow as he sank into the blackness. His last view was of Sabastian circling, waiting.

Transformation always began the same way, with the thread of creation locked within his soul. Blended with the design of another, he could become any beast he knew. Focused on the creatures he'd studied and the animals he knew, Kai imagined a serpent-like creature. It was bigger than any dragon with scales black as night, with a body able to glide through the water and eyes capable of seeing even in the dimmest of light.

The waves provided an abundance of energy. Kai pulled every ounce he could from their crashing. They gave freely. As if with a pen, Kai drew the serpent in his mind: the dark red eyes, spine-frilled neck, ridged spine, black diamond-shaped scales. Wings to serve as fins and a broad tail to help him slip through the water, and a sharp, menacing horn.

Inspired by his design, the golden braid coalesced into a spiraling coiled ladder. Magic-infused light swirled around Kai's body. His arms stretched and flowed into long wing-like fins, legs pressed tight they grew together as his body became longer and his tail unfurled. Taking a breath, he sucked water in over his new gills, and he felt the expanse of his head and the change of his eyes.

As he slithered from the deep, his head rose out of the water. Higher and higher he went, up into the sky. Still pulling from nature, the wind died with the waves. Studying his reflection in the dark waves, he beheld his creation, down to every detail. The beast was just as he hoped. The one surprise was his serpent tongue, pointy and forked, but it felt right.

His elongated body rolled out behind him. Elegant wing-like fins fluttered at his sides, and a fin-like tail swooshed through the water. Feeling complete, he stretched and recoiled. His new form slithered through the water, leaving little trace he was ever there. The sounds of an eagle's cry rang in his ears, and the gold tips of an eagle flashed by his eyes.

He watched the bird swoop and dive and transform into a man landing on his third protruding hump.

"Kai!" the man shouted. "Remember who you are, your mission— save Rayna!"

Kai slithered and bobbed in the water. Pictures of a girl flashed in his mind. He repeated her name in his head—*Rayna*—*Rayna*—*Rayna*. He remembered everything, his feelings for her, her predicament, and his mission to save her.

Thank you, he said in his mind. Return to Kendra.

Sabastian bathed in moonlight to regain his power and Kai sensed a shift in magic as his friend reverted to his eagle form and disappeared into the night.

Concentrating ahead, he held his head high while his body slithered through the water. With his massive size and speed, he was within view of the *Dragaron* in less than an hour. Easing his pace, he slowed, letting his body sink below the surface; the tip of his black horn just missed the hull of the *Dragaron*.

Kai's glowing red eyes watched the ship pass. He could not speak to Rayna in this beastly form, but he had to get her attention. His horn rose from the depths, piercing the wake behind the *Dragaron*. His winged head, nearly as large as the entire vessel, made a new wake. He watched from a distance, searching for a way to get her attention.

Two guards approached her. One was rail-thin, and Kai saw him pointing. Rayna shook her head in disagreement, and the other heavyset guard grabbed her arm. Rage boiled in his stomach, and he felt an uncontrollable instinct take over. His rolling body propelled him from the water as he lunged at the ship. Water drenched the deck as he passed over the top. Using his wing-like fin, Kai snatched the man from the boat and plunged back into the darkness. Rage consumed his mind as he swam in a downward spiral. Air bubbles poured out the guard's mouth, and his eyes bulged in fear.

Realizing the man was suffocating, Kai swam for the surface and flung him into the air. He landed on deck in a fit of coughs as Kai rose high above the ship. The white sails were soaked in water. Men shouted, drawing their swords. The captain pulled a crossbow and aimed at Kai's writhing form. Rayna screamed, her hands held out to the captain. "Don't shoot!" she begged.

Kai did not want to hurt the men on the *Dragaron*, but he wanted Rayna. A roar rolled up his throat, and he blasted the ship with the frightful sound. Men screamed in fear, and the captain let loose his arrow. It struck Kai's diamond black scales and bounced off without a scratch. Rayna ran to the rail and dove into the water.

Dumfounded, the crew watched as the leviathan sank beneath the surface. Rayna floated beneath the water, basking in the glow of Kai's red eyes. Kai nudged her with his horn, and she took hold. Anxious to put distance between them, he swam away from the *Dragaron*, rising from the depths so she could breathe.

The *Dragaron* bobbed motionless in the middle of the lake. Kai imagined it would not take long before the crew came to their senses and sail for Diu. They would arrive emptied-handed, with no bait to lure Kai back into captivity. He thought about Nola's anger and the added intrigue behind a mythical monster spotted in Baden Lake.

Rayna perched behind his horn between his winglike ears as he swam into the darkness. Dawn's rays cut through the fog, and the shoreline unfolded before them.

Kai eased into the sandy shore. Rayna slipped from his head, and he transformed. Standing in knee-deep water, he looked at her, wondering how furious she might be.

Her eyes held no anger; only a small tear ran down her already wet cheek. She ran to him, and he welcomed her with open arms. He could not thank Alenga enough for keeping her safe. It felt good to have her back.

"I should not have left you," he admitted. "I thought I knew better, but I was wrong." Scooping Rayna into his arms, Kai lifted her from the cold water and carried her to shore.

"I knew it was you," she confessed. "You are becoming a very powerful Beastmaster. The leviathan is your fourth animal, and second new creation—or are there others I don't know about?" She crossed her arms and raised an eyebrow at him as he walked.

She had every right to be mad. Lowering her into the tall grass along the shore, Kai tried to smooth the tension. "Leviathan," he offered with a smile. "That was the name I thought of, too."

The gesture fell flat.

"I am sorry," Kai admitted. "I have made so many mistakes, but one just led to another. It's as if I cannot stop."

Her eyes softened, and her shoulders relaxed. "It means a lot to hear you say you are sorry, but you need to stop taking risks with your magic."

Eagar to share his latest discovery, he changed the subject. "You know, I finally see now how the crystal channels our magic. The stone amplifies and softens the raw nature, and if we find the balance to let it flow freely, we can do anything."

She pushed his shoulder. "Seriously, Kai, you look exhausted. Not magically, but emotionally. How are you doing?"

"Don't worry about me," he said, shrugging off her concern. "We need to get going. We should be a bit south of Chenowith but not close enough for anyone to spot us. I want to get in the hills before I..."

"Before you what?" Albert shouted from the shadows. "Traitor. MURDERER!"

Kai peered in the trees. "Albert Chenowith, is that you?"

Rayna stepped close to Kai. "Be careful," she whispered. "Albert is the one who turned me in."

The possibilities danced through Kai's mind. What had Albert seen? Rayna and Kai came ashore only moments ago, less than fifteen feet from where they stood now. Did his friend see him transform? Did it matter? With a protective hand, Kai pulled Rayna close. "Albert, I know what you've heard, but it is not true. I did not kill my father. Please let us go. I need to find the people who took my father's body and return him to Diu."

"Liar!" Albert dropped the reins of his horse and drew his sword. "Our Queen commands that we turn you over. You are a murderer. You are a traitor to the crown and must pay."

If Albert were anyone else, Kai might have thought twice, but his friend was no swordsman. In three quick steps, he disarmed Albert.

"Come now, Albert, how long have we been friends? You know me, the *real* me. I would have no motive to kill my father. Only someone who wanted his crown would benefit from killing him, and you and I both know that being a king was never my ambition."

Albert started to speak but stopped—twice—as if caught between the sword's tip and the truth. With his friend pondering the facts, Kai relinquished the sword back to its rightful owner. "I am returning this to you as a symbol of trust. Believe me when I say I did not kill my father."

What appeared to be a mix of skepticism and relief caused Albert to slump and sheath his weapon. Trust was a precious gift, Kai wanted to relax, but Albert had tricked Rayna and was planning to hand her over to the dungeon masters. But, if he wanted to earn Albert's trust, he needed to trust him first.

"I need time to prove I didn't kill my father. I believe—"

"Let us leave, Albert," Rayna interjected. Then she whispered to Kai as she pulled him toward the trees. "We do not have time for this . . ."

"We need to go to Port Anahita," Kai agreed. "I hope to find Iver's body there. He was not on the ship with Keegan, and I have only today left to search. Tomorrow, I must return to Diu, with or without proof of my father's fate."

Albert followed them. "Keegan?"

"Why is he following us? There is no time for explanations. We need to go." Rayna tugged Kai into a quicker pace.

"I am sorry, Rayna," Albert said, jogging to catch up. "Let me prove my loyalty. You must understand, I had to turn you in. It was my sworn duty. You really did not kill Iver?" His begging tone left a speck of doubt in the air.

Kai stopped to let his friend take a breath. In as few words as possible, and omitting a few special details, he told the facts as he knew them from the moment he was with Queen Nola in his father's chamber, though Keegan's abduction, his promise to Dresnor, and today's rescue of Rayna.

"I could not allow Queen Nola to manipulate me," Kai explained. "I will return as promised to Diu tomorrow, but I could not allow the love of my life to go to prison because I was in the wrong place at the wrong time. Albert, tell your father that if he wishes to learn the truth, he should be in Diu tomorrow afternoon."

A moment of silence passed before Albert spoke. "Take me with you. Let me help."

Thoughts of Lord and Lady Chenowith's kindness rippled through Kai's memory. "I am sorry, Albert. I cannot risk being captured."

"I need a chance Kai, please. Let me prove my loyalty to you."

Kai felt his heart soften to the idea, and it must have shown on his face before Rayna pulled him back. "No, we cannot trust him. Plus, his mother will kill you. I have met the woman; she is strong-willed."

Years of friendship hung in the balance. Kai studied his friends face and saw the sorrow in Albert's eyes. His friend wanted to believe. He needed someone to believe in him.

"Rayna, please forgive me," Albert pleaded. "I only did what I thought was best with the information from Queen Nola. Rumors of Kai's disloyalty have poured into Chenowith for months. I should have trusted Kai, but the news of King Iver's death was very personal. Let me make it up to both of you."

Rayna's caution was understandable, but Albert's friendship meant the world to Kai. "I believe you want to make this right," Kai said, the choice becoming clear as he spoke. "We both seek redemption, but our paths do not converge. Rayna and I must go alone. I cannot afford another mistake—and taking you with us would be a mistake."

Albert's shoulders slumped in disappointment, but he continued to listen. "Albert, you could be of service. Speak with your father—inform him that you saw Rayna and I escape across Baden Lake. Mention our confrontation and my profession of innocence. Tell him if he wants the truth, he must come to Diu. By ship, you and he could be there tomorrow by noon. I want the world to know the I did not kill my father. Can you do this, Albert?"

Albert took a breath and nodded. "I want to come with you, but I understand. I would only slow you down or get you caught. Trust me, I will get my father to Diu."

They shook hands and parted.

With one short prayer to Alenga, Kai gleaned the area one final time to ensure there were no witnesses who might see him transform. In one direction, he saw Albert pushing the limits of his horse toward Chenowith, and in the opposite direction, the closest travelers were miles away, camping near a small fishing pier. On the lake, the *Dragaron* was sailing toward Diu.

Standing in the darkness, Kai thought about his chances of finding his father's body and about every choice he made in the previous days. A thin white ray of sunlight peeked over the mountains. They were out of time.

"As Sabastian told us," Kai reminded her, "there is a moment, just after dawn, when the sun's rays paint the sky white, then yellow. We missed the break of dawn, but the yellow rays coming over the mountain and down into the valley can still hide our departure. I must fly above the clouds. We will have to fly very high."

She nodded with acceptance.

Kai stepped back to provide space for him to maneuver, and then he transformed. Rayna climbed up between the two protruding horns along his back.

"I have missed you," she whispered as she kicked her heels as one would on a horse. "Take me flying. If this is our last day of freedom, make it beautiful."

THE TRAITOR

Kai took flight. The white and gold rays bathed them with light as they escaped the treetops. With a few strong beats, they were engulfed in the plump white clouds.

CHAPTER 17

One More Dead Man

Sleep had become a luxury Kai could not afford, but the lack of rest affected his ability to focus. Every flap of his wings took more effort than the last. If they were going to make it to Port Anahita, he needed to rest, even if only for a few hours. They were flying high in the clouds, searching for a safe spot to land. It had to be a place with no people—a place off the beaten path.

The first spot he recognized was the hunting lodge he had used every summer in his childhood. This area was very familiar to him. Although they could not stay in the lodge, he knew that the overlook provided ample landing space for a dragon's girth. The beating of his wings disrupted the low-hanging clouds, causing them to swirl.

Kai's landing was far from graceful, and the transformation back into his natural form brought pinpricks of pain raining down his body. Tears welled in his eyes as he fell to his knees, and Rayna rushed to his side, providing a soothing touch to the back of his head. Her keen sense of his suffering gave him the reassurance in their connection. Without asking, she placed another hand on his spine. The warm wave of magic bathed his vertebra, easing the pulse of agony he felt as his bones reset.

He raised his face to look at her. Her shocked expression was a cross between horror and sorrow.

"I rushed the change. I am sorry if I frightened you," Kai muttered in a gravelly voice, not entirely his own, with a mouth full of more teeth than usual. The golden hue of her face told him his eyes were still amber, and the weight of his head gave him the inkling he still had horns protruding from his skull.

Rayna continued to help him shift by touching his cheeks and covering his eyes. "You take too many risks with all these back-to-back transformations," she whispered, rocking back on her heels. "There, there, all seems restored. I didn't know a Beastmaster could get stuck between the change. When did you last sleep?"

The pain faded, and Kai rolled onto his back. "Thank you, Rayna. I did not know that could happen, either. I changed just my hand once to practice, but never have I been stuck like today." He shifted his head to look at her. "The lack of sleep is catching up with me, and I have no balance. The few hours at Robert Henley's estate was not enough. Creating the leviathan took more magic than you can imagine. I know all these new creatures put me at risk, but I must . . ." he let out a sigh too tired to finish.

The renewed confidence in Rayna's face eased Kai's mind. "I wondered why you chose this route." She plucked a blade of grass from his shoulder. "Around the lake instead of straight across."

Trust was a delicate thing, so Kai chose his words carefully. "I am sorry." He sat up straight, feeling his strength improve. "I owe you an apology." He searched her eyes for acceptance, but she remained indifferent. "What can I say?" He felt his words crumbled between them.

Several minutes passed before she spoke. "There is nothing to say." Kai noticed her withdraw. "You made a choice, and I will admit to being mad the first day, but then I made a choice, which turned out to be wrong. Both of us made mistakes, but it does not change how we feel."

"Not about leaving." He turned to catch her eyes with his own. "About kissing Nola. I know you saw us, and for that I am sorry. She cast a spell on me, and I should have tried harder to stop her. I love you, and only you."

Hot tears rolled down her cheeks, but her lips formed the hint of acceptance. "I know. It means a lot you told me." She cleaned her face and stood dusting the dirt from her knees. "Enough about the past. You need rest. We both do. I can create a natural enclosure to conceal our location. Perhaps over there." She pointed to a cluster of saplings.

The years visiting this location gave Kai an advantage. He gleaned the area for the Alpha, and he soon discovered that the pack was close. *Come to me*, he called with his mind. Other animals sensed him and moved in his direction. A mountain lion entered the clearing and sat near the overlook while a hawk landed in the trees above them.

"We can rest here," Kai said, "but not for long. The Alpha and his pack are coming to secure the area. I wish Smoke were here, but the animals around us will guard us while we sleep."

The saplings were pencil-thin, sprigs only three feet tall. Under Rayna's fingers, moss bubbled up through the pine needles and spread in every direction. The trunk of each tree expanded with a bit of her magic. Their thickening trunks shot up eight feet, and their lower branches interlaced, creating an arched shelter. From the ground, she urged evergreen holly to cover the arch and conceal the structure.

"What do you think?" she beamed.

Watching her create structures filled Kai with immense pride. "Wonderful, Rayna." He turned to see the Alpha. The wolf's heart pounded in Kai's ears; his friend was tired. The pack followed a moment later. They had come a great distance in a short time to answer Kai's call.

For most, it was not every day you called a wild animal to your side, and they came. Kai was honored, given all the pack had suffered in fighting for him last spring.

Thank you. I need your help, protect us while we rest.

The pack fanned out and started to patrol.

Rayna entered first, and Kai followed. Once inside, she sealed the entrance with more vines and foliage. Inside, the moss and pine needles provided a soft place to rest. The concealed space was nearly as dark as a cave, and Kai was asleep before his head hit the ground.

♦ ♦ ♦

Wind-blown embers jumped from rooftop to rooftop, and Diu became a sea of fire. Three-story buildings collapsed into piles of burning rubble. Ash fell like snow from the sky and the smell of death caught in Kai's dragon nostrils. Everywhere he looked, flames spread to engulf another structure. His city was ablaze, and his people were lost in the chaos.

Kai flew over the Central City Gardens—they were gone. Nothing but ash and cinders. On the east end of the park, the five large oaks had been reduced to smoldering trunks. Memories of Rayna burned alive in her tree flooded his mind. It stuck deep into his heart, so he turned away. He did not want to see any more.

Far across the city, he saw them—Milnos soldiers closing the city gates and locking the Diu people inside. Fury burned in Kai's throat. An explosion along the warehouse district caught his attention. Screams echoed on the wind, and yellow-orange flames licked at the heels of citizens running through the firestorm. Everyone was dying, and he could do nothing.

Kai woke from his nightmare with screams echoing in his mind. Drenched in sweat, he sat up and ran his hands through his hair. It had been years since a horrific dream had woken him like this.

"Did you have another bad dream?" she asked. "I felt your anguish."

Kai was thankful for their bond. They were true soulmates. Ever since Keegan tried to burn her alive in her tree, their connection was stronger. He leaned back on his elbows and sighed.

"About your father again?" she turned to look at him.

"No, this was something new." Sadness overwhelmed him again, and he swallowed hard before continuing. "I saw Diu burn. Milnos men torched the city and locked the people inside the walls. Men, women, and children screamed as the blaze engulfed them. There was nothing I could do."

"Are you sure it was real? Not sure if this will ease your mind, but I've done a lot of reading about dream interpretation. They say fire symbolizes destruction, purification, transformation, or anger. Forgive me for analyzing your nightmare, but you have struggled with your loyalty to Diu and your desire to live in Katori."

He wrestled with the idea this nightmare was only his inner battle to choose between the two, and not a vision of the future given to him by Alenga.

"It felt so real," he insisted.

"And it may have been. We both know you have undeniably accurate visions. But this is only one possible future for Diu."

Her truthful words soothed his spirit. He knew Rayna was right; at some point, he would need to decide. "I am not sure if it is a vision of what is to come or me trying to reconcile my heart to live in Katori or Diu. What should I do?"

Rayna tilted her head to the side, revealing her confusion. "You asked me to follow you to Katori, and now you are questioning your choice. Why?"

Kai sighed again. "I cannot lie. The peace I feel in Katori is undeniable, but I am torn. Am I, like in my dream, to burn the bridge behind me to Diu? Am I to forget what they meant to me?"

"I love my parents, but they live in Diu. It is a beautiful city, but not my home." Rayna patted her heart with her hand. "Port Anahita was not my home either, though I spent half of my life there. During the many months we've lived in Katori, I have never been more at peace. That is my home—I know it in my heart."

The usual kindness in Rayna's eyes melted into uncertainty. He knew she did not judge him, but his indecisiveness created doubt about their future. At a loss of words, he tugged the chain of his crystal.

Rayna stayed his hand. "Follow your heart. You are not saying goodbye to these people forever; you are simply moving to a new place. I cannot impose my choice on you, but you do have to make one. Now, you only slept about an hour. Rest."

She let her head fall as she closed her eyes. Kai was pleasantly surprised at how quickly he drifted off.

♦ ♦ ♦

The sounds of metal clashing on stone woke Kai. Disoriented, he sat up and looked around the cramped space. Rayna was asleep. Another sound hastened him outside, the sounds of low grunts and groans.

Rain mixed with snow put a new chill in the air and wet his head and shoulders. Down the slope, he searched for the sounds that woke him. He moved down the hill—the area was familiar to him, and he knew the sounds were coming from the direction of the hunting lodge that he had visited many times. Dread welled in his throat. Halfway down the hill, he spotted a man trying to climb over the large boulders.

"Come on, Marcus, slow down," the man shouted.

Kai's heart stopped. There was another man somewhere nearby. Was he so tired that he had walked right by someone and not noticed? Hidden in the trees, Kai searched the foliage for the other man. The glint of armor revealed a second man standing on the last boulder, panting.

"Don't be such an old man, Joshua, get up here. We are halfway now. The view from the top must be glorious."

Fear crept around the edges of Kai's heart. Soft-footed, he darted down the slope into a patch of broken branches. There were only two ways off this cliff: descending the hill to the lodge or propelling off the sheer cliff on the backside—the very place he had fallen all those years ago. Considering Rayna was asleep, and these men were closing in on the top, he needed to act without getting caught.

Unsure what else to do, he thought of scaring the men into leaving. Through his connection, he called out to the Alpha. Within moments, Kai felt the wolf approach. His low growl and barks brought the pack to his side, and they appeared on the rocks above the two men.

The unsheathing of a sword caught Kai's ears. "Get back, beast, or I will put you down," Marcus snarled.

A firm hand touched Kai's shoulder. Rayna knelt at his side. "You should have woken me. What is happening?"

"Soldiers climbing to the lookout," he said, motioning ahead. "We need to hide or get them to turn back. I will not allow anyone to hurt the Alpha or his pack, even if I must attack them myself."

She nodded in agreement, "Call the wolves back." She pressed both hands against a sturdy oak. "I hate to ask this of such a strong tree, but it is the only way." Her skin started to turn gray and craggy like the bark.

Kai did not understand her plan, but he instructed the Alpha and his pack to retreat. Then he watched her fade into the trunk of the tree, a curvy lump on the side of the oak. Her magic always mesmerized him.

Kai waited and listened. The men laughed and joked, shocked by their close and counter with the wild wolves.

"We should turn back," Joshua called.

"You're not afraid, are you?" Marcus challenged.

There was a sharp cracking sound followed by a dull thud, and Joshua was pinned by a large branch.

"Help, Marcus!"

Marcus came into view as he climbed down to reach his friend. "Easy does it, old man, I am here." He lifted the limb to help Joshua. "Maybe you are right. We should turn back."

Relieved they were undiscovered, Kai gleaned the area. The men were alone halfway up the ridge, but there were over thirty soldiers down at the lodge. As Rayna eased from the tree trunk, he held her hand to steady her. "We need to leave." He narrowed his eyes. "Where do you think they are going?"

As if certain, she pulled him up the hill. "By now, the *Dragaron* should have delivered me to Diu. These men could be searching for me."

Kai nodded, sure that she was right. "We should leave before the guards change their minds."

Now that his strength was returning, Kai slowly began to pull energy from his surroundings—a slow, easy drain to ensure he did not alert any possible Katori in the area. Not enough to make his crystal glow, but enough so that he felt the magic build. The Alpha and his pack ventured close, and Kai thanked them—then they disappeared into the forest, as did the other animals.

"What is the point of searching, we should be running away?" Rayna asked. "If we cannot find Iver's body, we are finished. How do we find a dead man?"

The question fell on Kai like a ton of bricks. His life, and now possibly Rayna's, depended on him proving his innocence. "There is only one place to find the dead—a cemetery. If you want to hide a body, do it in plain sight. Stash it where everybody goes, but blinded in their own grief they +-do not see. Iver would just be one more dead man. There are two graveyards in Port Anahita and three in Diu. Sabastian and Kendra are searching Diu and Thade Mountain. We will check Port Anahita and the forest below Diu, but I must go back to Diu alone if we cannot find my father. I will not risk your life for my choices. You must travel to Katori to tell them what happened and to prepare for whatever comes next."

His words were final, and he made sure his tone implied there was no room for discussion. Rayna stayed silent, and he regretted his tone. A small part of him wished she had challenged him; however, they both knew the likelihood of finding the person who was there the night Iver died and took his body was slim to none. And running was no life either.

CHAPTER 18

Graveyards

Above the dreary weather, Kai flew. The clear blue skies above the clouds felt serine, but he could not fly forever. Feeling rejuvenated, he was surprised when they reached Port Anahita within less than an hour.

Below him, the thick clouds dumped a mix of snow and rain on Port Anahita. Small breaks revealed a dark, sad city hiding from the weather, much like hiding from his troubles. Lost in the melancholy moment, Kai almost did not notice Rayna shivering; she was cold. The fire built within his body and filled the well in his throat. Resisting the urge to belch, he let the heat wash back down his throat. He felt Rayna squeeze his warm neck.

The view of Port Anahita from the sky must have been exhilarating, but Kai could not find pleasure in his descent. Outside of town, he drifted through the clouds toward a large cluster of snow-covered pine trees. Not wanting to leave giant dragon prints in the snow, he transformed mid-fall before he landed. Rayna clutched his neck tighter than he expected.

Rayna secured her thick coat around her neck. "Well, at least it stopped raining."

The lining in his coat, borrowed from Robert, left him wishing he'd taken something different. "We need to make this quick. We have little time left."

They walked hand-in-hand through the trees and down the small hill. The wet snow clung to his boots, soaking the leather. The cold never bothered him until today—now it seemed like everything added to the guilt he carried.

When they reached the road, he looked both ways; no riders approached. Every moment they could go without seeing anyone felt like a gift, much like the persistent storm clouds. If he did not know better, he would swear they were the handiwork of a Weathervane, an advantage to conceal his movements. *But could I be so lucky?*

"There are two cemeteries," Kai pointed as they veered right at the fork in the road. "This older cemetery is rather large since the Battle of Port Anahita and the many casualties buried after the fight." At least, he hoped that would be the case.

She nodded. "Agreed. We should go there first, because it is the most likely candidate."

Over the next crest, the rolling cemetery hillside came into view. At the gates, they saw Diu soldiers stopping mourners, lifting cowls and hats. Others ordered cemetery workers to dig up and open freshly interred caskets while they poked around at the remains. The macabre scene of disturbing the dead made Kai's skin crawl.

What are they searching for?

No sooner did he think it than it hit him. These men were searching for the same thing he was—Iver.

Rayna pulled him down another path away from the cemetery. "What do we do now?"

"We cannot risk these men being able to identify me." He answered her question, and then asked his own. "Do they really think I stashed my father here? They must. Why else would they search the dead?"

Rayna's stomach grumbled. Kai turned and motioned toward the left. "You need food, and we should get disguises. Maybe we can get some information from the locals."

"Disguises?" Rayna squeezed his arm. "Do you believe anyone would recognize me? You certainly, but I am nobody."

At first, Kai thought Rayna might be right; maybe he was over exaggerating their notoriety. Around the next bend in the path, they neared an outlying building. There was a large poster with their faces sketched in vivid detail pinned to the whitewashed wood next to the image of the King. It was labeled—*murdered and missing*. There was no denying they were wanted criminals and Nola was searching for them both.

Given the extensive distribution of wanted posters, he began to wonder if their trip was a fool's errand. And yet, it made him wonder if Nola had soldiers searching for Iver; there was still a chance Kai could find his father first.

Like any good spy, Kai had to acquire the necessary items to disguise their identities. The idea of stealing left a hollow pit in his stomach, but then Riome would say it was the life of a spy. In service to the King, she saw it as a small price to pay by the citizens. He found ground coffee and black tea from one establishment, and from another, he borrowed—to use her term—white flour.

"We need cloaks," Rayna recommended. "I found a shop across the street, we may find something there that fits, but there are several patrons, and I am no thief."

"I have an idea, but it will take both of us." He suggested. "If you can provide a distraction, I might be able to get what we need. Touch as many things as possible and pick a few small items. The owner will be drawn to watch you, even if he is helping others."

She agreed and together they entered a fashionable furnishing shop. Kai kept his hands in his pockets and one eye on the owner as he searched the aisles for patrons. The elderly owner polished his thick spectacles, ignoring him in favor of an attractive blonde woman inquiring about her order.

Deeper in the shop, Kai noticed two women, one slender and poised, her nose held high as if the air was better above the petite waif unfolding a bolt of pink flora silk for the woman to inspect. Beyond the wool racks, he spotted a black fabric drape concealing another room. He gleaned the back room and found it empty.

With one quick look he spotted Rayna, she gently refolded a delicate lace sample before dipping her hand in a large bowl of glass beads. Her eye sparkled with delight as she pulled a large coin-sized red bead to hold up to her eyes.

Satisfied the coast was clear, Kai gave one final glance around the shop before slipping behind the partition. The space was rather large, with wire bodices on posts, bolts of material stacked on the table, and scraps of fabric littering the floor. One wall of the workroom had spools of thread and a variety of colored ribbons. Beside the desk, there was a series of wooden slots filled with what appeared to be sheets of paper. Curious, he pulled one out; the image was a detailed sketch of a dress with measurements in the margins along with various notes about the design. Lady Crutchfield's name was scrolled across the top.

Worried that he had left Rayna alone too long, he returned the sheet and rifled through the coat rack near the back door. There were five cloaks. He took the black fur-trimmed one for himself and a smaller navy coat with white fur for Rayna. Hearing voices, he ducked out the back door into the alley. Before he reached the corner, Rayna stopped him.

She jutted her head back the way she'd come. "We cannot go back to the main street; Diu soldiers are there. There is a spice shop this way." She motioned to the left. "You mentioned we still need oil and colored powder."

Kai knew stealing from a spice house was extremely difficult. Most spices were kept in jars, barrels, or boxes, precisely measured upon purchasing. Shame was a most unpleasant emotion, and stealing the spices felt wrong, no matter how much he needed them. Spices were costly, and the two women he robbed had not gone a block from the shop before he lifted the items. As natural as breathing, he lifted brown and red spices from one woman's bag and oil from another's basket as he slipped through the crowd undetected.

Two alleyways later, in an empty loft overlooking the stables, he sat next to a bright six-panel window. The afternoon sun bathed Rayna in golden hues. He worked the flour strategically into Rayna's hair and eyebrows, changing her dark brown waves into a naturally aged gray around her face.

Over a small metal pale, he crushed the coffee and tea with his hands and added a few drops of oil. He rubbed the mixture on their hands and faces, giving them both a dark brown hue. The other spices he had Rayna rub through his sandy-blond hair.

An essential trick Riome taught him involved tattoos, age marks, and scars. The details mattered more now than ever. He added age spots and two birthmarks to Rayna's face using charcoal bits from the stable's wood burner and ground coffee. He went more drastic to his face, with a dark birthmark beside his eye and a reddish-purple scar along his cheekbone.

Suitably transformed, they strolled into an outlying tavern. Inside they lowered the cowls on their hoods. The patrons did not give them a second look as they took the last empty table in the corner. The establishment benefitted greatly from the bay of windows catching the midday sun and the crackling stone fireplace on the opposite wall.

When the barmaid approached, Rayna placed all the coins they had on the table. "Two meals and some ale, please."

The barmaid took all her coins but one. "You've only enough for the meals and one ale."

Rayna nodded in acceptance. Moments later, the woman returned with two steaming bowls of hearty beef stew and a hunk of bread, and one cup of ale.

Excessive hunger does strange things to the stomach. The smell of spices and beef drifted to Kai's nose. He knew he was hungry, but he could not bring himself to eat the meat in his bow. He dipped the bread into the stew and nibbled on the vegetables. Meanwhile, he gathered information. Focusing from table to table, reading lips, and listening to those nearby, he learned a great deal.

Unable to eat another bite, Kai pushed back his bowl. "We should go if you are ready."

Rayna nodded and started to rise but sat back down. "My goodness, it cannot be." Rayna nudged Kai's foot with her own. "I know that woman. She used to help in my parent's bakery here in Port Anahita—her name is Gretta."

Gretta was a round woman, as most good bakers should be. Her gray-streaked auburn hair, pinned in a loose bun, sat like a plump pillow atop her head. Kai decided her pale complexion meant she did not spend much time in the sun, and her thick glasses and callused finger meant she spent hours reading and writing.

Taking note of them, Gretta approached. Rayna grabbed Kai's hand and squeezed. "Just breathe, the woman cannot possibly recognize you," he assured her. "She has not seen you in years, and I do good work. It may not up to Riome's standards, but even I would glance by without knowing it was you."

They watched Gretta walk straight to their table. Her glare was soft yet suspicious. "My dears," the older woman smiled sheepishly, "I hate to be so bold, but you appear to be leaving. Could I have your table?"

Rayna nearly knocked her chair over as she bolted upright. "Certainly, madam, we are leaving. Here, please, have my seat."

Confident the woman did not recognize either of them, Kai leaned toward Gretta. In his best Bangloo accent, he asked. "I am new in town. If I may ask, who are the Diu soldiers searching for?"

Gretta's eyes swelled in surprise, and her hand wrapped around Kai's arm as she pulled him into the seat beside her. "Let me tell you, dear." She leaned in close enough Kai could smell her rose perfume. "Our once beloved Prince Kai has murdered his father, our beloved King Iver Galloway, in his bed. I heard he escaped prison, killing four guards and maiming three others."

That's a lie, Kai thought—or at least he hoped it was a lie. There was no telling what happened after Keegan knocked him out and abducted him. His father quite possibly could have murdered countless people breaking him out of prison. Curious about what else Gretta knew, he continued to listen, hoping to learn something useful.

"Now, I would never believe it possible of the young man, but the word is, the Queen witnessed the whole thing. Word is he claimed innocence to his jailors, but when questioned by the King's council, he did not even defend himself."

Kai wanted to tell her it was not his fault, that there was more to the story than she knew. "Maybe the Prince was in shock? His father did die, after all. Perhaps he was in the wrong place at the wrong time."

"I suppose you're right, but why did he run? And now the King's body is missing, as is the Prince. They say he had an accomplice. Someone else in the palace helped him. The news I heard this very morning, the Grand Duke is questioning Prince Seth about the escape of a maid who is said to be close to the children, a Katori woman. It seems Prince Seth was lurking around the entrance to the dungeon the night before."

The more Gretta talked, the sicker Kai felt. He wanted to leave, but her firm grasp and incessant whispers pinned him to his seat. "Maybe this other person knows what happened, and maybe he could absolve the Prince. I have heard of the Prince's dedication to his father and Diu. Could he truly fall so far the citizens no longer have faith in him?"

His question gave her pause, and Gretta fell silent as if the idea had merit. "We all loved Prince Kai. He saved this very city, and his Aunt Helena, during the battle for Port Anahita, but he has since taken up with the Katori mountain-people. As I hear, he spent these past nine months hiding away with them and refused to return to Diu. I, for one, was shocked to hear that he even engaged in a battle against his own men in a scuffle north of Baden Lake."

A scuffle, Kai fumed. *Is that what they are calling it?* No, it was so much more. And he did not attack his men; he only fought against Milnosian soldiers. Men who deserved his wrath. Before he could speak, Rayna spoke for him. "Thank you kindly for the information, madam, but we really should be going." She pulled on Kai's other arm, and Gretta let go with a slight smile and a nod.

Kai grabbed their cloaks and followed Rayna outside. They walked for several blocks without a word. He knew he had pressed his luck questioning the woman, but he had to know what the people of Diu knew about the situation. So far, it was all rumor and speculation twisted with a few facts to make it believable.

The silence gave him time to let go of his anger and frustration, and it also made him appreciate Rayna's compassion. She did not chastise him for the risk, nor did she harp about what he could have said. Around the next corner, two guards stopped them.

"What is your purpose in the city?" the tall one asked.

"Visiting family who were killed during the Battle of Port Anahita," Rayna responded in a thick coastal accent as she pointed north. "We are headed to the graveyards outside of town."

The guards let them pass, and they continued in silence for another block before Kai spoke. "I'd say our disguises work. For a woman who spent years seeing you nearly every day, she had no clue who you were." He puffed up his chest, proud of his work.

"Well," Rayna looked up at him and put her hand on his chest, "I would know your blue eyes anywhere, even behind all this brown makeup and dust."

"Blue, you say," Kai focused on her brown eyes and felt his change.

"Why you green-eyed sorcerer." She kissed him quickly and pulled him through the crowded street. "So, what are we looking for? A newly dug grave? Any disturbed ground indicating a recent burial?"

"Well, we should get our facts straight," Kai suggested. "Before speaking to Gretta, I learned that Diu soldiers started searching for the

King's body the morning after they threw me in prison. Given that Nola's men had days to search, I am not sure what we expect to find now."

Rayna picked up the pace. "We have to try, and since we can glean beneath the soil, we may see something the soldiers did not. We should check any that look suspicious or newly tended."

They passed through the cemetery gates and Diu soldiers approached. "What business do you have here?" the man questioned.

Rayna patted Kai's hand. Just as before, she responded in a thick coastal accent. "Visiting family killed during the Battle of Port Anahita." She touched her heart and sighed. "The Wittels and the Moores," she added, letting her shoulders droop as she leaned into Kai.

The guard let them pass. Out of earshot, Kai whispered. "Are those real people?"

"Indeed," she responded, motioning up the hillside toward two disturbed graves. "They died in the fires. Good people, both families."

Her tone felt solemn, and Kai did not ask anything more. He had no idea she knew people who suffered or died in the battle. "I hate to say this, but we should consider separating to cover more ground. I will take the graves on this side if you search those." He jutted his chin toward the left.

Rayna nodded, and they parted.

Gleaning into his first grave, he instantly regretted the task; it felt like an invasion of privacy. The decaying corpse of a one-armed man made him shutter. The shriveled man had only four teeth and long, stringy white hair.

He did not think it could get worse, but the next nearly made him retch. The grossly swollen woman had foam leaking from her mouth and nose, and he suddenly felt grateful there was no smell from his point of view.

After searching several other graves near the perimeter with no success, he worked his way back down the hill. Two graves were soldiers, men buried with honors—the graves were marked with a white stone carved with their names, followed by their rank and years of life. It pleased him to know someone would remember them and honor their service.

The next site brought him to tears. The young baby could be no older than six months. It appeared peaceful and fresh, as if he could be taking a nap. This one had no name, a forgotten child. Who could lay their baby to rest and leave no marker? He shook his head and walked away.

Wanting to see no more forgotten souls, he searched the hillside for Rayna, hoping she was not struggling as much with her search. He found her walking with two young women between the stones. Their voices carried, but he could not hear their words.

Spotting one last mound of dirt, Kai wormed his way across the hill. Like the baby, there was no marker. No sign of who lay beneath or proof that anyone cared they were gone. The man inside lay perfect, as if only asleep—just one more dead man—no other signs of a second body buried beneath.

Waiting for Rayna to finish, Kai gleaned as many graves as he could, searching for signs that there was more than one body interred. He also searched for a site with unusually fresh foliage given that a Kodama could hide any newly buried body with new grass. Finding nothing, Kai turned to see Rayna headed his way.

"What did the young ladies tell you?" he asked.

"Their mother died ten days ago." Rayna pressed her hand to her heart. "They come every day. I asked if they noticed any strangers, but they have not. Although to listen to their grief, they would not notice a purple cow if one walked over her grave."

The story reminded Kai that he owed Rayna's parents his life. "Rayna, I need to tell you something. It may be difficult to accept, but I made a promise. When I was on the ship with Keegan, your parents were there. They saved my life and freed me from my shackles. They wanted me to tell you and your sister that they were sorry."

Although he believed her parents, he could not speculate their truth or sway her to feel differently. "I appreciate the information," was all she said on the matter. "Shall we check the last cemetery before traveling to Diu?"

Kai nodded and led the way to his Aunt Helena's home, the Avar Estate, and the small gravesite along the perimeter reserved for noblemen in the port. Could he dare to get that close? By the time he asked the question, the setting sun kissed the hillside and a small group of people. He did not have to glean to know it was his Aunt Helena and Uncle Kaeco.

CHAPTER 19

Helena's Pain

Under a large oak tree, Kai kept his distance, watching his aunt and uncle mourn over an empty plot. It seemed strange to him that she would make a memorial for Iver, but then again, he was her twin and their bond was strong. A pile of flowers showed the daily torment of Helena's pain. *She must come every day*, he thought, looking at the clumps of flowers in various stages of wilting. He wanted to comfort his aunt, tell her his truth, but she would hate him like the others.

Disturbing the dead even with his ability to glean felt every bit as wrong as digging them up. Still, Kai searched the hillside, grave by grave, hoping to find something, anything out of place. There was only one new grave, and the body was female. Everything was as it should be.

Rayna tugged at his arm. "We should leave before they come this way. No point risking getting caught," she warned.

Kai knew she was right, but he could not bring himself to leave. This was probably as close as he would ever be to his family. He loved them, and they hated him. It was foolish of him to believe he could change Iver's destiny. He did not listen to others' warnings, and now he was a traitor—murderer. He wanted to stay and confront them, but their sorrow ran deep. They would never give him the chance to explain or solve his father's murder.

Before he realized it, his Aunt Helena and Uncle Kaeco were nearly on top of them, venturing on the path back to the Avar Estate. There was no use in running; he could see the details of Helena's lacy black veil covering her face, and it could not hide the tears on her cheeks, the redness of her eyes.

He knew he should not look at her, but he could not turn away. Their eyes met, and Kai knew instantly that his aunt had seen through his disguise. Helena was a strong woman, and she held her composure walking away. She never said a word, only kept walking down the path.

Compelled to follow, Kai pulled Rayna down the path a safe distance behind his family.

"What are you doing?" Rayna whispered.

A jumble of feelings and thoughts battled in his throat. It was impossible to admit he knew this quite possibly was the biggest mistake so far, but he owed his aunt an explanation. "She deserves to hear the truth from me, not some report from Diu," Kai finally answered.

When Helena and Kaeco reached the estate, Kai held back as his family entered a small side gate. Wondering how close he could get, Kai paced near a large cluster of snow-covered pine trees. If his aunt wanted to speak with him, she would have to come back outside. As much as he hoped to talk with her, leaving Rayna alone did not seem safe.

He waited for nearly an hour and was about to give up when Helena came to the gate, alone. She stood clutching the iron bars, behind a prison of pain, and stared at him. Her black lace veil still covered her face, which held a new emotion, something Kai decided was a cross between anger and fear.

Helena did not lift her veil, but even through the tears, Kai thought she was beautiful. Knowing she was Iver's twin sister made him wonder if she also physically felt his loss. "Aunt Helena," Kai started, but then he stopped. Saying sorry did not feel enough. Overwhelming her with his true parentage also sounded wrong in his head. What could he say?

"Kai," Helena croaked, opening the gate between them.

New tears streamed down her face. And Kai started to reach for her. She did not back away, but he withdrew the affection. "There are no words . . ." Kai began again.

"Words, you think I want words from you?" Her tone seethed with sudden anger. "Words will not set things right. Nothing will bring Iver back to me. Do you know where my brother is? I felt his pain the night he died, sharp and quick, then I felt nothing. I will not accept that he is gone, I cannot . . ." Helen broke into tears.

There was no denying the shared connection of twins. Iver and Helena were always very close; he remembered stories of Iver feeling her pain during the birth of her son. "I do not know where they took Iver," he responded. "I know you miss him, and I wish he were here too, but words and wishes cannot change the truth."

His guilt bubbled in his throat. How could his words bring any comfort? This was a mistake, yet he continued to speak. "The night he died—I was there, but I did not stay as he breathed his last." His mind stubbled and his mouth felt dry like cotton. "I am sorry, I ran. Nola screamed for the guards." His explanation came out all wrong, but he could not help but try. "I believe there was another person in the room, someone hiding in the darkness. He or she knows the truth of what happened and the location of Iver's body. I believe it was possibly a man named Keegan."

His rushed retelling felt forced and factual, then he noticed the mention of his birth father's name sent a shudder down his aunt's spine. "I know his name . . ."

"Yes," Kai acknowledged. "The man who instigated the attack on Port Anahita last year."

"Keegan hurt your mother," Helena mumbled. A faraway look took her into the past. "Mariana was my best friend, and Iver, my twin. There are no secrets between twins or best friends. Keegan is your father. I have always known."

Helena's knowledge shook Kai to his roots. If she knew as Iver knew, all these years, she never let it show. The love she gave him felt overwhelmingly intense. "Who else knows?" he asked.

"Mariana only told me." In a display of affection, Helena reached out and touched Kai's arm. "Iver asked me not to tell Kaeco. Secrets between spouses cause a rift—small, but it is there. A burden I chose to keep."

Tears welled in Kai's eyes and streaked down his cheeks. "You know I did not kill my father, right?"

"Best dry your tears, my dear. They are ruining your disguise." She offered a hand to Rayna, pulling her close. "Take care of him, if you can. Take care of each other."

Like a clockwork keeping time with their suffering, the winter weather returned. Snow fell from the night sky. The sorrow and pain bubbled up like a volcano to bring them all to tears. For one moment, his family did not hate him. Kai felt his aunt's arm around his waist, holding him close. "I am sorry, Kai. Go find Iver and bring him back to me."

Letting go of the pain and the sorrow, Kai stepped back. "Don't be sorry. I know what I have to do. Thank you, Helena, for believing me. I only wish I could prove what really happened that night."

There was no warning, no sound; Helena's pain had masked their arrival. Twelve Avar Estate guards and his Uncle Kaeco approached through the snow. Kai looked at his aunt, searching her eyes to see if she had betrayed him.

She had.

"Did you believe anything I said?" Kai called out as he took Rayna by the hand and pulled her toward the path. They did not get far. Bitter winds whipped around them, ruffling their cloaks. "Stay close," Kai whispered to Rayna.

Twelve armed men would not be an easy fight on his own, but he could not discount Rayna's power. She was not as good in a fight as him, but she was fast, faster than these men. Weighing the options, Kai decided he only needed to give them an opening. Better to run and survive than fight and make a mistake.

Kai thought about what they had to work with. No weapons, only a pouch full of seeds and Rayna's dagger. He took notice of the largest man in the group who took a position behind him.

"Do your seeds work in the snow?" he whispered to Rayna, squeezing her hand and nodding to the right.

She squeezed back. Kai saw her slide her hand into the pouch on her waist. A handful of seeds dropped in the snow, and Rayna closed her eyes for a moment. He felt her pull of power from the storm, and he saw her free hand swirl at her side. New plant life rippled beneath a blanket of snow. Kai saw the vines slither and grow, ready to do Rayna's bidding.

Everyone paused. In an instant, Kai spun on his heels, catching his chosen man the throat, disarming him, and kicking the side of his knee at an odd angle. Using the butt of his newly acquired weapon, he struck a nearby man in the temple. The man dropped in the snow with a grunt.

Kai kicked the next man twice, once in the gut and then in the head. This was followed by a series of jabs and whacks with the butt of his sword, which dropped two more in the snow before they were able to land a punch. Dark green leaves popped up through the snow, climbing the legs of four men and yanking them to the ground.

Meanwhile, Rayna lurched at Helena with her dagger, pulling his aunt around like a shield with her blade near Helena's throat. "Back off. Call them all off!" Rayna shouted. "I have little to lose, so back off."

Kaeco shook his head. "How can I trust anyone who has a knife to my wife's throat? Kai is not the boy I knew. How could you do this, any of this?"

Rayna pressed the blade into the veil against the skin, drawing blood. Kaeco grabbed a sword from one of his men and stepped forward.

"Kaeco, no!" Helena stayed him with her hand. "Let them go. I will be fine, but you must let them all go."

Kaeco wavered, flexing his fingers around the sword.

Rayna said nothing, she only pressed the blade farther into Helena's neck, causing her to flinch in pain. Finally, Kaeco retreated, pulling the remaining guards with him. "I will not forget this, Kai," his uncle called. "You will pay for the blood you spilled today. You both will."

Kai cringed at Rayna's aggression. How had they become so desperate? He touched her arm. "Let's go," he whispered, then he called out, "Do not follow us, Uncle."

Rayna released Helena, and then they took a few cautious steps backward before turning and running into the storm. Helena watched them go with tears in her eyes.

◆ ◆ ◆

The storm ebbed and flowed throughout the day, changing the visibility from complete whiteout to clear and back again. Now moonlight peeked through the clouds, highlighting the wintery landscape.

Kai and Rayna ran down a back road behind the Avar Estate, avoiding the groundskeeper's house, stables, and guardhouses. They moved quickly, but not too fast, keeping their distance from any of the servants or workers. Their goal was to reach the outskirts of town and the road to Diu without being discovered.

A speck of a rider crested the knoll along their chosen path, and Kai pulled Rayna from the road and down the embankment. Tiny snow flurries and the lack of trees offered zero coverage, leaving them exposed. When a second and third rider crested, Kai sank to his knees into the snowdrift. Time was not on their side. If they hoped to go unnoticed, they needed to decide what to do fast.

The three riders came closer, and Kai sank as deep as he could into the snow and leaned into the embankment in front of Rayna. The thundering horse hooves matched the pounding in his heart. He had no idea how much trouble they were in until their uniforms became visible. With the slightest bit of moonlight piercing the clouds, he noticed their midnight blue uniforms with a silver spear through a crescent moon— the symbol for Fort Pohaku. He held his breath as they came within fifty feet. The lead man stopped and gazed in all directions before turning and galloping back toward the waiting group at the top of the hill.

"Scouts," he whispered as if it mattered at this distance. "There will be more men, many more."

"I recognize their uniforms," Rayna said. "Navy men from Fort Pohaku. Roark's men are here. Your uncle must have sent them to search the estate grounds. Our clothing is too dark against the snow; those men will spot us if we run."

Kai frowned. "I agree, our disguises are useless."

Rayna rose again to look over the knoll. "The estate is behind us, but what is across those fields?" She pointed to over the road.

"Farms. Too flat and far to run. They will spot us long before we reach those trees."

"Your snow wolf is mostly white. From a distance, you would be near impossible to see." Rayna pulled opened her dark cloak, exposing her bright white blouse. "If I remove my cloak and you shield me from the road, we could make it."

Kai studied the rolling slope leading toward the estate. "Maybe, if we walk over the knoll." He looked up the road again. "Could be worse, at least these men are not Roark's elite unit. They do not have the Galloway symbol on their coats. It would mean Roark would not be far behind them."

His confidence sank when the silhouette of Dresnor came into view. Perched high in the saddle, his friend stopped at the top of the hill and waited for the returning scouts. More men crested the hill, forming two lines behind Dresnor.

"We need to move now." She gave him little choice by taking the cloak from his shoulders and balling it up around her cloak. "When we reach the top, we should run. I know you will not be able to speak to me once you transform, but I will keep up."

Kai nodded. "It may be a risk, but I think we should walk at an angle toward the men." He used his hands to demonstrate a parallel movement. "The sooner we pass them, the better. They should continue to follow the road and we can reach the tree line to hide."

Taking hold of his crystal, he transformed while remaining low along the ground. Giving a quick shake of his fur, he stood tall and glanced up the road. The scouts fell in line, and Dresnor took the lead as the group started down the hill. An uneasy feeling swelled as he watched them until Rayna's hand touched his side.

Letting his fluffy tail brush the snowy trail behind them, he held his ears back and head down, hoping to hide the blackest parts of his snow wolf's coat. It was a risk going back the way they came and getting closer to the estate grounds, but he could not risk crossing the road into an open field. Instead, he eased away from the road and walked toward Dresnor and his men.

Rayna nestled near his front leg, her head leaned into his wolf's shoulder. His massive size hid her from view as she hopped through the knee-deep snow while he walked at a comfortable pace up the slope. Each step took them closer to safety, although he knew no hiding place would be safe as long as they were in Port Anahita with Roark nearby. Meanwhile, Dresnor's group came closer.

A sharp whistle caught Kai's attention, and his wolf ears perked to the sound. Stopping, he instinctively turned his head toward the road. He stood parallel with Dresnor. A tightness formed in his chest as he stared at his friend. Were they friends anymore? After all, he asked this man for help, and Dresnor had threatened to turn him into the authorities.

Rayna whispered in his ear. "We need to go, Kai."

He knew she was right, but he felt paralyzed by the past. There were so many lies and half-truths between them now. The deceit lingered between him and his old friend like an invisible wall they both knew was there but had no idea how to tear it down. *I am so tired of running. There is no escaping my fate. Should I turn myself in now, save everyone the trouble?*

Dresnor eased his horse down the embankment. Frozen by sadness, Kai stared at his past, torn between staying and running away. *I am ready to give up*, he wanted to shout.

Moving slow and easy, Dresnor rode closer. "Hello there, you beautiful beast," his friend called, riding slow—getting closer. "I have never seen anything like you before, you stand as tall as my horse."

Kai stared. *Take me away, I do not care anymore*, his insides screamed.

A guard called from the road. "Dresnor, this is foolish, look how big the wolf is . . . Come back, man, please."

Rayna grabbed handfuls of wolf hair and pushed Kai. "Please! Please, run!" she cried.

An uneasiness rolled in Kai's stomach, and his hackles rose. Rayna's plea touched his heart, and he shook his head, mane, and body. *I have something—someone to live for*, he remembered.

Baring his teeth, he growled at Dresnor's horse. As loud and fierce as he could, he barked and growled and stepped toward his foe. The horse reared, but Dresnor held the reins. "Easy now." Dresnor wrangled his horse under control. "Easy boy."

"Dresnor!" another man shouted. "Should we kill it?"

Kai lowered his head and growled again as his friend back away, directing his horse onto the road. "No, leave it be!" Dresnor waved them off. "Let's go." He led his men down the road.

Kai lowered his head and felt ashamed for his foolishness.

Rayna wrapped herself in both cloaks. "Come now," she put her hands on either side of his muzzle and let her head fall against his. "You will be alright. Roark is coming, and we still needed to check the woods between here and Diu. Probably best if you stay in beast form. If I ride on your back, we will make better time than walking. Not sure there is any safe place for you to become a dragon."

In agreement, he lowered into a crouch so Rayna could climb onto his back.

New snow fell from the sky, hiding them both in the rebirth of the storm. Kai hated to admit all the doubt swirling around in his head. The usual four-hour horseback ride to Diu took him less than an hour. And once again, the storm eased, revealing patches of the clear stary night through the clouds.

CHAPTER 20

The Gravedigger

The moonlight danced between the rolling clouds kissing Baden Lake. Standing at the edge of the snow-covered forest, Kai clutched Rayna's hand. In the distance, he could see Diu beyond the Stone River Bridge. The sound of rushing water below Baden Lake dam was serene, but the lights of his city mourned its king.

Snowflakes and bitter cold ripped through the trees, and Kai felt Rayna shiver by his side. They both knew starting a fire was out of the question, but they needed to find a warm place to spend the night.

She rubbed her arms. "I am usually not this cold, even in the mountains. Maybe I can build something off the ground with a surround to block the wind and keep the snow off our backs. We can search the forest from the treetops."

"Good idea, I could transform back into my snow wolf. I can still use my gleaning ability, and you would have two cloaks and my fur to help keep you warm. Can you make something large enough for me?"

Her hesitation left a gaping silence between them. She wormed through the woods, looking up and down several tall oaks and pines. "I suppose, but I will need to ensure we have a strong tree to support you. We should get at least fifteen feet off the ground to go unnoticed, should anyone pass by. Here, this spot already has a few vines."

She pulled seeds from her pouch, knelt to clear the snow, and dug a hole for her plants to grow. Three different vines sprang from the ground, twisting and snaking up the largest of two oaks: one thick and woody with brown and orange leaves, another mossy and dark, and the last covered in large evergreen pine-scented narrow leaves. Up and up her foliage grew, taking her with it. "Is your snow wolf afraid of heights?" She shouted down from the center of three oak trees within the pod she created.

He took hold of the thicker vine and climbed after her. "Very funny." When he reached the top, she stood and worked the walls of the nest. Her latticework mimicked the pods back in Katori, minus the stonework used to hold a fireplace and distribute heat around the home.

"This is much larger than I thought from the ground. I hope it is strong enough for me once I transform."

She huffed a puff of white into the cold air. "You doubt my work?"

"Well, no, I just . . ." He waved his hands around as if to show the size of the snow wolf in relation to the space.

The curl in the corner of her lips stopped his protest as she continued to soften the hardscape with the mossy vines and encourage the thick garland to conceal their location. "There, that should do the trick. No time like the present. Either it will hold, or we will find ourselves on the forest floor." She motioned to the center of the space and stepped back to give him room.

Kai handed her his cloak for extra warmth. "Here goes nothing." He took hold of his crystal and started to transform, slow and easy in case he needed to change back. The tips of his ears reached the arch above his head, and the vines heaved. He crouched down as low as he could as his transformation completed.

"You are bigger than I thought!" She laughed, stroking his mane as he laid down.

The platform was just large enough that his paws did not hang over the edge. "I will search this side of the forest," Rayna pointed, and then she started sealing shut the opening with the thick garland vines from top to bottom. "You can search the other side."

The moonlight disappeared behind the vines she created to seal the opening. Kai shook his head and grunted, hoping she would understand his meaning as he began to search the surrounding landscape. He gleaned over and around felled trees, into a fox den, and through an abandoned shack, but no signs of anyone trying to hide a body. Deeper still, he searched under a pile of leaves and down a frozen creek bed.

After hours of searching, Rayna yawned and leaned into him, resting her back against his fur-covered shoulder. He liked the weight. *I am so sorry I brought you into this*, he whispered to her with his mind.

"I love you too," she whispered, pulling his extra cloak around her knees. "I have not found anything, have you?"

He could only shake his beastly head no.

The vines parted slightly at the touch of Rayna's fingertips. "You are terribly quiet," she said, nudging him. "Mind sharing your thoughts, or are you staying like that all night?" She sat up, and he could almost feel her looking at him.

This would be his last night of freedom—and his last night with her. The thought sent a shudder down his spine. He could see things so clearly now, but it was too late to go back and undo his choices. Kai transformed and sat cross-legged next to her, staring out the tiny opening. "My mind is a jumble—everything from you to my mother and both of my fathers. Even my destiny haunts me. Not sure I can organize my thoughts."

"I do not mind listening." She turned to him and him to her. "Sometimes, saying your thoughts out loud helps make sense of them."

He knew she was right; he had kept everything boxed away in his mind for far too long.

"I lied to you, and myself, these past few months. I was not working with Basil every day. And I was not imitating my mother's magical journey to help her recover. Truth be told, I mimicked my mother's experiences to understand why she did not choose to come back to me. Did she love being a dragon more than being with me?"

A lump formed in Kai's throat, but he kept going. "Every choice she ever made was usually for the benefit of someone else. Instead of running home to Katori after her escape, she started a new life in Diu with Iver. Maybe she thought returning to Katori would bring Keegan back into her life. Concealing my identity and hiding me from my real father gave me a chance to have a normal life with a man who loved me and treated me like a son."

New tears welled in his eyes and spilled down his cheeks—Iver was dead, and it was his fault. "Alenga showed me Iver's fate. Saving my father was never my mission; I now believe that my vision was to help me let him go. I had every opportunity to embrace my future in Katori, but I thought I knew better. In my arrogance, I imagined I could best Nola. Even Riome tried to warn me that Nola's brainwashing was unbreakable. I wanted to be the hero and save everyone, but instead, I lost everything."

Unable to control his own words, his inner pain poured out. "Alenga asked me to bring her people home, but I ignored my mission to reunite Katori. Because of my choices, I have lost Katori, too. Rayna, I left you behind because I thought I had to do everything on my own. I was a fool."

Guilt was a funny thing. It had a way of giving your mind clarity while punishing your soul. Kai pulled his stone from inside his shirt and let it dangle between his fingers. "Now that I know a Beastmaster can transform without their crystal, as painful as it is, it means that my mother chose to stay trapped. All this time, I thought she did not have a choice, but she did."

Rayna touched his arm. "Your mother was thought to be dead. You know as well as I that she could not return to Diu without revealing the Katori secrets. What other choice did she have?"

Hearing the truth did not make it any easier. "Recently, I imagined what would have happened if my mother did come back and stole me away. We would have spent our lives on the run unless the Elders welcomed us back. Which I am sure Keegan's spies would have discovered us, surely he would have returned to Katori for my mother and discovered me."

They sat in silence for a few moments. There was so much raw emotion bubbling inside Kai; he felt as if he would crack if he opened his mouth again. Rayna seemed to know his next thoughts, and she let them out slow and easy so he could accept them in small bites.

"I cannot begin to imagine the shame Mariana felt given what Keegan did to her—knowing what her country thought of the man, and how she carried his child. I understand why she never returned to Katori, and why she lied about your origins. She was lucky Iver found her." Rayna must have sensed that her point had settled in his soul, and she continued. "I cannot presume to know her reasonings beyond keeping the Katori secrets, but your mother spent a decade trapped by men who used her as a weapon. What a terrible life."

His mother's sacrifices were etched across his imagination. Was he strong enough to make the same? His time on the ship with Keegan showed him the horrific life he might have lived had his mother not given up her heart's desire to live in Katori—and maybe even return to Ryker. All to save him from his father.

"There is something I do not understand," Rayna said, interrupting his thoughts. How did Mariana's crystal force her to become a dragon and pull her across the ocean to Iver?"

"When I first awoke on Keegan's ship, feelings of anger and hate overwhelmed me. The room was thick with desires that were not my own. The scariest part was when my dragon claws sprouted from my fingertips, then receded as though they were never there. Our crystals are connected to our magic—to us specifically. For us, the stone amplifies magic; it softens the raw nature of power and provides the ability to enhance our gifts. And, it would seem, the wielder: us or another can control part of our magic."

Panic bulged Rayna's brown eyes. "Do you mean to say, with our stones, anyone could control us—use our own magic against us?"

"Unfortunately, yes. I thank Alenga nobody has discovered this—otherwise, all Katori could be weaponized against our will. If Keegan had witnessed my hand change while he held my crystal, we would be in a totally different sort of trouble now. My father seemed to hope he could use the power within my stone to his advantage for more power; his disappointment was obvious. I asked my grandfather Lucca what happens to the crystals after death. He said the stones are crushed and the magic returns to Alenga. All of Katori believes they only channel magic, and while that is true, the crystals are also tied to the owner."

More truth poured from Kai's thoughts. "My mother was in a no-win situation. She must have understood the same thing when it happened to her. When I was old enough to listen and not cry, my father told me a story. As he sailed across the Caprizian Sea, maybe a half a day's journey out from Port Anahita, pirate vessels attacked his ship. They outnumbered him three to one. Fearing he would not ever see my mother and me again, he held her necklace and wished for the old days when dragons fought alongside Diu. And as his story goes, a dragon came to him and saved him and his crew. I never knew he kept the dragon and wielded her like a weapon. I guess that explains his success. He and his dragon secured trade routes and brought in wealth to our kingdom. No ships dared attack a Diu vessel in those early days for fear of his dragon."

"What a miserable life." Kai could see the empathy in Rayna's eyes as she spoke. "Torn between keeping the Katori secrets and being with her husband and son."

The weight of his mother's decisions and his own made it hard to breathe.

"Are you sure you want to return to Diu without proof?" Rayna asked. "We did not find Iver's body, we did not find this third person. They will hang you tomorrow. Can we not run? Disappear?"

Rayna's urgent plea and fear were understandable, but he knew that would be no life for either of them. "I failed to understand the loyalty my mother demonstrated to the Katori people all those years ago. Now it all makes sense. I am ready to stand up for my mistakes, but it is not my place to reveal the Katori secrets. My mother spent a decade of her life in torment to prove her loyalty. Could I not do the same? I promised to return to Diu, and my word is my bond."

Rayna grabbed his hand and squeezed tight. "Kai, I found something—or rather, someone. A body buried in the woods. He is fresh, if you know what I mean." Her other hand slid through the vines like a knife through butter.

Mind racing, Kai took hold of her elbow. "Where? Show me."

"Take hold," Rayna pointed to one of two hooked vines dangling next to the opening. She grabbed one and the vines wrapped around her as she stepped off.

Anxious to follow, Kai grabbed the woody hook and stepped off. Thick vines slithered down his arm and around his waist, easing his descent. As his feet touched the snow, the vines retracted, setting him free to chase after Rayna.

She was nimble and quick on her feet, considering they had not slept since yesterday. She darted around trees and rocks with lightning precision. Vaulting over felled trees and stomps, she ran farther away from Diu. Before Kai could glean the area, she dropped to her knees without a sound and pulled him down beside her.

"Shhh," she whispered, pointing into the shadows. "Do you see him?" Rayna directed Kai's attention to the thick underbrush in the woods in front of him, but he saw nothing, only snow flurries dancing amongst the shadows.

Thump, thump, thump. Kai heard someone pounding the ground. "This is our last night together," a man's voice resonated through the trees. "I am done watching you rot. Nobody will ever find you here. I promised to hide you well and bury you deep. She made me promise, and I always keep my promises."

Controlling his pounding heart, Kai gleaned the darkness. Deeper into the woods, a man scooped dirt with a shovel and pounded the ground to flatten the clump. Curious, he gleaned what the stranger had buried—a man with a stab wound on his left side just below his heart, his face too damaged to be identified. Goosebumps covered his skin and pricked the hair on the back of his neck.

The stranger heaved the last of the dirt over the unmarked grave and brushed a few sticks and leaves for good measure. "Good riddance—you will not be missed." The man stood and dusted his hands and knees.

Did this person work for Nola? Was this another person doing her bidding? Had she been the one to arrange the removal of Iver's body from the palace? A million questions shot through Kai's brain at once, and unable to control himself, he darted into the night after the stranger. Fear and excitement pounded in his chest with each step. Could this be Iver? He did not want to lose this person, a possible witness of Iver's murder. Without care or stealth, he stormed through the woods, focused on the grave and the gravedigger.

Smack! Something struck Kai on the side of his head, sending him to the ground. "Darwin, you idiot!" the man standing over Kai shouted.

Kai squirmed on the ground. Stars danced around his head.

"Carter!" Darwin, the gravedigger, yelled with a Milnosian accent. "What are you doing out here?"

"Looks like I am saving your hide," said Carter with a thick Port Anahita draw, towering over Kai. "What do you want, boy? Who sent you? Speak, or I will put you in a grave of your own."

Scattered moonlight offered a meager glimpse of Carter's features. Covered in hunting gear and furs, he was an ox of a man with stark-white hair blending into a long, white beard. A short wooden staff bounced in his hand. "Speak, boy, or I will thump you again with my stick."

Head pounding, Kai tried to stand, but Carter knocked him back to the ground with his boot. "I said, what do you want, boy? Tell me or this is as far as you go."

Considering Darwin spoke with a Milnosian accent, Kai decided to do the same. "I came for my father," Kai gasped, pointing to the makeshift grave, thankful his disguise hid his true identity. "Who is in that grave?" He tried again to stand, this time ready for the blow that never came.

Carter chuckled. "You are a long way from the streets of Milnos, boy. I doubt he could be your father, illegitimate maybe, but I doubt it. You are too filthy to live the way this man did, I am guessing you grew up in the navel district by your twang. Trust me, this man had fine things, and you, well, look at you. Go home to your mother. You have no business being out in this storm. I do not know you, and you do not know me. Let us keep it that way."

The more Carter spoke, the more Kai needed to know who Darwin had buried ten feet from where he stood. Could they be speaking of Iver? These did not look like Keegan's Caroco men, and they were not Katori. Darwin's Milnosian accent confused him. Was he one of the Regent's men? Maybe Keegan was not involved. Had Nola arranged these two men to dispose of the King to further the war?

Kai looked at Darwin, hoping this man might be more reasonable. "My father was very well off, and his wife had him murdered, stabbed in the side." Kai pointed to his ribs. "I need to know if this is my father. Please, sir."

Darwin stepped back, and Kai got a better look at the other man. His navy cloak had a fine edge, embroidered in gold and silver, and his trimmed auburn beard angled to a point below the chin. "I am sorry for your loss, boy—but you are not his son. She is a powerful woman, and removing this man was the only way I could get close to her."

"Shut your mouth, Darwin," Carter snapped. "We do not know who this sewage rat is, but there is no way he is this man's son. Do you want him turning you in? You hired me to help you bury a man, not to become an accomplice in a highborn murder. I will not be locked away, even if I have to kill you both." He swung his short staff, preparing to strike the first man to move as he retrieved a large hunting knife from a leather sheath.

As Carter's gaze passed from Kai to Darwin, Kai stuck the hunter in the knee cap. The sweeping motion knocked Carter's leg out and sent him falling backward. In the same movement, Kai liberated him of his weapons and pinned him to the ground. "I do not care what you think of me—I am nobody—but I will have my answers. Who lays buried in this grave?"

Darwin's eyes swelled with fear, and he turned to run. Kai tossed the short staff, striking the man in the head, dropping him to his knees. "Answer me!" Kai shouted.

"I do not want any trouble, young man—" Darwin rubbed the newly formed lump on his head and raised a hand in submission "—but Carter is right. There is no way this man is your father. To say this man had status, well, again, no offense, but you do not appear to move in the same circles."

Rage boiled beneath Kai's skin. He was so close to freedom he could almost taste it. These men were the proof he needed. Carter squirmed; in desperation, Kai applied more pressure. "I only need one of you," he seethed, dragging the knife along Carter's jawline, carving deep enough to draw blood. "The first one to talk lives another day."

"The man buried there is nobleman Barton Manzini, his wife is Louisa Carmelo-Manzini, cousin to the Grand Duke of Diu, Dante Carmelo," Darwin blurted. "Please do not kill me!"

Sadness and disappointment broke Kai's heart in half. Carter took advantage of Kai's relaxed grip, tossing him to the side and freeing himself. "Not the name you were hoping, boy? But now that you know, well, I am afraid I will have to kill you." Carter pulled a cylindrical metal device with a solid wooden handle, a familiar weapon from Kai's past.

There was no time to think. Unwilling to kill Carter, Kai tossed the hunter's knife at the man's kneecap—it sank deep, dropping Carter to the ground. The unfired hand cannon fell into the snow as Carter writhed in pain. Kai retrieved the blade. "I have no time for your misdeeds, but now you will have a permanent limp, if you ever walk again. Justice will find you, both of you. This much, I promise." He turned to Darwin and cut free one of the monogrammed buttons securing the man's cloak as proof before darting away into the shadows to find Rayna.

He found her hidden in a thicket a few yards away. As he approached, she motioned, and he followed. They ran for miles, putting distance between them and the murderous Darwin and Carter. The speed blurred the tears in his eyes. Heartbroken, he wept, not for Barton Manzini , a man he knew well, but for his father. He was faced once again with the realization that his father's death was his fault, and he had no proof to show otherwise. Tired, he stopped and dropped to his knees.

Holding his face, he sobbed. This had all been a waste of time, and now as a wanted fugitive, he could not even turn in the murderers of a family friend. He felt Rayna wrap his cloak around his shoulders. She never said a word, just held him tight.

CHAPTER 21

Precious Moments

After a long, emotional night, Kai held Rayna's hand as they wandered through the woods, headed for Diu. "How, by the way, did you find yourself in Chenowith?" he attempted to fill the silence and avoid the thoughts twisting his insides.

"Well, let's just say that after you flew off without so much as a goodbye—I was angry, about a lot of things." She tilted her head to look at him. "Considering there was little I could do to stop you, I watched your dragon fade into the night. Your grandfather, Lucca, charged up the hill, insisting Simone chase after you. She refused. Like me, she hoped you would see reason and return on your own. Unsure what else to do, I even begged her to take me to follow you. Again, she said no."

Thankful that her tone held no malice, Kai took her other hand in his. He could tell the pain behind the memory was fresh, but he waited for her to continue. "Then Lucca ordered Benmar to bring you home, but your other grandfather would not respond to anything Lucca said. It was like Benmar was in a trance, focused on the sky. Your grandfather muttered a few incoherent words and then turned to Lucca and said, 'Kai needs my help.' In a flash, he transformed and charged after you. We all stood there in shock. Lucca again pressed Simone to follow, but she insisted two people forcing Kai home would only make matters worse. She felt you had to want to come back on your own. Naturally, they both tried to get me to go with them back to Katori, but I insisted that when Benmar managed to bring you back, I would be waiting. Mostly I wanted to give you a piece of my mind, and then I just wanted you back safe."

"Again, I am sorry for abandoning you. I was wrong about so many things, but mostly about not trusting you."

Her eyes softened, and she continued. "The following day, I decided one way or another I would get to Diu, to stop you or save you—I did not care which. I knew you hoped to save your father, and I only wished to arrive early enough. It took me about four days: walking, running, and camping, but I finally reached Chenowith. It took me a day to find Albert since I knew him, I felt he was the one to trust. He escorted me to his father, and they offered to let me stay with them while I recovered from traveling."

It felt like a fist crushed Kai's heart. "I am sorry the Chenowiths misled you. They are good people, very loyal to Diu. I cannot blame them, but it does anger me. I hope they did not mistreat you."

She shook her head. "Not really, not at first. I must admit when they would not let me leave, I was less than cordial. I might have broken a few glasses and a vase." She winced in guilt. "They did not restrain me, but when Lord Oliver could not get me to settle down, he sent in Lady Clair. I only met her once two years ago before the Winter Festival, but she is a commanding woman for one so delicate."

Kai nodded in agreement. Lady Clair's statuesque frame and golden locks, matched with her elegant clothes, gave the impression she was a fragile porcelain doll. Instead, she was anything but. The woman had a way of setting you at ease while ensuring there was no doubt who was in charge. "What did she say?"

"Well, Lady Clair reminded me that a lady commanded more respect when keeping her head than when showing her anger. She was kind enough to explain that Queen Nola hoped that by bringing me to Diu, I could convince you to turn yourself into the authorities. Lady Clair was not convinced it was right to use me to lure you out, but she did agree that you would come to Diu if you found out I was there."

"Do you remember when Lady Clair found us dancing in the gardens?" Kai laughed, hoping to lighten the mood.

Rayna blushed. "How could I forget? A second later and she would have found us kissing."

It was true. Kai had meant to kiss her. Their lips were so close, but then he heard a woman clear her throat. "She must have known, but she only commented on the late hour and said something about a lady's reputation is defined by many things, including the hours she keeps."

Rayna pulled Kai's hand, trying to continue their journey. "I cannot imagine what she would say of our current hour."

He pulled her back into his arms. "Seems to me, she interrupted a moment." He kissed her on the lips, then twirled her away before he lost himself in the moment.

◆ ◆ ◆

Dawn trickled across the snow-covered landscape as they neared the edge of the forest. Kai glanced down at his appearance and then to Rayna—neither of them were at their best, but Rayna never seemed more beautiful. Perhaps it was because this would be their last morning together, or perhaps because he wanted her to know how much he loved her, but either way he could not let the moment pass. "I love you, Rayna." He took her hand in his and cupped her face with the other. "I loved you from the moment we met. I have no right to ask, now that I am sentenced to death, but I want to spend my life loving you."

Rayna blushed. "And you will." She rose on her toes and kissed him. "When this is all over, you will ask me properly, and we will live wherever you want."

Her sincerity stirred his spirit. Time was a precious gift, and he did not intend to squander it, so he kissed her again.

CHAPTER 22

Convergence

The warmth of Rayna's hand sliding into his stopped Kai at the edge of the forest, and her strength added to his. Today he would need every ounce he could get, even if it were not his own. Part of him was glad she was here; he did not want to stand alone, but he also wished she were safe in Katori. If they took him away in chains, how could he guarantee her safety?

His eyes drifted to the bridge, a hundred feet from where he stood. Over the past few days, they spent more time running and hiding than searching. It would be the hardest walk of his life, but this was the only way he could think to end a war.

I am so tired, he thought. *Just a few steps left, and it will all be over.* Words cluttered his mind; if only he knew the right combination to save himself and send Rayna to safety, but she was stubborn, and she loved him. "Are you sure you want . . ."

She squeezed his hand, and he let the rest of his question drop in the cold snow at his feet.

Before the moment passed, he swept her into his arms. "I love you, my dear Rayna. Never forget that." He cupped her face with his hand and kissed her sweetly.

Then Kai noticed they were no longer alone. The Alpha and his pack approached. Deep in the forest, their nature called to him, but he held them back.

This is not your fight, Alpha, Kai said to the wolf's mind. I will not let you fight for me, not this time.

He gleaned the woods, allowing his mind to wind through the trees to see his old friend one last time. Snow-covered branches gleamed with his magic, giving the gloomy day a much-needed brightness. Stopped in a thicket, the Alpha stood proudly with his pack. They heeded his request, but they did not leave.

Stay hidden, he told them. I must speak with the other humans.

Kai's thoughts betrayed him, and he knew his true desire was to run away and start over.

Come with us, Beastmaster, and we can show you places no human ever treads.

Tempted by the thought, Kai took a few steps back into the forest, still clutching Rayna's hand. Then a rustling sound brought Kai's mind back to his body. Twisting his head around, he searched for the sound again. Rayna jutted her chin to the right. He raised his hands, ready to fight his attacker.

"You are off your game, boy," a familiar voice shouted.

The tension level in Kai's neck and shoulders relaxed, but only a little, when he heard his friend's voice.

"Sabastian?" He craned his head to see around the tall snowy pines. His friend stepped out of the shadows with another familiar face. Kai could not believe his eyes. "Kendra? You both came."

They were alone, so he assumed the worst, but hope still lingered. "Did you find Iver's body?" he asked and knew the answer from the sadness Kendra could not hide.

"I am sorry." Kendra took Rayna's hand in hers, keeping her gaze on Kai. "Every rickety shack, abandoned farm, and cemetery between here and Black Bear Fort has turned up nothing. I questioned many travelers, even a few Katori, but nobody saw anyone trying to hide or dispose of a body. If you searched from here to Port Anahita; there is no place left to look. Whoever took Iver is simply—gone."

Not wanting to be ungrateful, he looked away as he asked, "So, what are you doing here?" He hated saying it, but he did not want more people to suffer because of his mistake. "There is nothing left you can do for me. Being here could put you both in danger. I am not sure I can stop what is coming."

"Sabastian and Kendra are here for the same reason we are," Yulia called through the gloom. "We stand with you. You are our family."

Kai turned to find Yulia and Riome trudging through the snow. A lump caught in his throat. Riome had warned him not to come back. What could he say to her? As she neared, he saw her expression held its own burden. Did she blame herself for not saving Iver? They both let the moment pass with a slight nod.

"Thank you for coming." Kai's eyes wandered to the gloomy sky, and he asked Yulia, "Any chance you could make my last day sunny?"

She laughed and rolled her hands in a familiar motion. "Who do you think has been making all this snow?" Kai felt Yulia pull fiercely at the energy around them. "It is exhausting work; every few hours I stoke the clouds with new moisture. If proving your innocence meant coming back to Diu, I knew you would need cover. Your silver dragon shines in the moonlight, and I have made it snow nearly every day since I heard you broke out of prison, from here south to Port Anahita and west to Henley. My storm spread like none I have ever created."

The clouds parted, and the afternoon sunshine warmed Kai's face, making him almost feel hot with his thick cloak. "I do not suppose you were able to discover any clues about what happened to Iver's body?"

Yulia shook her head. "My network did report your father Keegan came to Diu with six Beastmasters and two Kodama, and left carrying you from the city. The woman who witnessed your abduction did not interfere because your father has the reputation of a madman willing to murder anyone who gets in his way. Even we Katori avoid engaging with anything he does. She reported no other signs of anyone else being suspicious."

"As best I can tell," Riome said next, "your father never left the palace. He never left his bed. There is no blood trail—not one drop of blood around his bedchamber. Sure, I found stains on the rug next to the bed, supposedly the spot where his murderer stood and withdrew the blade. There were a few drops on the tile leading to the hallway, and a large spot where Nola fell and dropped the blade."

Riome's clinical response left Kai cold as he thought about standing in that very spot. He could almost feel the bloodstain on his hand, and he tried to wipe it away once more. "But how is that possible? There was so much blood. Maybe they wrapped him up in a cloth?" More questions bubbled up in his throat, too many to verbalize.

"The real question is: if Iver bled to death, where did all the blood go? Not into the bed. There was not enough to convince me he died in his bed, so where did he go?" She glanced around the group as if giving them time to soak up her conclusions. "Instead, I found singe marks on the canopy fringe. Silk burns slowly and recoils from fire, leaving behind a dark bead of gritty ash on the edge. There was a fire in that room—a small, controlled fire."

Theories swirled around the group like a tornado. They had more questions than answers and no time. Kai interrupted the speculation. "So, we have all searched Diu and the surrounding towns and found no evidence of Iver leaving the city, so you would have us believe he is still in the palace?" Kai looked around to ensure his account was accurate. "And because there is no trail of blood showing where he went, we are to consider he never left the bed? Or at least when he did, he was no longer bleeding? I am not sure where to go with this."

"I am not saying your father went up in a ball of fire," Riome said, "but something else happened in that room. He may have left his bed, but he was not bleeding out as you would expect from being stabbed with a blade only moments before."

A low rumble of thunder emanated from the ground. Kai could feel their vibrations before seeing them—the rhythmic march of many horse hooves. Eyes closed, he gleaned the approach of multiple groups.

Admiral Roark Raebun and Kempery-man Philip Dresnor led the Fort Pohaku army along Port Anahita's southern road. They were close but not yet within eyesight. The first group had mounted warriors followed by men marching five-wide along the narrow dirt road, and there seemed to be no end to the trail of men pouring into the area.

High on the hillside across from Kai, Drew and Robert Henley led a small contingent of men. They were riding at a brisk pace through the trees. He imagined they would arrive first, and he could only hope Drew might stand with him.

Within the Diu city walls, he also noticed movement; a horde paraded through the palace gatehouse and into the streets. Milnos and Diu soldiers merged like coordinated ants, with Regent Maxwell riding beside Queen Nola near the front. Their sight made him clench his jaw.

On Baden Lake, Kai watched Lord Chenowith and his son Albert stand at the ready with thirty men set to disembark the moment their ship reached the Diu pier. His friend had done as he promised. Now the question on Kai's mind was on which side his friends would stand. Would Albert continue to have faith and stand with him? Would Drew or Dresnor believe his innocence?

They were surrounded, and Kai knew there was no turning back now. Even if he wanted to change his mind, everyone came to see if he was a man of his word. Ready to face his fate, he climbed the hill to the road leading to the Stone River Bridge. The sound of water rushed down the partially frozen spillway below Baden Lake dam.

Sabastian pointed behind them. "We are about to have company. Men and women. Lots of them. Not warriors, but they carry weapons."

Kai pivoted with his mind and searched the valley behind them. "It is Lord Eugene Sknash, and he is leading around one hundred people. He must have nearly a third of the population from Town Hope with him."

Lord Eugene Sknash soon arrived with the large group. It was odd to see a man in a suit ride, out of place atop his noble chestnut horse. His old friend eased out of the saddle, and Kai noticed his awkward waddle. Eugene was not much for riding, but the man's composure let him know a friend approached.

Sweat poured down Eugene's forehead, and he looked exhausted, as did everyone else in his group. Kai offered a hand to Eugene. "Lord Sknash, what brings you to Diu? Is there trouble in Town Hope?"

Eugene accepted his hand but slipped by him to Rayna. "My dear lady, you are not in prison?" he questioned, reaching for her hand. "We came to Diu to protest your capture. Days ago, word came from the town of Chenowith that Queen Nola was taking Rayna to Diu. Knowing everyone searched for Kai, I surmised the Queen meant to use the dear girl as bait. King Iver was a good man, and Nola is our Queen, but I do not trust her. Not to mention, she rescinded my invitation to the Winter Festival because we were too small to merit attendance. King Iver would never exclude Town Hope. Mind you she will take our taxes, but not accept us in the palace."

Rayna hugged Eugene. "Thank you for coming," she blushed at the attention. "Kai means to turn himself over to the Diu authorities today." She motioned to the bridge, letting her eyes swell with tears as though a looming presence waited to spirit Kai away.

Horses' hooves thundered across the bridge. Kai separated himself from his group and approached the lead rider. "Drew, have you come to escort me to Diu?" He watched his friend slip from the saddle before his stead even came to a halt.

Drew's doubt clung to him like a wet shirt. "I did not think you would come." He turned back to the other riders just reaching the bridge.

Kai stood tall and proud in front of Drew, his head held high. "Of course, I am here. I gave my word. I searched for my father's body, but I am afraid I could not find the person who took him. I have no proof against Nola. It is a Queen's word against mine. There was a time my word meant something, but as you said, I spent the last nine months lying to everyone. You have lost faith in me, my friend, as have so many others."

Robert Henley joined his son. "We have little time, Drew. You must make up your mind before it is made for you."

All eyes turned to the city, where hundreds of soldiers spewed out of the Diu gatehouse. Another army approached from the south; Admiral Roark and his sizeable army had arrived. There was no mistaking his well-groomed ginger beard in stark contrast against the winter snow and his midnight blue regimental surcoat.

Robert was right—they were all out of time.

"I can walk this on my own." Kai patted the air to make the others stay behind.

Drew pulled on Kai's shoulder to draw him away from the bridge. "I am sorry, Kai. I should have believed you; helped you, even. I can only guess my grief blinded me. I could not see past the anger and all the broken promises, but despite all that, I know you could never willingly hurt your father. I stand with you. Let me convince Roark to see reason; perhaps we can get Cazier to help. We may yet stop this nonsense and find the truth."

Kai wondered why Drew had had a change of heart; he could only guess years of friendship and faith still held them together. "It means a great deal to have you here," Kai said, "but Queen Nola will not see reason. After all, she was there the night my father died. Her hand pushed the dagger into mine and then into my father. There is no reason for her to let you search for a third person. The Queen and the Regent think war against Katori, a presumably peaceful nation, will be easy. They have no idea what is coming; Admiral Roark's men and the Regent's Milnos soldiers will not be enough. The only way to stop this war is to turn me over. I would be willing to die to stop this war. But, if I am honest, I doubt this will be enough. Please, save yourself. If you march with me, you only put your life in danger for a lost cause."

Robert padded his son's shoulder. "The choice is yours, my son. Let me go with you to speak with Roark. We three, Iver, Roark, and I, were very close once, and he may be willing to listen if I go with you."

Drew nodded. "Thank you, father."

It was time to go. The Stone River bridged once symbolized the beginning of responsibility, and now it would mark the end of his freedom. Rayna took his hand, and they climbed the hill. Yulia, Riome, Kendra, and Sabastian also joined him on the road.

Leaving Drew with Eugene and Robert, Kai led the rest of his friends, thankful he was not alone. The melted snow left the road a muddy mess. Kai's stomach burned with disappointment that he could not find the truth or his father's body.

Behind him, Eugen and Drew's argumentative voices caught Kai's ears, but he did not stop or turn back. He kept his eyes forward and continued to close the distance between him and the bridge.

Drew charged to the front, taking hold of Kai's arm. They stopped five feet shy of the bridge. "You are a Prince, Your Highness." Drew waved to Eugene. "Lord Sknash tells me that you have certain rights. First and foremost, you have a right to be heard. You never spoke at your sentencing. Not one word. Before they pass judgment, a council of your peers must hear you out by law."

The use of his formal title surprised Kai. "What would I say?" He looked to the others. There was little chance he could ever find any proof, even if he had weeks to search.

"The truth," Rayna insisted. "You have nothing to lose, so tell the truth. Queen Nola is a murderer. She brainwashed you, poisoned you and your father. Her hand forced the blade."

Riome stepped forward. "Drew is correct, Kai. Diu law states that royalty has the right to plead their case. You only need the majority of the council to agree on your innocence; Nola has no vote, and Aaron is an uncrowned King, so he has no power yet. Roark, Sigry, Dante, and Cazier decide your fate. Convince them, and you may yet have time to prove your innocence."

"Should he not present the facts?" Rayna repeated. "The Queen is guilty of murder."

"If Kai mentions the Queen, she can speak," Riome explained, "and you do not want her derailing your support. His best bet is to incriminate a third man in the room, the person who took Iver away. The council must address the questions: who is the third person, what did they witness, and what was their involvement?"

Once again, knowledge was power. If there was any hope left, Kai needed to heed Riome's advice. Relenting, he agreed to confront the council. Acting as his ambassadors, Drew and Robert Henley met with Admiral Roark Raebun and Kempery-man Dresnor. Even from a distance, Kai could tell the conversation with Roark sounded heated, and it was almost unclear who argued for or against him. But in the end, they parted and Drew reported that Roark would follow the letter of the law— nothing more.

His second group, Eugene Sknash and Riome Tamika, approached the Queen's army requesting a conference with the Grand Duke Dante Carmelo and Master General Adrian Cazier. In addition to asking for his right to speak, Kai requested a private council with the Grand Duke, hoping to inform him of his cousin-in-law's demise.

Dante accepted the terms to allow Kai to speak to the council in his defense, as was the letter of the law, but he refused the private meeting. He informed Eugene and Riome that any news the prince wanted to share should be delivered to the council as a whole. He would extend no favors.

CHAPTER 23

Last Words

Despite the fact that it was the middle of winter, the heat was rising. Many people had begun removing fur-embellished shawls and overcoats and fanning their faces. Without Yulia's influence, the cold weather faded and the snow melted, but this heat seemed unnatural, and Kai imagined his dear Weathervane friend was up to more tricks.

Watching the sweat pour off the armored men, he surmised their extra gear and furs left them taxed by the heat. He chuckled to himself. *Yulia, you are devious.*

While everyone waited with their respective groups, Diu soldiers erected a large white tent. They hoisted up thick poles at two points while others pulled out the corners and added more supports every ten feet, each drawn out by ropes and anchored by large metal spikes the men drove into the ground. Inside they unrolled two decorative carpets, upon which they placed tall thrones for the Queen and her two boys and smaller chairs for the council members.

First, five Kempery-men, each with four Mryken sentry dogs, approached the newly constructed tent. Unsure of their purpose, Kai reached out and sensed their confidence and dedication. Their ears perked to his probing, and they turned their heads toward him, yielding to his Beastmaster's will. If the Mryken were meant for more than show, they would no longer heed anyone's desire but his.

The second set of guards formed an outer ring around the tent, a mix of Milnos and Diu soldiers with Regent Maxwell in the lead. He and his men were a surprise to Kai; given the nature of this meeting, he expected Dante and Cazier to keep this event restricted to Diu council members. Still, he understood Nola would keep her one true ally close, and she clearly had sway over today's proceedings.

As the council assembled, Kai's heart pounded in his throat. It was now his turn. Eugene, Drew, Robert, and Riome approached alongside him. Holding his empty hands up, he eyed the Mryken dogs with the Kempery-men standing guard at his entrance. While his friends held back just inside, Kai stood closer to the center of the vaulted tent facing the council.

On his right, Sigry, the palace physician, offered his usual scowl, followed by Grand Duke Dante Carmelo, who appeared unforgiving with a touch of sadness threatening to overtake his typical pleasant nature. In the center, Queen Nola sat with her two sons Aaron and Seth. She oozed confidence below her smug expression.

Beside Seth was Master General Adrian Cazier, who stared at his daughter Riome. Kai imagined it was difficult to be on opposite sides. In the last seat was Admiral Roark Raebun, the Red Warrior, sitting on the edge of his chair with his fingers dancing on the hilt of his sword.

Lastly, near the tent's edge, Dresnor stood, seemingly unwilling to commit to one side. His body was rigid, and his gaze held a thousand-yard stare.

Nola's indifferent, bored expression worried Kai. Was her confidence so strong that she did not even worry about what he might say? The other faces and hateful expressions burned a hole in his heart. Seth appeared broken and empty. His gaze was hollow, and he stared at nothing near his feet. The boy wore no embellishments befitting his royal title. The cuffs of his white shirt did little to hide the scaring and deep bruising from his prison restraints. Why was Seth marched out here for this? Kai found it difficult to stomach the pain his mistake had caused—and the idea a mother could be so cruel.

On the contrary, Aaron displayed a self-righteous expression, holding his head high as though he was already the crowned King of Diu and everyone should bow to his presence. The crown perched on the boy's head was grander than it should be for a prince—another bit of Nola's handiwork on display.

Grand Duke Carmelo addressed the group. "According to Diu law, Prince Kai has the right to be heard by the council. Tell us why you murdered your father and where you have hidden his body."

The contempt Kai felt the last time he stood before these people felt was nothing compared to how they looked at him today. Each one no longer held even an ounce of feeling for him. Even his cousin Cazier's narrow gaze swelled with hate. How could he possibly hope to win them over? Should he even say anything? The gray line between guilt and innocence blurred, leaving him unsure he deserved forgiveness.

Roark rose from his chair and growled, "He is wasting our time. Seize this traitor. He murdered the King, and I will serve justice."

Drew stepped next to Kai. "You will let the Prince speak. No disrespect, Admiral, but sit back down." His voice carried as much weight as his stare, and Roark sat but continued to seethe.

"Before I address the court regarding my father," Kai finally said, "I have news for the Grand Duke. This is personal information, and I did request a private council, but Dante refused. In my search to prove my innocence, I discovered the murder of Barton Manzini, husband to your cousin Louisa Carmelo-Manzini. Two men buried him in the forest between here and Port Anahita, about five miles from here—a well-dressed Milnosian man named Darwin and a hunter who goes by Carter from Port Anahita."

"Lies!" Roark shouted, rising up in his chair but not standing. "He aims to distract the council. You will not garner trust with your lies, boy!"

"How do we know you speak the truth, Kai?" Dante asked, sounding hesitant to trust.

"When you last saw Louisa, how did she act?" Kai posed the question feeling confident he gained ground with Dante. "If I remember correctly, she was like a sister to you and came to the palace daily. Could they use her against you?"

The concerned look on Dante's face hinted the Grand Duke felt concerned.

"The man, Darwin," Kai continued, "should be sporting a large contusion on his left cheek where I struck him with a short wooden club. Also, I have a button I cut from his cloak. The initials D.W. embossed into the button may be proof enough if your cousin's wife knows such a man. I have no idea if she is a victim or if she conspired with Darwin to remove her husband or what Darwin hoped to gain given access to you through Louisa." Kai handed the button to Drew, who offered it to Dante.

He then continued. "The hunter, Carter, did not fare as well. During questioning, I modified his jawline with his hunting knife. When the man pulled another weapon on me, I stabbed him in the knee with the same blade. He should be easy enough to find." Kai pulled the blade from his belt and offered it as proof.

Dante inspected the large hunter's blade, still stained with blood around the hilt. The button raised the Grand Duke's eyebrow, and he called Captain Strauss forward. Kai could not hear what they said, but when the captain departed with the blade and button, he imagined the soldier would follow the clues provided.

"Now, Prince Kai, please address the matter at hand. Tell us why you murdered your father." The Grand Duke remained stoic, holding his chin high, offering no signs that Kai's discovery carried any weight.

There were no words that would clear Kai's name or absolve him of his guilt. He knew Nola controlled the council, and she would never let him go free. What mattered, at least to Kai, was the faith of one person sitting before him. He spoke directly to Seth. "I did not kill our father. Do you remember our last conversation, Seth? I asked you to trust me."

Nola reached for her son's hand. Seth did not move. "Do not speak to my son. You murdered my husband—you murdered the King. Arrest him. I will not tolerate this nonsense." Her shouts roused the guards, who took a step closer to the tent.

Dante stood and raised his hand, stopping their approach. "We will hear him speak." The desperation behind the Grand Duke's unshaved face gave Kai hope he might have at least one ally on the council besides his cousin. There was no question this man's loyalty for King Iver ran deep.

With a nod of respect, Kai continued. "Brother, I asked you to remember something. This is very important. Do you remember?"

Seth whispered inaudible words.

The crowd hushed and turned to Seth. Everyone waited for the young prince to speak. "Go ahead," Cazier said, leaning into the young prince to hear his response.

Tears ran down the boy's face, and his eyes rose to find Kai's. "I am here, Seth. Remember what I told you. Once simple truth, no matter what."

"You said," Seth croaked, "you said, you loved our father and me."

Nothing else mattered but his brother's faith. A tear ran down Kai's cheek. "I do love our father, as I love you. I did not kill our father. Do you believe me?"

Seth stood. Kai held his breath.

The young prince ran to his brother. "I believe in you, brother." He shouted, hugging Kai. "I believe you. Please forgive me for hitting you. Mother locked me in prison. She thinks I helped you."

"Seth, get back here," Nola instructed, but Seth clung to Kai's side as he rose to his feet. "Do you see? Kai has brainwashed my son against us. Seth did help Kai escape, and his innocent protests were but another lie! They are both traitors—arrest them!"

"Her tears are not real. I saw her with the Regent laughing and holding hands." Seth whispered so only Kai could hear.

Kai put a protective arm around his brother and surveyed the change in the tent. Dresnor chose a side, joining Drew and Kai. "I should have believed you," Dresnor spoke, but focused on the Queen. "I should have helped you. If what Seth just whispered to you is true, we must prove her guilt."

Emotion pursed Kai's mouth. He knew Dresnor could read lips. So, it took Seth's words to convince his Kempery-man, not years of friendship. "Thank you," was all Kai could say.

Roark rose from his seat, clasping the hilt of his sword. Sword drawn, Cazier stepped closer to the Queen with a protective arm in front of her, his eyes wild, fixed on Kai. Dante held his hands in the air, trying to calm everyone, and for the first time, Sigry pulled his sword and positioned himself to protect the Queen.

Guards closed in around the edges of the tent. Kai knew there was no use. These were all men that Nola most likely owned in one way or another. Even Cazier seemed changed; was he compromised by the Queen too, or was this an act to feign loyalty should this all go horribly wrong? Kai had no idea what or who to trust anymore. Considering Nola had brainwashed him to do her dirty work killing Iver, he wondered if each man here stood against him. They all seemed ready to kill him and anyone who got in her way, even her son.

There was no disputing that Nola had a certain air about her, but today Kai noticed something new. There was a substantial amount of magic emanating from her. He continued to study the movement of her magic. No, not from her, but something on her person. She reeked of darkness and hate. It oozed from her, but it had no real structure. The power hung on her like the very dress she wore but it did not build from within her.

Why had he never sensed it before? It was dark magic, weaker than most Katori magic, but it was there. Gleaning her person, he found a crystal hidden within her dress. A black stone, barely a shard, which he presumed was a Katori crystal. The dull glow was less than a spark, but like all Katori magic, it was noticeable. One by one, heads turned to gaze at her, and the council seemed to fall under her spell.

Unaffected by her words or her magic, Kai's body locked into fight mode. His mind was free of her spell, for now, but he needed to warn Sabastian. But how? Then it came to him. Searching the forest for the Alpha, he told his wolf friend—*the Queen has magic, go to Rayna, tell my friends the queen wears a crystal.* The Alpha responded, darting from the trees. Glancing over his shoulder, Kai saw the gray wolf bound up the hill for Rayna. He knew she would not understand the wolf, but the Alpha knew her, trusted her, and would protect her for Kai's sake. The rest was up to Sabastian and Kendra, as Beastmaster they would be able to speak to the Alpha.

Trying to buy time, Kai focused on Grand Duke Dante Carmelo, one of his father's closest friends. His brawny stature sagged as if he carried the weight of the world, and his tired eyes pleaded for the truth. Kai could not yet tell if he acted under his duress or if Nola's desires influenced the man.

"Please, Dante, let me speak."

Sweat ran down Dante's temples since he refused to remove his decorated winter overcoat like many of high rank. The Grand Duke shook his head and glanced at Cazier. "Sheath your weapon, Master General. We will hear the Prince speak. If it is the last thing we do today, I will learn the truth."

Yielding to the Grand Duke, everyone went back to their respective seats. Even Maxwell drew a chair behind the Queen's throne.

Although Kai knew he could not accuse Nola directly, he had to distract them. Somehow, he needed her to remove the necklace so he could destroy the crystal. "I did not kill the King," he said, following Riome's advice, "and I can prove it because there was a third person in the room."

Nobody would ever question Admiral Roark's loyalty to the King, and since he spent his days in For Pohaku, Kai hoped he remained uncompromised. "Name your accomplice," Roark shouted, again drawing his blade as if prepared to kill the guilty person the moment Kai or some stranger uttered the actual murderer's name.

In the next breath, a wave of pressure flooded Kai's crystal. It struck Kai hard. Looking at Nola, he noticed she felt it, too. Unaccustomed to significant shifts in power, she swayed forward, clutching her chest, and Maxwell rushed to her side. Steading herself upright, she continued to hold her chest. Kai glanced over his shoulder—Rayna, Sabastian, and Kendra were collecting magic and shoving it toward the tent.

"My queen, are you unwell?" Maxwell held her hand in his and knelt at her feet.

Everyone turned to Nola, but she waved them off. "I am fine, continue," she ordered.

Feeling the magic's weight, Kai allowed it to build slightly and flow through him. It continued to flow like a river into his crystal and out toward Nola. "The other man in the room spoke to me before I ran out . . ."

"Lies!" Nola shouted, cutting Kai off midsentence. The power Nola held floated outward on her voice, controlling the others. "Do not listen to his lies! Kai is a murderer, and he intends to assassinate me. Protect your queen!" she demanded, crumpling in pain.

This was how Nola manipulated those around her. Kai watched her bring each person within range to heel with her words. Regent Maxwell drew his blade and stood in front of the Queen. Sigry, Dante, Roark, and Cazier all advanced a step toward Kai.

Robert, Drew, and Dresnor unsheathed their weapons and closed in around Kai and Seth. Riome slipped Kai a set of throwing stars, and he caught a glimpse of three more, two daggers and three other throwing blades on her person. "Really, not even a dagger, I thought I taught you to be prepared? You could have hidden something from the guards." She jutted her chin, shoving a sword in his hand.

"Who was with you, Prince Kai?" Cazier challenged, holding his sword in one hand and holding the surge back with the other. "Let him speak. I will have my answers. We all will if you let him finish!"

The tent felt suddenly small with so many drawn swords. Friends pointing weapons at friends. "So, you do care about the third person, what they witnessed?" Kai stalled for time, feeling a second surge of power rush into his crystal, and again he let it wash over him toward Nola.

"Of course we care!" Dante stepped forward, pulling on Roark's shoulder. The Admiral did not budge to give him space, forcing him to talk over the taller man. "We must know. I must know what happened to Iver. Roark—let him speak!"

The Grand Duke's forceful tone made Roark step aside. Dante rubbed his head and appeared visibly confused as he sheathed his blade. He eased around Roark to stare through Kai as if the knowledgeable person might be among them. "Please, Kai, if your father meant anything to you, tell us the truth. Where is this third person?"

"This is a trick." Nola pressed her hand to her heart, and more dark magic swirled around the tent. Even Kai felt her anger and hate seep into his pores. "There is nothing you or some stranger can say that will undo what I saw you do."

When the next wave of magic stuck, Nola doubled over in pain, grabbing for the chain around her neck. Even Kai's crystal started to burn his skin as it surged with unrequested magic sent by his friends. Using some of the power, Kai called to one of the Mryken sentry dogs.

Tears welled in Nola's eyes as she yanked the chain free from her bodice and ripped it from her neck. She panted in relief. "Kai killed the King! Do not listen to his lies!"

The smoldering crystal dangled from the chain within her grasp only for a moment before a Mryken guard dog sprinted through the crowd, snatched it from her hand, and ran from the tent. Kai saw the beast run to Sabastian and his friend smashed the tainted shard on the rocks.

The shattered magic dissipated like the morning mist in sunshine. Her control over everyone was dispelled, and they drooped like puppets on cut strings, free to think and move for themselves. Everyone but

Cazier and Roark—that is. Both held their swords upright. They remained focused on Kai, taking a step forward.

Queen Nola stood with renewed strength, no longer burdened by the stone. "Enough of this nonsense!" she shouted. "I am Your Queen. Hear me and seize this traitor."

Maxwell charged forward, and Cazier twisted in place to block his advancement. "Regent, you have no place in these proceedings. Stand back, or I will have you arrested."

Cazier took three steps back toward Kai's huddled group, but he kept his eyes on the departing Regent and the rest of the council. "I want to know the truth, Kai." He glanced over his shoulder. "I am now and have always been your loyal friend. Riome can attest to my clarity, but I must know the truth. I know you could never kill your father, but who did? Who took him? Who was the third person in the room?"

"I am still your queen!" Nola screeched. "You will defend me against this traitor. His seeds of doubt do not erase what we know to be true. He killed Iver. I saw him with my own eyes, and Seth supports his treachery. Arrest them both," she ordered again.

Wanting to speak, Kai placed a hand on Drew's shoulder, and the huddle parted, allowing him to step forward and address the group. Seth clung to his side, unwilling to let go. Prepared to tell what he remembered, he took a deep breath. He knew he had no proof. No name to shout and deliver witness.

"I was there that night," he started, "and my blade did stab my father, but . . ."

CHAPTER 24

Roark's Fury

Grabbing Kai by the neck, Roark separated the brothers and shoved Kai through the crowd into the open field before releasing him. "No more lies—you will not return to Diu. Hanging would be too easy a death. You will die by my hand, slow and painful. And do not spout your lies at me, boy. In your own words, you admitted to killing Iver, for that you will pay. Tell me where you put Iver, return him to us, and I might end your life quickly."

"I cannot tell you what I do not know. I wish I knew who took my father. I was a prisoner moments after, and there was no way for me to steal his body. And if I knew who had, I could prove my innocence. I could prove Nola was the one who pushed in the blade. Please believe me. I want to know the same as you who took Iver."

"Enough lies," Roark charged, delivering a solid blow with his entire weight behind the motion, and the strike forced Kai to bend and shift to avoid falling to the ground and getting killed on the first assault.

Words are pointless, Kai thought. The Admiral would not take time to listen to any more useless words. He should have noticed the Admiral's intent earlier. Ever since Kai uttered his first word, the man had seethed on the edge of his seat, waiting to avenge Iver, and he would wait no longer. Although fighting his friend felt wrong, and Kai wanted to protest, he knew Roark's quick temper would not allow him to see anything but red.

A glint of polished steel flickered as Roark slashed with his sword and attacked Kai again and again. His skilled footwork and rapid thrusts kept Kai on his toes. The blade Riome gave him blocked each strike, but he quickly realized, blade for blade, that he was in trouble. The quality of the Admiral's sword and the man's skill would test Kai's limits.

It did not take long to notice that Roark's attacks were strategic, meant to test Kai's reach, balance, and strength. Clearly, the Admiral was searching for Kai's weaknesses. He would show him none. Maintaining as much distance as possible, Kai shifted to a more level location on the hill while forcing Roark to face the sun.

Kai kept his distance, eyeing the dagger within his opponent's belt. He knew all too well if the opportunity or misstep brought them close, Roark could quickly draw his blade and strike before Kai could block the second weapon.

Acting on pure instinct, Kai kept on the defense, letting Roark do all the work. Although hoping to exhaust the man was hardly a strategy, he could not bring himself to attack. The Admiral, on the other hand, showed his skill and proved he did indeed deserve the Red Warrior title. Each decisive blow started to fracture the blade in Kai's hand. The edge was no longer sharp, and he was sure it would only take a few more hits.

On the next strike, the blade broke, leaving Kai with a useless weapon. Faced with death, Kai thought only of Rayna. He did not want her to watch him die, not like this. Sidestepping a lunge, Kai dodged an attack, pivoting around his opponent and punching Roark in the ribs. Without a weapon, his chances of finishing the fight were slim, and he refused to use the throwing stars from Riome.

"Kai!" he heard Dresnor shout, and he turned in time to see a sword fly in his direction.

He caught the weapon midflight and felt the balance of the blade as he twirled the sword forward and back, followed by a figure eight and a few cut-twirls. Pleased with the weapon, Kai inspected the pommel—a silver wolf. It was Dresnor's sword. Roark charged before he could thank his Kempery-man.

As he deflected and dodged another round of attacks, it dawned on him that holding back was no longer an option. He needed to fight. Using his knowledge and speed, he switched his footing and charged Roark. While the Admiral deflected the blow, Kai got in close and punched the man in the wrist, followed by a jaw hit.

"Please, Admiral, see reason! I do not want to hurt you. I did not kill my father. I tried to save him."

"Lies!" Roark shouted. "You sent my son into the lion's den of Milnos, and I have no news since the wedding. And then you abandoned Diu. You attacked your men for the Katori, and now you killed my best friend—you must pay."

For the first time, Roark exposed his grief and fury. While Tolan's journey to Milnos started in celebration, the lack of recent news left everyone, especially Tolan's father, Roark, worried.

Another round of aggressive blows forced Kai on the defense. Given the Admiral's armor, there was little room to land a solid punch and strike muscle and bone. There were only a few exposed areas, areas Kai made quick work exploiting. A few more hits to the Admiral's sword hand forced Roark to switch hands.

Following Roark's next attack, Kai landed a kick to the knee as he dodged Roark's blade. A pommel strike to the temple while he was on one knee shocked Roark, but he did not yield; instead, he punched Kai in the ribs, quickly putting distance between them.

Bent over and catching his breath, Kai eyed Roark. For a man without an ounce of Katori blood, he held his own and at times made Kai think twice about not using his speed or sword to stop the fight. They both dripped with sweat. Although Kai could outlast the Admiral, he had no choice but to decide if he could stomach permanently maiming a man he held in such high esteem.

Once again, Admiral Roark delivered a combination of strikes and blows with the same pounding fury. His blade was swift, and his decisive thrusts put Kai back on the defensive. Unfortunately, the Admiral also embraced Kai's tactics, adding brute strength to his arsenal; Roark landed a dizzying punch to Kai's cheek, followed by a kick to the gut. Kai slid across the grass, gasping.

Rebounding with a renewed fury, he charged Roark with a series of blows to put his opponent on the defensive and delivered the first cut to the Admiral's cheek.

The sight of blood stunned Kai, and, in his hesitation, Roark returned the favor, cutting him on the arm. The pain surged up to his shoulder, and he parried the next two attacks before regaining his composure to resume his assault.

Shouts from the crowd danced around the outskirts of Kai's mind. He kept their cries distant, focusing on his next set of moves, which bounced between offensive and defensive.

Tired of the repetition, Kai knew there were a limited number of moves one can perform with a sword, and most ended with someone dying if they made even the slightest mistake. He was most certainly not willing to die today, and he did not want Roark's death on his hands, either. If the battle must continue, Kai needed to remove the swords from the equation. Without them, there might be a chance of subduing the Admiral and rendering him unconscious or temporarily paralyzed with the techniques he had learned from the Guardians.

Upon Roark's next round of strikes, Kai grabbed the Admiral's weapon at the hilt and pulled against the man's thumb, removing the sword from the Admiral's hand. Then Kai pushed back, putting space between them, ever mindful of the dagger when something caught Roark's attention. The Admiral looked to the skies, and his expression became fearful as he stumbled back, leaving Kai the high ground.

A darkness fell over the land, and Kai spun to follow the Admiral's gaze. High in the clear blue sky, a thunder of dragons filled the air. Surprised, Kai swirled around to take note of his surroundings. The vast circle of men dispersed in fear, leaving him standing alone. Even Roark retreated toward the tent. Nola and the council stood watching the creatures. By Kai's count, there were eleven in total, surrounding him in a circle: four black, three red, one blue, and three various shades of gray. There was one dark metallic gray dragon—Raijin, among them. The memory of meeting his first real dragon brought a chuckle to his lips, remembering how Raijin disapproved of him at first. Still, he eventually took Kai flying, allowing him to create his first Beastmaster connection.

It pleased Kai to see the real dragons support him. For the first time, he noticed the subtle differences between natural-born dragons and Katori Beastmaster dragons. Their size, coloring, and spines were smaller and more organic. The Katori-created dragons were intense and armored, and their wings were thicker and covered in a glinting layer of something akin to folded metal.

The ground continued to shake and moan as more dragons dove from the sky, landing with a thunderous thud in various locations around Roark's soldiers, near the lake, and on both sides of the river. There were now so many that Kai counted at least twenty additional dragons dotting the landscape. Still, high above, one remained circling. A silver flash pulled at Kai's heartstrings.

Benmar, grandfather, you came.

Kai could not help but feel glad that his grandfather came. Even after every mistake he made, they came as dragons—for him.

The silver dragon swooped and circled lower and lower until he, too, landed with a thud. The massive beast lowered his head to Kai. Thankful for the show of support, Kai held up his hand and touched his grandfather's dragon scaled head. "Thank you, grandfather. I am happy you are here, but you should not have come not for me, not like this."

Hot smoke blasted out of Benmar's dragon's nostrils at Kai, followed by three varied warbles and shrill tones that Kai understood. *We are family, always.* Then Benmar lifted his dragon head and spewed fire into the sky. The show of strength sent gasps around the hillside, followed by clangs of armor from freighted men taking a few steps back. But they drew their swords all the same, ready for a fight.

The first Katori Kai saw was his grandfather Lucca, followed by Haygan, who hopped down from the back of a black dragon, which Kai instantly recognized as Simone. Ryker, Liam, and the rest of the Katori Elders joined Kai around Benmar's silver dragon from the remaining dragons.

Never in all his imagination would Kai have thought they would leave their sheltered side of the world to stand with him. Lucca greeted him first. "Grandson, I am sorry we did not help you sooner. I knew you were struggling, and I should have listened more." Lucca raised his hand to Benmar's dragon. "Fortunately, Benmar acted quickly. His faith in you saved us all, and he did not think twice about following you."

Kai looked up, and the sun blinded his eyes. He raised his hand as the silhouette of a man stood up on the back of Benmar's dragon. As his eyes adjusted, the man slid down Benmar's wing and stood in front of him.

Tears flooded Kai's eyes and ran down his cheeks. His health restored, Iver looked five years younger. His gaunt, pale form was now tan and flush with muscle. "Father!" he cried. "How? How are you still alive?" Kai ran to Iver and hugged him with all his might to be sure he was real.

Iver released his son. "I have your grandfather to thank." His father pointed to the silver dragon. "Benmar was the third man in the room, a witness to the truth. While I slipped in and out of consciousness, he cauterized my wound. I do not remember anything until I awoke in Katori with Haygan, our old stablemaster, which I have since learned is your mother's brother. Anyway, I was initially in a lot of pain, but many people came to pray over me. Each day I became stronger, and then they gave me something called sacred water. When they told me the Queen accused you of my murder, and planned to start a war against Katori, the Elders offered dragons to come put an end to this nonsense."

The dragons parted to give Iver room to step into the open for all to see him. Roark was the first to drop to one knee and bow his head. In quick succession, every Diu warrior on the field followed his example.

Iver approached his Admiral. "Rise, my friend."

"Your Majesty, King Iver Galloway." Roark started to bow again, but Iver touched his shoulder. "How is this possible? I thought you were dead. Queen Nola said she witnessed Kai stab you with her own eyes."

Iver's eyes shot up the hillside to the tent. An intense glare passed between Iver and Nola as Regent Maxwell and his Milnos warriors swarmed around the Queen, escorting her back to Diu city. Aaron shouted for his father, but the Queen held him to her side as she retreated.

"Dearest Roark," Iver responded, "I thank you for your loyalty, but my wife is mistaken on many counts. First, she ordered Kai to kill me, and her hand forced the blade that pierced my flesh. But as you can see, I am very much alive. Our Katori brethren saved my life, and for them, I will be eternally grateful. It seems our Queen was also poisoning me with something the Katori call sinder root and bella bitters."

The mention of the plants used to poison Iver grabbed Sigry's attention, and Kai noticed the man mentally searching his memory for any knowledge of their existence. "Your Majesty," Sigry approached with another bow, "I have no experience with either plant. I will research their origins and add it to my journals, and I will not be caught unaware again, Your Majesty."

"Sire, no offense," Roark grumbled, "but you would trust these outsiders? They brainwashed your son into staying with them, fighting for them. Kai turned on his people." He glared at Kai, still acting wary.

"I have learned much from our Katori brothers and sisters," Iver responded. "There was a time our two nations were united, almost one nation. The Prince's responsibility is to establish relations with foreign countries, but lest we forget, his mother, Mariana, was from Katori. My son has every right to visit family and call Katori his second home, even. His trip renewed a new hope for our future, and the Katori Elders intend to extend talks, due in part to Kai's conduct and good character. Well done, my son." Iver offered a nod to Kai.

The pride in his father's eyes and the sincerity in his voice lifted Kai's spirits. He had so many questions, some he feared he could never ask, not in a public setting such as this. "How did you convince the dragons to fly with you?" he asked, settling on a safe question.

"First, in any relationship, there must be trust. Benmar understood this and offered me his truth. Son, my words played no part in bringing the dragons out of hiding. They came because of you. Benmar said that Raijin—" Iver motioned to the dark metallic gray dragon "—calls you friend, and it is clear to me they respect you, even if I do not comprehend them myself. We thought the dragons retreated to the Mystic Islands, and their numbers diminished. We were wrong. The Katori Mountains are home to many dragons, who no longer wish to fly over Diu. We must change this."

The sound of an explosion followed by thunder and screams drew their attention. The remanence of a flammable cloth trailed behind a burning boulder, spreading a yellow-white blaze through the wet grass. The first trebuchet strike fell short of everyone on the hill, but the second volley struck two rows deep into the Admiral's army, smashing men beneath the stone's weight and casting Arkin oil onto others.

Men screamed in pain as they burned—anyone who attempted to douse the fire only spread the oil to themselves. Kai had always thought the ancient siege weapons were mere decoration perched on the Diu walls, not viable threats. The third assault struck the pier, engulfing two vessels tied on either side of the blast. White and yellow flames floated on the water's surface. The smell of Arkin oil, a sticky syrup that floats, caught in Kai's throat, a smell he remembered from the battle for Port Anahita.

A dozen dragons took flight moments before a fourth trebuchet struck, and another Arkin oil-soaked ball flew into the air bound for the white tent. Three airborne dragons sprayed fire on the black-and-orange blaze as it hurled through the sky. A bright white glow blossomed around the boulder, and it blazed like the sun before it struck the ground. The projectile hit beyond the tent, creating a sizable crater, but the consumed oil had nothing left to give and burned out.

Roark's men responded to his call and retreated out of the line of fire. All but three of the remaining dragons burst into the air: Raijin, Benmar, and Simone. A few circled over the gatehouse, and Kai spotted the point of a dragon killer—a massive crossbow big enough to take down a dragon in midflight. When did Diu install a dragon killer? He watched in horror as a bolt was launched from the wall, but Simone rolled, and the iron point missed its mark. Kai knew all too well how it felt to have such a weapon rip scales and crack bone.

The remaining Milnos men and a few Diu soldiers continued to retreat through the gatehouse into the city's safety—men pushing and running as if their lives depended on hiding within the thick city walls. The Regent and Queen Nola's appearance on the gatehouse parapet surprised Kai.

Does she mean to orchestrate this battle personally?

Shouts and commands volleyed around the field, bringing the orderly chaos around Kai into focus. A launch of arrows turned the sky gray, but a blast of dragon fire turned the projectiles into embers before they peaked. Simone flew over to the gatehouse, preventing the dragon killer from aiming as she singed the banners blowing in the wind, encouraging men to run away.

Kai watched as Simone flew to a safe distance and the men returned to take aim. Queen Nola's defiant stare burred across the field as if she could will Iver dead once more.

CHAPTER 25

Exposed

Cannon fire and a flurry of arrows sent everyone running for cover and the safety of the forest. As Kai searched for Rayna, he found her running with Kendra and Sabastian. She was safe, for now.

Iver dragged Seth and Kai through the swarm of soldiers while the remaining dragons took to the sky. Their massive forms cast an eerie rolling shadow across the field.

While Roark and Iver discussed strategy, Kai studied the battlements along the walls. As the trebuchets cranked backward to reload, Milnos banners fluttered in the wind. He noticed someone was fighting against the retreating mass but could not see who disrupted the orderly flow filing into the gatehouse when the Admiral's words caught his ears. "How do we use the dragons?"

"You do not!" Kai barked, letting go of Seth's hand. "Dragons are not tools you wield like a sword, nor are they under your command." The sounds of battle pulled Kai's gaze to the gatehouse as the last few men disappeared into the city, and the young prince emerged before the gates slammed shut, leaving him alone on the outside.

Tears streaked down Aaron's cheeks as he removed his royal crown. His expression turned sour, and he glanced up above the massive archway to his screaming mother. Although Kai could not hear their words, he imagined that Nola demanded his loyalty. The young man's response came as he tossed the unwanted symbol aside and ran away from the gatehouse.

Soundless shouts chased after the runaway prince, but he did not stop. The Queen waved her hands in anger, but he would not turn back. Through the men, Kai searched for Seth when he caught a glimpse of his brother darting away from the protection of the King's men. The twins, two halves of one soul, shouted and cried desperately, trying to close the gap between them.

Worried about his brothers and their exposure on the open field, Kai pushed through the soldiers when an uneasy feeling washed over him. Thoughts of death surrounded his brothers and gripped his chest, forcing him to run toward the unsettling moment. When he saw Regent Maxwell and a line of Milnos soldiers nock their arrows and take aim from the parapet, Kai gasped at the sight and increased his speed.

The arrows let loose, arching high before gliding downward. Kai's heart pounded in his ears, and his mind warped forward in time, showing the possibility of the next moment. The edges of his vision blurred. Only his brothers remained in focus. As he took his next breath, three arrows pierced Aaron—one in the shoulder and two in the back, straight through his heart, dropping him on the field. Seth reached Aaron's dead body and wept as the Regent's men let loose more arrows. The fierce projectiles cut through the air, arching high in the sky, striking Seth. It was as if the arrows had stabbed Kai through his own heart as tears streaked down his cheeks.

Then Kai's mind cleared and he snapped back into the present moment. It had to be a vision of one possible future. He looked to the sky and saw the arrows reach their peak above Seth and Aaron. As gravity took over, Kai held on to the moment, altering time, which slowed their descent. Propelled by fear and anger, he begged fate. *Please let me stop this.* With the perception of time within his grasp, Kai held his breath and pushed against the thick temporal distortion. There was little distance left between the deadly arrows falling toward Aaron and Seth.

Kai struggled, holding every second close to his chest, unwilling to take a breath lest a deadly fate befalls his brothers.

Knowing he, no better than Aaron, could survive the piercing arrows, he had to consider the only part of him that could deflect such a blow— his dragon. These were no dragon killer bolts from a giant crossbow, merely average arrows. As he leaped into the air and dove over his brothers, Kai took hold of his crystal and focused on the golden braid of his dragon. While taking a needed breath, allowing time to commence, he transformed.

Thick dragon scales erupted across his back seconds before the arrows struck his spine. The metal tips plinked against the hardened skin bouncing off into the grass, useless and broken. Wings expanded and curled around the twins, protecting them from the Queen's hatred. Head angled around his wing Kai, glanced at his father. Roark was holding Iver back as the King anxiously shouted for his boys.

Kai raised his head ever so slightly, hopeful he had blocked every arrow. He opened one wing to find Seth staring at him in shock. Seth reached up, almost able to touch Kai's dragon chin; his eyes filled with tears, his mouth agape.

"I . . . I always knew you were special, Kai."

Opening his other wing, he uncovered Aaron, who looked at him with speechless wonder and a touch of fear. Kai wanted to let go of his magic, and tell them he was sorry for keeping secrets, but they were still in danger. Shouts and threats rang in his ears along with an audible thud, causing Kai to turn his head as the deadly dragon killer clicked into position. In one vast spray of fire, he engulfed the weapon in a blaze of flames. Fury and rage at the attempted murder of his brothers overtook him, and he turned his head, continuing to spit fire down the long line of men armed with arrows. Nola was no longer among them.

Enraged with the Queen, Kai rammed his head into the blazing gatehouse. Men shouted and ran, the stone groaned and cracked but did not break. Shouts from Roark and Iver caught in Kai's ears. His father touched his wing. "Hurry, son. We must save the city and stop the Queen. Let's do this together."

Understanding his father's request, Kai extended his wing to Roark, hoping he would join them. Roark did not hesitate. He ran up the offered wing and jumped from Kai's head to the fire consumed gatehouse. Within moments, the thick wooden gates partially ablaze began to open.

All sounds of the outward attacks fell silent, and a new battle within the city slipped through the opening gates. Who was fighting whom? Ducking his mighty dragon head, Kai peered into the city and caught sight of the Queen fleeing on horseback.

Unable to speak with his father as a dragon, he transformed back into his natural form. Letting go of the final bits of magic, he heard a familiar voice beside him. "So, this is your secret?" Dresnor stepped beside Kai but kept his eyes focused on the departing queen and her Milnos men.

"It is one secret," Kai responded as the Queen disappeared in the haze of the rolling city streets. Realizing this was one battle he should not fight alone, he turned to see who was with him.

Roark exited the city gatehouse. "The Queen and Maxwell will pay for their crimes, but we must hurry. With the gatehouse on fire, it will not stand long. We will need to get as many men inside as we can before it collapses." At the Admiral's command, men slipped through the fiery gates.

"Your Majesty, we dare not risk attacking the city until we know the conditions inside," Cazier said, approaching Iver. "My scouts report skirmishes along the south wall, but if we hope to capture the Queen, we must act now. We need to get to the palace."

"King Iver," Benmar bowed ever so slightly as he approached, "I believe we can help by landing on the other side of the city. We can keep the Queen and the Regent from escaping."

Roark muscled in and took the measure of Benmar, who did not flinch under the glare of the Red Warrior. "Sire, who is this man?" he asked, still overly protective of his King.

The sight of Benmar softened Iver's expression. "Benmar, thank you. Roark, this is Kai's grandfather, the man who saved my life. He is the silver dragon who brought me here."

The Admiral took a step back and offered a nod. "We are most grateful for your heroics in saving our King, but . . ."

The hand of the King stayed Roark's inquiry. "Benmar, I am most appreciative to have your support. Anything you can do to help, we thank you."

Before his grandfather left, Kai whispered to Benmar. "You showed him our secret. Why now?"

"There is no time for questions, grandson. We all do what we must. But understand the strongest relationships require trust." Benmar hurried away down the hill to Raijin.

Simone dropped from the sky, landing behind Cazier, startling the Master General. "News of the King spreads," she spoke to Kai and Iver. "Diu soldiers turn on their would-be allies, your city has erupted into civil war, but they needed reinforcements. Milnos men stir chaos in the streets, setting fires across the city, while citizens hide in fear. We must get the Admiral's army inside now. Since the gatehouse is on fire and is going to collapse, we need a second entrance, say fifty feet down from the gatehouse."

"How exactly are you going to open a section in the wall?" Dresnor asked, looking between Simone and Kai.

Rayna laughed. "There is so much more you do not know, Dresnor, but you will see."

Liam stepped forward. "We three Stonekings—Jin, Rochelle, and I— can make short work of your wall if Yulia and the other Weathervanes can squelch the fires."

"Thank you, Liam," Kai said. "I will fly Iver, Dresnor, and Drew to the palace as Roark and his men take back the city."

"No, you are not leaving me behind," Roark insisted. "I have little wish to fly, but I go with my King. Dante can lead my army into the city."

Dante nodded and ran along the wall as the two Elders and Liam touched the stone. Thunder rumbled from the ground, followed by a plume of dust as the wall slowly wobbled into the ground. Followed by the shouts of men, the Grand Duke led the men through the gap into the city.

From the sky, Kai surveyed the city and the spreading chaos below. Hundreds of Fort Pohaku soldiers flooded the town, overrunning the Regents' men. Random fires burned, and, in the distance, three dragons faded into the horizon, bound for the other side.

A fierce draw on his magic drew his attention moments before a flash of light bloomed on the city's far side. Sabastian. Kai worried about his friend, who would only use his special Lumen gift in dire situations. Although he wanted to help, he knew the other dragons would be there well before him and could undoubtedly contain the problem.

At the center of the palace grounds, Kai landed in the courtyard. Milnos men attacked with swords drawn—their metal blades sparked across his scales. They did not have the force to pierce his thick hide. Using his spiked tail, he swatted the men away or crushed them where they stood.

Iver, Roark, Dresnor, and Drew jumped into the fray, swords at the ready. Men on the inner walls fought amongst themselves—Milnos versus Diu. Blade against blade they battled until a row of archers fired, Milnos men willing to kill both sides to ensure victory. Kai spat fire at the projectiles, burning them in mid-flight.

The sound of metal striking metal drew Kai back to his father. Engaged in battle against Milnos warriors, Iver's fluid movements were swift and precise, and he fought like a much younger man. He deflected attacks from one man then delivered strikes against another. It made Kai wonder if his father's time in Katori and the water-infused healing had sparked his dormant Katori bloodline.

At first, they made quick work and dispatched most of the men surrounding the palace. There was no sign of the Regent or the Queen, but soon more and more men flooded into the courtyard. From where

Kai stood, he saw them fleeing to the inner gatehouse. Something or someone was forcing them back.

Their escape cut off, the Milnos men swarmed back to the palace, presumably forced back by Sabastian and the arrival of Benmar and the other dragons on the far side of the city. Milnos men poured through the gatehouse like rats.

A barrage of arrows plinked off Kai's back, and he turned his head to a cluster of fearless Milnos archers on the palace wall, who were taking aim and firing another volley. Three men heaved a dragon killer into position, while a fourth cranked the bolt into place and fired. The bolt flew straight and true but only scraped Kai's neck, taking shards of dragon scale with it but drawing no blood.

The second round of arrows bounced off his wing and neck, a mere distraction for the next oncoming bolt they intended to launch. In response, Kai screeched in anger at the unwanted invaders, but the archers did not yield or run away. Instead, they nocked another arrow as if unaware their tiny sticks were useless against his armor-like scales.

As the giant crossbow turned for better aim, it cranked into position with a new bolt positioned to fire. An immense heat rolled up Kai's throat, and he blasted fire, consuming every man around the lethal weapon. Set ablaze, the Milnos warriors still managed to launch the bolt, aimed at his head. Shrinking his dragon form, Kai managed to dodge the bolt; but it struck the crowd behind him, running through four men before striking the ground. With the threat dispatched, Kai turned back to the courtyard.

The next round of Milnos soldiers pouring back through the palace gatehouse contained the Queen. Surrounded by loyal Milnosian men, Nola looked like a damsel in distress backed against the wall. Her once elegant gown, now trimmed in mud, sagged under its burdens, and her stylish blonde curls contained bits of dirt and ash and blew in the angry breeze. Kai almost felt bad for her.

Surrounded by a new swarm of men, Roark moved closer to Iver. In response, Kai took hold of his inner dragon, and like a cleaver, he hammered his tail down across the palace courtyard. In seconds, he crushed dozens of Milnos men and sent the rest scurrying against the walls, dropping their weapons and exposing their queen.

Nola stood in proud defiance, her chin held high. Strolling toward Iver, her expression appeared happy to see him after a long voyage. Without hesitation, Kai transformed and landed a foot in front of his father, blocking her path. Joining him, Dresnor handed him a sword, which he quickly pointed at the Queen.

"You have gone far enough, Nola." He stepped forward and raised his blade, stopping her advancement. He scanned the Milnos men but did not see Maxwell. "Where is the Regent?"

Everything in the courtyard fell silent, and all eyes landed on the Queen. Despite her coy demeanor, Kai did not trust her getting close to his father.

"What a difference a day makes, my dearest Kai." Nola removed her gloves and cloak, letting them fall to the ground. "Are we no longer friends? Look at you, redeemed in the eyes of everyone because your father stands here, but you held the blade the same as I, willing to do as I asked and kill your father. Any clarity you might have found in those final moments did not change the fact. Part of you was willing."

Her words stung, and Kai let his eyes wander to those next to him. Dresnor and Roark on either side glanced out the corner of their eyes but never lost sight of the Queen. "Enough talk, Nola. You are under arrest for treason and the attempted murder of your King." Kai held his blade, tracking her movements.

Trapped, Nola screamed at the top of her lungs. "I hate you—I hate you all. You killed my father, and you must pay."

"You nearly killed our son, Nola," Iver shouted back. "In fact, you have been killing me for years. Slowly, but you were killing me. My mind, body, and soul. And now it is time you pay for your crimes."

Tears ran down her face. "ME!" she screamed. "What about your crimes against my father and me? You killed him."

The confusion on Iver's face prompted Kai. "Nola is the illegitimate daughter of Milnos King Bannon Penier, the man who murdered your father and uncle. She is a half-sister to Landon Penier."

Memories of loss washed over Iver. "Bannon was a murderous, twisted man, filled with hate for every nation but his own. I loved you, or at least I believed I loved you, and all this time, you plotted to kill me and take my kingdom for vengeance?"

Nola laughed. "Love? What do you know of love? Men love money, power, and control, but nothing else. No, there was no love between us. I spent years tricking you into gaining the wealth and power I needed to crush you. It was not enough to murder you; I wanted you to suffer. I wanted to take everything from you."

"You are a madwoman, Nola," Roark spat. "Just like your father."

"You have no right to judge me. You can't understand me, after all the lies men tell themselves, seeking power at all costs. If a man acquires riches and power, you make him your king, and if he gains too much power, another will come and take it away. That is the way of men, and my father was such a man of power. The Galloways sought to take away his kingdom and cripple the great superpower Milnos was becoming. Well, let me assure you Milnos will show you her might and destroy you all."

Iver stepped between Roark and Kai. "Surrender, Nola. It is over; you lost, and now you must face justice, same as your father. His men found him guilty, and they sentenced him. I only provided solutions. Diu and Milnos wanted peace, and I have kept it all these years."

Her cold stare offered no remorse. "I will never surrender."

"You must—there is nowhere to run." Iver took a step toward the Queen, then everyone heard the cries of Cordelia.

"Mommy!" she cried as she ran to her mother.

The Queen scooped the little girl into her arms. "Let me go, Iver. I will not go to prison, and you could never kill me. I know you too well." She laughed and pulled a small dagger from her sleeve. She held it low against the girl's bodice, aimed at her heart.

Cordelia squirmed. Seeing Iver for the first time, the girl started to cry. "Father? Father, is that really you? Let me go, Mother!" She squirmed again, but Nola pressed the blade into the fabric, and the girl went stiff.

Fear forced Iver back a few steps, but Kai stepped forward. Could he possibly move fast enough to split them apart before Nola ran the blade through his sister? He dared not take the risk.

"Do not do this, Nola," Iver begged.

"I do not care," Nola seethed. "Not for you, not for her, not for anyone. You will not put me in prison."

Nola's eyes burned with rage—and in that instant, Kai knew that she was about to murder Cordelia before their very eyes. Kai took another step forward, desperate to stop her . . .

But then Nola's face twisted. A hollow stare consumed her as the life drained from her eyes. Her arms went limp, dropping the blade and Cordelia to the ground. The little girl ran to Iver's open arms, and Nola sank to her knees with her last breath.

Behind the Queen stood Kendra, her blade dripping with the Queen's blood. Kai saw the sadness as a tear rolled down her cheek. "I am sorry." Kendra covered her heart with her other hand. "I could not let her kill Cordelia. Not my little lady."

Iver covered Cordelia's eyes and laid her against his shoulder. "Kendra, thank you for saving my daughter." He carried her away into the security of Roark's men.

Kai bridged the gap, catching Kendra before she transformed flew away. "I know you love Cordelia as any mother would. You did the right thing—saving her. She will understand, someday." He hoped his words softened the pain he knew would tear his dear friend to pieces.

"Maybe." Kendra's eyes had a faraway stare. "But I think it is time I leave my position in the palace. Start a family of my own, if we can. I have always wanted children, but our inability to be close to home over the years makes it impossible. Lumens cannot typically procreate unless paired with a Kodama healer, or unless the mother drinks the sacred waters regularly."

This was news to Kai. "But then how did Lucca manage to father my mother and uncle?"

"Your grandmother was a Kodama, bless her soul. She was able to bear the light, but she was unable to pass on the Lumen gift. Mariana surprised us all when she was able to deflect light, but she could not create it like my husband. Please explain my departure to Iver, but I believe my leaving is for the best." She turned to go before Kai could respond, not that he had any words imbued with wisdom enough to change her mind.

CHAPTER 26

New Beginnings

Today was a sight Kai would have never dreamed possible. All eight Elders stood in a circle in the palace gardens in Diu; while they spoke of the future, Kai could see their uneasiness. The Diu council stood among them with a similar awkward countenance. Although Roark wanted to talk peace in the King's council chamber, the Elders insisted the garden's open air would provide clearer minds. Kai also assumed it allowed for an easier exit if things didn't go well.

Each Chief and Unie wore the color of their discipline. Their robes rustled around their feet in the breeze: Lucca, Yana, and Kam in shades of yellow—Lumens; Jin and Rochelle in shades of red—Stonekings; Wilda wore purple—Weathervane; Zook in blue—Beastmaster; and Noreen in green—Kodama.

While living with Lucca, Kai had come to know each elder well; they preferred tradition above everything else. Even though they decided to show the world their truth, he presumed some wanted to hold firm to the old ways. Although Kai had no idea how this would go, he worried with Keegan still on the loose and ramped up for war, there was no real way to know who from Katori Diu could trust.

As the talks continued, Kai found himself distracted by other concerns. It felt terrifying to know people would look at him differently. Would they see his Katori gifts as a hidden disfigurement, curling their nose at him or shying away? Worries over his newfound paradise suddenly struck him. What of the pristine cities and harmonious lifestyle of Katori? Currency, among a vast many otherworldly desires, did not exist there.

Lost in thought, Kai flinched at Iver's touch. "Sorry if I startled you, son. If we may, I wish to leave the palace. Dante is preparing a small escort to take me to the Central City Gardens. Would you consider joining me?"

"Certainly, father." Kai nodded, noticing everyone else had already departed.

◆ ◆ ◆

Saying today was beyond imagination felt like an understatement. The Diu Central City gardens teemed with Katori enjoying a pleasant afternoon and communing with nature. Frolicking like children set free in a sweet shop, they performed magic without a care in the world. Kai paused, caught in the surreal realization of everything that happened the past few months and how this came to be.

"Simply amazing, my son," Iver said, standing with Kai gazing down the length of the gardens. "Never in my wildest dreams would I have considered magic, if that is what they are calling it, possible. The Katori are very blessed to be so close to the foundation of nature."

"Yes, father." Kai wanted to celebrate, but another instinctual feeling crept through his mind. Nature and people kept a respective distance, and the balance of the relationship felt genuine, but now the rules were changing, and he was unsure if this was for the better.

The Diu citizens seemed curious and happy with their new magical benefactors. He could not help but wonder how long the euphoria would last. Sure, the Stonekings repaired the city walls and various other structures in a single day, the Weathervanes brought pleasant summer weather while the rest of the world lived in winter, and the Kodama restored the multiple gardens around the city and grew crops overnight, helping to replenish the cities food resources.

But the Beastmasters performed no such offerings. They were oddities at best. The children were amazed, but the adults displayed a range of emotions that he found troubling. Some cowered in fear but watched anyway, and some argued, curious or radical, over the science behind their transformations. But those were not the ones who concerned him. The men and women who whispered and nodded and poked and befriended or even separated one here or there. Those were the people to watch, who were most apt to take advantage or see them as creatures for study.

"Shall we walk?" Iver motioned, cutting his eyes down the pebble path and back to squadron of King's Guards. "They give me little room to breathe." He took in a long, deep inhale and released it as if it cleansed his mind further and gave him with the needed courage to speak.

"Give the men more than three days, Father. Their dead king is now restored, hale beyond measure, and father to a boy who can become a dragon. It is like a fragile piece of glass in their hands. Their world is upside down with the Queen's conspiracy, and they have yet to determine what parts to accept."

"Wise words." Iver started down the path, putting distance between them and their guards. "Over the recent years, we have not been as close as we once were. I blame myself for allowing Nola to come between us, and I was not the understanding father you needed after your mother passed away."

The inevitable conversation Kai avoided four times over the past three days was now upon him. His father was an intelligent man, and it did not take a professor to piece together the details surrounding his mother's fate. There would be no running away this time. Thankfully Benmar's words—*understand the strongest relationships require trust*—offered him a place to start.

"Since you are one of them, a dragon, will you tell me the truth behind Mariana's . . .?"

Iver could not finish, and Kai understood why. The very question bothered him not so long ago; if there was trust between the Katori and dragons, why would one kill his mother. He started in a whisper, as if the secret still mattered, and explained as much of the truth as he felt necessary.

His mother was a dragon, and she transformed that day; unfortunately in her confusion, she killed a guard and fled. Although it was technically a lie, Kai omitted the fact that his mother was the red dragon that served Diu all those years. It was preferable to the truth; not to mention he had known before he traveled to Katori that his mother did not die that day. Yes, there would be several details to remain untold about his gifts and how he knew the things he did.

Finally, he explained that as all Katori children reach adulthood, the pull of Katori calls them home, but he also omitted the power within the crystals and Alenga's blessing in the sacred water.

"I guess your crystal and your mother's crystal explain how you can communicate with dragons?" Iver asked more than surmised.

"The stones are more symbolic of our gifts," Kai suggested, offering an alternative that felt less threatening and less powerful. Allowing his father to believe a false truth seemed better than the truth that his stone could control him. There were some secrets too valuable to share. This little lie needed protection, and Kai was willing to ensure it stayed that way.

When he shared his experience with the dragons and the truth of his mother's change, he noticed a well of emotion bubble in his father's eyes, but he did not interrupt. Altering the sequence of events, he continued to share his realization and mission to find his mother and restore her to her true self. He could not bring himself to explain how long he had known his mother was alive or how he lit up the world to find her trapped in her dragon form when she held prisoner by Iver's very own Diu soldiers.

As much as others might want, he knew he could not leave the story unfinished, so he continued to share his quest to find Mariana and her final discovery off Dragon Spine Island. The knowledge she was still alive, only sleeping, left Iver's expression sadly happy.

"May I see her?" he asked, removing the tears from his cheeks.

"Father, she is not as she once was," Kai whispered again.

The furrow across Iver's brow told Kai his father's heart wrestled with his mind. "I want to see her—I must see her. Will you make this happen?"

Kai nodded, "I will make the arrangements, but it would be best if we waited. Let Diu settle before their King goes missing for a few days."

Iver reluctantly nodded and offered the occasional wave as they walked on in silence back through the excessive entourage of lords and ladies cheering at the sight of their restored King. Holding back the throng, the Diu soldiers surrounded the King's carriage, which sat at the ready to escort Iver and Kai back to the palace after the King's outing.

◆ ◆ ◆

The morning dew felt cold against his bare feet. He missed home, and the palace gardens gave him the most comfort. Enjoying his surroundings, he noticed the area had prematurely bloomed—under the influence of the Kodama, he presumed.

Like him, those Katori who stayed within the city each night preferred the outdoors to the palace, and his grandfathers were no exception. Seeing them stroll through the rose-covered arched trellis, Kai raced after them like a desperate child.

"Why now after everything?" he asked, stepping between them. "Why reveal our secrets so openly?"

Benmar clasped his hand behind his back. "In truth, hiding becomes increasingly difficult each year. As people look for ways over the Katori Mountains, they get closer to our secrets. Three such groups made it up and over before we turned them back. Trade routes force more ships to our shores, and it is difficult to refuse shelter from storms or overnight respite along their journey." He took a breath and looked to Lucca.

"Our people are tired of hiding," Lucca concurred. "Each generation becomes more restless, and while we live far longer than the average person, and experience tells us to stay hidden, others are curious. Katori has become a forbidden fruit in the eyes of the world. We find ships crashed on the rocks along our cliffs—ten or so a year because they are trying to find a way up our cliffs. Over my lifetime, four groups have managed to scale the bluffs and reach the top. They were dealt with and returned to whence they came."

Kai did not ask how, he could only hang onto the notion they were returned, and he hoped it meant safely. "But I thought . . ."

Lucca held up a hand. "The Elders know what we have preached, and there are many Katori who might disagree with our decision. And if I am honest, I may need to step down as an Elder. I let my love for you as my grandson cloud my judgment. Yes, it was the right thing to do, coming here. We Katori must keep up with this changing world. People are resourceful, and they will find a way. How many adventurers can we continue to stop at our borders? How many could we miss? Instead, we hope to implement a pass of sorts that would allow people to visit and leave with oversight."

"Why?" Kai stopped their stroll. "Why would you step down as a Chief? I thought the position of Elder was for life?"

"I fought with my heart, not my head." Lucca motioned them forward. "If this were any other young man in trouble, would I argue as fiercely to break with tradition?" Lucca sighed in a way Kai knew he was tired of talking.

Kai dropped the subject, and they continued through the gardens in silence until he spotted Rayna entering the gardens with his father and little sister. "Excuse me, grandfathers. I know we are leaving in the coming days, and I would like to spend as much time with my father as possible."

◆ ◆ ◆

On the morning of their departure, Kai found himself standing on the palace's inner walls, looking out over the waking city. The sunrise was a golden hue with a hint of cold blue around the edges—signs the Katori no longer held back the winter weather left a touch of frost on the city rooftops. His beloved city felt restored with a new sense of optimism, which made it difficult to leave.

"I do not apologize well," Roark broke the serine moment and addressed Kai. "I am glad your father is alive and that I did not kill you." Roark's puffed-up chest and his raised chin spoke of his pride and authority, but what surprised Kai was the hand the Admiral offered. "I am proud to call you my Prince," he added.

Kai shook the Admiral's hand, but he let Roark continue without interruption—not that anyone would dare interrupt the man when he so clearly had something on his mind.

"The Regent was nowhere to be found. I am not sure how he escaped after he abandoned the Queen, but he is not among the dead or imprisoned, as far as we can tell. I doubt he was among those released, either. Your friend Sabastian claims that many Milnos soldiers were pouring out of the gatehouse when he arrived. He was able to drive the majority back through the gates—do not tell me how, I am not ready for anything else magical—but a great many blinded individuals wandered outside the city after the battle. Dante assured me they were healed and left to us for punishment."

"First chance he gets the Regent will return to Milnos," Kai explained, agreeing to not say more about Sabastian. "The Regent spent time in Diu, and he may have friends here willing to hide him and sneak him out of the city when the time is right. Would you like me to search for him?" he offered, knowing it would take time—but if Maxwell remained, he was their best hope of capturing the man.

"As you say, he may have friends here in the city. We will find him if he remains. I appreciate your skills, but this is not a mission for our Prince, Your Highness."

"Kind of you to use my formal title. Will you feel the same after I return to Katori?"

"Typically, a princess through marriage secures peace between two countries, but you were offered to Milnos for the same purpose. I believe it a wise choice. Plus, how can I argue with my King?" Roark continued to gaze out over the walls.

Changing the subject, Kai turned to watch the procession of men gathering near one of the three-story barracks behind them. "What is all of this?" he gestured.

"The Grand Duke is accepting any disbanded or retired Diu soldiers," Roark explained, "and he is even considering individuals who left without permission when the Milnosian horde moved into the city. Which brings me to the matter of your Kempery-men—Dresnor, Albey, and Redmond. Dresnor is a proud soldier, and he will not ask for a return of service like the others, but we both know it is his wish. You will have to formally request his return if that is your desire."

Without hesitation, Kai responded. "I would speak with Dresnor first. I offended him the last time I spoke without his permission. I will not make the same mistake. He must understand I plan to spend most of my time in Katori, returning to Diu now and again."

"Wise move," Roark said with a nod. "The face of the world is changing, and if the Katori allow strangers into her borders, it may no longer be the tranquil paradise it is now."

The thought of change worried Kai. "The Guardians, as we call them, may well need a different understanding to keep the peace in our cities. I have ventured deep into Katori territory, flown over many cities. There are no walls, no armed guards walking the streets."

"Well, whatever you decide, put the request in front of Dante, and I will approve the transfer." Roark's expression turned serious, with a furrowed brow and narrowed gaze. "And finally, while we must repair Diu and restore her security, I have not heard from my son in months. I mean to travel to Milnos in early summer. I trust I can count on you to travel with me to Milnos to inquire about Tolan and Amelia? The rumors of war between Diu and Milnos spread like fire through our streets. The Master General's spies report unrest and men on the march. The horde of Milnosian men seek to return to their city. We must prepare for war if that is what comes next."

Curious himself about his friends, Kai could not refuse the request. "I will come when you call. But we must be ready considering war is on everyone's lips. Milnos will retaliate; dragons or no, they are thirsty for battle." Kai could only wonder where Keegan would fall in the battle. Would he stand with Katori or Milnos in his quest to rule the world?

"Return to Diu on King's Day, we will be ready." Roark nodded and left.

◆ ◆ ◆

Rayna played with Cordelia, picking the remaining white and purple blossoms from the palace gardens. Kai walked with his father, both in a somber mood, knowing this was his last day. Caught by his stare, Rayna blushed and waved at him behind a bouquet of fresh flowers. It pleased him to see her happy.

Knowing the remaining Elders were about to leave, Kai felt anxious about their departure. He planned to go with them to see the ramifications on Katori, considering the world knew of their gifts. Katori was vast, and the Elders could not be in every city to reassure the people. Rumors and fear would spread like fire across this great nation. He imagined each city set ablaze with light, like the spokes of a wagon wheel—the typical design of each city across Katori—would burn through the night, people toiling over their new freedoms and new risks.

Unaware of Kai's serious contemplation, Iver spoke with a joyful tone. "How long do you plan to wait?" he asked, and Kai knew that he spoke of Rayna.

The thought of his desire to marry, talk of war, and his need to travel with Roark tore him apart. "We spoke of marriage a few times, but this is not the right time." He tossed around the idea, unsure he had the right to such happiness in this upended world. "Diu is in recovery, the Regent runs free, there is talk of war with Milnos, and we have no word from Tolan and Amelia. Katori, I am sure, is struggling to adjust to new liberties and new fears. There will be a better time, but not now."

Iver left a moment of silence between them as they circled the garden, away from the girls. "Time moves on, my son—cherish every moment. Life will not wait for the timing to be right. Seek to enjoy every tiny moment with Rayna, as many fall in between life's adventures and its trails. I would give anything to have my time back with your mother or to be with her now, but I understand she may never wake."

"Do you still plan to visit?" Kai inquired, hoping the answer was yes.

"After you spoke with them, one of your Elders—Wilda, I believe— assured me I would be able to visit Mariana, but she can never return to Diu. Like you, the Elders believe it will be too confusing for a deceased woman, magical circumstances or not, to return from the dead."

The acceptance Iver demonstrated on the matter did not surprise Kai. He knew his father understood the burdens of leadership and the tenuous nature of civility. "We spoke of marriage," he took the conversation back to Rayna as she came back into view. "But if I am honest, neither of us desire a large spectacle. Many traditions on both sides of Diu and Katori are appealing, but I think a simple woodland ceremony is more befitting. The difficult part will be keeping it small and intimate without offending anyone."

"Were you thinking here in Diu or Katori?"

Kai could tell his father's question came with an assumption and a hope. "There is a special garden in Katori, and I hope to take Rayna there to ask her to marry me. I can only guess she would choose the same location for the wedding, but I will let you know and bring you there myself if you would do me the honor of attending."

"It would be *my* honor, son."

The End.

EPILOGUE

S unshine sparkled throughout the Kodama garden. Birds sang and the trees swayed in a delicate breeze, each adding to what Kai hoped would be a perfect day. Although he and Rayna wanted a simple ceremony for just the two of them, they soon realized that those closest to them needed this happy moment as much as they did.

Dressed in all white, Kai stood proudly with his arms behind his back, waiting for a glimpse of Rayna through the foliage. Next to him stood his father, Iver, and his friend, Dresnor.

In his nervousness, Kai let his eyes wander around the small crowd gathered to celebrate this day. Kendra and Sabastian held each other close. Haygan and Simone stood cooing over baby Neveah, while Lucca and Ryker stared quietly ahead. As his eyes fell on Drew and Riome, Kai noticed a kindred connection between them. Rayna's parents, Dori and Levi Kendrick, stood with her Aunt Mina and Uncle Taner alongside Marduk, Shane, and Julia.

His family and friends partially blocked his view of Rayna meandering through the trees. He first noticed her crown of white and pink flowers which decorated her long dark hair. As she came through the crowd, he noticed the silhouette of her sparkling white dress slowly flaring out across the ground, which was strewn with hundreds of tiny pink and white flowers that matched her headpiece.

Kai's heart raced at the sight of her. She had never looked more beautiful. As she walked down the aisle behind her sister Imani, several guests offered her different colored roses to create her bouquet. As she came to stand at his side, it was all he could do not to kiss her in the moment.

Benmar stood ready to perform the ceremony. He raised his hands out to his side and said, "We are gathered here at the dawn of a new day to unite this couple in marriage. We, your family and friends, are the foundation upon which your union will grow. Our promise to you both is to love and support you through good times and bad."

Gesturing to Rayna's bouquet, he continued, "Each flower given to you represents an essence that you will use to build your relationship. Red signifies passion, courage, and security; may it strengthen your union. Orange represents optimism, playfulness, and symmetry; may it provide balance without control. Yellow, the color of the sunshine itself, represents clarity of thought, wisdom, and joy. Green denotes fertility, growth, and trust; through it, you will find wealth in each other. Blue is the color of the sky and the vast oceans; hence, it is your spirituality and faith; may it be limitless. Indigo is calming and peaceful, may it help you to be self-aware and enhance your sensitivity towards others. Lastly, violet combines the depth of blue and the intensity of red; may it strengthen your devotion and ignite your imagination in every aspect of your lives together."

Hands raised above the couple. "Will you offer all of this without measure and without limit? If so, let us all say, 'I will.'"

In unison, Kai and Rayna said, "I will."

Benmar then reached into his white robe and pulled out two rings, giving one to each of them. "You hold in your hand your rings, the symbol of your enduring promise. Kai and Rayna, please recite your vows to one another."

Kai turned to face Rayna, and as he placed the ring on her finger, he said. "My vow to you this new day is to be your companion forever. You are the love of my life. I will dance with you in the rain, warm you when you are cold, and share in your pain or joy. My beloved, may Alenga bless us each day, as we will walk together hand in hand from this day forward, united in love."

As Rayna repeated the same vows, Kai looked at her, desperate to hang on to this one happy moment as long as he could. Still, a cloud lingered over his soul. Keegan was still out there, intent on bringing Diu to ruin and transforming Katori in his twisted image. A dark storm was coming, and he feared they would not be ready.

"Now, by the power entrusted to me by the blessed Alenga, I now pronounce you husband and wife. You may seal this promise with a kiss."

Kai gently touched the side of Rayna's face and pulled her in close. Smiling, he paused. "I will love you, forever." Then he gently kissed her.

Printed in Great Britain
by Amazon

46392405R00169